The Man
Who Rode
Ampersand

The Man Who Rode Ampersand

FERDINAND MOUNT

CARROLL & GRAF PUBLISHERS
NEW YORK

THE MAN WHO RODE AMPERSAND

Carroll & Graf Publishers
An Imprint of Avalon Publishing Group Incorporated
161 William Street, 16th Floor
New York, NY 10038

First Carroll & Graf edition 2002

Library of Congress Cataloging-in-Publication Data is available.

ISBN 0-7867-1007-1

Printed in the United States of America
Distributed by Publishers Group West

For Julia

Acknowledgement is made for excerpts from songs reprinted by kind permission of the publishers:

For 'Green Carnation' from the musical play *Bitter Sweet*: composer and author, Noël Coward. Copyright 1929 by Chappell & Co. Ltd., London; Chappell & Co. Inc., New York. For 'Two Little Babes in the Wood' from the musical production *Paris*: composer and author, Cole Porter. Copyright 1928 by Harms Inc., Chappell & Co. Ltd., London; Warner Bros. Music, Los Angeles, U.S.A. For 'I'm Gonna Get Lit Up': Peter Maurice Music Co. Ltd., 138–140 Charing Cross Road, London, WC2H OLD.

CONTENTS

CHAPTER ONE   *page* 1

   Early Morning   29
   Weighing Out   37
   The Off   52

CHAPTER TWO   62

   Night Life   77
   On the Rails   91
   Flagrante Delicto   105

CHAPTER THREE   118

   Silesian Bliss   132
   Intercessional   156
   The Last of England   170

CHAPTER FOUR   183

   Barrack-room Ballad   185
   Mussolini's Tits   194
   Back of Beyond   204

CHAPTER FIVE   214

CHAPTER ONE

DAN was my father's keeper. That was not how it seemed at first glance. They were an unlikely couple. My father affronted the street, the weather, the other pedestrians; he sniffed cold air like a connoisseur called in to describe its bouquet, he bore into the rain as stoic as a lifeboat skipper, inspected passers-by with friendly but lingering gaze. When he stopped to look into a shop window or to wait for the traffic from a side street, an invisible regiment stamped to a halt behind him. He seemed all exuberance and will.

From a long way off, with his glaring tweed overcoat and weathered red face he could have passed, if there was passing to be done, for a big farmer come to town for a cattle show. Closer up, this air of commercial gusto dissolved. There was nothing shrewd about him. Though oddly unlined, he did not look at ease with himself. The way his head was drawn back into his shoulders as if expecting a blow undermined his panache. Yet it may have been this very shadow of unease which lent magnificence to my father's overcoat and thick grey hair and gave a crozier's dignity to his umbrella with its silver band inscribed 'Dr J. McKechnie, Kirkintilloch, 1897', picked up not entirely cheap in some den of serendipity. When his hair grew long, people sometimes said he resembled a minor prophet, which pleased him although he would remark later that it only showed how little they knew about minor prophets. In any case, his hair was usually cut short, not because he wished to present a respectable profile to the world but because he liked going to the barber.

He had been told that the hairdressers at the Army and Navy Stores were known by number rather than by name and, taking perpetual delight in the rituals of unfamiliar worlds, would ask for cryptic telephone messages to be relayed to the barber's shop from the food hall or the haberdashery department to which he had been wrongly connected, the messages couched in telegraphese—'Number Three, 11.30, confirm soonest'—as if he were a *capo mafioso* transmitting instructions for the elimination

1*

of a troublesome rival. I later heard that this system was a fantasy, the Army and Navy hairdressers being known in the ordinary way as Mr Clive, or Mr Frederick, but they politely humoured my father's whim in referring to each other by number when he was present—'Number Three is engaged just at the moment, but you will find Number Two will look after you very well.' This power to impose a language of his own flowed entirely from my father's zest; he was in no way domineering. People acceded to his fancies out of sympathy not fear. On the other hand, this zest had something reckless and inflexible about it. He could not bow with the wind.

By contrast Dan submitted meekly to the elements. A gust of wind would send him scurrying past my father, his shoulders hunched, a curled autumn leaf. If the wind was against him, Dan tacked into it like a dinghy on a ruffled estuary. But in the sunshine he would dawdle, open-shouldered, slant-hipped, taking his pace from the other strollers on the King's Road: bickering leathery American couples, mind-blown loafers, puzzled matrons. Dan occasionally turned a little to catch an eye or flip a faunish wave, posing almost with neck turned and legs sketching the third ballet position. This fluid, cool pantomime—half designed to attract attention, half the unconscious imprint of his training—made him a part of the crowd from which my father stood out so unnervingly. They rarely walked side by side.

Sometimes my father had stopped to remark on some object of interest—the soldiers drilling outside the Duke of York's barracks, a grimy painting in the antique shop window set out to catch the tourists but pronounced by my father to be probably a Julius Caesar Ibbetson. Then Dan would walk on, hardly concealing impatience, looking backwards like a relay runner waiting for the baton change, repeating softly, 'Oh, Harry.' Less often, the roles were reversed. Dan stopped to exchange a few words with an acquaintance, muttered, furtive, so brief as to suggest an inconsequential meeting arranged for a few hours later, though in fact he might not leave the house again for days, crouching in front of the fire, motionless except for the thunderous blink of his black lashes.

While waiting for Dan, my father would stand quite still with complete good humour, relishing his own exquisite patience, perhaps even looking back with amiable regret on a lifetime of missed appointments, trains seen steaming out of stations and notes pinned to doors by people who had got bored of waiting. He radiated the perfect manners of someone who would not dream of reminding his dawdling companion that they were expected the other side of the river at half past twelve sharp. As they were in fact expected nowhere, there was no reason for him to be other than good humoured; all the same, his patience came from temperament not lack of occupation. When Dan caught him up, my father would continue this display of courtesy, looking straight ahead, perhaps even humming, behaving as if Dan had merely paused to do up his shoelace and had spoken to nobody. This ostentatious refusal to pry would throw Dan into a more than usually brooding silence, so that when finally my father reopened the conversation, it could be an occasion of some shock to the people walking in the opposite direction. The elderly man with the umbrella looked decidedly unattached; so in a different way did the tousle-headed dancer in thigh-length boots. The revelation that they were in fact together seemed to send a thrill of pleasure through visitors looking for the exotic side of metropolitan life. Was the elderly man trying to pick the boy up or had they arranged to meet on the trot at precisely this time and place? Sometimes, my father, swaying a little as the morning wore on, appeared to be echoing Dan's sinuous hesitant gait as if they were together mimicking a soft-shoe duo, carried away by high spirits.

They shared a taste for reflection upon the passing scene, though from differing viewpoints.

'It's fantastic the things they have in the big stores now,' said Dan staring into the window of Peter Jones. 'The paper says in the States you can even buy a midget submarine.'

'I don't want a midget submarine,' my father said. 'I am not a midget.'

'No, no, it's just a small submarine big enough for one or two people.'

'If I needed a submarine, I would want to take all my friends out in it, but I do not need a submarine. My life is already full enough.' Dan was frequently on the receiving end of similar didactic reproofs. On the whole, he took them sceptically but without resentment.

'You cross a zebra crossing like a woman, Dan. Women always cut off the corners. If I was driving a big lorry, I would not be able to see you jumping out from the kerb like that.'

'Have you ever driven a big lorry, Harry? Well then, how do you know?'

'It's a question of angles.' My father felt strongly about the rights and duties of pedestrians. Ever since he had given up driving, to the relief of his friends no less than of the police, he had become a professional pedestrian. He looked with exaggerated care to right and left before crossing, always between the studs when there was no zebra. He reproached strange old women for failing to do the same. On the other hand, motorists who neglected to observe the Highway Code down to the last particular might, if delayed by the traffic, be startled by the rattle of my father's umbrella on their bonnets. On one occasion, stoutly standing his ground on the black-and-white stripes, he met his match and was carried fifteen or twenty yards on the bonnet of a mini driven by an impatient model in granny glasses. 'It is an extraordinary and rather wonderful experience,' he explained later as he sat in bed receiving wellwishers. 'You are swept up and for a moment hang in space, entirely weightless, glaring at the bad-tempered face the other side of the windscreen glaring back at you like a fish in an aquarium.' In the violence he wrought upon the motoring classes, he totally disregarded the armour at the disposal of the enemy, as tribesmen with bow and arrow might consider a tank as merely another kind of juju whose superiority was unproven. For him the moral issues at stake outweighed base calculations of relative strength. Dan disapproved of these quixotic assertions of principle. He regarded crossing the road as something to be achieved only by alertness and low cunning.

If their attitudes were different, their interests were more divergent still. When my father let go one of his more morose aphorisms—'all dress designers secretly hate women' or 'only small men and masters of foxhounds like Wagner'—the exasperation in Dan's, 'Oh, Harry, come *on*, really', revealed a world of difference. Yet it must not be assumed from this lack of shared enthusiasms that they did not get on together. Their occasional spats were more in the nature of work-outs. In general, their association, although freely chosen by neither of them, was marked by a certain mute communion. They showed one another a particular sort of recessive courtesy and when they walked side by side without speaking there was a sympathy between them as of companionable strangers on a train temporarily lapsed into silence while passing through a tunnel.

They had drifted into each other's company rather than having sought one another out. Dan had started to accompany my father on his daily round because he had nothing better to do and perhaps to his surprise soon found himself established as a bodyguard-cum-psychotherapist, in return for which services he was fed, lodged and given a home. After two or three years of this arrangement, his situation had become not unlike that of a trusty palace eunuch; his loyalty unquestioned, his grasp of reality considerably superior to that of his master's.

Since I had moved into that part of London, I often used to catch sight of this conspicuous couple. Only a few weeks earlier, I had seen them making their way through the holly-laden crowds, dazed by the blasts of muzak carols from the super-market. Ghosts of Christmas Past spoke to me then. Mythic, nearly forgotten simplicities swept my mind clean of the worries of a minor civil servant. I remembered how I panted to catch up with my father, crunching through the thin ice into the brown puddles, my wellingtons as usual leaking at the ankle where the rubber joined. The wind rattled through the rusting tin of the War Department 'Keep Out' notices, posted at intervals along the barbed wire fences, the white arrow on the red ground pointing ever upward as if to draw the attention of potential trespassers to some celestial military police post. The straight, chalk-scarred track split a landscape that was still half-prairie, rolling, patched with plough only at the edges, an eternal nursery for war toys—prehistoric camps, Roman forts, Centurion tanks. My father, with his torn, dirty sheepskin coat and his long shepherd's crook, looked like a pastoral refugee driven from his ancient grazing grounds down a demilitarized corridor. As it happened, he knew nothing about sheep but he would spend hours talking to the local shepherd on the steps of the latter's ramshackle caravan. To be accurate, it was more a question of listening to the shepherd who talked in a strange, unceasing monotone as if he had not seen another person in months, although he rarely spent more than two nights on the downs before descending to the village pub. But then my father said that shepherds were always like that; he claimed once to have seen a shepherd run the length of a field in order to pass the time of day with him, or had he read it somewhere, in W. H. Hudson perhaps?

Memory jinks and fades like a woodcock in the bare woods; I can remember only the wind beginning to whip my chapped legs and the boots rubbing my ankles raw. For me these mid-winter walks were an uncomfortable mixture of running and waiting, of fear and boredom, the child always out of step with the rhythm of adult life just as the civilian is alternately bored and terrified by life in wartime. Besides, flat-footed and asthmatic, I was bound to fall behind, however kindly my father spaced his pauses to review the landscape. In panache too, I fell behind, or rather I never began to compete. In these blank, unembroidered days it is implausible at best to recall that as we serially breasted the highest ridge of the down my father would burst into song—no other phrase will do—the song as often as not the drinking song from *Don Giovanni*, its invitation to the feast bellowed to the downland sky. This aria, all light and dash, yet printed its underlying melancholy upon the empty fields the more memorably because it called up crowded squares and faces heated by wine and feet stamping time. The compressed gaiety rang forlorn in the unbounded winter landscape. The wind blew the notes back to me . . . *vo' amoreggiar, vo' amo-oreggiar* —a flowing counterpoint to the call of the peewits flapping over the rare ploughland.

Once or twice my father borrowed a gun and took me shooting across the fields of a friendly farmer. He would splash through the marshes, crash through the brambles, clucking encouragement to the sluggish birds. Occasionally he would flush a pigeon or even a bedraggled wild pheasant and I would fire in the general direction of the fugitive if my numb fingers could shift the safety catch in time. As the darkness crept on, I would loose off at anything that moved, partly in hope of rewarding my father's enthusiasm, partly out of humiliated rage. Once I shot a lapwing at dusk, hardly able to see what I was doing. I thought it was a snipe, although even to my ignorant eye its flight was slow. I rushed forward to retrieve my trophy, boots sucking in the wet ground. My father shouted from the other side of the stream: 'I'm afraid it's protected.' 'What?' 'Pro-otected' . . . The syllables rolled slowly across the cold air like the savoured verdict of a hanging judge; they still bring back as fresh as a wet print the image of the bird cradled in a tussock, its soft white breast trembling warm and its sleek crest bowed like a widow praying. I do not know whether there really is an Act of Parliament protecting the peewit—my father was not always reliable on such matters—but even now the sound of a human voice through a winter dusk revives that feeling of having made a mistake so terrible and irreparable that there can be no forgiving or forgetting, just as the Mozart aria still stands for an exuberance unattainable and unattained.

It is mere melodrama to suppose that each man kills the thing he loves, but often, I think, a man is drawn to love the thing he has killed. It seems to me now that I have never felt for any living animal as I did for the murdered lapwing, or is it only that hindsight softens guilt for the deed into affection for the victim? Certainly the embarrassment that my father's singing caused me at the time has been elevated by the years into admiration for anyone who could sing so loud to an empty horizon and a stumbling child. But there is more to the operation of time than the soft blurring of distance. The mythical perspective never ceases to alternate with the factual. This demanding, ferocious giant, a legend of caprice, a tower of strength and love, shrivelled under the glare of my growing self-esteem. The fairy-tale ogre dwindled into a tiresome but manageable obstacle to my plans, a thing to be thwarted, humoured, coaxed, spoken straight to, ignored or even avoided. My father became a case to be compared with other fathers amongst my friends, like doctors discussing their patients in the staff-room. But suddenly to my surprise I found my patient had taken up his bed and hopped it. And there ambling down the King's Road was the old fabulous monster, the last survivor on the whole flat earth of the age of ghosts and kings, his sceptre now given for a palmer's walking-staff, now bent and milky-eyed, but still exacting reverence and love. The myth had been made flesh again and trod the crowded pavements. The fact that my father should actually be walking past the Safeway Stores on Christmas Eve seemed to me as incredible as the legend of Glastonbury. That my father should walk past the Safeway Stores almost every morning, that his existence was not an occasional intrusion into my life like a comet which passes once in a millennium but rather itself amounted to nothing less than a life was not only incredible but intolerable.

Yet I knew in my mind that Dan and my father set out at half past ten sharp most days, as regular as a postman on his rounds. To start with, they walked briskly, looking neither to right nor to left, no dawdling here in the dry country. There was nothing to see but the occasional twitch of a curtain and a bleared face peering out to see what sort of a day it was or an old woman twirling a mop in a bucket on the doorstep. At best a dog-lover, with curlers veiled, letting her pooch sidle up to a lamp-post, might stir a wordless grimace from Dan and my father, hatred of dogs being one of their few common passions.

Inertia blanketed this dormitory of solitary bourgeois transients: middle-aged women separated from their husbands and behind with the rent, artistic Australians having difficulty with residence permits, thirty-five-year-old public-school men between jobs—will go anywhere, do anything legal—single ladies attending classes in bookbinding, widows come to London to die interestingly, and all sorts of people recovering, convalescing, undergoing treatment, in analysis, taking up theosophy, into encounter groups, taking things easy for a bit, making fresh starts or old endings. Morning rarely lightened the windows of their dusty basements (or garden flats, as the letting agents liked to call them, though no flowers could have bloomed there since the time when my father's great-grandmother was said to have skated on the Pimlico marshes) and even when a ray of light did manage to straggle through they were not there to greet it. Some had already left in the dark for the travel agencies, photographer's studios and interior decorating shops where they watched the day slip by in a gentle procession of snacks—coffee-and-biscuits, yoghurt-and-salad, tea-and-biscuits and a quick one round the corner on the way home. Others were still savouring their power-assisted sleep, the last traces of mogadon, kif and highland cream sweetly flavouring their dreams of past extravagance and future sobriety. Today they would sand the floor, visit their trustees, get the place really cleaned up, start their exercises, but for the moment they would have one last lie-in.

Dan and my father would stride undeviatingly along this familiar path until the first signs of life broke in. At the main road, choice reared its head, the day began to define itself.

On that January morning, a small boy was pulling back the iron grille in front of the Prince of Wales. 'No, I think not. Too many pansies in the Prince these days and it's too dark.' My father liked a light pub where he could see what he was drinking. Across the other side of the road, the doors were already open at the Duke of Connaught. 'Too draughty.' Further on, the Duke of Teck, rarely favoured with custom: 'I don't much care for the publican. I left my umbrella there once, he pretended he'd never seen it.' The whole line of minor royalty rejected with the solemnity of a sovereign choosing a son-in-law, only after having passed the town hall did my father announce his final destination, like a ship's captain who may not break the seal on his orders until he is on the high seas.

'I think,' he said reflectively, 'that we had better go to the library first. I must look something up.' My father was fond of the library but at the back of his mind there seemed to be a slight feeling that the place needed cheering up. There was something about the manner of his entry which suggested not so much the seeker after knowledge as the well-known entertainer making a Christmas visit to the chronic ward. Without ever raising his voice above the appropriate level or banging books about, he contrived somehow to disturb almost everyone in the building. 'Good morning,' he whispered to the attendant pushing a trolley of books along the passage. 'Hello, sor,' the attendant replied, startled by this approach. 'And what part of Ireland do you come from?' 'Clonmel, sor, County Tipperary.' 'Clonmel—I coursed a dog there once, during the war, against a priest.' 'Now that's a shame, the bishops won't let their priests run the dogs now. It was the betting that was giving them a terrible name.'

My father nodded vigorously, delighted to have marked up his first Irishman of the day. He was always quick to seize on a brogue. Sometimes even a vaguely Irish aspect—a hint of jug-ears, a reddish cheek, a button nose—would be enough to lure him across a bar or over to the other side of the street. Occasionally, he got the brush-off from an indignant Welsh-man, but more often the timeless warmth of camaraderie was established as quickly as lighting a gas fire. It was the timeless-ness rather than the camaraderie that spoke to his depths. He was at his best with surly hall-porters from County Monaghan or Fermanagh, holding their reluctant attention with stories of fishing on Lough Erne.

This flagrant defiance of the temporal imperative, this spitting in the face of the business of the day was in striking contrast to my father's lightning speed of attack. In any public place, I had only to fall behind him for a second to buy a ticket, lock a car door or get rid of a coat and by the time I caught him up, he had already established his audience's native region and was well launched on some anecdote which was apposite only in the geographical sense.

The library attendant, though still friendly, was looking increasingly uncomfortable as if under examination and liable at any moment to be called upon to give the crucial answer which would decide his fate. For the time being, he cautiously mumbled, 'Well now, is that so?'—a response which, like any reaction short of outright rudeness, my father took for shy encouragement. With his experienced sense of the rhythm of these things, Dan gently led my father on down the passage, giving him time to take his leave of the attendant with the grace and affection suitable to the hour's good talk he would have liked.

Already, inside the reading-room, the girls in thick skirts behind the desk were looking up uneasily, aware that they were next in line. They appeared almost to feel that their unwavering attention to duty, admirable from one point of view, was also narrow, spinsterish. There was more to life than moving little cards from one file to another. My father's manner, though neither breezy nor falsely intimate, gave unsettling hints of this wider world. Dan, already a little impatient as he himself later admitted, made the atmosphere worse by shifting his weight from one leg to another. A book on sauces? A life of Marshal Macmahon? A guide to the Upper Rhine? While my father listed his requests, the girls became still more agitated. As if to answer their fears that he might ramble on all night, he explained, rather slowly in the manner of a lecturer to a foreign audience, the reason linking these requests. He wanted to find out the origin of mayonnaise.

Some held that the sauce was German in origin, deriving from the town of Mainz—or Mayence as the French called it— and was first used, oddly enough, as an accompaniment to sauerkraut. Another school of thought maintained that it was first made in the Mayenne region of western France to coat the lobsters from the Bay of St-Malo. My father himself had inclined to the theory that it was so named in honour of Marshal Macmahon, the hero of the Crimea, but Sir Harold Nicolson, who had once written on the subject, had produced evidence that the term went back to Port-Mahon, the capital of Minorca captured by the Duc de Richelieu in 1756. One of the girls, desperately catching at the name, looked up a biography of Cardinal Richelieu and gave my father the shelf number.

As he roamed along the shelves, occasionally turning to whisper to Dan, readers started to shift in their seats. The light from the high windows glinted on upswung pairs of spectacles. Even the old men who had just come in to keep warm, accustomed in the manner of professional egotists to provoke disturbance rather than to acknowledge it, recognized a superior performer in my father and screeched their chairs through a quarter-turn in salute. Their greatcoats, ancient, overlarge, thick-collared, were thrown around their scrawny necks like robes. They looked as if they had been parachuted into their chairs, catapulted into alien thrones by fate, exemplars of that class which has greatness thrust upon it. The whites of their eyes, red-veined Italian marble, twisted up from their newspapers to follow my father's ramblings round the reading-room, like a chorus of baroque saints rapt in a vision of the infinite. My father did not himself look too far removed from the old men, apart from his garish overcoat and the gleaming, buckled shoes he affected for his small feet. The same red-veined marble in red sockets, the same silver stubble outlining his chin, like the silhouette of a moonlit field of corn, the chin itself defiantly thrust up, the same impatient, compressed lips—he shared the marks of the lost tribe.

For a few moments the whole library was a flutter of apprehensive little movements. Then all at once my father, no dedicated browser still less a taker of notes, had had enough. The discovery of some curious not necessarily relevant detail had quenched his thirst for information. He abruptly abandoned the comprehensive research programme he had planned during the walk and made for the door, to be dragged back to the desk by Dan in response to the muffled appeals of the girls to be allowed to enter the books he had under his arm. At this point, my father's good humour suddenly broke. He gave a brief imitation of an ordinary citizen driven to distraction by red tape. How, he implied, could sensible men get on with their work if they were to be continually harassed by pettifogging bureaucrats? Then with a magnificent effort he rallied himself, thanked each of the girls in turn for her help and departed in a blaze of *bonhomie*, pausing on the way out only to greet the Irish attendant, his nerve now fully recovered from their first meeting. 'That's a fine boy you have there, sor.' My father smiled and shrugged his shoulders without committing himself.

Such mistaken guesses at his relationship with Dan were not surprising. To hit upon the truth would have been far from easy. Certainly it was made no easier when Dan, asked what he did, said in his reluctant whine, 'I'm a dancer.' In fact though he did get occasional work, dancing was neither a vocation to him nor did it provide a steady income. The practising in dusty rehearsal rooms till muscles throbbed with exhaustion, the austere abnegation of the grosser world—Dan's life did not accommodate itself to these narrow intensities. He had undoubted talent, had once even auditioned for the Royal Ballet, but recoiled from the necessary effort. These days he was more often to be seen backing some middle-aged singer on a television variety show. While the raddled thrush was belting out 'I could go on singing' or 'What the world needs now is love, sweet love', Dan and his blank-faced accomplices would be shadow-pedalling or skating from side to side, arms flailing as if they had hit a patch of black ice. It was upsetting to catch Dan's eye during these numbers, for he glared at the camera with a demoniac melancholy as if defying the viewer to be distracted by such gimcrack frivolity from the contemplation of mortality. Suddenly the world seemed a sadder place. You felt that something appalling had just happened in the studio and that at any moment the singer might break off in mid-song to inform the audience that she was sorry but she just couldn't carry on in the circumstances and she knew they would all show their respect by filing out quietly to collect their refunds at the box-office.

At teatime once, watching *Playpen* with the children of some friends, I was startled to see a giant toy kangaroo hop on to the screen with Dan's face peering grimly from its pouch. The kangaroo came to a halt, bouncing up and down in time to the music. Dan then clambered out of the pouch, revealing himself to be clad in beige leotards and sporting a droopy tail, a rather sketchy salute to macropodomorphism, and began to hop along behind the kangaroo, singing with bleak finality:

> *'Bouncy-bouncy whee*
> *Just in time for tea*
> *I'm a kangaroo*
> *Don't you wish you were too?'*

These sombre cameos cannot have taken up much of Dan's time. He was always around. Sometimes, on the bus home from work, I would see him leaning against a belisha beacon in the Tottenham Court Road, being talked at by men in heavy coats while his gaze travelled slowly up and down the wide pavement. From the lighted top deck of the bus, I could not see his face in the gathering dark. Another time, he was serving behind the bar in a strange, cold pub in Camden Town. I called in for some cigarettes. He greeted me without being either friendly or unfriendly. We did not have much to say to each other.

'What does Dan do?' I asked Pip Parrott, war hero, antique dealer and last of the Bright Young Things. He answered, off-hand: 'Well, I hear he plays the Lady Bountiful.' 'What do you mean?' 'Oh, he takes soup to the cottagers.' Again meeting with incomprehension, Pip continued rather irritably, 'Cottages equals public loos, cottagers frequenters of same. Sorry to use homintern jargon.' 'How do you know which ones to . . . where to go?' 'Same way as other tramps and vagabonds. The word gets round, and then there are . . . *certain signs.*'

We sat in Mossy's dark, crowded house in which it seemed always afternoon and where Mossy herself played hostess to ageing lotus-eaters and offered sanctuary to menopausal drop-outs. Pip Parrott crouched on one of the dwarf sofas, his great green head sprouting out of a tangle of limbs like a cabbage gone to seed. He talked in burbling rushes, which were punctuated by occasional throat-clearings followed by one or two words given funereal emphasis. He hit 'certain signs' like a cathedral organist pulling out the big stops for the 'Dead March' in *Saul*. This melodramatic delivery usually derived its absurdity from being out of all proportion to the mundane topic, giving tragic intensity to the difficulty of getting his newspapers delivered or the untidy habits of his lodger, a shadowy figure whose role in Pip's life was, perhaps intentionally, never made clear. Yet here his manner seemed no more than the matter demanded, just as the most exaggerated adult narration cannot spoil the surrealism of a fairy story.

I had a vivid image of these 'cottages': thatched, round and comfortable as cottage loaves, nestling, almost beckoning, in the midst of the alien urban forest like the witch's cottage in *Hansel and Gretel*, their walls daubed with rough signs by past visitors, crow's feet perhaps, broad arrows, phallic symbols, all the arcana of the queer world. Even the verbal graffiti, being couched in the language of the underworld, would be cabbalistic, inaccessible to outsiders. This fabulous kingdom had the thick outlines and primary colours of a child's picture. Its tales of beating up and rough trade were as remote from my demure reality as so many dragons breathing fire or Red Queens shouting, 'Off with his head!' There was even something miraculous in the way the silken thread of deviance wound its way through the labyrinth of straight society almost unnoticed by the local residents. The talk of fairies and faggots and bent and straight seemed to belong in a medieval romance.

Here, wishes were magically made reality just by going underground, down the little steps leading to the cottage. Here be giants and sailors and blond-rinsed nancy boys and monsters in macs. Here too were transformations like in a pantomime—a thin man in jeans with a waving palm tree embroidered on his left buttock locking himself into the little cell and coming out dressed as a Roman Catholic priest: 'Just getting back into harness, officer.' A world of sidelong glances and lightning changes, of tremblings soon done with and quizzical goodbyes.

In retrospect, Dan seemed to me too fastidious to knock about in these promiscuous haunts. Puzzled, I later asked Mossy whether Pip's imputation was likely to be true. 'Of course not, my dear,' she said. 'The old thing's just eaten up with jealousy. Dan would never need to go out and forage like that.'

Reluctant, however, to miss a chance of prolonging such an interesting controversy, she in turn asked Dan who said, 'No, never', which ended the matter, for we knew by experience that he always spoke the truth. At the time though, Pip's claim had a certain seamy force which deterred me from rejecting it entirely.

'As they say, he's a good boy, goes and sees his mother every Sunday,' Pip went on, grinning at me now. Again the image of the nursery, the loyal pilgrimage to lay flowers on the grave of his childhood. I pictured Dan sitting bolt upright on the top deck of a bus, holding a carefully chosen seasonal bunch—snowdrops and chionodoxa at this time of year—or perhaps chocolates, she might have a sweet tooth. 'You know mother?' I had not had the pleasure. 'In Camden High Street, the Mother Redcap, all the faggots go there on Sunday morning. Does a roaring trade in every sense of the word. Every pouf in town yelling his head off. Drag shows, unisex strip, go-go boys, all the fun of the fair, if you like that kind of thing.' Again a transformation scene. The lights went down on that strange, deserted bar and with a clash of cymbals, a glare of strobe lights, hey presto! fairyland.

There was something uneasy, defensive about Pip's manner as if I had accidentally pushed open the door of his bedroom before he had time to smooth the rumpled blankets. My casual question about Dan had caught him unawares. He had answered as a fellow member of a hidden world, which was not how he wished to appear, at least not exclusively. Pip did not intend that outsiders should gather the impression that he assessed or talked of young men from this aspect first or only; he found the notion of homosexual solidarity callow and paranoid, the mirror image in fact of that narrow world which the deviant had so thankfully fled. But it was worse still that it should be Dan about whom he was bitching as it were fraternally, for he had as little to do with Dan as possible, dismissing him as 'another of Mossy's waifs and strays'. He would like to have spoken of him with the asexual detachment which befitted their differences of class, intellect and above all age. 'A rather slow young man . . . on the dull side . . . doesn't seem to know what to do with himself'—I had heard Pip use such dignified phrases on other occasions; they would have suited his self-image better than the insider's sly tit-bits he had been unable to resist serving me.

Dan represented most of the things Pip disliked about modern youth. His painstaking caution, his refusal to say anything he did not mean, usually resulting in refusal to say anything, his slow, shy movements, his ducking away from a steady gaze, his tentative kindness—all this was too artfully sincere for Pip, who responded only to the old-fashioned grand manner, camp gossip screeched through the gin-laden air. 'I'm the last of the alcohol generation, my dear. When we're high, we don't giggle, we *cackle*.' If anyone else mentioned Dan, he would say,

'Oh don't let's talk about that tiresome boy.' On the other hand, he could not refrain from bringing up the subject himself: 'Where on earth do you think he comes from? Somewhere amazingly suburban, I should think, Godalming perhaps, or Beckenham.' Mossy, squat, indomitable, fringed and jewelled in the Egyptian manner, sitting straight-backed on a hard little sphinx-armed chair, as Pip said, for all the world like a tableau of what would have happened to Cleopatra if the asp had turned out to belong to a non-poisonous sub-species, groaned, 'Come on, Pip.' 'I'm sorry, darling, but I honestly can't see why you have him in the house.' 'Why are you so obsessed by him? He's just a ballet boy.' 'I'm *not* obsessed by him.'

But this split attitude was a sure sign that Pip was in fact gripped by a fresh obsession. His life was a series of surrenders to enthusiasm. He threw on new identities like a quick-change artist, trotting from one ideological cottage to the next. During the Spanish Civil War, he had volunteered to drive an ambulance but had been arrested by the French at Perpignan on suspicion of being a German arms dealer on a mission to the Nationalists. He had changed his Christian name to Phil which he thought had a more proletarian ring than the Pip which had clung to him from his twenties days. About that time he was also known as 'Party' Parrott, nobody was certain whether because of his energetic social life or because of the CP card which a girl once claimed to have found in the trouser pocket of his dinner jacket. This was to distinguish him from his cousin 'Piccolo' Parrott, also baptized Philip, who had once earned his living in the London Symphony Orchestra but asserted, typically straight-faced, that he was strictly a flautist and had only once helped out on the piccolo when the other flute player, who had a better 'mouth', was off sick. Piccolo Parrott, combining as in so many cases mathematical with musical talent, had abandoned music as a profession in order to support his growing family. He was now a Senior Principal Inspector of Taxes at Somerset House. He and Pip used to get drunk together once a year in memory of the time when he had advised Pip on how most painlessly to be received into the Roman Catholic Church —a step he himself had taken a year or so earlier. They shared a cell during a weekend retreat. During this time, Pip asked to be known as Philip.

The Catholic era ended abruptly when Pip's wife demanded and obtained a divorce for reasons which he dismissed with seeming nonchalance either as 'the acolytes, my dear' or 'the demon al-co-hol', depending on his mood. His latest speciality was describing freakish incidents at meetings of Alcoholics Anonymous. His talk, though as high-spirited as ever, had taken an increasingly savage tone. He would conjure up the revivalist fervour—'yes, my friends, I was an alcoholic and I can tell you even now, that's a hard thing to say'—describe with precise self-observation how carefully he himself would dress for the meeting as for a Chelsea Arts Ball in the old days, recount with relish the cross-purposed conversation over the tea-cups and then shatter the whole image of a comforting if odd social structure by one terrible detail—the neat man beside him in the front row suddenly stricken with the shakes and clawing at his cheek till he drew blood, the middle-aged woman on the platform losing control of her bladder: 'A little pool formed under her chair and began to trickle remorselessly in my direction.'

Here was a desolate vein; its black outline stood out starkly against the amiable meanders of Pip's old gossipy ways. In this new mode he acknowledged only the irreducible facts of physical existence. X-ray plates and cardiograms were the true scriptures; the rest was phoney, mere dust on the dark negative of reality. The only worthwhile news of friends came not from their lovers but from their blabbing specialists; affairs of the heart concerned not passion and its cooling but systole and diastole; where once Pip and his circle had exchanged unreliable whispers about the private parts of mutual acquaintances, now they whispered about the size and hardness of their livers.

He had shared in the hope of his contemporaries, had seen it disappointed as they had, and now found himself getting on a bit without the domestic comforts that padded most of them. He had never liked being alone. He liked it even less now. Not only solitude itself, but the fear of solitude, of being caught in solitude, of imposing his solitude upon other people, of becoming so wedded to solitude that he was awkward in company—the dragnet closed in on him, made him savage and sly. He dared not allow himself a free evening. He would refuse to answer the telephone after seven o'clock on Friday night for fear that people would find out that he had not been asked away for the weekend, although in fact he hardly knew anyone who was now in the habit of either issuing or receiving such invitations, this image of social normality surviving from a much earlier period when he had been a spare man in demand for conventional parties. There was little pleasure to be had in looking back to such times. For the carefully tended relationships which had gilded his halcyon days dissolved in retrospect into a fragile compound of lust and habit, each working to destroy the other— habit dulling the edge of lust and fresh lust corroding the habit of affection.

'Cut it out.' Mossy could not tolerate talk of physical malfunction or of any process which might imply mortality. Mention of grey hairs or stumbling step was forbidden. She would not allow it to be said even of an enemy that he was slowing down a bit, retorting tartly, 'Oh, he never had much go anyway.' Impotence in men of seventy or more she attributed to psychological problems. At the same time, youth caused her no envy. When Pip pointed out a good-looking young man, she would drawl, 'Don't be silly, he's just a boy.' Her world was curiously timeless; she refused to come close either to birth or to death. Her fear of hospitals was merely the most commonplace aspect of her rejection of such things. There was a peculiar fierceness in the way she would say of an old friend, 'He's dying, you know', as if he had committed some unexpected crime and she was not going to let him get away with shamming innocent. As far as Mossy was concerned, people entered the world in their early twenties and continued in it unchanged until they were called away by some random contingency, just as she herself might loll in her bath for ever if it were not for the telephone or the window-cleaner or boredom or the water running cold.

Her distaste for the passage of time was not inspired by vanity.

She was well aware of what she looked like and didn't mind very much. The extravagant curves of lipstick and eyebrow pencil seemed intended to divert attention from her rugged features rather than to emphasize them. She dressed with an imperious bravura which was not so much a serious effort to project a particular personality as an exercise in fancy dress to enliven the scene. Today her role was Cleopatra Thirty Years After. But a different combination of beads, fringes, bracelets and ear-rings might give the effect of She Who Must Be Obeyed or The Queen of the Night or Hiawatha's Mother. Her purpose was not to repair the ruins of a beauty she had never claimed but rather to do her best to keep the show on the road.

To be ill or alone was for her to suffer the feelings of an actor on that night when he first sees a small patch of empty seats in the auditorium, the dread that the patch will spread until the audience is a mere enclave looking nervously round at the emptiness and the producer says afterwards, 'Well, we could give it one more week; you never know, business sometimes picks up around this time of year.' My father, seeing Mossy fidgeting when the weather was too bad to go out or upset by her complaints that he was always leaving her alone in the house, would say, 'You know, she suffers badly from claustrophobia', taking comfort in a psychological term which in other circumstances he might have scorned. Yet this fear of being shut in was not really neurotic, if by that is meant irrational, baseless. She was simply terrified of wasting time. That may sound unlikely in someone who rose so late and did so little; in fact, on occasion Pip, uplifted after a session with his 'alkies', would accuse her not only of over-indulgence but also of wasting precious time. Yet each minute not spent to her satisfaction was a catastrophic loss; only the hedonist counts the ungathered rosebuds with such exactitude. In her own way she showed an iron discipline in the pursuit of pleasure, a refusal to be deflected by ill-health or insolvency. To say, as people did, that she was easily bored implies a carping temper which she had not. In her own line she was content with very little, but the entertainment offered had to be in her own line. Though she appreciated wit, the conversation could be unrelievedly pedestrian so long as it touched the subjects that interested her—gossip, antiques, the theatre, the old days. My father demanded a little more. On the other hand, she shared his disregard for time when things were going well.

I had come for lunch at one o'clock, hoping that we might eat at half past. Pip let me in. We talked, a little uneasily. Towards two o'clock Mossy came down, ready for action. I asked, stiffly, after my father.

'Oh, he's gone out with Dan.'

'It's nearly two, you know. I'll have to get back to work soon.'

Mossy flapped her hand in a movement of indifference and wandered into the kitchen to get a drink, offended at the mention of time when the day had such a promising look to it. On her return, I tried to get the show moving.

'We could go on wherever we're going and leave a note here . . .'

'Or we could wait here.'

'Or we could wait here.'

'Let's wait here for a bit. Pip has been so looking forward to seeing you.'

Pip tried to give his grin a sort of boyish complicity to indicate that he too thought this last assertion rather exaggerated. His conversation certainly made few concessions to my presence:

'The chair, my dear, ah if only you knew the saga of the chair. The bottom's fallen right out of it. I told him if he was so keen to get rid of it why didn't he sell it as a *chaise percée*. By the way, I met one of your exes the other night . . . three guesses which one . . . no, not Arturo, no it was Geordie . . . I'm afraid he's fallen off the wagon again . . . well, he was always clinging on by his fingertips . . . No, I missed *Scrubber*, I must have been away, a tiny cure, my darlings . . . oh I remember, the one about the whore with a heart of Eurodollars symbolizing the spirit of capitalism . . . I still can't quite see why the part had to be played by a man except I suppose capitalism is so awfully *masculine* and *penetrating* . . . have you noticed how everyone these days is talking like poor dear Carlos Marx? . . . no of course I never met him, I may know everybody but he was *long* before my time, you must know that ... I went into that *antiquaire* on the corner and the little poofter behind the guichet showed me some old tat—an ivory swizzle stick, and a moustache-cup—and said, "marvellously late-bourgeois, don't you think?" ... well, I was a trifle irked—after all, six months ago he couldn't even pronounce *art deco* ... so I told him I'd imbibed Marx with my mother's milk and he could stuff his swizzle stick up his moustache-cup for all I cared ... anyway, it's all very well to talk about surplus accumulation but I don't know where on earth the surplus is supposed to come from. I run my own tiny shop purely for the *thrill* of commerce. The word profit never crosses my lips ... every *sou* that trickles into the till goes to pay the enormous wages the State chooses to lavish upon my dear kinsman Piccolo ... there's simply not a grain of birdseed left on the floor of the Parrott's Cage at the end of the month ...'

The bang was loud and flat, like a door slamming at the other end of a long corridor. A loose pane in the window shook and the ever-drawn venetian blinds briefly fluttered to let in the January light.

'Oh dear, the ghastly micks again. So tedious having to keep one's upper lip stiff at my age.' Within minutes, as if released by a delayed action of the same fuse, a chorus of sirens began to bray, alternately growing and fading, drawing the beat of the listening heart into their rhythm. Pip knelt on the sofa and raised a blind. He squinted through the chink like the patron of a speakeasy trying to see if the joint was about to be raided.

'Ambulance, fire engine, another fire engine and a rather sinister police van with SPECIAL UNIT on it. Dull words absolutely paralyse me with terror.'

'Oughtn't you to go and help, Pip? Weren't you in Bomb Disposal?'

'It's so awful being a bugger. You're always expected to be so much braver. Anyway, I don't think they'd exactly welcome me if I turned up and said Major Parrott reporting for duty, sir. The jeans would be all right, but the silver boots?'

'Couldn't you be like the Red Devils ... the Silver Sods?'

It is hard to say whether passers-by would have recognized a superior officer if Pip had appeared on the scene. He had something imposing about him; on the other hand, neither the floppy scarf nor the mauve Norfolk jacket, let alone the silvery suede boots and the long silver hair tied in a pony-tail, exactly suited the part of Major 'Polly' Parrott, late the Royal Engineers, despatches twice, wounded, prisoner of war, escaped. Even thirty years earlier and fatter round the cheeks, he must have stood out in a sappers' mess. Now he looked less like a guardian of the peace than a messenger of death.

There was another bang, louder than the first, this time as if a giant had slapped the world to put an end to the buzzing of the sirens.

'Where can Harry have got to?'

'The Potter? The Queen's Elm? Who knows, depends where he started.'

'I suppose he's quoting Keats to some mad Irishman.'

'Would Keats soothe the hard men of the Provos?'

'Yeats would be better.'

'No, Yeats was a Free State man. Safer with Keats.'

'Keats is a bad sign though.'

More sirens . . . further away, then nearer, then in all directions, near and far together . . . and the bells of the older fire engines ringing, drowning the sirens, and then the braying again. The noise of voices from next door through the thin walls, then louder voices in the street, and terrible running feet. The blood throbbed at the back of my head, then over the crown, beating above the eye-sockets, trying to invade my skull, beating in time to the sirens, no, faster. Pip sat still, watching me. 'Don't worry,' he said.

But worry was on the rampage, contemptuously demolishing the carefully built barricades of indifference, tearing up the paving-stones, smashing windows, banging open impassive shutters, letting air into musty rooms. The old fears were back on the loose. It was dusk again and the bare light-bulbs were switched on over the market stalls. Some of the traders were already packing up to go home, offering perishable or half-perished goods—tomatoes, lettuces, the rare luxury of bananas

—at knock-down prices. It was cold, wet. The pavements were covered with sodden wrapping paper and cabbage leaves. I nearly slipped several times as I ran up and down the lines of stalls looking for the torn sheepskin coat. He had not been under the bus station clock at five, there was nothing unusual in having to wait twenty minutes or half an hour, but it was nearly six. In all the rapidly rehearsed mental scenarios—my father in Casualty, behind bars, grappling with a runaway horse, electrocuted by a high-tension cable—fear for myself intensified concern for his fate. What was to become of me, desolated, virtually orphaned, while he was serving ten years in Dartmoor or lay in a coma for nine months, never again to be much better than a vegetable?

These visions, recognized as fable even while they spun their way through my mind, still increased my panic. The sense of doom was unavoidable. Even if this crisis was resolved, there would be another and another—an endless chain of inescapable panics, not the least cause of which was my knowledge of myself, the knowledge that even after my father finally appeared, the fear would go on reverberating, breaking out in an asthma spasm a day or two later, a spasm made worse by my irritation when I heard them saying, 'It's a funny thing, he always gets these attacks *after* he's been under strain', this irritation carried further still by my foreknowledge of the waves of self-pity that would wash over me as the spasms receded, leaving my resistance to the next panic even lower. I cursed my ability to see what was happening to me and what was going to happen. I longed to be dumb, insentient. It was easy enough for Roosevelt to say that the only thing we had to fear was fear itself, that was indeed precisely the thing that I did fear and I was well aware this was what was wrong but knew no way to put it right.

Since growing up, I had begun to forget what that kind of fear could be like. Besides, at the office it was not our practice to stare into the abyss. We were, after all, established civil servants; we had tenure. Occasionally, we would hear of a colleague being left by his wife, less often of him doing the leaving; sometimes other minor frailties raised their unofficial heads. But in general we were as well guarded from tragedy as from temptation. We handled no money, promotion was almost entirely by seniority at least at my own level, there was no expense allowance and the secretaries were plain. This is not to say that life was dull or the work uninteresting. On the contrary, it was a stimulating exercise in interdisciplinary restructuring. In other words, we were extremely busy, but we didn't have much idea what we were supposed to be doing.

The correct title of the group to which I was rapporteur, secretary and teamaker was the Under-Secretaries' Policy Analysis and Review Staff. In essence, it consisted of a number of persons of Under-Secretary rank on secondment from their various ministries who came together to assess the cost benefit of inter-departmental trade-offs. Although naturally we shared the manner and inevitably the jargon of the service, UPARS was divided into two distinct camps: the senior and rather staider fraternity who referred to the group as 'Yew-parze' and the somewhat more raffish element who called it curtly 'Up-arse'. I belonged to the latter, but I do not want to give the impression that our irreverence was unrestrained. We did not make a habit of returning late from lunch, for example; at worst, our cheeks might be a little flushed the last afternoon before Christmas leave. Sometimes we might smoke a second cigarette with our tea or even talk about girls. But such indulgences were no more than the most cursory bow to our youth. We were as keen to get on and as dedicated to the austerity of public service as any of our seniors.

Having fallen so easily, even thankfully into this vocation which might have been designed for me, I did not welcome the return of these giddy childhood fears. In particular, I did not like the fantasy which jumped uninvited into my mind of my father ambling into a post office to buy stamps and being faced by a crazed Irish bomber high on purple hearts and the legend of Seamus Twomey . . . 'And what part of Ireland do you come from?' 'Mullingar, sor, and stand back or you'll be sorry' . . . 'Mullingar, well now, I caught a great pike on Lough Sheelin once—why don't you let me have that thing?' BANGGG! arms, legs, envelopes, postal orders flying in all directions just like in the comic strips, my father's mouth spouting blood, the IRA man sprawled in a heap of belted raincoat and broken glass, the police turning him over and exclaiming at his fifteen-year-old babyface . . .

Dan came in, breathless, paler than ever.

'Quickly, could you help? Harry's had an accident.'

My father hung over the railings outside the front door like an empty sack. The blood poured from a star-shaped cut on his forehead, trickling down the side of his nose. One eye was closed and swelling fast, the other blinked yellowish, dog-tired, suppliant. He tried, I think, to smile, but his lips would only stretch far enough to give a faint snarl. His face was a dull purple, lolling across the railings like a mottled plum on a branch. In that instant as we stood on the doorstep looking at him, the blood began to come from his mouth, bright and fresh against the darker crimson now mantling his face and straggling through his hair. He tried to move, to walk towards us, but his legs splayed, buckled and he fell forward, his head catching the edge of the railings in the fall. I thought he lost consciousness when we caught him, but he was still mumbling as we carried him awkwardly up the narrow town stairs. I cradled his head and arms, the blood spotting bright for a second on my sleeve before fading to the colour of rust.

The no-parking lines on the new-laid tarmac outside, the dirty stock brick of the back wall opposite, the leafless sycamore leaning over the pavement—all were still. The world was flat and numb. Only the irony of fact disturbed the silence, ticking as coldly as a metronome: bombed, yes, bombed out of his mind . . . get an ambulance—sorry, sir, they're all out on a bomb scare, we've none left for a person scare . . . get a doctor—sorry, we don't make house calls after closing time . . . it's the third fall he's had since Christmas, congratulations, three falls equals one submission, please accept this gold medal with the compliments of the management. At any rate he was breathing, unevenly, noisily, calling out incoherently to start with, then sinking into deeper sleep.

'He's often like this. Sleeps for twenty-four hours. Then gets up, a bit groggy but otherwise all right.'

'But why is he like this?'

'Well, it was a long morning and he must have had a drink when I wasn't looking.'

'No, I don't mean why today, Dan, that's not your fault, you can't watch him the whole time, but why is he like that generally?'

'Darling, why are any of us like that . . . generally?'

'Excess, that's what does for the dear boy.'

'He can be so amusing.'

'Excess, my dear, excess.'

'So amusing.'

'And when you're here, Aldous, he usually makes such an effort.'

'He's bored you know, hasn't got enough to do.'

'Did he ever?'

'That's the trouble with us. We weren't brought up to do a job, not like you, Aldous, we didn't know what work was.'

'I'm not sure I know even now, darling.'

'There, you see.'

'But there must be more to it than that.'

'Yes, of course. All sorts of things. You'll find them out as you go along.'

Find them out, find out what? From my father's own finely embroidered words, from shaky memories ransacked, from illuminating stray remarks, epithets even—'ah, so that's what he was like'—from occasional documents, summonses, bills, something could no doubt be retrieved, but what would that something amount to and how could it shake itself free from the sensuous weight of childhood experience? Even after twenty years peasants can say of a dictator little more than that he smiled or frowned and saw they had enough bread or didn't. Can children say much more of their parents without thereby ceasing to be children? Each perception of grown-up character and motive is a retreat from magic, not a disappointment but a disenchantment. Yet it is a disenchantment that we ourselves have sought. Our parents' world may seem tedious and un-appealing, but we cannot rest content in our ignorance of its real nature. It is not because grown-ups do not play that we know we cannot go on playing for ever but because we have to get to the bottom of the vast and extravagant conspiracy which has landed us where we are.

And supposing I choose to be disenchanted, to affect an impersonality I do not feel, how can I be sure of capturing correctly the rhythms of a dead language? In our electronic age we have surrendered the illusion of conversation. We know that our voices are no more than the humming of so many defective computers printing out their random assemblage of clichés, sentiment and malice, to do with ourselves only and not the other person. Proximity but no communicating. As I wander home in the summer evening I see the well-to-do standing in a cloud of scent on the steps of a theatre chattering to one another about the divine inconsequentiality of what they have just heard, the stimulating, *authentic* refusal of one tramp or madman ever to listen to, let alone answer another, the inner truth of the fantasist's monologue. Dialogue is the last refuge of middle-class morality, strictly for the straights.

In burrowing back to my father's youth, I am trespassing upon a time when people communicated without talking so much about the difficulty of communication. They did have difficulty of course; the channels were already furred; words and feelings got lost in transit but broken phrases, closely guarded emotions still trickled through under the escort of irony. These staccato interchanges are now poignantly dated, for they turned out to be dialogue's long-drawn-out death rattle. It is hard to rehearse them today without regret for possibilities which are no longer available to us. To reopen such a terrible old wound demands a better excuse than filial piety. And that is certainly not my justification for what must inevitably be a series of motorized vignettes, an album of loose-leaf fancies, a period piece (with all the patronizing sentiment that phrase implies)—tag it how you please.

If I set about trying to reconstruct the life and times of Harry Cotton, it is not to build him a monument. I am well aware that lapidary tribute is as out of date as the storyteller's art; narrative is for hayseeds, discontinuity is the thing now. Nor am I hoping to achieve the truth, or a truth, or the real truth—or any of those high ambitions with which people like to dignify their diverting fictions. I cannot hope for much more than to dust off a few old sporting prints. After all, I am neither a social worker nor a psychiatrist and I have no great urge to have my father explained to me or to himself. In reality, I want something more.

The light is dimmed. The memory of how it shone upon me will dim too in time. I must try to re-create the source of that light. I can draw no warmth from its fast fading reflections in old photograph albums, the sepia reliquaries of our past. In any case, time's secret police have erased the figures from the frame. Where once a young man in a Shetland jersey and riding breeches squinted into the camera, there is now only a blank doorway crudely blacked in. If they can fake the records, I have at least the right to trace the outline of what might have been the reality, not because I wish to satisfy my curiosity but because I want to entertain my imagination. I want to people my world with resurrected bodies, to snaffle from the tomb the creatures of affection, to blow colour back into the pressed rose. Is that too much to ask? Yes, but not too much to try.

Early Morning

Waking was a slow delight. Faint echoes of the night before still hummed at the back of Harry's head. The creatures of his dreams—a gaggle of bawdy old women, two jockeys in a pulpit, some Scottish cousins singing hymns in ragtime—shuffled off stage, leaving blackness or not quite, for the gas lamps already lit in the dark street outside made the windows paler blurs. He stretched in the creaking bed, then still drowsy snuggled down again. The old women tiptoed back on stage to join in the hymns. They took off their shoes and banged them on the table in time to the organ played by the two jockeys in the Sefton colours, 'O God Our Help in Ages Past', knock, knock, who's there? Harry—Harry who?—haricot vert—groan, groan. You don't need two jockeys to play that organ—please sir, they're only little ones. Knock, knock, open that door in the name of the law. Suspended an immense distance away in outer space,

Harry surveyed the hills and valleys of the quilted counterpane, a stray feather tickling his nose. For God's sake who will rid me of this turbulent knocking? Something must be done. From the further reaches of the Milky Way, Harry launched a grunt.

The click of the door opening, the little clatter of cup on saucer as the tray knocked against the door-post, a stifled murmur of annoyance, shoes clucking on the parquet then clunking on the worn carpet, the slither of stockings rubbing against each other and as she bent over him, the scrape of starched apron on the counterpane. Her soft breath slid past his nose. As she stretched her arms to put down the tray, he caught the scent of sweat, still fresh from the heat of the hotel passage, edged with a slight sour early morning smell. She settled the cup in the saucer. He sat up and kissed her on the lips. She grinned, leaning half over him. She had big white teeth.

'No biscuits, sor, is that right now?' She drew her heavy eyebrows together in exaggerated concern.

'That's right. I'm banting.'

'You're a thin man already surely.'

'No, I have to. I'm riding in a race today.'

'Mind you don't fall off.'

'What part of Ireland do you come from then?'

'Tralee.'

'You must be the rose they talk about.'

She groaned and told him not to be so sharp or he'd cut himself. On the way out, she patted the racing saddle he had hung over the armchair: 'That's a dreadful thin saddle. Won't it make you sore?' She laughed as she closed the door.

In the second-hand bull-nosed Morris piled high with saddles and boots, the windows steamed up as snug as a nautilus in the black waters of the early morning, Frogmore O'Neill, horse-coper's son and himself horse-coper-elect, sang:

'Fad-ed boys, jad-ed boys, Womankind's
Gift to a bull-dog nation . . .'

They roared out of the stable yard of the Black Boy, engine coughing loudly, into the silent streets of Nottingham. Froggie's bulbous eyes peered through the darkness, his sandy hair standing up straight as if he had just seen a ghost, his lips wide as a mouth-organ. Harry pulled the grubby rug up over his knees, which were knocking together in the cold, scarcely protected by his thin breeches. He cleared his throat, sat forward to rub the condensation off the windscreen.

'Froggie.'

'In order to distinguish us from less enlightened minds,
We all wear a green car-na-tion.'

'Froggie, I kissed the chambermaid.'

'Where?'

'At the Black Boy.'

'Just as well you didn't kiss the black boy. No, I mean whereabouts did you kiss her?'

'On the lips.'

'Ah, so did I.'

'The one with the big teeth?'

'She did have rather big teeth.'

'I don't believe you.'

'No, I promise you. I always kiss the maid.'

'Do they like it?'

'Usually. It gets the day off to a good start. Thing is, it doesn't matter if they're pretty or not. It's just like a goodnight kiss from your mother.'

'I don't think my mother ever kissed me goodnight.'

'She must have.'

'I don't think so.'

'Oh well, thing is, it's all quite innocent.'

'You never get any further?'

'No, that's not the idea at all. It's just a cheerer-upper.

'Fad-ed boys, jad-ed boys . . .'

Froggie's enormous mouth spread into a pillar-box grin, his broad chin pushing the polo neck of his jersey down towards his chest. They were driving down a long, twisting street of low brick houses. It was still dark. There was no sign of life, nobody about, no trees, no grass, only now and then the lighted windows of a newsagent with the blurred outline of a bent man undoing parcels. The car bumped on the cobbles, occasionally slewing sharply on a wet tramline. Harry, gazing sleepily at the empty pavements, was startled by a mass of still, dark shapes. As they got closer, he could see that they were men, about fifty of them, standing quite motionless, shoulders hunched, chins pressed down into their chests.

'What on earth are they all doing up at this time of night?'

'Wake up, old boy. They're going to work. Miners probably.'

'Poor sods.'

'They're the lucky ones.'

'I suppose so.'

'What you going to do, Harry?'

'Go on riding as long as I can.'

'But afterwards? Will your father give you a job?'

'No, you have to be good at maths to be an actuary,' said Harry. 'Anyway, we don't get on.'

'Thing is, none of us do. We are the generation that don't get on with their parents. That's why they're so close with the cash.'

'Fleas can only expect fleabites.'

'Ah, 'tis a blithe parasite you are,' said Froggie irishly. 'I'll say this for my da, he likes a jar.'

'More than I can say for mine. I was brought up on thimblefuls of dry sherry.'

'Made up for lost time then, haven't you? Hey, safety first, Stanley boy!' Froggie hooted at an old man who had stepped out from the kerb without looking.

'All together now, why are we like the man who wouldn't wear braces and didn't have a belt?'

'Because we have no visible means of support. Oy.'

'Oy.'

The straggling streets died away. They began to climb out of the flat Midlands. The road ran between quickset hedges where the old man's beard hung like a mist in the slow dawn. The hedgerow elms leant into the swelling hills, haphazard sentries nodding at their posts. The fences were broken down, the sedge invaded the pasture. The gates were patched with anything that came to hand—barbed wire, odd pieces of wood from carts and sheds; they swung askew from old pit props pressed into service as gateposts, decaying industry propping up depressed agriculture. A red winter sun broke out over the rim of the hills and glistened on the dirty dew. Harry opened his eyes wide and yawned, feeling the staleness at the back of his mouth. The brambles humped themselves over rotting tree trunks, the bracken sprang unmolested across the woodland ride. The land had the fairy-tale curse upon it; even the cobwebs were left over from the former life, hanging ragged, blacker than the grey morning. Yet the sleep, though sad, was also gentle. The poverty that shaped these soft outlines was at the same time consoled by them. The brambles on the rusting quarry railway bore fat blackberries in September and in summer willow herb hid the discarded plough in the corner of the field. Men driven from this land saw its beauty blossom even as they blocked up the pithead and slammed the cottage door.

'Look, it's a miracle, a pub open at nine in the morning.'

In a village up in the hills they sat becalmed, the Morris entirely surrounded by sheep. The flocks stretched as far as they could see in every direction, shepherds and dogs noisily trying to keep them separate. In the great barn just off the road other sheep were already restlessly turning in their pens, and an auctioneer was gabbling in the middle of a ring of men, some perched on straw bales, others leaning forward on their sticks. Across the road, the lights were on in the Three Drovers, making the best of its special market licence.

'Five-a-five-a-five, finest ewes off the east daleside . . .'

'A little stout will warm us up, two pints, please.'

'Twenty-six-six-six-six-and-a-half, you won't see better than these, hardy Cheviot crosses these are . . .'

'Same again, landlord, if you will.'

'Six-and-a-half, to you, Mr Matthews, sir, do very nicely down in the Cotswolds these will . . .'

'Must have a decent breakfast, old boy. Have a chaser now, always have a chaser to settle the stomach, doubles, my friend.'

'Now then, now then, you all asleep this fine morning, I haven't seen ewes like these since I was a lad . . .'

2*

'Chase the chaser, that's the thing, better than toast and marmalade.'

'If I must, I must, going, going at twenty-seven-and-a-half. . .'

'Same again, please. Nice pub you've got here.'

'*Very* nice pub.'

'Gone.'

'Pity Kate's not here.'

'Kate would have liked it.'

'Kate likes a good breakfast.'

'She always did. I remember when we were children . . .'

'You had breakfasts like this when you were so high? I never believed that story about the thimblefuls of sherry. Now I see why your growth was stunted.'

'Would the owner of car number WV 271 please remove it from the middle of the road where it is obstructing the traffic.'

'On the contrary, the sheep are obstructing my car. Would the owner of sheep number . . .'

'I say, look at the nancies in their knickers. Don't they look just too feahfully tophole, what?'

'These, my dear sir, are breeches and kindly don't make fun of my accent. Took me years to learn to speak like this.'

'Go oan, git out of here, you big fat——'

'Look here, this is a *public* house, isn't it?'

'Want a proper hidin' then?'

Froggie answered by taking off his coat with gusto and squaring up like an old-fashioned prizefighter. In his breeches and stockinged legs he recalled a hand-coloured print of Tom Cribb delighting the Fancy. His great pale eyes bulged with pleasure as he shouted abuse at his opponent, also stocky but black-haired and dark-eyed, bellowing back with equal zest. Harry ordered himself another drink and leant back against the bar, elbows propped on the greasy wood as the two pugilists launched wild swings at each other. The local man seemed to have a lead of a few minutes' drinking on Froggie. On the other hand, Froggie had made up for lost time. There was not much in it and the two of them landed among the enthusiastic spectators more often than they landed on the target.

The stout began to warm his empty stomach, the whisky

sang in his head. Harry floated out of the low-beamed smoky tap-room, first hovering like a sozzled angel over the heads nodding and wagging their flat caps and billy-cocks, then soaring into realms of pure freedom where Tom Brown eternally knocked out Flashman and Teddy Lester rescued smaller boys from cads and townees; there was no quarrel that couldn't be settled by frank manly fisticuffs. You're a fine Christian gentleman, Frank Manly, sir, and you've got the finest straight left in England, put 'em up, sir; David was a public-school man, Goliath a common sort of fellow, half past ten in the morning and drunk in the Derbyshire hills. Mr Burrows was light-heavyweight champion of the army, you know, sir—nonsense, Cotton, Mr Burrows wasn't even in the army—well, sir, that's what he told us in Maths this morning, half past ten in the morning and drunk in the Derbyshire hills. Nobody knows where we are, nobody cares where we go and we've got enough stout inside us to sink a battleship if we had any battleships, half past ten in the morning and dead drunk in the Derbyshire hills. Come on, Froggie, come *on*, but Froggie had lost his balance again and collapsed into the arms of two elderly shepherds who bundled him out through the double doors and dumped him in the mud beside the road where he sat staring over the hills like a sightless prophet.

'Come on, I don't want to miss my chance on Rubber Band.'

'Look here, old boy, I'm riding Rubber Band.'

'No no, I'm riding Rubber Band.'

'Didn't you think that was a nice pub?'

'A very nice pub.'

'Aha trick question. Caught you. Thing is, it wasn't a nice pub at all. It was a bloody awful pub.'

'All right, it was a bloody awful pub.'

'Don't humour me.'

'I'm not humouring you.'

'Thing is, you suck up the whole bloody time. Why don't you speak out straight and say it was a bloody awful pub.'

'I said it was a bloody awful pub. Now shall I drive?'

'You will not drive. This is my car for better or worse and I am driving it. Even if it were your car, I would not permit you to drive it because you are not reliable in a tight spot. I go into a pub to have a few quiet drinks, I am set upon by thugs who mock my speech and molest my person and what happens? Do you stand shoulder to shoulder with your comrade in arms, trading blow for blow, do you call for the police, do you even ask the landlord to eject my assailant? Do you hell. You stick to the bar like fly-paper, drinking yourself into a stupor with an idiot grin on your face. And then to add insult to injury *and* insult, you say what a nice pub, what a charming place. I suppose if we'd been in the trenches, you'd have said what a delightful spot, so snug and warm. Hey, you *are* driving. Well, I only hope they catch you. I can tell you the court's bound to take a very serious view. I've never seen such a drunk man at the wheel. There's too much of this sort of thing going on, hopelessly tight jockeys careering across the country murdering innocent pedestrians. As soon as they see the saddles in the back, they'll have you inside. Five years without the option and take his licence away and give it to the poor.'

Harry planed over the blank day, rolling through the unbounded space of youth, a hawk over the hills above the amiable meanders of the River Dove. To be open, free-floating, unbounded was the only way to stay alive. You had to keep moving, the wind slapping at your cheek, the branches thrashing your legs. The old engraving of the Four Horsemen of the Apocalypse which hung above his bed when he was a child showed the horses white, or so he thought and deduced them to be of the pure Arab strain, slow but tireless, purpose-bred for eternal, implacable pursuit. They were always hard behind, but they could catch you only if you stopped. On, on, faster, faster, but Harry's foot was already flat against the floor. The Morris was not much good on hills, particularly into the wind.

'She's a lovely girl, Harry.'

'Who?'

'Kate. Your cousin Kate. Who else? He's a terrible cold man. Never thinks about his little cousin Kate.'

'She'll be there. She's on driving duties this week. C. L. says she corners well.'

'I love your cousin Kate. But she doesn't love me.'

'Amazing.'

'It is amazing, how right you are. But then the thing is, I don't think she loves men at all.'

'Wounded vanity.'

'Not a bit, old boy. Just profound knowledge of human nature. I don't think she cares for men.'

'It *is* wounded vanity.'

'Well, you wait and see. She'll declare herself soon enough.'

'Have you told her of your great discovery?'

'God no, I may be a bounder but I'm not a shit.'

'Matter of opinion.'

'For example, have you taken in the C.L. set-up?'

'It's just a job.'

'Mmm, just a job ... I wonder if you would mind not treating my car like a dodgem.'

'Twisty road ... Good Lord, what was that?'

An enormous green racing car overtook them as they came out of the bend—in the middle of the roar and dust two pink faces in goggles and fur helmets as motionless and identical as the twin headlamps on the long belted bonnet.

'C.L.'

'And Kate?'

'And Kate.'

'Wow.'

Weighing Out

'The Bumper's cut.'

'What'd you say?'

'Never you mind, wasn't talking to you.'

'If you mean to imply that the gentleman jockey is drunk, you may be right or you may be wrong, but *Speak Up!*'

'If you heard what I said, why'd you ask?'

'Now, now, Frogmore.'

'No question of now now. This pimple-faced chalk jockey has gratuitously insulted me.'

'I am not on the chalk.'

'Only because they don't even know how to spell your bloody name.'

'Come along, sir.'

'Don't call me sir. Only chalk jockeys call me sir. I am of the fraternity.'

'Morning, Mister.'

'Ah, Joe. I seem to be having a bit of trouble.'

Froggie softened, beamed. Joe Johnson ironed out ill-humour like he ironed breeches, exuded balm from every wrinkle. Only a slight twitch around the mouth let slip his impatience with the petty fracas. He would have no brawling in this refuge from hard knocks, for the ramshackle low room was his temporary kingdom. The rest of the year, it lay empty, uncared for. The wind sneaked in through the broken panes; tramps sneaked in through the door to sleep on the dusty benches. Sweat and urine still clung to the place like the fog clouding the old gas-lamps. But overnight Joe and his fellow valets had created a haven for the three days of the meeting. On the long middle table lay freshly laundered towels, bandages, soap, brushes, embrocation, razor strops, folding mirrors, basins of hot water; along the sides neat piles in each jockey's place, breeches, underwear, jersey or silks, cap and skull-cap, all shining and clean; ditto the riding boots under each seat; above, the saddles hung from their pegs like stags' heads with the weight-cloths dangling below them. At the end a fire snorted in the grate, the senior professionals sitting either side of it, cathedral saints in their niches, gaunt, bent-shouldered, their white skin scar-slashed and bruised. Everything here was brushed, gleaming, polished, in its place. Yesterday the racecourse valets had dismantled a similar haven three hundred miles away; next week they would recreate it two hundred miles in the other direction. They were fairy cobblers; nobody ever saw them at work, they were always free to brew tea or console a faller, but next morning all mud would be gone, all tears mended. Within this community each valet lorded it over his own. Joe's boys swore by him, he by them. Together they derided the poor horsemanship and insolvency of other parishes. The jockey inherited his valet's history, had it kept warm for him by the

ripple of reminiscence as he stamped on his boots; Joe had done
Morny Cannon, or was it Tom Cannon? No, Tom would be a
hundred if he were alive.

'Used to wear boots up to their armpits, they did. None of
your American low-cut rubbish. Them's no better than galoshes.
Fred Archer used to say . . .'

'You never did Archer, did you, Joe?'

'Didn't say I did, did I?'

'Joe Joe.'

'Who's on the favourite then?'

'One of Joe's.'

Even in the few nervous moments before each race, the
parochial spirit flickered. The presence of Joe, companionable,
dwarfish Munchausen, loomed vast and sheltering over the
assemblage of broken-boned waifs, adventurers and bankrupts.
The facts of his life—a sequence of stuffy rooms like this interrupted by long journeys in draughty vans, thirty smokes a day
and damn the bronchitis, a couple of jars down the road and
stumble back to bed down on the dirty towels along these
benches unless the ditch felt more comfortable—well, they were
facts, but they were not to be talked of. No family, not much in
the way of wages, a pauper's grave in a strange town after a
foggy November meeting—these might be facts too, but not
worth troubling an audience with. If misfortune was to be
mentioned at all, it had to be on the grand scale: princes of the
turf gone bust, jockeys caught coupling with duchesses, bones
broken in a dozen places.

This affable guild of valets faced outward, concentrating its
half-bright, half-bleary gaze on the passing accidents of its own
world, as uncaring of the world beyond as of the world inside
their own skulls. A set of silks left behind at Wincanton would be
wafted overnight to Catterick on the fingertips of friendly
railway guards; a boot split on the rails at Ayr would turn up
fine-sewn the next day at Worcester. The pleasure in working
these marvels, in arousing such astonishment gave these slow,
bent men that self-assurance that comes from contentment in
the exercise of power, such contentment depending not so much
on the conspicuousness of the power as on the neatness and

completeness with which it may be exercised. Joe stopped to
look at Harry, consultant pausing to examine patient.

'You don't look so good, Mister.'

'Been wasting too hard, Joe.'

'Wasting—well that's one name for it.'

'Joe, could you get me twenty on Rubber Band?'

'Can't leave the room, you know that.'

'Send one of the lads out then.'

'You're in a hurry to lose your money. Fancy yourself, do you?'

'Well, I think I've got a decent chance.'

'Never saw a cut man win a good race yet.'

'You don't have to get the cash to the ring. Just pass the word
to Cod.'

'I hear you're in deep with old Cod. He's a hard bugger is
Cod. He'd sell his own mother, that one.'

'Not unless the price was right. Anyway, I'm more or less
breaking even.'

'In my book even's as long as a piece of wrist elastic. Hey,
Mister, you're shivering.'

'Look, you must get it on. We'll be weighing out in a minute.'

'Shivering like a bloody jelly.'

'Well, I have had a bad-ish run recently. Got to recoup.'

'All right then. I'll send the lad out. But you want to watch it.
I'll have some hot blankets ready.'

Harry thanked him. The nagging throb stopped. He was on.
He felt a glorious absence. Someone had said it was like sniffing
cocaine. For the next few minutes he was flying free. Nothing
mattered. He could settle down to ride the best race he knew
how. There were people who fussed about the odds, rejoiced
in having caught a hundred-to-six shot at twenties. That was
nothing. Being on was all that counted. He stretched himself on
the bench, twiddled his boots. The toes winked back at him.
At his side, Froggie was still slowly undressing in preparation
for the race after this one.

'Extraordinary thing is, I feel rather sleepy.'

'Extraordinary thing is you're still conscious at all.'

'There is that.'

Froggie drew off his socks with the seductive languor of a

stripper, right leg thrown over his left knee, foot pointing to the ceiling. Harry gazed numbly at the foot. It seemed to be bleeding. Drip, drip, drip from one toe to the next. Everything was all right. He was on. Perhaps he was seeing things. No, not all right exactly. He was buzzing like a bee. He was on. Poor old Froggie with his bleeding feet.

'Bumper's painted his toe-nails.'

'Go on.'

'No, I swear it.'

'Fuckaduck, so he has. He's painted his bleeding toe-nails.'

'Bumper's painted his toe-nails.'

Froggie sat, eyes half-closed, with a faint smile on his broad mouth. Jockeys all round the room stood up, craning their necks, leaning on one another's shoulders to get a better view of the outrageous extremities. One haggard horseman of mature years hopped up on the bench and shaded his eyes from the gas-lamp like a punter trying to follow a group of horses on the far side of the course.

The toe-nails were painted a deep crimson.

'Now I know what Lily Langtry felt like.'

'They didn't stand on chairs to look at her nail varnish.'

'Ah but to have all eyes upon one, now that's the thing.'

'Tell me, Mr O'Neill, when did you first take up this original habit?'

'Some girl fooling about, you know how it is, I scarcely remember. Rather fetching in its way, don't you think?'

'Bloody nancy boy.'

'This seems to be a common delusion. Must I defend my masculinity yet again?'

Froggie rose to his feet. He stood in a menacing posture, swaying slightly on his scarlet toes. The opposition subsided, busying itself with boots and saddles, still grumbling beneath its breath at this exhibition of epicenity. Joe came round with his little canvas quiver of whips. He was in a state of ambiguous excitement. He did not like ill-feeling among his boys, but he liked Froggie's red toe-nails. They were good copy; they showed the detachment of the racing world from conventional standards of conduct; he liked people who didn't give a damn.

'Red toe-nails. I'd never have believed it. You youngsters. Now here's a long tom for you, Mister, or I've got a little whalebone switch if you'd prefer.'

Some jockeys brought all their own tack with them, including whips. Harry liked to choose from Joe's quiver, although most of the whips, being cadged, discarded or left behind, were well worn and curved like bows. There was something Homeric about the choosing, a reverent concentration upon the practical. Joe hovered in front of him, tilting the canvas bag towards him. Harry tried a couple, holding the whip delicately between index and middle finger, twirling it through a lazy arc. The leather and plaited cord which covered the spines of metal or whalebone were greased with sweat, the tassels frayed by long wear on the steaming flanks of tired horses. Although he carried his whip like the rest, Harry did not hanker for the licence of being told, 'Give him a tap if you like, the owner's on a bundle today,' not through excessive tenderness for the horse's feelings (an animal which crashed through hurdles and battered stiff brush fences would hardly mind his imitation of a man riding a hard finish) but because the moment a jockey took out his whip half the crowd cursed him for his cruelty and the other half cursed him for not keeping the horse straight, both curses provoked by prejudice rather than observation.

'Look sharp now, here's the senior steward . . .'

An elderly man in tweeds came in. He stood on a chair and made gather-round-me gestures. They stayed put on their benches. The hum of conversation moderated only marginally as he limped into his harangue, the jockeys continuing to dress at a leisurely pace. They were unmoved by such rhetoric, having heard similar advice at the beginning of each meeting since time began. The senior steward laid into the apathetic sunken-shouldered crew, like a superannuated Ulysses attempting to revive the energies of his weary mariners. Unfortunately, his voice, though melodious, had itself a tendency to the effete.

'I regret to say that in previous yeahs there has been an awful lot of boring in the dip . . .'

'Lot in here too.'

'. . . so I want you to know that this yeah we have stationed a man there . . .'

'What's he say?'

'. . . to keep an eye on you chaps. So you've had your warning.'

'So help me Gawd, I swear I'll never touch another drop.'

'What's that, Mr O'Neill? Are you ill?'

'Never better in my life, Sir George.'

'In your what? What's wrong with you, man?'

'Life, sir, a well-known fatal disease.'

'What have you done to your toes, man? Better let the M.O. have a look at them before you go out. Can't have blood all over the paddock. Now then, I want a clean meeting. Jump awff sensibly, hold to your line and keep your hawss straight round the last bend.'

'You can't always stop a tired horse rolling, sir.'

'I think you can trust us to tell the difference between rolling and crawssing. Anyway, I hope I don't have to see any of you again.'

'Feeling's mutual.'

'Now awff you go and jawlly good luck to you all.'

As Harry trooped out to the weighing-room behind the other jockeys, he looked back and noticed that Froggie seemed to have gone to sleep.

'Red toe-nails,' said Joe, chuckling to himself.

Down the deep-carpeted stairs they strutted, cocks descending a midden. Frogmore's winged collar sticking out from under his wattles like a ruff in the pride of his crowing, Harry still slight and bony, even now not quite fledged, a late developer. They knocked on the door of the suite, smirking at each other. Froggie did a little fancy-work with his feet, patent-leather pumps twinkling. Harry slumped against the doorpost pretending he had been sandbagged, letting his legs gradually slide together away from the wall until he was sitting on the floor.

> '*Vedrai carino*
> *se sei buonino*
> *che bel rimedio*
> *ti voglio dar.*'

Tingling from his bath, thighs still aching from a hard finish, at first Harry thought the singing on the other side of the door was another buzzing in his head. Slowly, as in the twilight between sleep and waking, he recognized the tune and wondered who was offering that sweet embrocation against life's hard knocks, whose voice it was ringing so finely through these egregious halls.

The door opened. His cousin Kate put her head out.

'Oh God. You. What are you doing on the floor?'

'The doctors say I may never walk again. You know my good-looking friend Mr O'Neill?'

'Come in, Frog. But don't be a bore. C.L. can't stand any spooning.'

> '. . . sentilo battere
> toccami quà.'

They stood in the doorway while a dark girl with round shoulders standing by the piano threw out the final notes as if she hoped her breath would slam the lid on the accompanist's fingers. Kate appraised her sharply.

'Stella, your seams aren't straight.'

'Don't nag.'

'I warn you, C.L.'s in a foul temper.'

'Are *my* seams straight, please?' The accompanist's voice was ingratiating, soft. He stood up from the piano and tugged at his trouser bottoms, twisting his head to inspect an imaginary pair of stockings.

'Your lipstick's smudged, Evelyn. This is Evelyn Henriques, C.L.'s racing manager.' The accompanist bowed with theatrical restraint.

'You play very well.'

'I used to be all right, but I've become somewhat rusty since the days when I had my Wigmore. But Stella now, she really does have a lovely big voice.'

'Can I try the last phrase again, please?'

'Of course, darling.'

'. . . *toccami quà.*'

'Stop that garbage.' The breathless voice gabbled, shouted

the words. C.L. stood in the doorway to the bedroom, gargantuan, thyroid-eyed, munching a chicken-leg. Although her tweed skirt was the size of a bedspread, it was drum-taut. Her pasty face bulged around her small features. Only her legs, firmly planted wide apart, seemed, massive though they were, to be constructed on the human scale.

'But C.L., Stella has a charming voice. Rather like yours in the old days.'

'Shut up. I don't want any of your soft soap. And who asked you to talk about my voice?'

'Well I thought our young friends . . . she was at the Conservatory, you know.'

'No I wasn't. I was in the lavatory.' The great cheeks trembled—too much to call it a smile. 'I've got a bone to pick on that one as it happens. I thought I had made it quite clear on Stable Orders this morning that all loos were to be personally checked by Blue Label before leaving for the races.'

'You did, C.L.'

'Well, Kate, let me tell you that I went downstairs when we got back and it was bloody disgusting. No paper and smelled like a sewer. Ruined my whole afternoon. I won't tolerate it. It's bad enough having to stay in this—who the hell are these *men*?'

'My cousin and Froggie O'Neill. They're riding at the meeting.'

'Of course I know they're riding. I've got eyes in my head, haven't I? What I want to know is, do you think they are any good, Evelyn?'

'They ride very nicely, my dear.'

'Soft soap again. Which one's better?'

'They're both good.'

'Come on, Evelyn. Are they as good as Sears?'

'Sears is more experienced.'

'For God's sake, I know all about his experience. I've been paying for it, haven't I? Sears rides like a bloody grocer. I'll never let him on Ampersand again. Never.' She hammered on the piano with her chicken-leg.

'Well, you could do worse than try one of these gentlemen.'

'They're too big. I don't want that horse to carry a single pound in overweight.'

'Mr O'Neill, what weight do you ride at?'

'Round about eleven stone five.'

'And Mr Cotton?'

'The same.'

'Near enough. Perhaps we could put them on the scales, my dear, and may the lightest man win.'

'I'm not having them in my bathroom.'

'In my room then.'

Henriques led them down the passage. There was a skip in his stride.

'Down to the essentials please, gentlemen.'

They stripped to their underpants and stood waiting while Henriques brought the scales out into the middle of the room. The soft light of the bedside-lamp fluttered across Froggie's body as he mimicked himself squaring up in the pub, Knockout O'Neill, the Terror of the Drovers, scoops of shadow brimming over his collarbone twice broken in falls already, his rib-cage as clear as the skeleton of a fossil in amber. Walls, carpets, counterpane were all delicately pastel-shaded, no colour quite itself. In this anonymous commercial blur, Froggie was white and hard as a bone bleached by the sun. The freckles across his back and the bruises below his ribs, brown like the bruises on a peach, only marked how white he was. Harry stood very still, startled by this nakedness. Then he saw Evelyn Henriques looking at them both with a smile and he turned away. Off the piano stool Henriques seemed smaller, older. As he bent down to look at the scales, the light drew a network of wrinkles across his cheek.

'I make Mr Cotton two pounds the lighter. I wish you luck. But I wouldn't count too much on all this if I were you.'

Back in the other room, Kate was taking dictation.

'. . . Bentley at hotel door 10.30 a.m. Also the Lagonda as first reserve. Blue and Red Labels to stand by. Have right-hand window of Lagonda open. All cars must have radio tuned to Home Service. Food for journey—three wings of chicken, salad with fresh lettuce—very important about lettuce and raise hell to get it—and the new fruit cake, the one without the icing. Cake-knife must be sharp. Refill flask. Check loo in member's stand. Nine race cards, pencils and *Sporting Life* to be handed over at gates. Tell—what colour did I give that new girl— Pink? Pink Label to have rugs properly folded. Warn the police I am coming, also loo lady. Most important: cross your fingers for Ampersand. I have not been feeling well all this week and I need a win to pep me up. Get tickets for new show at the Adelphi, but check that Binnie Hale will definitely appear, otherwise no good. Order table at Savoy for three for 10.15 precisely. Tell manager, head waiter useless, that Miss L., must repeat must have a corner table and will not repeat not sit on top of the band which was where they put her last time and was deafened by the noise. Say I am rather fussy if you like. Now put this in capitals: Urgent repeat urgent. In stable orders last week all colours were warned to report any illness immediately. This morning Pink Label comes into Miss L.'s room with a hacking cough, breathing germs everywhere. This must not happen again. With Miss L.'s gastric history we cannot afford to run any risk of infection. Well?'

'Mr Cotton is the lighter by two pounds.'

'All right. He rode a good finish on that Rubber Band animal today. Give him a gallop on Ampersand tomorrow morning. And tell Sears I'm finished with him.'

Harry babbled thanks like a man who has fallen down a gold mine.

'I said no soft soap.'

'Will he be running tomorrow?'

'None of your business. I don't want any gossiping round the stables. If you're the sort that goes tattling to journalists you had better get out now. Kate says you can sing.'

'Not really, not like—'

'Stella thinks much too much of her singing. The truth is, it's just highbrow garbage. But Kate knows some good songs, don't you, Kate?'

Kate did not change her expression. She put down her note-pad and pencil, got up and went over to the piano. She was tall and thin. Her features were regular, unremarkable, but something

about her—the naked pallor of her complexion, her thin lips—
gave her a sealed look. When she spoke more than a few words
or unleashed her gurgling laugh, it was like the rattle of a
convent shutter opening. A strange bright eye blinked out. Then
abruptly the shutter would close again as if the eye had not
exactly liked what it saw or as if she needed time to think about
it. Harry could never guess what she was thinking but then he
had never tried very hard. She was four years younger, still not
twenty. One afternoon when her mother had gone off to the
local magistrates court to deal out justice with a hand which was
only marginally sterner than it was impartial, Kate, still a
schoolgirl but home for the holidays, had packed a small suitcase
and fled. She wanted to work with horses. Jobs were hard to
come by. To be one of C.L.'s secretaries was at least within
smelling distance of the stable.

'Come on now, Harry. Two little babes in the wood.'

> *'There's a tale of two little orphans who were*
> *left in their uncle's care,*
> *To be reared and ruled, and properly schooled*
> *Till they grew to be ladies fair.*
> *But oh, the luckless pair!*
> *For the uncle, he was a cruel trustee;*
> *And he longed to possess their gold;*
> *So he led them thence to a forest dense,*
> *Where he left them to die of cold.*
> *That, at least, is what we're told.'*

Their voices tripped along in talentless unison, Kate decidedly
sharp, Harry a little flat but making up for it by mugging like a
ukelele player, throbbing with outrage at the uncle's rapacity,
whispering the narrator's scepticism behind cupped hand,
drenching the refrain in sentiment . . .

> *'They were two little babes in the wood,*
> *Two little babes, oh so good!*
> *Two little hearts,*
> *Two little heads,*
> *Longed to be home in their two little beds . . .'*

C.L. beat time, slumped on a sofa, legs apart. Henriques crouched at her side, notebook in hand. Harry caught snatches as he and Kate paused for breath:

'Enter the filly for the maiden at Haydock and I'll have a good bet if the price is right. Yes, banco . . . want that mare whatever it costs, of course I know they'll bid me up, don't care . . . go on singing you two . . . pretty little thing but a bit soft, what I'd call a mooner and spooner type . . . I'm not being hard on her . . . no good talking to me like that . . .'

Never had Harry seen power so nakedly displayed. He had watched many people giving and receiving orders, but there were always certain veils of decency, certain prescribed limits. In this bizarre caliphate there were no rules. Fresh servitudes were invented from hour to hour, tasks of ever-increasing triviality laid down in minute detail, old retainers were flogged or freed according to whim, the rewards were vague and unpredictable. Kate told him that in C.L.'s household there was no distinction made between day and night. C.L. herself went to bed whenever she felt like it, which was often, and stayed there for as long as she liked, which was a long time. Two complete kitchen staffs were maintained to make sure that meals were available twenty-four hours a day. There was always to be a fresh pot of tea standing on the Aga, always a roast chicken freshly cut up and placed in a bed of crisp lettuce, always a pile of hard-boiled eggs in the china dish with its cover shaped like a hen. C.L. had a passion for hard-boiled eggs and delighted to crack them in unexpected places—on her secretary's head, on the ebony elephant in the hall, on the silver statuette on the bonnet of her Rolls.

Yet the effort to manufacture such a precisely repeating life inevitably engendered a stream of failures. The most frequent setbacks revolved around the change-over between the day and night staffs. To remedy this, dozens of memos suggesting fresh arrangements had passed, some to All Colours, some Private— For Distribution to Orange and Red Labels Only; but the new procedures thus promulgated never ended the quarrels and misunderstandings between the tired rabble going off duty and the nervous wrecks coming on. Stable Orders repeatedly exhorted All Colours to work together as a team, to have some consideration for C.L. who was snowed under with commitments and in general to get off their backsides. But in vain. There remained in almost every day a moment at which the brocade bell-rope was pulled and no tea appeared nor anybody to explain its non-appearance. Blue Label, dispatched to the kitchen, would hear the back door slamming and find a flustered kitchen-maid struggling with her galoshes while the giant kettle whistled unheeded.

Race days imposed a more conventional timetable on the household, but this only made the situation worse because the change-over tended to coincide with C.L.'s calling for breakfast in the morning and her return from the races in the evening. The day thus both began and ended in an atmosphere of chaos and recrimination. The pressure on C.L. at these moments was so great, or she thought it was so great which came to the same thing, that she sometimes issued contradictory orders within a few minutes of each other. Lying in bed behind thick curtains, she would visualize a fine sunny day in which she would roar through country lanes in the Lagonda with the windows down, warm as toast in her old fur coat referred to in Stable Orders as The Hearthrug, then, momentarily distracted by the lack of fresh rock salt on her breakfast tray, a few minutes later she would imagine a bitter east wind and order the Daimler with the windows tight shut. The question was often further complicated by the arrival of the typed transcript of the BBC weather forecast which was never brought in until she had finished her breakfast and already issued the first batch of orders.

Smooth running was made still more difficult by C.L.'s insistence that there should be no 'bumping'. She considered it perilously bad luck to meet on the stairs or in the passage anyone whom she had already dismissed for the day or night. Most of her employees therefore scuttled off duty and took good care to stay out of sight, ensuring that the incoming shift could not be briefed about their duties. Sometimes the latter arrived in the kitchen to find it virtually bare, C.L. having decreed that the existing food stock should be destroyed, as it had been contaminated by contact with some infected person such as a butcher's boy with a heavy cold.

But the danger of 'bumping' was not confined to employees. Once in the same room as C.L. guests were best advised to stay there until they wished to take their final departure, as any reappearance might be considered presumptuous intrusion; even a visit to the lavatory was liable to be criticized as 'popping in and out as if this was a bloody hotel'. On the other hand, C.L. herself often left the room in the middle of a conversation without a word, leaving the other person to finish his sentence in solitude. The worst kind of bumping was for a visitor to come back into a room by a different door from that through which he had gone out of it; this was known as 'popping up like a jack-in-the-box'; offenders might stay in the house for days without ever being spoken to again.

It was not surprising that guests were few and the turnover of staff rapid, though there was a core of the high command which had been with C.L. for some years—'sticking by me' she called it, in the tones of the leader of a hazardous expedition to the interior who has been deserted by all but the trustiest bearers. She had known Evelyn since she was a music student. Kate and Stella were comparatively new to Nuts Grove. They shared rooms in the annexe beyond the stables and gossiped about the power struggle in the big house. Even now they could not refrain from continuing their conversation, though in lowered voices, in the corner of the hotel room while Henriques buzzed around C.L. like a fly on a melon. Harry sat between the two girls in a happy daze.

'I hear Orange Label's moved up to the second floor.'

'Red's sick as hell.'

'C.L. says Red wears old woman's suspenders.'

'How divine, Stella.'

'Your friend Froggie—he's sweet.'

'He's all right.'

'He's got a charming face.'

'Not much to him, though.'

'You're a hard woman,' Harry said, coming dozily to his friend's defence.

'He rides beautifully, doesn't he?'

'He can ride.'

'She's always sparing with her praise,' Harry said.

Stella turned to him. 'It's wonderful for you to be riding Ampersand, isn't it?'

'Wonderful.'

The Off

Once, just once, perfection. Like sitting in an armchair, the trainer said. That, yes, but much more, almost as if sitting in an armchair was the best sensation the human body could ever know, shrivelling to nothing the pleasures of love and wine; as if his whole life he had been bumping up and down on camels and switchback railways and pogo-sticks and motor-boats in a high sea, his vertebrae all jangled together. Ampersand even looked rather like an armchair, with his massive shoulders and quarters and rather plain head; perhaps not a club armchair (too redolent of lethargy and wasted afternoons) but something strong and spanking new from Maple's—'see our Ampersand model, sir, not fast or showy but guaranteed to last a lifetime.'

Harry took him slowly at first over the dew-soaked ground. His stride was smooth, easy like the stride of the old Cup horses; he could go on for ever with a dead man in the saddle, as steady as Brown Jack himself. Harry caught the cold damp air in his nostrils, the sting of the morning in his eyes. Ampersand rose to take the plain brush fence and Harry flew, crouching low in his stirrups, riding short for a tall man, stylized homage to Tod Sloan and the Australian Seat. The fence was nothing, an irrelevance. It was as if Ampersand, like a flying armchair in a children's story, had suddenly taken it into his head to spread his wings for the fun of it. They landed on sweet turf beyond the mud and broken twigs pounded by other horses. No jarring, no break in the rhythm of his stride flowing on and on and up and over and on and on like a bird soaring and swooping on a summer day. There was no fleck of sweat on his dark neck, no change in pace, nothing that was not grace and pleasure.

As his heart stopped thumping at the thrill of it, Harry began to sense the virtue flowing through his own limbs. His legs felt strong, his hands firm and delicate, his body balanced, knee, hip, shoulder, elbow all flexed at the proper angle; he sat beautifully still, the reins as gentle on the mouth as if he was stroking it with his hand. The imagination chattered of a line of Gold Cups, even perhaps a National, of an unbroken, almost legendary partnership: 'Ampersand (H. Cotton) over the last' in a hundred newspaper photographs, 'Ampersand—Mr H. Cotton up' in a flash of vermilion silks and umber flanks at the Academy by Munnings or Lionel Edwards or even Ted Seago, 'The Big 'Un, Harry Cotton in the saddle'—cheap engraving, horse and rider stiffly arrayed in the stable yard, tacked above the bar of every racing pub, fly-blown and yellowed by the smoke of years, joined but never displaced by champions of the future. Ampersand had only just won the Gold Cup the year before. Sears was blamed for holding the young horse up too long and losing control in the gruelling uphill straight. 'Flapping all over the place at the finish he was, and the horse still going like a train. Jockey shagged out, horse as fresh as paint. Never off the bit. Pulled the whole bloody way.' With Harry on him he would win by a distance because Harry knew how to ride him. Ampersand was the kind of horse who needed to be nudged not yanked. The harder you pulled, the harder he would pull. Tact was the answer—a dialogue of friends, not a contest of strength. Already Harry could hear the shouts of 'Well ridden, sir' as they trotted back towards the winner's enclosure, he himself turning in the saddle to see what was going to finish second.

A green shooting-brake bumped over the grass towards him.

'Get off that horse.'

'What?'

'Get off that horse. I don't want any bloody amateurs riding him.'

C.L.'s swollen face hung out of the window fringed by her fat fingers like some overripe tropical fruit. As she drew back in again, she hit her head and swore. A chicken-leg fell from her fingers on to the grass.

'Pick it up.'

The face swelled even further. She looked as if some unseen attendant inside the shooting-brake was inflating her with a bicycle pump. Harry jumped off the horse.

'You could say please.'

'I don't take cheek from young men who flog my best horses like hired hacks.'

'I took him as gently as a baby.'

C.L. wound up her window and glared through it just as Harry twitched the chicken-leg at her. It hit the glass and fell back on the grass, leaving a greasy smear at which C.L. jabbed her finger in silent rage. She let in the clutch with a jerk and the car bumped away. Harry caught a glimpse of Kate looking out of the back window as a stable lad rode up and took the reins from him.

Ampersand had won by ten lengths. Sears had ridden a good race. Everybody said so. C.L. had had a big bet on him and although the odds were so short as to be almost invisible, she was exuberant (she never minded laying out a thousand pounds to win a hundred). Everyone was to be happy. There was to be no sulking.

'Get that cousin of yours to come and join the party.'

'I'll ask him but . . .'

'Go on, get him.'

Kate was tentative.

'She asked me particularly.'

'Why should I go?'

'There might be other rides.'

'If that's her usual behaviour, I wouldn't ride a donkey for her.'

'She has a thing about donkeys. Well, it wasn't much of a job I suppose, but it kept me off the streets.'

'Blackmail's an ugly word, Miss Cotton.'

'So's the dole.'

'Oh all right then.'

The lights were already blazing in the dining-room at Nuts Grove, its brocade walls glumly glowing and the polished mahogany sideboards reflecting the display of trophies crowding over every available surface, a cornucopian assortment of cups, statuettes, shields, salvers and towering above them all a giant silver pineapple, the fruits of a victory secured by an undistinguished two-year-old in a race in South Africa whither it had been sent on some obscure veterinary whim of C.L.'s. Kate and Stella had dragged two crates of champagne up from the cellar and the eight or nine men who had tagged along from the races prised them open with unrestrained zest.

'A trifle *chambré*, I fear,' said Froggie, handing Harry a bottle.

'God bless you, your honour, it's a terrible thirst I have on me.'

'I need a shampoo,' said a small bald man, holding out a glass.

'Thank heavens, a waterhole at last,' said a very large bald man.

'I told you so, follow old Tiny and he'll lead you to a drink. He's got a nose like a bloody beagle has Tiny.'

Stella brought in a gramophone and put some records on. She began to dance with one of the other secretaries. Kate looked on, arms folded. She had a gleam in her eye.

'Lovely party.'

'C.L. always gives lovely parties.'

'She's got a heart of gold underneath, you know.'

'I always said her father treated her badly.'

'I thought it was her mother who treated her badly.'

'No, her mother died, I think. Or was it her father?'

'Anyway, underneath . . .'

'Yes, exactly.'

'Heart of gold.'

'I've always said so.'

'Where *is* C.L.?'

'Must congratulate her.'

'Absolutely.'

'Upstairs probably. Giving out Stable Orders.'

'No she isn't. Here she comes.'

'Well done, C.L. Wonderful race.'

'Your very good health, C.L.'

'What the hell is all this? Kate, *Kate*.'

'You said lay on a celebration.'

'I said a celebration not an orgy. Who asked these men to drink themselves potty at my expense, and what's that cousin of yours doing here? I've seen him off for today. You know how I hate bumping with people. Can't you have a little consideration, Katchen, just for *once* can't you think of somebody besides yourself?'

But it was not so easy to put the party into reverse. The racing men surged forwards.

'Jolly good of you to ask us back, C.L.'

'That's a cracking good jumper you've got there.'

'Can I offer you a glass of your own excellent bubbly?'

'Cracking good jumper. Have you got space here for any more Gold Cups, C.L.?'

'You would have room if only Tiny would shift his carcass.'

'Do you know old Tiny, C.L.? First-rate chap. Used to be the fattest man in India bar the Buddha.'

'I do not know old Tiny. Nor do I want to.'

'Oh. Ah. Pity. I think you'd like him awfully. Most people do.'

'Sorry to butt in, boys,' said the very large bald man. 'I just wanted to introduce myself to my hostess. Name's Tupholme, Miss L. Tiny Tupholme.'

Harry stood in the corner of the room, looking at the two tethered barrage balloons: Tiny Tupholme, pink, sweaty, beaming, C.L. pasty and unyielding. At his side Stella said:

'Miss L. is two pounds the heavier I think.'

'It's a close thing.'

'I'm glad I'm leaving tonight.'

'Tonight? This is so sudden.'

'No, I have to go back to Germany. I'm only here because Evelyn arranged it. He's an old friend of my father's.'

'You're German?'

'Stella Slonimski . . . Polish I suppose. But we live in Germany. My language is German.'

'I wouldn't have known. Your English is so . . . so you're not a permanent fixture here.'

'No, it's just a way of seeing England.'

'Well you're seeing it, though I wouldn't want you to think this is an entirely typical slice of English life.'

'I guessed that.'

'What train are you going on?'

'The next one.'

'When is it?'

'I don't know.'

'I'll go with you.'

'That'll be nice.'

'Let's go now.'

'Now.'

In the train two men were playing Find the Lady.

'Now then, now then, where is she? Well, I'm blowed. Got X-ray eyes you have. There you are then, that's another quid for you. Now then, try again, flip flop flip, where's the lovely lady? Stone the crows, do you want to see me in the workhouse before me time? Perhaps I'll do better with this gentleman here. Care to spot the lovely lady, guv'nor, I should say the other lovely lady, now shouldn't I?'

'I'll have a go,' said Harry. He put a pound note down on the table. The man with the cards matched it. The other man looked moodily out of the window.

'Off we go then. Flip flop flip. Now then where is she, sir?'

'There.'

'Stone the crows. There she blows again. You're ab-so-lutely right, sir. The Queen of Hearts it is. There's your two pounds. Care to try again, sir?'

'No, thank you very much.'

'Pardon.'

'No, thank you.'

'Come along now, sir, you're a sportsman surely. You'll let a fellow-sportsman have his revenge. Why, this other gentleman here and me have been going at it hammer and tongs all the way from Manchester.'

'No, thank you. I don't think I will.'

'Just one more go.'

'No.'

3

'Would the lady here like to try?'

'No she wouldn't.'

'Certain?'

'Certain.'

'Well, come on, George. We know when we're not wanted.'

The two men got up and went out of the compartment. The moody one raised his hat to Stella as he closed the door.

'Where to now?'

'I don't know.'

'You must know. You must have a hotel room or something.'

'No, I have no money, only my ticket.'

'That makes two of us.'

'Don't try to be kind. You are the *jeunesse dorée*. You throw pound notes about in railway carriages.'

'I had one pound in the world. Now I have two, plus a cheque for a fiver signed F. O'Neill which is not exactly a liquid asset.'

'You're exaggerating.'

'I promise.'

'I don't believe you.'

The great vaulting echoed to the lazy clank of the last engine backing out to its shed. The steam billowed up to the giant ribs. Single footsteps sounded on the almost deserted platforms. A man in a ginger tam-o'-shanter was vomiting against the next pillar. Stella shivered, laughed, drew closer to Harry. He put his arm round the stooped curve of her shoulders. She held herself like somebody who was always cold.

'Come and help me spend my millions.'

'All right.'

'I know a place—'

'You see, he knows a place.'

'I don't really know the place but Froggie told me about it.'

'What's it called?'

'I don't think I'll tell you.'

'Go on.'

'Well, it's called um . . . the Pyjama Club.'

'There you are. *Jeunesse dorée*. High-life.'

'Wait and see, as Mr Asquith said.'

'Or as the bishop said to the actress.'

'They did teach you something at Nuts Grove then. Come on, we can't hang about all night.'

The Pyjama Club was at the end of a wide alleyway lined with dustbins. A grimy sign showed the bottom half of a pair of pyjamas capering in an abandoned fashion; the bulb illuminating the top half seemed to be broken. Harry rang the bell. Feet clumped down the stairs. A short woman in her late twenties with a square face opened the door.

'Yes?'

'Froggie sent us.'

'What a perfectly sinister greeting. Have you been rehearsing it for ages?'

'Isn't this the Pyjama Club?'

'Yeah, buddy, but this ain't no speakeasy joint. Come in all the same. Mind the little step, fill in the form on the landing, you can be my guests until you're members. The drinks are five bob each and filthy at the price. You can even dance if you're out of your mind.'

Halfway up the stairs the lino changed to carpet, the smell of cold and cabbage to warmth and whisky. The wall on the landing was decorated with a poster advertising the Dolomites, a few cards, mostly out of date, for exhibitions at the Leicester and the Mayor Galleries, the Monteverdi String Quartet's Winter Programme, notices in various hands—Please pay your subscriptions PROMPTLY. We do *not* cash cheques at the weekend, LOST down the mews, ARTHUR beautiful black-and-white cat, Guests must sign the book—letters stuck behind the crisscross tapes on the noticeboard for Dr R. B. T. Dunbabin, FSA, and a picture postcard of Cassis addressed in violet ink to 'darling Mossy'. In the long, low, main room, deep-red striped wallpaper, gilt wall-brackets, a zinc bar, red plush stools, attempted elegance already beginning to fade. In the darkness of one corner two couples were revolving very slowly round each other, the bright yellow hair of one woman coming into view every thirty seconds like a lighthouse beam. Harry could not hear any music. The other two dozen people in the room were crowded around the bar making a lot of noise. They sat down at a table and waited for ten minutes. Nobody came. Harry got up and thrust his way through the mob. The woman who had let them in was working her way along a line of impatient customers.

'Sorry, darlings. That bloody boy's let me down again.'

'You're a terrific barmaid, Mossy.'

Eventually Harry got to the front.

'Two whiskies, please.'

'That's a quid, darling, and another quid for the entrance fee.'

'You said the drinks were five bob each.'

'It's gala night, sweetie.'

They danced. There was no music.

'You've got a wonderful sense of rhythm.'

She twined her legs firmly round his right thigh and rubbed her crotch against his. He grunted in surprise.

'Don't you like it?'

'Yes, very much, but I didn't know you were that kind of girl.'

'I'm all kinds of girl.'

'I like this kind.'

'Not too cheap?'

'In my condition, the cheaper the better.'

'I like to excite men.'

'Are you a tease?'

'What's a tease—oh I know. No of course not. You look a little pale.'

'All this exciting.'

'Perhaps we ought to go home now.'

Harry went over to Mossy who was now sitting at a table.

'Nice place this is.'

'Don't go overboard.'

'We've enjoyed ourselves very much.'

'That's wonderful news.'

'The only trouble is . . . you couldn't lend me a quid for a bed, could you? I'm broke.'

Mossy looked at him carefully, then handed him two pound

notes. 'Try just round the corner. Come back here tomorrow if you like.'

'I certainly will. I can't say how much—'

'Don't. Goodnight. Girl's pretty.'

'I'm not used to this kind of thing.'

'What about all those other men you excited?'

'Who? Oh, I made that up.'

'Really?'

'Yes, to impress you.'

'Well, I am impressed. I'm not used to this sort of thing either.'

'Don't believe you. Don't . . . believe . . . you.'

'Beginners luck.'

'Same to you too.'

'As the bishop—'

'Not that again.'

'No, this again.'

CHAPTER TWO

MY FATHER had a taste for custom and ceremony. He responded with delight to the incapsulation of feeling in symbol. He liked parades, processions, fêtes, protest marches, harvest festivals, inductions—anything involving ritual and uniform. At the sound of horses trotting or tanks rumbling on the road outside our house, he would start to his feet like a soldier jumping to reveille, not for love of the military but for the display of it. In this taste he was anything but a man of his time, for today ritual, custom, ceremony—all these words have a stale crust to them. Even now they are stamped with images of Victorian humbug, of hollow men kneeling, bowing, standing to attention. We have ceased to think of ritual as a means of intensifying experience and come to resent it as an imposition of form upon the essential formlessness of life, therefore as a timid defence against the richness and freedom of reality. We take care to prevent the self from plunging carelessly into ritual, from finding in the here and now of ancient regularities the high points of life. Our lives are too full, our world too overstuffed to let us listen to the slight tremble, the accidentally diminished interval in the sound of a passing bell or its occasional reinforcement by a pigeon crooning in the trees.

As I lay in bed having my afternoon rest, I could hear the bell tolling through the open window. The solemn remorseless sound dulled my ears to the sparrows twittering outside. I snuggled down under the covers, awaiting with dreadful pleasure the still more solemn sound which was to follow. It always came abruptly, with no fade-in. At one moment there was nothing but the twittering in the laburnum trees and then there it was: the crunching, clanking sound as they rounded the bend in the road, already close enough for the noise to bang my ears as if they were in the next room. The hand-cart was new; its polished wooden frame gleamed even in the dun light; the dull oak coffin lay on it as snug as a chrysalis in a cocoon; the iron rims to the wheels shone as they clanged through the afternoon silence. After they passed the next house to ours, I could begin to hear the tramp of the feet. Was there time for a quick look? As I measured the risks, it was already too late. My father was up the stairs and through my bedroom door, pulling both curtains to with one great sweep of his arms, the ends of the curtains fluttering to rest like the wings of a pigeon settling. Far from spoiling things, this thrilling gesture of respect for the dead made my pleasure more intense. I thought with awe of the grief and gravity of the unseen cortège which must be protected from indecent prying. On the rare occasions when I did manage to sneak a look, it was so brief that I retained only a vague impression of the gaggle of black mourners, the white vestments of the rector and the creaking hand-cart piled high with chrysanthemums.

Love of such ceremonies is not now in fashion, but it is not as rare as convention pretends. Even in the common change of modern condolence it is sometimes possible to detect a note of suppressed regret in expressions like 'thank heavens it was all quite simple . . . there was no fuss . . . such a relief for the family'. My father would have none of this austerity. Reading through the deaths in the newspaper, he was pleased to discover that some old enemy had not only died but was to be buried with 'no flowers by request', which seemed to him a suitably poor way to go, an index of the mean-mindedness of the dead man. For himself he liked a good funeral. 'They can't mess it about,' he said, meaning that it was impossible to imbue its uncompromising message with any more prosaic social purpose.

On a summer afternoon some years later, we were clipping the front hedge from the road side when a funeral procession came past. I froze to attention and bowed my head as long instructed, so as to avoid charges of impious curiosity. The birds flew out of the hedge as the bell tolled. The hearse rumbled past. I watched the dust fan across the tarmac pavement. It was hot enough for the tar to be sticking to my gym shoes. Suddenly I heard the clatter of clippers falling on to the pavement. Looking up from under lowered brows, I saw that my father had joined the tail-end of the procession. Worse still, he was beckoning to me to join him. I held my ground, pretending not to notice. He beckoned more insistently. For a second or two I went on standing there, holding my own clippers in front of me like a sentry with arms reversed. Then two or three of the mourners started to stare at me. I could see them wondering who was this irreverent clod publicly shaming his father. To continue to show such reluctance to pay my last respects to the deceased, or in this case my first respects as I had no idea who he might be, was clearly worse than joining in his obsequies at the halfway stage. I put down my clippers carefully to make no noise as if I was laying a wreath and hurried across to my father's side. The mourners were still looking at me with white, inquiring faces. I became conscious that while my father was wearing the jacket of an old suit, admittedly well worn but in an aptly funereal shade of grey, I had on a bright red sweater. The rubber toes of my gym shoes were frilled with sweat. I wore no tie. Worse and worse. After conferring with the men marching beside him, my father whispered in my ear:

'It's old Arthur Poole.'

A woman in front of us turned round angrily, then looked mollified as she saw my father apparently scolding me for my sullen manner and slovenly dress.

'Seventy-seven he was. I thought he was older.'

I nodded, keeping my head well down. I had never heard of Arthur Poole.

'Last man in the village to fight in the Boer War.'

The woman looked round again and said 'ssh'. The afternoon seemed oppressively hot.

'They used to call him the Flying Elephant. He didn't know what fear was, didn't know anything much, as it happens.'

The woman said: 'If you can't keep quiet, you shouldn't have come.'

My father walked a little faster so that he could breathe over her shoulder, 'I was just saying what a fine old man your father was.'

'My grandfather, thank you very much.'

The man next to the woman turned round and said, 'Would you mind not breathing down my wife's neck?'

My father said 'ssh' and fell back into step beside me. He

bowed his head and as the cortège slowed to turn up the path leading to the church he shortened his stride to an old man's shuffle, humble in the sight of the Almighty.

At such moments his surrender to the spirit of the ritual was complete, encompassing yet transcending the ironies of the situation and tending to leave his companion sheepish and impatient. I was not the only victim. Adults found it no less embarrassing to be with him when he came upon morris dancers in the square of a country town. Yet such sights were rare. We did not often go to the town. Our village was small and isolated, and its main street not much frequented. And if public ceremonial was hard to come by, my father's life afforded even less scope for institutional ritual. He held no official position. In fact he held no position at all. He belonged to no clubs and to none of those freemasonries, formal or informal, by which men assign to themselves a place in the social structure. Just as families were said to make their own pleasures in the days before wireless and television, my father had to invent his own rituals.

He endowed every excursion with monumental significance. A day's fishing was a crusade. To prepare for its rigours took the whole of the preceding evening. My father detailed the necessary steps as if he was reading a manual to himself: 'First select your tackle.' He pulled out of a cupboard a pile of black tin boxes wreathed in tangled wire, intertwined with a pair of musty khaki puttees. 'Paternoster tackle . . . we'll need a couple of these . . . then these twist weights for the smaller fry and the penwiper floats for the surface feeders . . . grease your lines well . . . we might run into a pike so we'll take these ferocious big spinners, we can always spin from the landing-stage . . . eel-trap, well, there might be an eel about, just as well . . .' he paused, entranced by the vision of the eel wriggling at the end of our line, the hook halfway down its throat. Smoked eel perhaps, we would need woodshavings; that old apple bough might do. And a sauce, we must make a sauce, with capers. I did not like capers. I did not like eels either; I did not like their slimy, feathery energy; I did not like the way they continued to thrash about even after they had been skinned and cut in pieces; I particularly disliked the way they tasted. My father

3*

loved all fish—the black and green speckled dace, the delicate bearded gudgeon, roach, perch, chubb, pike—all he claimed to find not only beautiful but delicious if prepared by an expert hand, all would fall prey to our immense armoury. In the end, we took the entire contents of the cupboard including a set of watercolours and an old army dagger. But my father's enthusiasm went beyond the angler's normal mania for equipment. He constantly emphasized that his concern was not merely with the refinements of pleasure but with the dictates of practicality. He insisted on both of us taking a complete change of clothing including two spare pairs of trousers each and a day's supply of food in case we were becalmed by some disaster whose exact nature even he could not be expected to foresee.

The storm-clouds of drama thus accumulated were not to be lightly dispersed. From the moment we arrived on the river bank we were to converse only in whispers, although the shouts of two fellow-anglers a few yards downstream made it difficult to hear. Nor was the fishing itself a crude matter of dropping the line in the water. For the first hour all that happened was that my father crept up and down the bank throwing crumbled bread upon the waters as ground bait. Whatever its effect upon the fish, this attracted a host of moorhens which splashed across the river like a fleet of tiny motor boats. The fishermen downstream said if we wanted to feed the ducks why didn't we go to the park. My father riposted with all the fury of the impugned expert, but as he was still whispering they couldn't hear him.

These expeditions were often the object of vicarious envy on the part of older persons. 'You are lucky, Aldous. Your father always makes everything such fun. I wish I'd had somebody to teach me how to fish when I was your age.' I did not know how to explain what I felt, let alone dare to give vent to my feelings which were approximately that it was not that I minded going fishing or being taught how to fish but that I could not stand all the fuss. Even then I was dimly aware that such an attitude was not only ungrateful but deeply philistine; by now time has taken the edge off that resentment, left high and dry the grudges of adolescence. Whenever I drive past the water where we used to fish, I pause to look at the piers of the old bridge standing naked in the stream. The road now goes over a new bridge designed by the brutalist county architect. The new bridge makes little of the river. There is no bump in the road, no change in its width or surface or gradient. There is now no need to brake or to peer forward to see if anything is coming the other way. The old bridge gathered the road and bunched it between high stone parapets like a hand grasping a piece of cloth. As we drove slowly across it, we used to peer over the parapet on each side to see if we could spot a fish lurking in the weeds. An omen, my father said, like passing over a railway bridge when a train was going under it. And although I wanted to complain so much at the time, it seems to me now that what I really liked was the fuss and not the fishing. The car bumping off the road on to the grass track, the squeak of brakes which needed relining, that sick smell of petrol and old leather suddenly cut off by the smell of the river, and the damp silence, and my father jumping out of the car like a man who had five seconds to defuse a bomb.

If age sets us in our ways, it is vacant, errant youth that gilds routine with the dignity of a sacrament. As a fisherman I have no vocation, I am lapsed, but I bear the marks of my training. I see a man fishing on a bank or I pick up a word out of context —'paternoster', 'float', 'reel'—and I tremble at the thought of all that concentration of being, that burning focus. I do not long to go back exactly but for a minute or two I cannot think, I can hardly move. The feeling is so intense that I cannot place it—a feeling of regret, a fear that the best of life is gone and that there is nothing much left. Or is it the remembrance of pleasure, or only a sense of life, palpitating, exultant, momentary?

This displaced intensity begins to pursue me whenever I try to retrace my father's favourite tracks, repeat to myself his book of hours. Each rite was all the more charged with meaning because he had invented it but at the same time remained oblivious of its impact. He had, for example, discovered that the Inland Revenue would give free advice on how to make an income tax return. Upon this well-known fact he founded a stately rite. There was to be no dilatory exchange of letters, no dribble of telephone calls to clear up points of detail. The thing to do was to get matters settled at one go. Nothing less than a full-scale personal consultation would do. The appointment was booked. I was to accompany my father, in theory for my own enlightenment but in reality I think because he had at the back of his mind a picture of the team of experts from the Inland Revenue against whom he would need to deploy his own advisers; although the Revenue men were supposed to be helping him, there was a certain degree of pride involved. He assembled every document he could find which had the remotest bearing on his financial situation ranging from the variegated collection of cheque-books to a series of unpaid butcher's bills still stained with the blood of the meat they had been skewered to. Having no briefcase, he put these papers into a very large battered brown suitcase. As we stood on the doorstep of the local offices of the Inland Revenue, we looked as if we had come to stay the night or alternatively as if my father was dropping me back at the reformatory after weekend leave.

My suspicions that we were almost alone in using this personal method of consultation were strengthened by the fact that the waiting-room was always empty and that it was only a few seconds before the inspector who had been deputed to deal with my father's affairs called us in. He sat, this wan ascetic, in a bleak room: bare boards with a square of brown lino on which his table and chair stood as if they were part of a unit which could be moved out in one piece at the end of the scene. My father started by placing the suitcase on the table where it loomed so large that we could scarcely see the inspector, a man of modest stature, over the top of it. So the three of us stood up, grouped round the suitcase while my father opened it like successful burglars assisting at the share-out of the swag. Finally, it was agreed that the case was too big and we put it on the floor whence my father would draw up another handful of documents whenever the problem threatened to simplify itself. That there was a problem at all was a testimonial to my father's genius in these matters.

His income, drawn entirely from a small trust, unsullied by wage or salary, varied little, but the ways in which he fended off his creditors were legion. It was hard to conceive that there could be so many ways of borrowing money or of delaying its repayment. Even the Revenue itself seemed to have fallen under his spell. While he was several years behind in making his tax returns, he claimed to have already received a tax rebate for a financial year which had not yet begun. On hearing this, the inspector froze, his mouth sagging like one caught in the extremity of grief. 'But surely . . . perhaps . . . no, I can't,' he stammered, half plain incredulous, half guilty that by taking the assertion seriously he should appear to cast doubt on the capacity of his superiors to keep one jump ahead of my father. After sorting through a bitter correspondence with the local garage, my father eventually came upon the documents which proved his point. The inspector's furrowed features resumed their ascetic calm. All was well; Somerset House had not spun on its axis; there was merely a confusion between the calendar and the financial years. My father, however, pursued the question with undimmed enthusiasm and frequent use of technical terms which did not sound so much used wrongly as quite irrelevant in this context, words like 'contango' and 'plough-back'.

From his cogent and concentrated manner it would have been hard to guess his almost paralytic incapacity to settle the slightest matter of administration, let alone pay the smallest bill. In his brown suit and tie with foxes' heads on it he had the air of an entrepreneur whose work kept him in the country and out of the great centres of commerce but who was none the less as shrewd as any of your city sharks, a medium-sized timber merchant perhaps. From time to time he jotted down little sums on a pad, firmly underlining the total even if, as I could see by looking over his shoulder, the total was quite often wrong.

My head began to buzz in the bare room. As my father sorted through some old cheque stubs, I thought of him reading the lesson on Christmas Day. 'And it came to pass in those days, that there went out a decree from Caesar Augustus, that all the world should be taxed.' Had Caesar Augustus known what he was letting the tax-gatherers in for? They might be only publicans and sinners but surely they did not deserve taxpayers like my father. In any case, this inspector was clearly nothing resembling a sinner. Rectitude shone from his pale brow and, nobler than rectitude, a sweet patience. How gently he inclined his head as my father in his equally gentle, dwelling voice explained his difficulties. On reflection, I recalled that Caesar Augustus had something else in mind, something more like a census. That would have been little better, perhaps worse. The scars of the recent census were still fresh.

In completing his return my father had insisted on pedantic exactitude in every answer. He had tested the footnotes to their limit, crossed out his first entries and written over them in a different ink until at length all that was legible with any certainty was his own name—Harry Cotton, in his strange, wild hand, each letter separate yet giving an unforgettable cursive effect, 'H' like a wind-battered television aerial, a shrivelled cherry for the 'a', the 'r's like two cloves, then a savage, swooping catapult of a 'y'. He wrote as if he had been brought up on Cyrillic script and only recently converted to English.

Yet he read aloud with clarity and fine expression, rather too much expression at evensong after a heavy day. He smote the ungodly with appalling ferocity and saturated the lamentations of the prophets in acerbic melancholy. The promises of Isaiah had never sounded more exhilarating, Ecclesiastes never more autumnal. He was less at home with the New Testament. He used to grip the lectern with both hands, either because of the intensity of his emotion or in order to keep his balance, and launched the words on the outspread wings of the brass eagle high over the heads of the small congregation. A few feet from him, in the front row, the other Harry, startled by the noise, would take his nose out of his hymn book and look up to the ceiling.

The other Harry was squat, his head almost shaven, his lower lip thrust forward as he babbled and gobbled throughout the service. His head darted in and out of his overcoat like a turkey-cock, his eyes questing round the church. He was fond of church and had his own special hymn and prayer book which he brought with him, clutched tightly to his chest. He would change from one to the other, at first at intervals of five minutes, then quicker and quicker until he was nearly juggling with them and finally dropped them both under his pew with a bang. He would then disappear from sight and scrabble about under the pitchpine until he triumphantly re-emerged clasping the books with his overcoat up to his ears. During the week when there was no church service he held his own mattins in the barn at the back of the pub. He carefully arranged empty beer-bottles in pew-rows and hectored them with texts from a large bible which his mother had given him. Every now and then he would look up and give a loud, angry groan to reprove the inattentive, reproducing exactly the anguished sound of the parson starting off on a fresh tack. A new barmaid at the pub had once started tidying up the bottles and was knocked flat by an outraged kick up the behind from the other Harry. Since that time, everyone had been warned not to go into the barn when the service was in progress. This one gesture of outraged piety apart, he had never been any trouble. He ambled about the village, always in his long trench coat winter and summer, gobbling and making gestures with his stubby fingers. In church I used to watch him with fascination and a certain sympathy. Outside, I was both frightened of him and ashamed of being frightened.

My father used to send me over to the pub with a glass jug to get some beer for lunch. The journey was no more than three hundred yards, but it was bristling with perils. I might be arrested for going into the pub under age, or I might be run over crossing the road, or attacked by the pub-keeper's rabid sheep-dog or, worst of all (and indeed I had imagined the other dangers only in order to avoid thinking about this one), have the jug dashed from my hand by the other Harry with all the irresistible strength of a madman. Once, coming back down the narrow alleyway with my foaming jug, I did meet him. He smacked his lips and raised his hand with elbow bent. I mis-understood and lifted the jug as if to hit him although I would never have dared to do so. He shrank back against the wall. I heard him knock his head. I found myself running. When I got home, I told the story, half as a joke, half as a boast. My father was very angry; at first I was not quite sure with whom; when he realized this and made it clear that it was with me, I too was angry in the way that children are when they feel that too much has been expected of them.

Two years later, the other Harry's mother who had looked after him all his life died. He was lucky enough to be found a place in a home for the sub-normal set in its own grounds and quite near the sea. My father and I happened to be walking down the village street when we saw him being driven away in an old Rover by a woman in a hat. A little further on, I noticed my father had tears in his eyes.

'But isn't it, well, for the best . . . however sad,' I said.

'I have no time for a man who cannot weep,' he said.

I still dream, no not of the other Harry, but of the foaming jug and me carrying it and a voice dwelling and gentle but insisting that if ever the pitcher be broken at the fountain, then shall the dust return to the earth as it was, but the jug still escapes my fingers and dribbles the beer on the ground like an old man caught short in a pub passage. And I wake up, glad for a moment that my life is dry and simple. I think of that pale inspector, patronizing in my mind's eye his patience and honesty.

My father said: 'And then there are my expenses.'

'Expenses?'

'Unavoidable expenses.'

'I don't quite understand.'

'These for example.' He produced from a corner of the suitcase a bundle of my school reports tied together with garden twine.

'Mm yes,' the inspector said, going through them with professional thoroughness, careful not to be caught out in a premature verdict of irrelevance. 'Very good. Your son appears to be quite a scholar, Mr Cotton.'

'No, not those,' said my father. There was an unusual shortness about his manner as if the inspector had been rummaging in his suitcase without permission. 'Here.'

The inspector's eye rested on a brochure describing Woodland Manor Preparatory School.

'It sounds a fine school. There's nothing like country air.'

'No, no.' My father's finger jabbed the papers. 'The fees.'

'I'm sorry but school fees are not allowable against tax.'

'Extra milk. It's terrible what they charge for extra milk.'

'I'm afraid there again . . .'

'You have no children yourself?'

'Unfortunately not.'

'Quite right. The expense is appalling.'

'It wasn't really a question of choice. My wife's health did not permit.'

'I'm very sorry.'

'She is much better now.'

'That's good.'

'We play a lot of golf together.'

'Do you now?'

'For her health really.'

'You don't care for it yourself?'

'At Tenby, the sea air.'

'I know Tenby. Very pretty place. Augustus John was born there.'

'Was he? I didn't know that. Was he a golfer?'

'I don't think so. He used to wear an ear-ring.'

'Really? Augustus, you say his name was?'

'Just one ear-ring. He was pretending to be a gipsy.'

'Pretending? Why did he do that?'

'I don't know.'

'Of course I don't like everything about golf, I must admit. Some of the people who play are, well, rather loud, if you will excuse me saying so.'

'I know just what you mean.'

'My wife says I shouldn't mind. But I do. We eat our sandwiches on the beach. I don't really like going into the club-house.'

'Very sensible.'

'Some people would think it rather standoffish. Well, it is standoffish. It's supposed to be a club, after all.'

'Much nicer on the beach,' my father said.

'But I keep on thinking, suppose one of those men at the bar—you know they call the bar "the nineteenth hole", you knew that? —suppose he makes a joke about his bladder.'

'His bladder?'

'My wife has just had her gall bladder removed. But you couldn't be expected to know that.'

'No.'

'It's the sort of joke they might make, though.'

'Exactly.'

'And it could be very awkward. Perhaps I'm oversensitive, in fact I know I am, but I can't be doing with people who think money's everything.'

'Nor can I.'

My father relaxed. He had his man. I could already see him framing his judgment: 'very nice chap, the bloodsucker, wanders from the point a bit, but awfully helpful and friendly'. There would be in this assessment a genuine fellow-feeling spiced with a certain satisfaction not unlike that of the missionary who speaks of the sober and godly manner of his converts without himself claiming any credit for the instilling of these qualities. My father took paradoxical delight in reclaiming supposedly arid patches of humanity while pointing out, usually quite accurately, the falsity of the warmth attributed to some allegedly convivial spirit. He collected misanthropic innkeepers and unpleasant professional charmers in the same way as he seized upon warm-hearted civil servants and sensitive army majors.

There was a sense in which my father's theories tended to have something to them, reluctant though I was to admit it, but it was rarely the sense in which the theories were propounded. In assessing people, he muddled individual temperament with professional manner because he had no real idea of what work was, like. It was not that he despised work. Far from it. He had no particle of bohemian scorn for routine. He revered regularity without himself aspiring to it. In the same fashion he admired hard work and liked and respected quiet, diligent people. He just did not fully understand what they were up to.

Let loose in any place of employment, he roamed about picking up things with the magpie interest of a child, irritating beyond measure those who were immersed in the prevailing routine and unnerving even those who were ready enough to stop for a chat. Work to him was a kind of sympathetic magic.

Human beings performed these strange offices—sealing envelopes, tapping typewriter keys, soldering pieces of metal together, digging holes in the ground—and by some arcane process gold showered down upon them in return. This awe was distinct from my own amazement on first getting a job that anyone could actually pay *me*; it was a more general reverence for the mysteries of the social organism, not unlike the reverence of that legendary novice drama critic who, never having been to the theatre before, was so entranced by the beautiful ingenuity by which the curtain was raised and lowered that he failed to take in the substance of the play.

My father did, however, have a sharp appreciation of how routines, manners of life, experiences could shape people. He singled out certain jobs as more difficult to perform with grace than was generally recognized. He thought that to work in a box office must be a great strain on the temper; he therefore approached the window with an elaborate courtesy which was usually rebuffed, either because it wasted so much time or because the girl suspected lurking sarcasm in such sentences as 'I wondered if you might possibly have two three-and-sixpennies left?' The crude response he received only confirmed his diagnosis of the taxing life endured by the box-office girl in her insanitary cage.

These delicate approaches came from the heart. But they did not preclude a taste for the more blatant extremes of the human condition. My father liked freaks and freakish behaviour. He found it natural to let his attention dwell on the victims of nature or circumstance, unnatural in fact to turn away his eyes. 'Either you can take dwarfs or you can't. I can take them,' he said. By 'take' he meant regard them as interesting persons, capable of being either comic or tragic or both together, and not as objects of charity, beings too hideous to contemplate without disgust.

Once when he was sitting in the pub, a coach party of blind people poured in through the door. They were on a Mystery Tour. Coach parties often turned up as the innkeeper was the uncle of the bus-driver, and in default of precise instructions from the tour organizer the party usually found themselves at our pub with at least an hour to kill before they could decently start for home. The strategy of regular customers on these occasions was not quite to block the way to the bar but to stand close enough to prevent the visitor from getting a drink without bumping into them, apologizing and in due course standing his round.

The arrival of the present group, however, embarrassed the regulars. Not only was it hard to conceive how to persuade a blind man to pay for the drinks; the smallness of the bar and the largeness of the coach party made it difficult to avoid bumping into them. There was even a risk of tripping them up with their own white sticks. Most of the regulars sidled out, leaving the bar to the visitors and my father who was wedged in the corner and would anyway have been hard to dislodge. He assumed that the new arrivals needed cheering up and tried a few words of welcome. He had a vision of old men holy in their suffering, leaning on their sticks, fumbling quietly for their mild-and-bitter, heads meekly upturned towards him as he showered them with local lore and wit. Unfortunately, he failed to make himself heard in the surge of querulous voices.

'Thought we'd never get here.'

'Worst bloody driver—'

'Call this a Mystery Tour, it's a sodding disaster area.'

All the imagined serenity of the kingdom of the blind was shattered. They shouldered their way to the bar like a victorious football team, puffed cheroot smoke in my father's face and finally turned their backs on him to form a crater which periodically erupted in volcanic mirth.

'I'll tell you one thing,' said the pub-keeper, 'I'm never having any blind coach parties in here again. Paraplegics, yes, they're a decent sort of customer, but not these conceited blind buggers. You ought to be more careful, Ted. It's always the stone-blind ones that are the worst.'

'I'm sorry,' said the bus-driver, 'but I understood this lot was to be partially sighted.'

'Took me two hours to clean up after the last time, it did.'

'They let 'em out of that holiday camp for the handicapped and they're like wild animals.'

A blind man with a pear-shaped face and a regimental blazer turned to my father.

'Nice little place this.'

'I like it.'

'Must be a bit slow in the winter though. Where do you go for your fun?'

'We make our own,' said my father grimly.

'That's the way, old boy, that's the way.'

After he had recovered his temper, my father began to treasure the experience and to start forming in his mind an axiom about the conceit of the sightless. At the same time, he started to admire their zest. The blind men's Mystery Tour became a collective odyssey, a heroic journey through dark seas. The malign fate which had put out their eyes had not put out their spirit. They were unyielding world-conquerors in their dark glasses and regimental blazers. When I came across to the pub to ask if my father wanted any dinner, he was staring at them with a smile on his lips, as if it was he who had lost his sight and was warming himself at the fire of their revelry, solacing his isolation.

Night Life

There was a flounce on the dirty pillowcase, one touch of elegance in the threadbare room. Harry's eye, hard and staring, traced its path. At the edge it had come away, the beaded seam ripped like a piece of paper torn along the dotted line. The loose ribbon of linen wandered up the pillow till it vanished into her clenched hand. The milk-white side of her forearm lay flat and open, tensed for the jab of the hypodermic. Her head was twisted into her shoulder like a broken-necked bird. Her back arched, stretched; her upper lip thinned, quivering, the lower rounded for the silent cry. For a moment they remembered that they were strangers. Then in anarchic dissolution, they flooded into one another's arms and his gaze dwindled from its stern pursuit of the flounce to meet her eyes. The curtain flapped away from the open window as the cold air rushed in over them, fanning their slippery skin.

He slept. He woke to hear her bang the window shut. She stood with her thin arms stretched up to the sash. Her shoulder blades were bat's wings; the bones of her back marked her skin like the veins on a leaf. This frailty sorted oddly with her sturdy legs and the strong curve of her bottom, that ancient conversation between weakness and strength which stirred him to the edge of alarm. He thought of other women with upstretched arms: his mother brushing her hair, a hundred strokes night and morning, head cocked sideways against the brush's arc; Flo cleaning the glass front of the bookcase in his father's study, reaching up on tiptoe so he could see the white glimmer at the backs of her knees where her stockings stretched. He watched Stella rub the dirt from the window off her forearm. She peered anxiously at the smudge like a woman trying to keep an eye on a distant child and rubbed it again.

'Well then?' she said.

'Well.'

'Go to sleep.'

Stella shuddered in the cold, stooped, huddled her arms about her. He struggled to bring to mind something a long way away. A stooped figure reflected in the water. He got it. The engraving hung in a dank passage at home, the girl's thighs already invaded by mildew, as if she had risen from the lake modestly girt with duckweed. He laughed.

'September Morn.'

'February night. Oh I see. We have it in our dining-room. It's terrible. Kitsch.'

'What's kitsch?'

'Bogus. Bourgeois. No good.'

'The comparison doesn't appeal to you?'

'I hate it.'

'Would you rather be the Nude Descending a Staircase?'

'It's much too late to talk about modern art.'

'Never too late to talk about Art.'

'What do you know of these things? You are just a simple gentleman jock.'

'Jockeys are never gentlemen and rarely simple. They are mostly hollow-eyed, tormented creatures like myself. On cold Newmarket nights they up and kill themselves.'

'Now don't you go killing yourself,' she said turning towards him. At the sight of her nakedness he forgot what he was saying and gawped as if she had just sleepwalked out of the passage into this strange room.

'I can make no promises,' he said finally. 'These matters are beyond our control. Anyway the reason jockeys kill themselves is they are so hungry. How would you like to live on nothing but raw eggs, dry toast and champagne?'

'I could manage, except for the raw eggs.'

'Your guts,' said Harry warming to his tragic theme, 'feel like cat's-cradles of hot wire. You feel as strung up as the horse you're riding. Your mind goes first, then your spirit. You feel like all the failure in the world. I'm an amateur, only been through it once. Even then I,' speaking with simple pride, 'I toyed with the gas-tap.'

'But you had no sixpence for the meter?'

'Don't be so irreverent. You should respect a man's suicide attempt. In any case, it's mostly physical. Your resistance is so low. The slightest thing can bowl you over. A cough, a cold. Then bang it's pneumonia or typhoid. With Tom French it was consumption. And Arthur Rossiter, who rode Robert the Devil, cut his throat in the plantation near the Bury Hill. And poor Fred Archer, not thirty yet, his wife dead in childbirth, his other child dead too, a close secret man, shot himself after a bad go of typhoid.' By continuing to talk, Harry had achieved a certain sang-froid. He propped himself up in bed with the heroism of a moribund dandy and declaimed with a wealth of gesture:

'The shoppy slang of Turf is hushed today,
No cry of "Tinman won, sir, by a head!"
The dull November seems to all more grey,
For Archer's dead!'

'Who's Tinman—his horse?'

'No, Archer. They said he was close with money. They called

him the Tinman. But he was only a poor boy who was scared of losing it all. When he died, they cried in the streets of London. My father saw two old men blubbing in Piccadilly. Most shocking thing that ever happened. He had extraordinary grey eyes, and tiny feet, though he was so tall for a jock.'

'Tinman,' she said sleepily. 'Are you the Tinman?'

'He won his greatest Derby with one arm. The other was clamped in iron after a horse had bitten it. Robert the Devil was so far in front that the bookies had stopped laying odds and then Archer came like an arrow on Bend Or and seemed almost to lift him past the post with his good arm. It was like a miracle. Afterwards, the people who owned Robert the Devil complained that Bend Or was really another horse, a ringer, had been switched as a yearling and so on. But the stewards overruled the objection, the Duke of Westminster got his prize money and the Tinman got his tin. And poor Rossiter cut his throat because he had wasted too hard and the crowd said he should have won.'

'And should he?'

'Well, the Tinman didn't think so, he shouted back at the greedy swine "Don't say it, it isn't true, the lad rode as well as any lad could, but he met a better horse".'

'The Tinman ... the Tinman.' Stella lay down beside him and stroked him with solicitude till he fell asleep. He knew she would be gone when he woke. No note, however. She should have left a note. It was surely the thing to do.

'Good morning, good morning.'

'Good morning, sir. What is this exactly?'

'It's a grand morning. That is, as you see, a cheque.'

'I can see that. But Mr O'Reilly does not happen to bank at this bank.'

'O'Neill, O'Neill. Frogmore O'Neill, after the last resting-place of the late Prince Consort, in the neighbourhood of which he claims to have been conceived one summer afternoon after Windsor Races. His father, though an O'Neill, was a staunch Unionist and a good Church of Ireland man. But I must admit that his writing is terrible.'

'Well, as it happens, that's really immaterial.'

'It's kind of you to say so. But I fear that on the contrary it is extremely important. They mark you down in examinations for it. Sloppy handwriting is the sign of a sloppy mind.'

'No, sir, the point is this is not one of our cheques.'

'Ah nor it is, but I am one of your customers—or do you begin to weary of my custom? Putting it another way, has my custom staled my infinite variety?'

'Indeed not, sir. Unfortunately the fact remains that we cannot cash this cheque for you.'

'But this cheque is open as the day is long. Far from having crossed it with his spavined hand, Mr O'Neill has written, though I admit scarcely legibly, Pay Cash on it, there.'

'Just a moment, sir.'

Harry picked his nails and gazed at a leaflet depicting a man in a bowler hat being knocked down by a car. The strap-line shrieked 'What Would You Do Without Him?' In the ensuing text, the bank with a certain immodesty claimed to be adept in the administration of all matters concerning wills, funerals, insurance, trusteeship and investment, both equity and gilt-edged, drawing as it did upon a wide range of specialist advice and more than a century of experience. In the circumstances, it seemed decidedly callow of these financial solons to raise such timid objections to the disbursement of a mere five jimmy o'goblins.

'The manager will see you now, Mr Cotton.'

'But it was only a fiver . . . I mean I have another appointment . . . don't wish to trouble . . . busy man.'

'He particularly wished to see you.'

Yielding to the ineluctable summons, Harry followed the clerk into this local branch of the debtor's prison where a small man crouched behind his desk like a stunted ant-eater. His pendulous nose twitched wildly as he welcomed his old and valued customer.

'First-class race you rode on Rubber Band. I see the *Sporting Life* says that if Harry Wragg is the Head Waiter on the flat Harry Cotton bids fair to match him over the sticks. I cut that out, you know.'

'Did you now? That was kind of you.'

'Not many people associate bank managers with the turf. Chalk and cheese, you know. But I've always been a keen follower. I just wanted to congratulate you in person.'

'Thank you very much.'

'Not at all. Hope to see more of you—on and off the course, you know.' Exhausted by the effusion of this tribute, the nose began to throb as if a tourniquet had been applied to it somewhere in the region of the bridge for the purposes of measuring its mean blood pressure. A smell of peppermint strangled the room. Harry assessed the purple rings round the eyes, the swollen vein coursing diagonally across the bulb of the nose like the sash of some grand order of oenophiles and on a puckish, instantly regretted impulse, said:

'Would you care to pop over the road for a quick one?'

'Rather too early in the day for me, I'm afraid.' The bank manager laughed, ducking away stoat-wary from the clerk's inquisitorial gaze. He was angry. Harry's invitation had come too pat. The habit must be showing. Where did he keep it—a drawer in his desk, a filing cabinet? 'It's been a real pleasure to meet you, Mr Cotton, but I fear I must be toddling along now. I have some documents to consult in the vaults.'

Ah the vaults! As the great iron grille clanged behind him, what cool release he must feel. How his feet would scud along the cold lino, toddling towards the toddy. Past the filing clerks— Good morning, Miss Tytler, Mrs Critchley, good morning. There must be no hint of hurry as he clip-clopped down the little iron staircase into the holy of holies, the inner paradise of dust and dark. If you had the taste for it, there was nothing like browsing in the files: A-Bells, Buchanan-Haig, Highland Cream, White Horse and then those back files, with what rare irony labelled DEAD MEN, the cold unwinking rows of empties stretching to kingdom come. In banking premises storage space was always at a premium, but these vaults should just about see him out and the temperature was ideal for the purpose. And when he was gone, they would look upon the empties with the reverence due to a man's tomb, a personal Pyramid.

'As I say, a pleasure to meet you in the flesh, you know. In the flesh,' said the bank manager bounding to one side of the desk, barely pausing to extend a farewell paw in his determination to reach the door before he was denounced to the authorities. Harry opened his mouth to reciprocate these abbreviated courtesies; the manager forestalled him: 'Crowther, you will of course see to it that Mr Cotton has everything he needs.' Hush money, thought Harry, as he counted the five brand-new oncers with extreme deliberation to annoy the clerk.

'Your two pounds.'
  'I couldn't be more surprised.'
  'I couldn't be more grateful. I shouldn't have—'
  'Any time. Pretty girl.'
  'Yes she was, and is, I imagine, but she's gone. Anyway, thank you.'
  'Any time.'
  'I wouldn't keep saying that if I were you. I'm never too flush.'
  'Are you by any chance looking for a job? No, don't worry, your secret is safe with me.'
  'I'm not worrying.'
  'You went white as a sheet when I mentioned work.'
  'What do you mean? I have worked . . .'
  'I like the past tense.'
  '. . . and I may work again.'
  'Ah the dignity of labour. Would it interest you to know that strangely enough this establishment at this very moment stands in need of an experienced assistant manager, must be skilled in all the duties of the licensed victualler's trade, fiver a week and board and lodging?'
  'The bloody boy's let you down again.'
  'That's the kind of razor-sharp brain this place needs. You pierce straight to the heart of the matter. I didn't catch your name.'
  'Harry Cotton.'
  'We need a noo barman in this town, Harry Cotton. You could be the man.'
  This searching interview concluded, it was agreed that Harry should enter immediately upon his duties which were to be

strictly temporary, part-time and underpaid. He lost not a second in taking stock of his new surroundings, taking particular stock of the Pyjama Club's extensive range of fine malts, blending them in his gullet with all the skill of a master until Mossy, unnerved by this application, had to remind him that board, as in the phrase 'board and lodging included', referred in its strictest sense to solid sustenance only. Harry, having been shown the attic suite, riposted that not only was it his duty to assure himself of the quality of the beverages being served to his intended clients, he also had a right to some compensation for the shortcomings of the lodging which fell well below the minimum standards of space, hygiene and ventilation as laid down by the London County Council.

'I like your style, old-timer.'

'Are you American, Mossy?'

'No, just studying.'

'I'd rather you didn't. I don't think you've quite mastered the idiom.'

'As you like. I find it helps to keep the drunks at bay.'

'I am beginning to wonder if this post was really designed for a person of delicate breeding like myself.'

Lodged in this cave of slaking, seated cross-calved on his bar-stool as snug as a gnome on a mushroom, Harry began to feel the dusty coolth stealing over him. Across the bar, Mossy, scarlet-lipped, wisecracked imprecise American, her square face jutting from under her pudding-basin hair like an Angevin yeoman. Time, never required by either of them to move at much above walking pace, now obediently stood still. There was a suspension of haste. In this academy thinking ahead was forbidden, cere-bration in the wider sense discouraged except where it promised to help kill time.

'You train your barmen well,' said Harry, resuming his research into the malts.

'We insist on the highest standards.'

Outside, the distant rattle of traffic, barely the sound of voices. Inside, a brush knocking against the corners as the char-lady worked her way up the stairs. In the heartland of the club, indolence reigned, its legitimacy unquestioned. The few austere rays of morning that had got through the defences expired softly upon wine-stained carpet, greasy chairbacks, insect-speckled lamp shades blurred with dust. Nothing was here to affright the aching eye, no dispraise or blame, in fact nothing much except a militant lethargy. For, like the picturesque quarter of an old town, these seedy delights asked nothing of the visitor except that he refrain from trying to clean them up, reform them into modern conveniences, at the first hint of which interference they would pack up their inimitable atmosphere and decamp to more secluded regions. Leave us alone, they muttered, and we will leave you alone as you have never been left alone before; you want to get away from the pressures, here the pressure is as minimal, the air as thin as on the surface of the moon; heed our social contract and you will enter into the last true realm of freedom.

'Nearly time for the noonday gun.'

'What?'

'Tom Dunbabin. Always makes for the shade as soon as the clock strikes. Here he comes.'

There was a scrabble of footsteps on the stairs, then a crash and a brief babble of voices and a madman in a shabby topcoat, belt and lapels flying, limped into the room.

'Foolish woman. What an ill-considered place to leave a brush.'

'Tom, this is our new temporary barman, Harry Cotton. Dr Dunbabin.'

'Bloody boy's let you down again, has he?'

'What's your poison?'

'I don't think that's quite the right opening for a high-class barman.'

'Sounds more like one of his customers.'

'Someone at Skindle's.'

'With a large moustache.'

'In the Regatta Bar.'

'Exactly.'

'Well then ... What's yours, guv'nor?'

'No, no, that's the Nag's Head, Holloway Road.'

'Sorry, I'll try again. Good morning, sir.'

'That's more like it. A chaste and simple greeting. Leave the pleasantries to the customer. Your task is to soothe and mollify, not to amuse. You're not the cabaret.'

'Good morning, sir.'

'No need to be importunate. There's nothing worse than a barman who pesters one. You must give the customer time to reflect, make up his mind for himself. I think . . . I think . . . I'll have a large whisky-and-ginger.'

'It *is* cold for the time of year.'

'There you go, jumping to conclusions. I might be asking for a large whisky-and-ginger because I was cold. But on the other hand, I might equally well be acting on doctor's orders, it might be the only drink my single remaining kidney could absorb or I might have been drinking nothing but whisky-and-ginger-ale continuously for the past forty-eight hours or I might be a travelling salesman for ginger ale condemned to consume the stuff from here to retirement or I might belong to some muslim sect which took an individual view of the Koran for some reason regarding whisky-and-ginger-ale as exempt from the prophet's prohibition. You must await the evidence.'

'Well, what's it like out then?'

'As it happens, it *is* cold for the time of year. But the publication of this intelligence is my prerogative. I am, after all, the one who has been out in it. And I am also the one who is paying for the drinks.'

'Say when.'

'Ah now, there you find me out. If I have a fault—no, no, let me speak, let us at least embrace the hypothesis—if I have a fault, it is that I do not know how to say when. I cannot trace the reason. Jung, Adler, Ouspensky—all have tried and all have had to concede defeat, Freud won't even take the case. It is inexplicable but I just cannot do it. Stop, whoa back there, don't drown it—all these I can manage without the slightest qualm. But when—no, it is beyond me.'

Tom Dunbabin was as ageless as rust. The muddy orange of his skin, his red-rimmed eyes gleaming behind rimless spectacles, his crinkly ginger hair, his tensely beaming mouth made it difficult to establish whether he was an unusually vital sexagenarian or an adolescent with a hereditary predisposition towards alcoholism. In practice only the most clinical of intellects would have bothered to apply itself to this question, the subject's company being so overpowering that his audience was faced with the more pressing choice of surrender or flight. It was no more possible to preserve an analytical detachment towards him than it would have been to wrench open his jaw and, as with a horse, assess his age by the state of his teeth—the latter course being in any case futile because in the interests of economy he had had them all removed and replaced by un-nervingly regular dentures. This dramatic measure he also justified by explaining the nature of his staple diet—cakes and buns from Lyons except on Thursday afternoons when he patronized the ABC, his local Lyons being shut.

'Ordinary teeth would never stand up to the perpetual bombardment of butter icing, the hailstorms of angelica and stem ginger. Think of the pain, think of the expense—all avoided by my one decisive, almost Napoleonic stroke. I do not pretend that my present life is entirely without discomfort, but these pangs are sent to try us. I trust I can play the stoic as well as most. Was it not the Emperor Marcus Aurelius who first sported false teeth? Besides, in moments of stress I can always lay aside my cross. If I can be sure that the confidence will go no further, I will let you into a secret.' In default of heads eagerly crowding in to apprise themselves of this esoterica, he leaned forward himself, enveloping his hearers in a halitotic gas which was coincidentally reminiscent of the dentist's chair, though clinical analysis might in fact have broken down its components as: whisky-and-ginger-ale, Dundee cake, threepenny éclairs, a quantifiable deficiency in vitamins and a decided shortage of washing facilities and fresh air at Flat 1a (Basement), 181 Mecklenburg Row, Bloomsbury, where Dr Dunbabin profes-sionally pursued the vagaries of the Young Hegel and diverted himself in the byways of English genealogy. 'When I am by myself, at home, eating a light meal, I do on occasion, only on occasion you understand, take my teeth out and exercise my gums, subjecting each mouthful to positively Gladstonian mastication. I feel all the better for it. In fact, I sometimes think if I could subject every part of my body to equally rigorous stimulation how wonderfully well I would be.'

'Every part?'

'Every part. You must not mistake the part for the whole, Mossy my dear. That is the sin of synecdoche, sternly to be resisted by all men of goodwill. Anyway, you look quite adequately stimulated as you are.' The wrench he gave his lips failed in its mission of amplifying innuendo, *double-entendre* and general one-of-the-boysness, leaving behind instead the suggestion that he had some months earlier suffered a minor cerebral haemorrhage from which he was now pluckily recovering.

'My dear, I feel perfectly ghastly. I need ten years in the country.'

'I can think of no worse remedy. I can assure you the country would be disastrous. The first sniff of silage and you would immediately contract hay fever and severe melancholia . . .'

'But the air, the long walks . . .'

'Nobody ever goes for walks in the country except for townees down for the weekend, dabbling their stout walking shoes in the mire. The country offers no pleasures but eating and drinking and both of those are blighted by the inescapable bucolic constipation. You need pavements beneath your feet. So do I. We all need pavements. The decisive struggles of our time are fought out in the cities. What do you say, barman?'

'Of course they are.'

'Hegel.'

'Just so, sir.'

'He's getting the hang of it nicely. I like his slavishness.'

'That's what we pay him for.'

'Have we paid him?'

'He's young yet.'

'He's got a lot to learn.'

'Nobody's perfect.'

'Don't generalize.'

'I'm sorry.'

'Not at all. It is I who am sorry. I should be nicer. I should not be so abrupt. It is a fault, I know it. I think living alone may have something to do with it, a sufficient but not a necessary cause, I must rise above my situation. I may get nicer as the day wears on or then again I may not. These things are unpredictable. But then that is the glorious uncertainty of our predicament. At least *I* glory in it. For we are but the tennis balls of destiny.'

'Indeed, sir?'

'You should not greet these aphorisms with such an impassive mien. "Well I never" or even an enthusiastic "really" would be more fitting. You are after all in the presence of an educated man. There are not many of us left. We are a dying breed. We deserve somewhat of respect.'

'Quite so.'

'Still too dry. Where is the sap, the juice in you, man? Have you no heart, no feelings? A desiccated barman is an abomination.'

'I'm sorry.'

'Ah, this eternal exchange of apologies, as if life were some endless vicarage tennis party. But so it is, so it is, as I was saying, for we are but the tennis balls of destiny, no, don't interrupt . . .'

'I'm sorry.'

'No, it is I who am—I *will* be nicer. You shall not know me. And. Yes. We are only the tennis balls of destiny, but we can at least make a splendid plonk as we are smashed into the back netting.' He drained his glass and threw back his head violently, holding on to his spectacles with his free hand as if to shout defiance at some person appearing through a trap-door in the ceiling, perhaps a swashbuckler of the Douglas Fairbanks type. 'But then,' he said plunging forward again with equal violence so that his head nearly impaled itself on the soda syphon as if the Fairbanks phantom had planted a small but deadly throwing knife between his shoulder blades. 'In the great Centre Court of history how faint will be the echo of that plonk. It will hardly register on the Beaufort Scale—do I mean the Beaufort Scale?'

'Isn't that something to do with winds?'

'Or hunting.'

'On the equestrian Beaufort Scale we would be the merest yeomen, ostlers barely suffered to hold the horses at the mounting blocks.'

4

'Speak for yourself, Tom. Our barman is a divine horseman. He has ridden Ampersand.'

'I am confused. I apologize. This is indeed a divine horseman. He has bestridden a conjunction, sat upon a cipher. Phaethon himself never managed that.'

'Ampersand is a horse.'

'Of course it's a horse. Even I in my solitary basement have heard the thunder of its hooves. In time past it has borne upon its back a tithe of my modest resources—and borne it nobly. And you, sir, you have ridden this animal? My cup is filled by the man who has tamed this mighty part of speech? This is wonderful. I am a prince. You will not, I hope, think it indelicate if I enquire what has temporarily no doubt reduced you to the level of a common tapster?'

'Don't be so bourgeois, darling. Jockeys rest . . . like actors.'

'Forgive me. I am bourgeois, irredeemably bourgeois. You gilded butterflies dance upon the air, singing all summer long. I am the bourgeois ant, always busy, bustling from A to B on some senseless errand or other. And the worst of it is that my labour will all be wasted, for I belong to a doomed race, all my old maid's ways, my houseproud thrift . . .'

'Have you ever seen his place? Pigsty . . . a pig wouldn't go near it.'

'You are the wave of the future. I am the Last of the Bourgeoisie . . . I see it all, a huge tableau by Lady Butler—the little band of burghers down to its last round—no, I think this is your round, my dear—collars still stiff, umbrellas immaculately rolled and all around, the screaming dervish swine, bohemians in uniform, hashish-crazed cosmopolitans, libertines addicted to the worst sort of nameless practice, the tiny garrison of civilization swamped . . . the tattered flag of decency torn down by the barbarian hordes . . . wretched is the man who survives that battle, I would rather die on the ramparts. It is different for you. You have your life before you.'

'That's just the problem.'

'Come, come, man, no weakness, have you lost the will to live?'

'No, just six hundred quid.'

'Ah, I'm sorry, I did not intend to pry into your embarrassment.'

'On the contrary, it is you who are embarrassed. I am merely in debt.'

'Courage, remember that even the Prodigal Son was forgiven.'

'The Prodigal Son did not bet with Cod Chamberlayne.'

'Good old Cod—forgive me, a slip of the tongue, he is neither good nor nearly as old as he looks. But Cod Chamberlayne . . . how that name takes me back to my youth . . . happy days, I cannot repress a tear.'

'Don't believe it.'

'You're right, quite right. They were not happy days. They were hellish days. In fact I visualize hell as being rather like Hurst Park on a wet afternoon. I hated every second. It is a consolation to reflect that nothing in later life could ever be so utterly dispiriting as to watch a long-priced double go down in the last stride and to hear Cod whining, "ay, you 'ad me worried for a moment there, my dear sir." There is nothing . . . absolutely nothing quite like the deep, deep peace of being warned off the turf. The best years of your life lie ahead of you.'

'I shall miss riding.'

'There are donkeys . . . and rocking-horses . . . and merry-go-rounds. I have heard that in America they even have barstools shaped like saddles. And think what you will be saved from . . . that itch to have just one more bet . . . the piles of old *Sporting Lifes* marked with hieroglyphs whose meaning you have long forgotten . . . the insane scholarship of it all . . . getting up before dawn to pore over the results of the autumn meeting in some Irish bog in order to get a line on the form for Cheltenham where in any case the going will be bone-hard, and all the long agony of insolvency . . .'

On the Rails

Cod Chamberlayne sat at his desk, episcopal in his dignity, staid as a billbroker in his dress, eschewing the professional

vulgarities of outsize tie-pin and tattersalls waistcoat, his only
concession to the traditional flamboyance of his calling a monstrous carnation, resembling in its dimensions and inflorescence
a young cabbage. This bloom was the emblem of his standing as
both butt and monarch of the rails. Around it had sprouted a
herbaceous border of pleasantries mostly rooted in Cod's
speech—pure cockney of the old type, his vowels chastely
flattened with never a hint of a diphthong. Pointing with pride
to the carnation, he would whine, 'I plucked it from my green
'ahse,' to which his hearers responded eagerly 'must be wonderful soil, Cod', or in a variation, 'I grew it in my 'ot 'ahse'—'I
always said you were a passionate man, Cod.' On rare occasions
when the carnation was absent waggish patrons would shout
'Where's the flower then, Cod? It's like a garden party without
the blooming queen.'

It was as much Cod's size as his piscine appearance which lent
him such ambiguous dignity. On cold days he wore a belted
camel-hair coat so enormous that when it made its debut the
resident tormenters yelled 'What's up, Cod? Brought the family
with you?' Again, in enlarging on the delights of his new palace
at Stanmore he declared with modest satisfaction 'I like a nice
big 'ahse', a statement greeted with 'you got one already then,
ain't you, Cod?' He was wont to parade himself as a comfortable
man, indolent and pleasure-loving: 'I like a course which is 'andy
to the metropolis. You can attend to your business in the a.m.
and then drive dahn and you've still got time to take a glass of
wine with friends and associates. 'urst Park or Ally Pally, that's
my line. I don't care to go frigging all over the kingdom to places
like Aintree and 'aydock. Freeze your balls off, standing on the
rails at them northern courses, ay, that's young men's work.'

This parade deceived no one, may not even have been intended to, being perhaps a masque to divert the audience during
the transaction of more serious business. If that was indeed the
intention, it had the reverse effect because, far from bathing Cod
in a eupeptic glow, this assumed geniality merely threw into
higher relief the acerbic acuity which he displayed in his business
dealings. He skipped through account sheets with the magisterial
frown of a schoolmaster correcting an essay. Froggie had said it

was like being led through an interminable litany: 'From backing two-year-old maidens before Ascot, Good Cod deliver us. From monkeying arahnd with the autumn double, Good Cod deliver us. Remember not, O Cod, our offences nor the offences of our fathers; neither take thou vengeance of our debts.'

It was profitless in practical terms to acquiesce in this litany. Cod never abated a farthing and took pride in dealing with each man according to the length of his pocket and not the length of their friendship, if the latter word could even legitimately be used of his relationships. His clients agreed to be thus catechized not because they expected to gain financial advantage by it but because it enabled them to contemplate more fully the shrivelled state of Cod's soul from the carefree eminence of the debtor. Besides, they went away from the interview with a tale to tell which, as Cod was well aware, would soften the humiliation. The fact that he was a bit of a character was good for business; he knew this too and was not above embellishing the character that nature and circumstance had given him. There were after all other bookmakers, though he was not in the habit of acknowledging their existence. But none could dye the carnation like Cod, none could perform the less agreeable duties of the profession with such sadistic exuberance.

He even managed to imbue the grubby process of accumulation with a certain magic. To initiates he exuded a monstrous divinity, just as adepts were able to discern in the sullen figure of the Egyptian god Thoth—who sometimes took the form of an ibis, sometimes that of a dog-headed monkey—none other than the Thrice Greatest Hermes, the founder of all occult science. Cod himself often went by another name among those who had suffered at his hands. Froggie in particular never referred to him except as 'Old Winey', this sobriquet bearing a weight of almost hermetic allusion: first, to Cod's fondness for 'taking a glass of wine', his euphemism for the conveyor-belt of champagne bottles which passed before him all day long; second, to the quality of his voice, the wheezing of a distant nose-flute, and finally, to the gloria which rounded off his homilies, 'make the cheque out to C. F. Chamberlayne, if you please, Chamberlayne with a Y-N-E.' Froggie claimed that whenever he felt the drumming in his ears after a bad fall or listened to the train rattling over where the rails joined, sooner or later he always heard the old refrain 'Y-N-E if you please, Y-N-E if you please' and that these words should be graven on Old Winey's tombstone if by some oversight they should chance to bury him in consecrated ground.

The gloria was not yet in sight. In fact Cod was only just reaching the end of the passage where he was wont to threnodize upon the melancholy spectacle of young men gambling beyond their means. He then broke down this general dirge into three secondary themes—his own mistaken charity in allowing these foolish striplings such extensive credit, the importunate demands of the Inland Revenue which made the small businessman's life so difficult and the unscientific, nay, immature manner in which Harry had contrived to lose so much money: 'Backing a two-year-old before June and a maiden too. What was you thinking of, Mr Cotton? And this one here, a most imprudent wager, if I may say so. I don't like my gents to go messing arahnd with 'andicaps and well you know it. 'andicaps is for the simpletons that follows the scribes and Pharisees. Why, I've made more money laying the odds against our course correspondent's nap selection than I've 'ad 'ot dinners. Naps! Blooming sleeping beauties if you ask me. But that's all water under the bridge as the first mate said to the captain of the *Titanic*. We must . . . oh, this is a sad story, a sad story indeed—a pony at a hundred to six. If you will do it, Mr Cotton, I can't stop you. Another two-year-old. My dear sir, they're too young to know what their legs is for. They oughtn't to let them out the paddock without their mummies. Ay, I'm disappointed in you, I honestly am. And one of Miss L.'s too. Now then, Mr Cotton, you know that Miss L.'s purse is bigger than her brain. By the way, entirely by the way now, did I hear aright or was it only a story they was telling me abaht you and Ampersand?'

'Yes, I did have a gallop on him the other day.'

'Quite so, but that wasn't all they said. They said Miss L. 'ad promised you the ride on 'im in the Gold Cup, 'cos poor Dicky Sears was no good to man nor beast, and then she repented of 'erself and come up to the gallops and give you a piece of 'er mind and 'ad you pulled off the 'orse. And you threw her bleeding chicken bones at her and gave her a piece of *your* mind. Now is that right or is it the merest 'earsay?'

'Well, you know what C.L. is like.'

'I do indeed, Mr Cotton, I certainly do,' said Cod, ecstatic, gadoid mouth trembling with delight. 'But I also know that she is a very wealthy lady. And she has a quiverful of 'orses. Is it prudent, I ask you, to throw chicken bones at such a lady? Is them the right tactics for a young man trying make his way to in life?'

'Listen, Cod, have you ever been pulled off the back of the best horse in the world when he was going like a train?'

'No, my dear sir, I 'ave not 'ad that pleasure. I was never a riding man. And I appreciate your psychology. I only ask, is that the right way to get on in life?'

'Well, getting on isn't everything.'

'No, I appreciate that to the full, don't think I don't. Getting on isn't everything but it's better than nothing. To take an example, Mr Cotton, it's better than this what we have here. This is a lamentable state of affairs. Six hundred and fifty-seven pound is a great deal of money, even these days. A considerable sum. I don't wish to intrude, that's the last thing I wish and I know you will pardon me for asking, but 'ave you security, Mr Cotton, and if you 'aven't security, 'ave you expectations? A lot of young gentlemen 'ave expectations. Expectations is nowhere near as good as cash, but it's better than nothing.'

'Like getting on.'

'Ay, you're a serious man, Mr Cotton, I know you intend nothing humorous. But these are serious matters. And I must ask you just what your intentions are.'

'Oh you'll get paid in the end, Cod, you always do.'

'I wish I did, my dear sir, I wish I could be so blithe. I must ask you again, what is your security, what are your expectations?'

'Then I'm afraid you must ask in vain.'

'Ay, I'm sorry to 'ear it. This is a bad business, you know, a very bad business. I am to take it then that your net assets are present 'ere before me?'

'In person, in all their glory.'

'Oh dear, oh dear. No security, no expectations. What abaht your dear father?'

'I'm afraid we are not on very good terms.'

'What a misfortune. I am sorry to hear it, very sorry. Some other person of substance then who might be prepared to assist you?'

'Cod, you're a man of the world, you know persons of substance don't grow on trees.'

'You flatter me, sir, but you're right, no more they do. That's the pity of it. It would seem then that we 'ave reached an impasse.'

'I can't deny it.'

'We must take other measures.'

'We must.'

'Let me put my cards on the table face upwards. I believe in being frank.'

'There must be no secrets between us.'

'I am anxious to keep matters on a private and friendly basis. The last thing I wish is to bring the lawyers in on it.'

'Come off it, Cod, you know gambling debts aren't recoverable at law.'

'I'm glad you're a student of the law, my dear sir. The law repays study. As you rightly say, in my profession we 'ave no legal rights. We are despised and rejected of men. The courts do not know us. That is why when we distrain, we distrain informally.'

'Informally?'

'Quite informally.'

'I don't like the sound of that.'

'No more you should. It is a disagreeable business. I am sorry to say that our bailiffs are not pleasant men. Not pleasant men at all. That is why we keep them as a last resort. But there are of course alternatives.'

'Such as?'

'Well now, I might be able to help you out myself as a mark of personal esteem and regard. I like to help riding men. After all, without the members of your profession, where would we all be? This game 'as been good to me, I won't pretend it 'asn't. And I like to put back something of what I 'ave taken out of it.'

'That's a generous thought.'

'Ay, it's kind of you to say so, but it's no more than I ought to do. Now what I suggest is, and I put it forward purely for discussion with no commitment either side, that it might be possible for me to advance you the sum in question myself, as a private transaction you understand, nothing to do with the firm . . .'

'In which case, the debt would be . . .'

'Ay, you're a quick one. Exactly. The debt, being a private transaction pure and simple, would be recoverable at law. I have to look after my own position.'

'And there would, I suppose, be a small matter of interest.'

'You suppose correct. These matters are difficult to calculate in the head. My old brain is not what it was. Time was when I could balance the odds in a ten-'orse 'andicap before they'd finished putting the numbers up in the frame. But let me see . . . on the one 'and, no security, no expectations, no nothing . . . on the other, you're a riding gentleman, you like 'orses, you wouldn't want to be warned off the turf for not meeting your obligations . . . six of one . . . rather less than 'alf-a-dozen of the other. Yes . . . I think five per cent would be fair. My accountants will curse me for a foolish old man, but you 'ave my word on it. And Cod's word is—'

'Five per cent?'

'Paid monthly of course, in the usual way.'

'Sixty per cent a year.'

'Don't let's think in years, my dear sir. Let's look on the bright side. In a month or so, who knows? A fortunate investment . . . a chance meeting with a person of substance—and all this embarrassing business will be a bad dream.'

'I don't fancy it, Cod.'

'Ay, if life was what we fancied, we wouldn't none of us be here, would we? Necessity rides hard, my dear sir.'

'I would prefer to make some more enquiries first.'

'Please do. Make enquiries of our friends down the road if you like. They're a fine people, a fine people—but I doubt very much if they can suit you better. You see, the trouble is they can't give you the personal service. Now old Cod, he's a patient

4*

old sod. He likes to keep his regular customers. He'll be there waiting after you've made your precious enquiries.'

'Like the girl next door . . . always there to come home to.'

'Even the girl next door can't wait for ever. The stewards is very particular these days. Cod, they says to me, we can't 'ave these unpaid debts of honour 'anging abaht like a eunuch's kiss. You 'ave any trouble, Mr Chamberlayne, they says, and you come along to us sharp and we'll see you get satisfaction.'

'Where's the doctor?'

'Giving his lecture,' Mossy said.

'On?'

'From morality to history—the impact of Kant on Hegel or perhaps the other way round. He had to go early to buy some éclairs on the way.'

'I hoped he could give me some advice.'

'About your debts? How would he know? He never paid his. Still, it's a pity you missed him. You'd be the first man in living memory to ask his advice. You wouldn't dream of even asking him the time of day if you saw him in the street.'

'No, but he might know the best way of not paying,' Harry said.

'There is no best way. You just don't pay.'

'Ah, Frogmore. I cashed your cheque.'

'Congratulations.'

'Unfortunately . . .'

'Say no more, Harry. These things will happen. I'm sure it was a racing certainty.'

'No, no, I was referring to that small matter of six hundred quid still owing.'

'Ah that—rather out of my league, I fear.'

'Any suggestions?'

'You could always try Henriques.'

'That old—'

'Hush, never speak ill of potential benefactors. He is a kind chap and . . . lonely.'

'I thought he was just C.L.'s maid of all work.'

'Popular fallacy. He's as rich as she is. That's why they cling together. Two little rich babes in the great wood of life. By the way, I saw Kate again yesterday. There was something odd about her.'

'Her refusal to melt into your arms, I suppose?'

'No . . . genuinely odd. She spoke very strangely about C.L.'

'Strange not to.'

'Not as if she hated her but . . .'

'Pitied, was sorry for her? That's not surprising either.'

'As if it wasn't her fault.'

'Society had made her a parasite?'

'More or less. That kind of thing.'

'That's always been rather Kate's line. She keeps it on a tight rein, though.'

'Thing is, I rather thought perhaps . . . the rein might be on the point of breaking. That may be putting it too high.'

'She's always tense. It's hard to say. She's only my cousin.'

'Which means?'

'Oh nothing much. You think perhaps Henriques . . .'

'Might. Worth trying. Give him a ring.'

'Undignified though . . . distasteful at any rate.'

'He'd rather like that.'

'You're a hard man, Frogmore.'

'No, just realistic . . . in this case, anyway. When I say he's kind, I mean he's kind.'

Henriques was kind. He settled Harry in a chair, bathed him in a silken compress of courtesy. Drinks, cigarettes were wafted to him with the hesitant elegance of Gerald du Maurier fumbling for his lighter. Harry was immediately so relaxed that he felt like nuzzling down in the *toile-de-Jouy* till wakened by figs and wine. He could hardly prop up his eyelids. The business of keeping his affairs afloat seemed to him an absurd waste of effort. He was hypnotized by the dearly bought timelessness which pervaded these rooms: sound deadened by thick carpet and thicker doors, air refreshed without the vulgar intrusion of traffic, telephones answered, messages, bills, shopping all dealt with by invisible genii—another realm of freedom with a different price on the ticket of entry.

'How nice . . . you are good to say so . . . I am fortunate . . . your gifts as a horseman.' It was the sweetest embrocation but sweeter still was the manner in which Evelyn—'I hope you will not think it too premature if I ask you to call me Evelyn'— dropped the fiddle-faddle and put on a manner which was direct, even brisk. 'What bad luck . . . these problems are always so difficult for jockeys to avoid . . . I hope you won't think it impertinent but might I offer to help . . . a long-term loan, let me be open, it's really nothing to me and I would be delighted to . . . one condition only, as soon as you receive my cheque, you give up betting permanently . . . then you can forget all about it and get on with your riding . . . I think you have real ah, quality in you.'

The dreaded operation was so quick Harry hardly knew it had happened. A whiff of anaesthetic, a snick of scalpels, a twist of the needle and thread and it was all over—the surgeon peeling off his gloves and clapping the patient on the back with post-operative heartiness. Even in the rush of relief Harry felt the first twinges of suspicion, the first resentment of the obliged. Who was this man to be kind to him? By what right did he pour upon him this limitless bounty of tact and generosity, impose upon him one condition only, and that for Harry's own good? The world was not supposed to be made that way. Life was well known to be a struggle for survival. Softness was the texture of defeat. He waited angrily for the catch.

But Henriques—no, Evelyn, even the ingrate could not affect such brusquerie—burbled nicely on. He spoke of music and the poetry of riding and riding poetry, of Masefield and Adam Lindsay Gordon, of the English landscape and of that blot upon it, his friend, C.L. who, it seemed, was a person of sensitivity, musical talent, consideration and other gifts all hidden under this, ah, protective layer. Harry's experience in relations with her had been unfortunate; in that respect he was not alone; trainers and jockeys the world over nursed their bruises, but she too was bruised, deeply bruised. She was a good friend to Evelyn, they understood each other; they were both bruised. Here no doubt it came; the real price of release from the Fleet was to be inclusion in the brotherhood of the bruised, a little discreet showing of old hurts.

'I'm a lonely man . . . I expect you thought I would say that.' Harry felt that there had been enough of this second-guessing. If there were to be more conditions, formal or informal, he wished to hear them straight and react with all the honest candour of a bankrupt jockey. If it was to be whips out, the sooner he was allowed to make his distaste clear, the less embarrassment for all parties. 'I'm afraid elderly bachelors do tend to become maudlin . . . an occupational disease. We are nervous of boring the young, which is exactly why we always do bore them. We have so few resources of our own. The decay of the body is a melancholy enough business. You begin to fear the decay of the mind too. It's like a malicious trick being played on you . . . overnight your stomach seems to swell up and your backside goes flat and wrinkled. It's like somebody shifting a load from one saddlebag to the other . . . ah now—I'm sorry . . . we embarrass the young too. That's worse still. We need to talk, or rather, we like talking. C.L.'s a good listener, you wouldn't think so, but we have very cosy chats. I ask nothing of her, she nothing of me, well, I suppose I look after her horses, not very well though, it's a hobby. She'd do better to put her faith in a good trainer and leave it all to him. But she's not made that way. I'm very fond of her. I can't expect you to be. But then one can't expect one's friends to get on with each other. I hope you won't think it . . . this is perhaps not the moment but I hope I may ah, call you a friend without . . .'

'Good heavens, yes, of course.' In fact yes or no, depending.

'I am glad. I have so few young friends. But there is one to whom I am particularly attached . . .'

Harry looked down into his drink studying each vein and bubble in the ice-cube with a glacialist's devotion.

'I hope I shall not further embarrass you. I am so awkward in saying these things. . .'

Harry analysed the molecular structure of the ice-bubbles. Only the limitations of the naked eye prevented his gaze from splitting the atom.

'But I am extremely fond of Stella. I have known her since she was a child. Her parents are my oldest friends. When I lived in Breslau ah, at the turn of the century, we lived in each other's pockets. She is a lovely girl.'

'Lovely,' said Harry with all the exhausted gaiety of the reprieved.

'I would be desolate if anything happened to make her unhappy.'

'So would I.'

'You are fond of her too?'

'I don't know her very well but—'

'Ah I thought . . .'

'A very brief meeting.'

'You would like to see her again?'

'Very much.'

'You are sure? In the light of day these things . . .'

'Not always, not in this case. I am sure.'

'As you may guess, I do not speak from experience. You would know.'

'Far from it, but—'

'You have borne with me very patiently so far. May I go one step further?'

'I think I should say,' said Harry carefully, 'that you may have been wrongly informed. I am not quite sure what you have been told but I can only say that Stella said she had to go back to Germany. And she went.'

'Quite . . . I did not mean to imply anything at all. I only thought that if you really did want to see her again, you could go to . . . I am sure they would all be very pleased to see you— Stella and her family. And I would be more than pleased to see to the expenses.'

'This is really . . .'

'Let me finish by being ruder still. You look tired and run down, like a man who has been hard pressed.'

'Oh I've had a few late nights.'

'When the steeplechasing season ends, wouldn't a holiday— no, I won't press you now. Think about it. Please. It would give me pleasure.'

'Pleasure?'

'Pleasure. Breslau is, ah, not quite my home but the place where I have been happy . . . Many years ago . . . when my mother left my father, she went back to her people in Germany —quite modest you know they were, shopkeepers, but she was at ease there, they paid attention to her. My father had other things to keep his eye on. He had made a great fortune, he was almost the friend of royalty; with a little more effort, a somewhat bigger box at Ascot, a larger moor in Scotland, he might have done it. His house was vast, but was Belgrave Square a little too far west for Them to venture? Perhaps if only he could get Joachim to come and play . . . so many worries, then those fat cigars, those enormous meals. My father was a large man. I remember how he stood in his great tails, legs apart, head slightly backwards with his big red lips rounded to receive the dinner pill. The pill seemed such frail protection against his volcanic dyspepsia. Everything in that house was large and heavy, closed in. Going to Breslau, to my mother, that was light, not airy exactly but relaxed. Lime-trees . . . the open plain . . .'

'Do you ever go back there yourself?'

'No, I am too old, too stiff. My cousins would all be strangers. That's why . . . I would like to see it through your eyes.'

'It's very kind but . . .'

'I have no dependants. No nephews even. My younger brother never married either. He was killed in the war, a rather elderly lieutenant at Wipers the second time round . . . oh on our side we were more English than the English. Breslau was only for the holidays, not real life—I was in my father's ah, clutches. You know how my brother died—telling the second-in-command not to keep his head down as it did no good and set the men a bad example. I met his second-in-command the other day. He is doing very well in the insurance business. My brother was determined to be English. In the end he had his lines pat.'

'Hm, yes.'

'I know people your age aren't so keen on that kind of thing. The supreme sacrifice seems more like a senseless waste. I can only say that in comparison with ah, my own life it does not seem so wasted.'

'I once met the man who wrote that, you know, the Armistice Hymn. Nice old boy, but very sentimental. Hadn't weighed the odds at all.'

'Do you yourself . . . riding . . .'

'That's different. There's no sentiment in that. It's a question of enjoyment, nothing more.'

'I envy you there. I have never learnt to enjoy risking my neck. In theory I would love to be young and in debt and in plaster. But I have never broken a bone in my body, I step too warily.'

'And never a moment in the red?'

'I did my best. It is a sad story. At Cambridge all my friends had overdrafts, boasted of their debts. I determined to rake hell with the best of them. I spent money like water—Sulka shirts, Charvet cravats in dozens, jeroboams of Krug. I gambled, I bought horses. Surely I must be in the most terrible debt. But not a word from my bankers. More banquets, more horses. Still not a word. I bought a yacht. Nothing happened. I called at the Strand. I enquired after the state of my account. Perfectly satisfactory, Mr Henriques, a healthy credit balance. I bought a bigger yacht. I called again, said I was just a little worried as to whether some recent purchases might have strained my finances. Not the slightest cause for alarm, sir, *alles in Ordnung*. Finally I went to my father and had it out with him. What was going on? Rather shamefacedly he admitted that he had not wished me to worry about money and so had instructed the bankers to replenish my account regardless of what I spent, so that I was always in credit. I was furious. It was almost the only time I told him what I thought of him.'

'A tragic story.'

'As they say in Breslau, you should have such problems.'

'Was there no limit at all?'

'I never found one. It is a very distant world . . . a dead world. But Breslau is still there, much the same I expect. Consider it at your leisure. No hurry.'

'I will. To be frank, I had not thought about Germany.'

'Or about Stella.'

'Yes, I think about Stella.'

Flagrante Delicto

'You ought to go to America,' said Frogmore O'Neill. 'America's the place to make a fresh start.'

'I don't want to make a fresh start. I just want to get square.'

'But you said Henriques was going to pay anyway.'

'He will, but in return he wants me to pay a sentimental visit to this place on his behalf.'

'No visit, no cash?'

'Nothing so crude, Froggie. You lack the finer feelings. He has merely landed me with a debt of honour.'

'And are you going to pay it?'

'Well, it's all rather odd . . .'

Odd was less than what it was. Even in the lift speeding silently through the buhl-congested space Harry felt changed. The simpleton who had blundered into Aladdin's cave would never be quite the same again. To slam the heavy front door of the luxury block was to slam the door not on innocence—even his presumption was not boundless—but on something closely resembling his freedom or at any rate the illusion of freedom. He had touched the limit of his credit.

'Why is your leg all bandaged up, Frogmore?' asked Mossy.

'Thing is,' said Froggie, 'this chap—no names, no pack drill— this chap has got a bloody great greenhouse leaning against his house. Very fine vine crawling all over it. Said to be part of the Hampton Court Vine.'

'That's what they always say.'

'Chap swears this one really is.'

'Where is it then?'

'East Molesey.'

'Very close.'

'No, it's not. It's bloody miles.'

'Very close to Hampton Court.'

'Possibly. That is not the point. Thing is, I sweat the whole way down there by train, the car being laid up. I arrive at this palatial suburban retreat, crouch in the laurels as instructed.

There's a lot of complicated stuff which I won't bore you with. Wait five minutes and then I'll play the Jupiter symphony on the gramophone.'

'The Jupiter's rather strong meat.'

'She's quite musical. Anyway, at the end of the five minutes the husband comes rushing out. So far, so good. Give him two minutes grace, quite right, the old campaigner always knows, back he comes, forgotten his briefcase or some such rubbish, out again, wife pecks him on the cheek, whole thing played at Chaplin speed, two minutes later out jumps lover from laurels, dripping wet and cold as charity, into house, I'll make you warm, you're my hotwater-bottle-pottle, let me fill you up, smiles and kisses, love in the suburbs, nothing like it, the only way to spend the afternoon, you don't get that terrible hung-over feeling about half past six.'

'A cowboy film's quite good too.'

'Gives me a headache. I have these rather weak eyes, very sensitive to intense light.'

'About the only thing they are sensitive to,' said Harry.

'What do you think happens then?'

'I'd rather not speculate.'

'Sound of front door opening. Husband back, quick you must go. Where, how—shin over balcony, work of a moment. Only thing is, there is no balcony. Crash, smash, lover catapults through the greenhouse roof . . .'

'No doubt damaging priceless vine . . .'

'Not to speak of bedding plants . . .'

'Just pricked out . . .'

'Lover clambers out of the bloodstained begonias and staggers off into the dusk, having suffered critical injuries. Husband probably impressed by wife's story about a masked intruder for just long enough to allow the scent to go cold. Doctor round the corner patched me up, told him I'd had a bad fall while gardening. Roof gardening? he enquired with a Hippocratic twinkle, removing the slivers of broken glass from my leg. Told him I'd have him struck off for interfering with his female patients if he didn't watch out, gave him a false name and here I am.'

'Now what really happened?'

'I go through a living hell shedding my blood all over north-west Surrey and I am greeted with vulgar incredulity. Romeo never had to endure this kind of treatment.'

'He came to a sticky end, though.'

'At least he had a balcony to work with.'

'That's the weak point in your story. Surely your girl-friend would have known there was no balcony outside her window.'

'She's not very observant.'

'Of course she might in fact have known and . . .'

'That's an unworthy thought, Mossy.'

'I prefer to disbelieve the whole story from beginning to end.'

'Disbelieve away. The truth is written in blood, all the way from here to East Molesey.'

Froggie hopped away from the bar in search of a more lenient audience.

'That man uses London like cats use other people's gardens—as a fornicating ground open to all-comers with no restrictions on hours, noise or decorum. It's extraordinary. Great men have passed through this city. Sheikhs from the desert entrust their hernias to nimble white fingers in Harley Street. Almond-eyed princesses buy their cardigans in Knightsbridge. Cattlemen from the Chicago stockyards sack the bazaars of Bond Street. But to Froggie all the city's mighty hum is nothing, nothing at all. It means as little to him as my neighbour's tulips to the cats. Does he behave like this in Uttoxeter or Catterick?'

'He does his best.'

'I don't believe it, Harry. I see him as one of those eternal provincials for whom London is synonymous with sin. He gets into a state of high sexual excitement as soon as he passes Potters Bar. In his language, "going up to town" is simply a euphemism for committing adultery . . . Ah Boy, do you happen to know Frogmore O'Neill, the last of the great cocksmen?'

Tom Dunbabin gesticulated more and more violently as night gathered and the club began to fill up. At the same time his swaying back and forth became less violent, more rhythmical, beginning to suggest the steadiness of a man on a rowing-machine or even perhaps of Froggie during one of his alleged

forays within the metropolitan area. Nevertheless, there was a
certain extravagance in the way Tom threw out an oar to arrest
the stately progress of a large man with a very smooth face.
Harry was startled to hear him speak to this imposing person like
a mere coolie. But it was soon made clear, and on inspection
hardly needed making clear, that the appellation was a piece of
unbridled meiosis. Boy Kingsmill was not a boy, had never been
a boy, had sprung from his mother's womb aged a vigorous
forty-five. It would no doubt have saved time if he had skipped
childhood and puberty and been equipped at birth with his
resonant baritone and macadamized raven hair.

He had the equable temper of true maturity. To be compelled
to talk to someone who could be of no conceivable use to him
was almost the only circumstance which stirred him to anger; a
prolonged conversation of this kind, say, with an elderly person
of slender means might leave him weak with resentment. He
would begin to suspect some complex plot against him, of which
the scrawny old woman babbling nervously must be the spearhead and his two colleagues chuckling at the far end of the room
the instigators. It was not so much the ridicule he feared as the
loss of influence, that fragile commodity so lovingly stored over
the years and so easily dissipated; ridicule was in fact one of the
occupational hazards of collecting influence, the stings un-
complainingly suffered by the bee-keeper in the pursuit of
honey. There were always people ready to laugh at one, or to
pretend to laugh, because one had the minister's ear. Boy
secretly thought that the sense of humour which people made
such a fuss about was really just the way they concealed their
failure from themselves.

Tom loved this man's company, hung around him, perpetually
trying to distil his secret as a chemist might have tried to isolate
and analyse the odoriferous components of his hair-grease.
Given Tom's untidy manner, this hobby was inevitably
accompanied by considerable importunities, noisy greetings,
much bobbing and swaying and unexpected standing of drinks.
So often did Tom ask Boy for his opinion, bring friends across to
meet him, declare in eaves-shattering tones, 'Oh, Boy's the man
to ask about that' that Kingsmill unconsciously began to assume

that Tom was his most devoted follower. These were after all not unlike the ways in which he himself was accustomed to show respect and loyalty to worthwhile persons. In strict logic—and protocol in these matters was nothing if not logical—he was bound to reciprocate these attentions in the manner that his own attentions were reciprocated, by a mixture of rough chaff and flirtatious caresses, thumps such as 'who's paying your debts these days, Tom?' being followed up with little dabs and pats—'You're looking very fit . . . what would you recommend as a good book on war reparations? . . . you *are* an amusing chap . . . where did you get that tie?' Tom listened enraptured. The flattery itself did not come amiss. 'I have often thought of writing a History of Flattery. After all, it's flattery that makes the world go round. It is a great mistake to underestimate how far flattery will get you, as long as it is sufficiently craven and laid on with a trowel. At the same time, there is something special about Boy's obsequiousness. It has a kind of solidity. It's like clay or putty, some substance which responds to the slightest pressure of finger and thumb but which given time sets surprisingly hard. No, that's not quite it . . . What is it that makes him unique—his bottomless ignorance . . . his complete indifference to everything except himself . . . his unflinching eye for the main chance? No, there is something else. It is not even that his *bonhomie* is false. He hardly reaches the stage of pretending to be *bonhomous*. The answer must lie in the recesses of the will. There may be a phrase somewhere in Schopenhauer which will illuminate the problem.'

Boy Kingsmill seemed unaware of this obsessive quest for his essence. He turned his head towards Tom very carefully, like a driver guiding a limousine through a tight bend, determined not to scratch the mudguard on the kerb. 'Of course I know old Froggie. He's one of my wife's few lovers.' There was no suggestion of bitterness or betrayal. He was simply conveying a piece of information; and the truth being relative to the importance of the speaker, he would have been quite prepared to defer to superior authority. If some grizzled senator had protested, 'Nonsense, Kingsmill, I've known your wife since she was a baby and I know she would never think of such a thing', Boy would have chuckled serenely and said, 'I dare say I've got the wrong end of the stick again,' passing his hand gracefully across the tarmac hair like a glider coming to rest on a rainswept runway.

'She's a funny girl, my wife. No sooner had I left the house this afternoon than she puts the gramophone on full blast, Mozart I think, but loud enough to waken the dead. Why do you think she does that now?'

'Isn't she rather musical?'

'But that's just my point. No musical person could bear to listen to that racket. Then another thing . . . I had to go back home again to pick up some papers to take down to a meeting. Just as I put my key in the door, I hear a great crash in the greenhouse. What the hell's going on? She tells me some lunatic story about a masked intruder in her bedroom—as if any intruder in his right mind would jump through the greenhouse roof in broad daylight when there's a perfectly good balcony and fire escape outside the other window.'

'He might have panicked.'

'Not a chance with a pro. Of course I knew exactly what had happened. The children had been playing football on the back lawn again and smashed the glass and then made an even bigger mess trying to clear it up. I gave 'em such a walloping last time I suppose she was trying to protect them. Anyway, by the time I got there the little devils had cleared off. But it just shows, I only have to leave the house for a minute and all hell breaks loose. Pauline my dear, come and meet Dr Dunbabin and—I didn't catch your name?'

Boy looked slightly irked as if he expected to be given a proper dossier in advance on any person he was liable to meet, down to the merest barman, and his normally reliable staff, all hand-picked men, had for once let him down.

'This is Harry Cotton. When not acting as our locum here, he rides races. In fact he even rides Ampersand.'

'Afraid you've slipped up there, my dear Tom. Old Dick Sears always rides Ampersand. Your friend's been having you on.'

'No, no, I—'

'Promise you, old man. I know it for a fact. C.L. would never allow anyone else on his back.'

'Well, she did this time,' Tom said tartly.

'I wish I could believe you. But facts are facts.'

'Ampersand, Boy. *And-per-se-and*, as they used to write it in the old horn books. *Of all the types in a printer's hand commend me to an ampersand.*'

'You *are* a clever chap. But I happen to know a bit about the chasing game. I know that horse like I know my own mother. Sears is the man. Always has been. Now here's Pauline.'

Harry had remained modestly silent during this discussion, confident that the truth would out. He had ridden the horse, after all. Seeing, however, that Boy was not going to accept his claim, he stepped forward to deliver a dignified remonstrance. There would be no hard feelings, merely a statement of the true facts, possibly accompanied by the offer of a drink on the house to show the absence of umbrage. Most people would feel themselves honoured to drink with a man who had ridden the greatest chaser of the age.

This projected display of grace under pressure remained only a project. Words fell back into his throat. Catatonia bound and gagged him. Harry was, for want of a better phrase or in his case any phrase at all, struck dumb. Even so might Paris, normally cocky as a jay, have broken off his discussion with the dreary Spartan drovers on the contrasting merits of the mountain sheep and the valley sheep in order to feast his greedy little eyes.

She leant with her back against the bar, elbows propped on the high stool behind her. Fair hair, a boat-shaped face, eyes that were—no, this is not a model agency. Such a catalogue has little meaning and this is no place for one any more than the Pyjama Club was a place for her—although she seemed to like it there. Boy looked at her fondly. His eyes, though small, were avid. She surveyed the room, neatly avoiding his gaze.

'She's a good girl is Pauline. Tone deaf,' said Boy with satisfaction. 'Can't sing a note. Wouldn't recognize *God Save the Queen* if the whole room was standing to attention. I find her restful after my wife. You can have too much music, you know.'

'Bird-brained then?'

'Lord no. Pauline's extremely intelligent. I like intelligent women. We had a first-rate talk about Social Credit over dinner.'

'And what were her views?'

'She doesn't go along with all this Greenshirt rigmarole but she thinks there's a good deal to be said for a national dividend.'

'And what do *you* think, Boy?' Tom's questioning was relentless.

'I don't mind saying I think she's hit the nail right on the head.'

'My, my . . . and where do you stand on Kibbo Kift?'

'Well I'm not much of a hiker and that Kindred stuff is a bit over my head, but I shouldn't be surprised if there turns out to be more in it than we think.'

'I expect you'd like to have a go at her Dark Place, though, wouldn't you?'

'Steady on, old man. Lord, he is an amusing fellow.'

'You don't think . . . I put it to you, Boy, purely for the sake of argument that you might have suggested some of these deep thoughts to her yourself.'

'Lord no, Tom. I sat quiet as a mouse. I like to have a good listen whenever somebody's got something worth saying.'

'If only there were more people like you, Boy. What the world needs is good listeners, preferably to me.'

'I hear you're interested in Social Credit,' Harry said.

'What's that, oh the thing the man who brought me was talking about at dinner. He seemed keen on it.'

'And you?'

'I agreed with him. I usually agree with people. It saves trouble.'

'Even when they're boring the pants off you?'

'Particularly when they're boring the pants off you.'

'You know who I am, Kingsmill?'

'Of course I do, Froggie. We've met a million times. As a matter of fact, we've just been talking about you.'

'Don't smirk. I don't want any smirking—'

'Look here, we're old friends—'

'We are not old friends. I don't want any smooth talk. I want a serious talk.'

'Have you had a few, old man?'

'How typical. How typically English. How typically despicably English. A man suggests a serious talk. And another man, *if* you can call him a man, accuses the man, the first man, of being drunk. Do you know what's wrong with the English? I will tell you what is wrong with the English.'

'That's right, you tell us, Froggie.'

'You do not know how to be serious. And do you know why you do not know how to be serious?'

'No, why don't we know how to be serious?'

'Because you have not suffered.'

'Now that's quite true, Boy, in the art of suffering we are the merest provincials, hicks with straws in our mouths, ignorant Merrie Englanders.' Tom waved his glass as if to evoke this nescient bliss.

'You have not suffered,' Froggie repeated. 'You have not known pain.'

'Well, old man, I've taken a few knocks in my time.'

'I don't mean mere physical discomfort. I mean the pain in the heart. Kingsmill, do you know where your wife is?'

'Of course I do. She's in our new house in East Molesey.'

'She is not in East Molesey. She is in hell. She is not on the banks of the River Mole, she is weeping by the River what's it called?'

'Styx,' said Tom, stuffing a withered olive into his mouth.

'Thank you, the River Styx. You have made her live a lifing hell, or rather her life a living hell. You have never shown her the least consideration. You have abused her. You have traduced and betrayed her.'

'Well, come to that—'

'I know what you are going to say. You are going to refer to certain recent events. Those events have nothing to do with it. That is merely a matter of consolation. Certain recent events are not to be compared with your behaviour.'

'Look, I try to take a balanced view—'

'What right have you to talk of balances when a human soul

is in agony? Balanced, for God's sake! I will redress your balance!'

With this battle-cry, recalling in its aggressive opacity those scraps of Norman French with which certain families embellish claims to have mislaid their origins in the mists of antiquity, Froggie charged. His first rush took him, head lowered perhaps to reduce wind resistance, on a course somewhat to one side of Boy, who thus needed only the barest veronica, the most genteel of hand-offs to deflect him. He continued, speed unchecked, towards the telephone booth whose corner spun him round like a swimmer turning for home. On the inward journey he encountered Harry, who, feeling that a modicum of valour was the better part of a barman's discretion, had come out from behind the bar, towel flipped over his shoulder with professional nonchalance. Froggie, still maintaining the posture of a promising young bull, butted him full in the stomach. For a second, Harry felt himself carried like a feather on the breeze, feet scarcely brushing the ground, breathless and weightless, until a sharp blow behind his right ear knocked him sideways. As he toppled off the bull's horns towards the floor, he stared giddily up at Pauline. She was sitting on a bar stool, her outstretched arm frozen in wonder. Like Lucifer in his fall he gazed back up at the stars. A good deal of 'I'm sorry—I thought—I didn't mean' pummelled his numb consciousness.

'Wonderful timing,' he murmured to himself.

'He just walked on to the end of my fist,' said Pauline.

'Like Dempsey in the first Tunney fight. He forgot to duck.'

'We are all in the gutter,' said Tom Dunbabin, helping himself in the unavoidable absence of the club's popular barman, 'but some of us are seeing stars.'

Froggie returned to the charge, strutted up to Boy and seized the nearest available lapel of his coat. 'Wouldn't have believed it if I hadn't seen it with my own eyes. You refuse fair fight, you hide behind a woman's skirts, and then to crown it all you pick on a mere flyweight like my friend here. In fact this man wouldn't even hurt a fly. He is a lovely man and you have struck him when he wasn't looking. You are a bully, a bully and a brute.'

'I didn't lay a finger on him. It was she who—'

'Incredible, quite incredible. Now he blames it on his mistress. Are you trying to tell me that a slip of a girl like that could have laid out a fully grown man?'

'She is not my mistress.'

'I congratulate you, madam. I would advise you to go straight home while there is still time.'

'Come on, be a good chap, do let go.'

Froggie was convulsed by a fresh spasm of rage and jerked hard at the coat using both hands, Boy pulling the other way with his body so that they seemed to be executing together some complex dance step, the coat acting as a scarf whose intertwinings conveyed to initiates all the nuances of the language of the dance. Gradually the coat was dragged off the near shoulder; there was a moment at which there seemed a chance that it would come clean away and with a shout of terpsichorean triumph the two performers would leap apart and bow low to the audience. But when the sleeve had slipped to a point just below the elbow, the torque exceeded its tolerance and something had to give, in this case the armpit seam, spilling a sliver of the discreet padding which lent such majesty to Boy's shoulders. Opinion later differed as to whether the quality of the cloth or of the tailor was to blame.

Mossy, shepherding new arrivals to the bar, inspected the commotion with displeasure. 'I can't have my barman drunk so early in the evening. I knew it was a mistake to hire a jockey.'

'I was only trying to keep them apart.'

'What is that girl doing down on the floor with you?'

'She knocked me out.'

'The man's raving. Says the girl knocked him out.'

'Excuse me, did you say he was a jockey?'

'Yes, he rides Ampersand. Come on, get up, Harry. And stop bathing his brow you. You'll give the place a bad name.'

'That's most awfully interesting. It must be awfully interesting to ride a horse like that.'

'Yes it . . .' An epic peace came over him; he trotted off through fields of waving poppies to nestle down in the shadow of a haystack where a naked girl in a straw hat tickled his chin with an ear of corn. The summer noon dazzled him. The stubble scratched his bare arms. Somewhere he heard a voice saying, what was it saying?—that the whole thing was a stupid joke, the man had never ridden Ampersand at all, probably never been on a horse in his life. Too hot to argue. What were they saying now? Barman's passed out, that's good, barman's passed out. Not passed out, knocked out—there was a difference, people were so careless, they never noticed differences, that was why they always got things wrong. The girl bent forward, her face shadowed by the hat. What was she called, he must get her name right, people hated it when you got their names wrong even if you were only one letter out. How white she was in the stubble, she was called Pastern, why did he think that now, Pastern wasn't a girl's name, it was a part of a horse. You've got a pretty pair of pasterns there, no, no, to joke about a person's name was even worse than to get it wrong. He hated it when they called him Cotton Reel at school. How white she was. Pastern, O my darling Pastern, let us lie down together and watch the wind bend the poplars in the wood at the end of the field. He can't lie there for ever, you know. Plastered on his first night. Hopeless. Hopeless, my darling Pastern, hopeless.

He lay in his attic bed looking up through the skylight. Still more stars. Stars as far as the eye could see and further.

'For a barman you drink too much.'

'Oh, Mossy, my dear, if you knew how sober I was. A strange girl knocked me out. I would know her again if I saw her. What more can I say?'

'A sober man would stand his ground.'

'It's all a question of balance. Everything is a question of balance. Let me kiss you.'

She looked down at him and clicked her tongue.

'I had hopes of you.'

'So had I. Kiss me quick. Imagine I'm a sailor.'

'You're a wreck.'

'Cruel words. But there we are.'

'There *you* are. Goodnight.'

'Goodnight, sweet lady, goodnight. And goodnight to you, too.'

Harry woke up in the middle of the night and went down to the single bathroom shared by the residents of that blighted tenement. He crept past Mossy's bedroom, paused for a moment until the floorboards beneath his bare feet began to creak and then moved on.

On the way back he met Tom coming out of Mossy's room. He looked different without his spectacles.

'Would you mind very much if I borrowed your toothbrush?' Tom said.

'Yes.'

'Mossy says I have bad breath.'

'She's right.'

'In that case, I will borrow your toothbrush. Harry, would it interest you to know something?'

'What? I don't want to hang around out here all night.'

'So far this year I've asked eleven girls to sleep with me.'

'And how many have accepted?'

'Two, including tonight.'

'Well, it's only February.'

'March.'

'So it is.'

In the morning Harry decided to go to Germany.

CHAPTER THREE

MY FATHER's feet were small and high-arched. They were very white against the dazzling green of the spring grass. On still mornings in April, those mornings when a flat dawn promised a hot day, he used to walk to the end of the garden in his bare feet, cradling his cup of tea already gone cold. He picked his way over the 'terrace', a square patch of bricks outside the back door, which he himself had laid out in herringbone pattern. Either because the bricks were of poor quality or because he had failed to allow enough space between them, they cracked in the first and then in each subsequent frost. Instead of providing an arena for sunbathing and elegant meals out of doors, the place was like a corner of a deserted brickyard, a paradise for ants and woodlice. Snails blazed nonchalant trails across the red-sharded moonscape; humans had to watch their step. My father walked delicately as if in high heels.

His dressing-gown flapped about his thin legs. Unusually for a man with such a restricted wardrobe, he had two dressing-gowns —a thick, roomy affair vaguely suggestive of a badger and a rather more sharply cut model, seersucker with thin red-and-white stripes. The two garments were handy for illustrating the two sides of my father's character: the badger model standing for a traditional English countryman, the seersucker a more cosmopolitan city-dweller, a frequenter of Riviera beaches even. At other times, I took them more personally as emblems of his relationship with myself: the badger dressing-gown enveloping a patriarch or housemaster, a person set in authority over me, while the seersucker corresponded to my father as comrade and companion. Most often, I took the choice of dressing-gown as an indication of his mood, disregarding the possibility that he might have been influenced by the weather that morning or, less likely, though highly desirable, that the other one was at the cleaners. In this fancy, the badger dressing-gown represented my father in sober and therefore melancholy mood considering what past, present and future had to offer, while the red-and-white stripes promised a carefree day, flapping around his legs like racing silks or the awnings outside French cafés.

Both dressing-gowns had the simplicity of the robes worn by characters in the illustrations to Bible stories. The Lord God walking in his garden in the cool of the day must have looked not unlike my father. Joseph's coat of many colours would have been a jazzier version of the red-and-white stripes. These intimations of alien majesty depended on the dressing-gowns being plainly cut, without braid or quilting. Dressing-gowns which had these latter fripperies were effete indoor garments to be associated with cigarette-holders and Noël Coward. My father's dressing-gowns bore no such stamp of decadence, but nor were they mere cloaks for nakedness; they robed him in a strange dignity. Callers did not 'catch' him in his dressing-gown. He muttered no apologies for not being dressed. He was dressed. These were his robes of office. The butcher demanding early settlement of an outstanding account found himself at a mid-morning levee.

In seeing the badger model and the red-and-white stripes as symbolic of my father's two sides, I was perhaps only imitating that binary reverence by which primitive man is said to have ordered his experience. To stress the division between light and dark, raw and cooked, marrying in and marrying out of the tribe is to celebrate the world; but even this celebration is also a violation, for by chopping up the world and setting it in order, we are preparing to dominate it. So my ruminations on my father were a celebration of his patriarchal authority; but they were also the groundwork for revolt.

His feet broke the shimmering web of morning, leaving matt-green prints in the grass. He shivered very slightly as he trod the cold dew, and the tea-cup trembled. I looked up at the under-side of the saucer wondering whether the cup, now hidden, would suddenly come tumbling down out of the sky towards me. I had forgotten how young I must have been when first I watched my father take his morning walk and what long service the badger dressing-gown must have done, outlasting the seer-sucker by five years or more. I was crouched on the terrace, observing the ants march up what I supposed were to them interminable red-brick glaciers until the leaders reached the edge of the cliff and ordered a tactical retreat while the snails steamed to and fro below like great ships in a channel. Underneath the jagged shards the lice huddled and gossiped, their sleepy bourse only occasionally stirred into panic when I bombed them with a chip of brick.

Across my rose-red polity, my Lilliputian Petra, the white feet would tiptoe, hardly disturbing the manœuvres of the ants and too quick to divert the snails from their courses. He would move at an unhurried pace across the small lawn, ducking his head under the overhanging bough of the apple-tree at the far end, and then on up the path which led to the rubbish-heap. The apple-tree hung so low that his head once or twice knocked off a sprig of blossom which stuck in his black hair; at least I can remember this happening only once or twice; perhaps the tree was later lopped, or perhaps his hair had grown so white that the blossom no longer showed up against it, the tinge of pink being too faint to be seen from the terrace.

I myself, lying on my stomach, jersey covered with brick-dust, often felt irritated by his appearance on the scene. The white feet might not disturb the traffic flow of the ants; they disturbed me. They scuffed up half-buried humiliations which I was still trying to forget. At breakfast one morning I had dropped the marmalade, a new pot, a precious fraction of the jam ration; half an hour later, tears just dried, I had barely recovered my self-respect when the feet came tiptoeing across the terrace. A spurt of rage. A patricidal mist. A shudder of resentment. Words were not enough. Action. Through the red mist I saw a slat which had fallen from the lichen-damp seat and broken in two. There was a ball of twine on the seat, black, tarry, frangible. With frenzied, clumsy fingers ('Why are you always so clumsy, Aldous?') I tied the two pieces of wood together to make a dagger. My father was already out of range, but he came back to look at the wallflowers like the Archduke Franz Ferdinand returning home by another route, thus allowing the astonished anarchists a second shot, as if fortune had decided that the assassins no less than their victim deserved a fair chance.

As he turned again to walk on up the garden, I threw the

dagger as hard as I could. It brushed the edge of the dressing-gown, the red-and-white stripes (it was a fine day), making a scratchy little noise, imagined rather than sensed. My father stopped. Had he felt it, or was he just looking at the flowers? In a twinkling rage dissolved into terror. The whole garden shuddered with my fear. Excuses—'I didn't mean to throw it,' 'It wasn't meant to hit you'—excuses were futile, they would spill out of me none the less, get me into worse trouble. It wasn't my dagger, somebody jogged me, it jumped out of my hand—the drivelling litany would never end. The marmalade, and now the dagger; once you were in, you were really in. Resisting arrest, assaulting an officer, causing malicious damage; ten years on the Moor, this one's vicious. But your honour ... my father walked on. Perhaps the dagger hadn't reached him. I never had much of a throwing arm.

The garden steadied. Red mists fled. Adrenalin sank. A modest stillness settled over us, disturbed only by the occasional phutting of a tractor backing up into the farmyard next door. My father would slow his already easy pace, pausing every few feet, inches even, to inspect the flowerbed: the tiny beads of the grape hyacinths now fully blown, the last few buds of blossom on the prunus yielding to fresh russet curls, some of the early summer perennials—cranesbill, astrantia—already throwing glossy leaves up through last year's withered straws. The haze began to melt to unveil a pale grape-hyacinth sky, a temperate sun.

It is too simple to think of idleness as uniform or unvarying either in quality or pace. Idleness may be tempestuous or unremittingly busy as well as plain inert; it may even express itself in a state which is a kind of supreme concentration, paradoxically akin to that reached by the most diligent. Within his general idleness my father apparently managed to attain such gathered moments, states of being which were all the purer because they were dedicated to no ambition beyond that of taking a walk round the garden and could have been stated in no more mystical terms without evoking from him that noise halfway between a snort and a guffaw with which he dismissed pretentious or embarrassing suggestions.

5

It was from these moments that he burst forth, breaking off whatever he was doing or not doing, leaving the cup and saucer on the garden bench to rush back into the house as if summoned by some hidden intercom and reappearing minutes later, more or less normally dressed, to demand immediate assistance. He gave the impression both that some inner process of battery-boosting had been completed and that at the same time some inner balance, precariously achieved by a mixture of luck and effort, had broken down, that in fact the gathered moment was not, could not hope to be more than a moment. Its unassuming perfection was something to be grateful for; to expect more would have been peevish.

Impatience overtook him particularly towards evening. The steep hill at the end of our garden took the light away from us early. As soon as its shadow reached the terrace, my father became restless. The lateness of the hour gave a delicious urgency to his chivvying: 'We must hurry . . . hurry . . . they'll be closed unless . . .' The words pursued me round the house as I ran up the stairs to look for my coat or the keys to the car. We did have to hurry; quite often they were closed. We would arrive to find the shutters down and a man in a porkpie hat with keys in his hand closing the door behind him, or the window at the cash desk closed and the cashier making up her till in an inner room, or the foyer empty and laughter coming from the barred auditorium, or the station shut and the steam of the last train only a wisp in the night sky. This eleventh-hour perspective on life has its compensations. Without experience of such disappointments it is hard to imagine the pleasure to be gained from being in the right place at the right time, the satisfaction of seeing the opening credits come up on the screen. Yet this constant pleading with people who had already decided to call it a day had its gloomy side; it was like living in a perpetual twilight.

As we stumbled along the narrow, rutted path which led to the watercress beds, the sun would begin to sink over the slope on the far side of the stream, occasionally breaking back through a gap to gild a strip of water where the cress had already been cut. The honeyed light filled the air, making black silhouettes of the slanting willows which only a few minutes earlier had them-selves been dense shimmering masses. When my father saw the light going, he would start to run, his feet slipping a little on the muddy path. But the man who kept the beds was always still there. Sometimes he was standing in the bed itself throwing the bundles up on to the path, hardly visible in the darkness except for a pale moonface beneath the cap. The wreaths of cress scattered in front of us like nosegays thrown to sweeten a king's progress. Sometimes if we were later, we came up behind him as he scooped the cress into his big wicker baskets. Later still, we would find him leaning against the handle of the sluice-hatch smoking a cigarette, his outline an umber stump against the sky.

There was a kind of deception in this crepuscular idyll which even a good look at the watercress man in broad daylight did not dispel—rather the opposite. His jauntiness, his outsize handlebar moustache and his emerald thigh-waders with the tops elegantly turned back all seemed to indicate an affable, even exuberant character, the belly rolling over the belt only confirming the general air of rustic *bienséance*. This impression was quite mis-leading. Although it was the whiskers and waders which had made me think of him as Puss in Boots, his character corres-ponded closely to what that remarkable cat must have been like: an inventive and energetic temperament, impatient with the clods around him, able to appease his restlessness only by outwitting the ruling class on a huge scale. Unlike Dick Whittington's cat, an equally pushing operator on his master's behalf, it seems that Puss in Boots showed no particular affection towards the miller's son, indeed offered to help him only to save his own skin. There is no reason to suppose that Puss despised the floury youth any less than he despised the king and his toadies or the terrified reapers—all impressed with such pitiable ease by the threat of wealth. The miller's son was just a lever for turning the bourgeois world upside down, which appears to have been the one pleasure left to Puss in his fully awakened state of class consciousness.

The keeper of the watercress beds differed only in the degree of success ultimately achieved. He had come from the village, a farm labourer's son, and entered the Royal Air Force some time before the war. He became an officer, was said to be the only man in his squadron to have saved his pay during the Battle of Britain. He spoke with equal scorn of the idiocies of the Few in the air and of the many on the ground, reserving especial contempt for any display of social pretensions. After the war he had married and bought a smallholding cheap. He looked forward with no greater relish to what he called 'the featherbed state' than he looked back to 'the stuck-up idiots who let the place go to pot during the thirties'. Yet beneath the apparently unchanged acidity of his manner there had perished an unspoken assumption that things on the whole were bound to go his way. Although distrustful of the system, he had always been confident of his ability to outwit it and believed there to be a certain logic about its distribution of rewards. He was surprised and furious to find that he was wrong, that in this department, too, mistrust was the only sensible attitude. It was as if the reapers, when commanded by Puss to tell the king that the land belonged to the Marquis of Carabas, had blown raspberries and gone for him with their sickles.

In truth, his was a commonplace story of post-war failure. The land needed draining. The bills, twice as high as forecast, came in during a severe credit squeeze. It turned out to be the worst possible moment to start a small dairy herd. He had to sell up when land prices were still low, keeping only the narrow strip along the stream which he turned into watercress beds. With his RAF pension he just kept going.

He did not like my father much. He did not like anyone very much. Affection was not in his vocabulary, but nor for that matter was personal antipathy. He did not cling to or recoil from individuals, seeing them rather as representatives of class and period, though not in the abstract sense these terms usually imply. People were to him essentially obstacles to prevent him getting his deserts. The human race was a sort of motley barricade keeping Puss in Boots from the high place he would undoubtedly enjoy in a rationally ordered society. My father formed an insignificant part of that section which had been thrown up to defend monopoly capitalism; the merest cobble-stone, he nevertheless took his place alongside Sir Montagu

Norman and the Wall Street barons; he belonged to the king's court rather than to the equally cretinous brotherhood of reapers. At the same time, Puss liked talking to him because they shared a certain detachment from the big battalions, outsiders or misfits depending on your point of view; this shared detachment licensed a good deal of mutual frankness, or so Puss thought, though my father was puzzled by the candour with which he was pelted as by the dripping watercress exploding out of the beds. Puss also took pleasure in drawing a sharp distinction between what he felt to be his own genuine independence and my father's spurious, even parasitic position. The real savour of ideology lay for him, as for so many, in the opportunities it provided of unmasking the true motives behind the most seemingly casual act. Even Puss, however, shrank from trying a full-scale Marxist analysis. He contented himself with remarks like 'somebody in your position would be liable to say that though, wouldn't they?' It was then left to the victim to enquire exactly what Puss meant. Most people had neither the time nor the inclination. They just stared suspiciously and passed on. My father would have regarded such incurious haste as both a discourtesy and a waste of possibility. Also, he had more experience of fending off such accusations than busy people were likely to have. In a society still dominated by scarcity, the virtue of hard work is far more sternly enforced than that of kindness or continence; the idle are well practised in dealing with criticism.

'Well now, a privileged person such as yourself . . .'

'Privileged?'

'A man with advantages . . .'

'You're right. I've been very lucky, living in a lovely part of the world . . .'

'Having money of your own . . .'

'I suppose it would be nice to have money but you and I know . . .'

'It's easy enough for folk with private incomes . . .'

'I've met a few millionaires in my time. Miserable all of them. On the other hand . . .'

The conversation slid to and fro, each side refusing to fight on the same ground as his opponent, slippery elisions between money earned and unearned, between savings and inheritance, between wealth and competence serving to cover tactical retreats and fresh advances. At one moment, my father had almost convicted Puss of longing to live like a rentier, at another my father came within a whisker of admitting he had never done a hand's turn. Simultaneously, they decided to abandon the field, my father gesturing towards the cress basket to ask if the price was the same just as Puss, slowing into the owlish plod befitting a rustic philosopher, said:

'Women now, women are different.'

'Women,' said my father. He was still thinking about watercress.

'My wife now.'

'Yes.'

'I can never tell. Times she's all flint. Then just when you don't expect it she melts . . . melts like putty.'

'Putty, eh?' said my father. For a moment his mouth stayed open as if he had more to say. Perhaps he thought of disputing whether putty could be said to melt or of stating that he too had noticed this unpredictability in the female sex or even of questioning, though that would have been unlike him, how this was relevant to the matter in hand, namely, the justice or otherwise of possessing private means. In the event he said nothing.

'Then she cleaves to my bosom as the Bible says, but by that time I'm already halfway down to the pub. That's the trouble, when the mood is on you, they never want it. Not at all, they act as if they never wanted a man in their life.'

'Indeed,' said my father snorting and making a point of looking in my direction to remind Puss of the extreme tenderness of my years while at the same time indicating a general openness on his own part to a discussion of such things. In fact he did not really care for that kind of talk. His desires were no doubt as pressing as the next man's but a hedge of primness guarded his own conversation. This may have been left over from his upbringing, just as a sailor might assume clean underwear in deference to his mother's parting wish before going ashore for rough frolic.

It may also have been—he certainly said that it was—part of a plan for my own education. When I was with him, he would not touch on any aspect of love with which he felt my age and experience made me unable to cope. He would state this policy in violent terms—'How can a fifteen-year-old begin to understand adultery?' Far from calming me, this only agitated my incomprehension; just as I thought that my intense study of great literature and the frenzied efforts of my own imagination must be getting me somewhere near the truth of these mysteries, I was told that the thing could not be done. Only by living the struggle could I hope to understand it. There were obvious objections to be made: if this was so, what was the point of all these books? Besides, you did not have to commit murder to understand it, why should adultery be different? But even the most tentative efforts to put these objections were withered by condescension. I relapsed into conformity. Until age and experience should qualify me, I confronted only those aspects of love which my father chose to present to me, regarding the rest as mere book-learning, not excluded but postponed.

Thus I came at love from an odd angle. At least it seems odd in retrospect, though statistically it may be more the rule than the exception. I saw love not as desire but as enjoyment, not pursuit but possession. To me its occupational diseases were not jealousy, envy, greed but sloth, complacency, indifference. The bad fruit was not sour but rotten. I was born in autumn. The sudden spring thirst, the itch, the pang, seemed to have nothing to do with love, to belong to a quite different world, an ambiguous category of sensation, neither wholly pleasurable nor all pain. That kind of love, so the heroines of the less than great literature which I also patronized in the interests of research, were wont to muse, was like toothache or pins-and-needles; not an exact parallel—otherwise why stamp your foot or go to the dentist?—but giving some idea of the oscillation between pain and pleasure, the wanting it to go on and the wanting it to stop; that was something else.

My father's loves inhabited an eternal present. I could see nothing that he loved that he had not always loved. The yearling running on the lunging rein in the next field was its splay-legged, rough-coated self, but it was also the ghost of sire and grandsire, the image of strange horses long dead, glimpsed once across a foggy field, all but bought in a Kilkenny bar, destroyed after an unlucky fall or flogged to death by a rich fool; strong in the quarters like this one, with a way of twisting his head under your arm like the old cob that the doctor used to make his rounds on when my father was a small boy.

This unhurried mode of love had its fruits. The white feet left their prints in the dew. Yet there were also difficulties which amounted to a kind of language barrier. It was hard to translate from this slow, contemplative rhythm to the syncopated throb of desire, to make any connection between the two. I even remember wondering how anybody except old people and children like myself had the time to fall into anything that could properly be called love. At school I was glad to discover that others shared my emotional handicap. Were we all crippled by the same cultural fall-out, victims of the same mutation, or is this dissociation a timeless mark of youth? The rising generation claims, rightly I expect, to be more openly sceptical about the permanence and authenticity of romantic love; yet its attitudes are basically much the same as ours were, only splashed with a bold hand where we dealt in adolescent cabal. We too recoiled from the thought of our parents copulating because they were so old; we too ridiculed those persons a few years older than ourselves who covered their cowardly retreat into domesticity with talk of true love. It was not of course the institution of marriage that we scorned so much as the cant and gush that went with it. This impatience with sentiment led us to make vows not of chastity but of celibacy. We bet each other extravagant sums that we would never marry. The bet seemed like a sure thing, the stake a mere fleabite of the immense wealth which the world was bound to shower on us.

In a folder full of odds and ends I recently came across a stiff card recording one such bet in neat schoolboy's handwriting: 'I ——— ——— (the name would mean nothing, besides, he was killed years ago) bet Aldous Cotton £20, twenty pounds, that I shall never marry, the sum to be paid on my wedding day.' The card does not record how he was to collect from me if he kept his vow—on his deathbed, I suppose. The pure austerity of the gesture had stopped us from considering such a trivial point. At any rate it is too late now, and besides he had already lost his bet. I think I had made a similar bet myself, or had I just challenged him to put his money where his mouth was, a curving, ironic mouth, the wittiest in the world?

This language barrier was not to be dismantled overnight. Years later, looking at a girl's face across the table in the villainous dark bistro, I still speculated how the now familiar piston-feeling could ever be slowed down into love without entirely seizing up. I suppose the pretty face was trying to conceive how something recognizably human could be made out of the male smudge opposite. A stiff evening it was, like so many at that time.

'Watercress,' she said. 'I'd like some watercress with it.' The dark green leaves with their salt-fringed taste were nearly fresh, fresher at least than anything else on the table. The waiter poured the dressing with the solemnity of a priest administering extreme unction; it ran over the leaves and down the firm stalks. The oil fell in fat drops as her fork raised a mouthful to her lips. It was quite a performance. How carefully the lipsticked curves closed over the cress, convexing somewhat as they met; how delicately she twirled her fork to shake off the surplus dressing. Puss shook the water out of the bundles with the grim motion of a man wringing a bird's neck, and he just chucked the dripping bundles over the lip of the basket. Yet the dainty twirl and the careful convexing were in the end no less matter-of-fact than the chucking and the wringing. They were all part of the same cutting, binding, chopping, crunching, swallowing, digesting violation of the dark green leaves, the same purposeful predatory desire, both equally opposed to my father's purposeless contemplative affections (my father did not much disturb the earth). Desire and affection were in that way parallel motions of the heart, always sliding past each other like the two of them talking about money by the sluice-hatch.

The light died over the hill. Puss humped the cress basket on his shoulder, his other arm stretched out straight for balance. My father offered to help. They each took a handle, walking
5*

half-turned one in front of the other because the path was narrow. I followed, listening to the mournful suck of my boots in the mud and the flapping of the pigeons going to roost in the willows. This hill was the last wandering curve of the down which reared so sharply above our house. In my mind it was a feeler towards the world outside, the main road, the buses, the town. The watercress beds were a preparation for all that. Their mossy banks and gurgling culverts were familiar comfort; yet their keeper's presence, obdurate and alien as it was, gave more than a hint of the outside world's indifference, its perpetual possibilities of conflict and rejection. The beds were at best an outpost of the empire of intimacy. To walk back up along the hill towards the hut was to return to home ground.

The hut was mysterious too, but its mystery lay in being so familiar and yet so unexplained. It sat on top of the steepest part of the hill above our house. It was large enough to seat six in comfort and a foot or so taller than my father. There was no easy approach to the place where it stood. How had it got there? A tractor could not have done it. To hire a crane would have been beyond our means. My father was evasive. Sometimes he said he didn't know. Once he said that the village blacksmith might know. The blacksmith looked amazed when I asked him. He knew nothing. Nobody seemed to know. I suggested that God might have put it there. My father liked the idea of divine deposition, *machina ex deo*, but said we should not assume such things without evidence. Climbing the hill past the windblown hawthorns flecked with sheep's wool, clawing on to tufts of grass to keep upright, I looked for tracks. In my bedroom I doodled possible arrangements of giant levers and pulleys based on slight recollection of how the ancient Britons had drawn the blue stone all the way from the Prescelly Mountains to Stonehenge. In refusing to elaborate, my father left space for other possible explanations: perhaps the Germans had planned to drop huts by parachute as forward bases for the invasion of England and ours was the only one that had got through; perhaps the hut was originally a shooting box as mentioned in stories of high society (it seemed rather small for a weekend party but sportsmen were probably used to roughing it).

The side of the hut facing the horseshoe of seats was open to the wind. With its two white wooden pillars, it looked like a small verandah uprooted by a typhoon from the house behind it and dumped on this strange hilltop. Mice and lice infested its floorboards; bats lodged in its creosoted rafters; it was carpeted with sheep's droppings and cowpats. Humans used the hut for the same purposes; the wind never quite blew away the smell. Lovers sheltered there; so did the village children; sweet papers 'and worse' had been found. But the real feature of the hut was that it went round; in later years not very much and that only after a lot of pushing and creaking and clanking, but in earlier days there was a choice of views if you pushed hard enough. In front, you looked down on the smoke-blue huddle of the village, a cluster of trees and roofs; behind, your eyes could grow tired planing, dipping, rising, fading across the corn-gold or plough-brown downs.

Even this choice was exercised with difficulty. My father could not manage it by himself. He liked to take visitors up the hill to help him push the hut through the forty-five degrees required to change the view. Their reward was to be allowed to sit for a few minutes inside the hut and admire the new panorama. Quite soon they or my father, or both, would get bored and they would slither back down the hill with a certain satisfaction, as if they had themselves refreshed nature by their efforts. But when he was by himself, my father would sit for much longer, staring with his long sight at the farthest prospect. We sat together like this. He then spoke occasionally of an even earlier time when he still took the trouble to oil the hut's turntable and you could spin it right round with one hand so fast that anyone sitting inside would feel giddy. I could hardly imagine it . . . the landscape spinning round and the people in the village down below looking up open-mouthed at the whirling blur on the skyline.

'I do like a revolving summer-house,' my father would say happily, as if this were some tame pavilion on a lawn instead of a hut clinging to a windy hill.

Silesian Bliss

As Harry came over the rise, all he could see were the legs. They were brown and sturdy. They slowly bicycled across the sky; the lumps of muscle slid up and down the calves; the thighs pistoned to and fro. The ankle flexed on the downswing, straightened on the up so that the foot stabbed at the sun. The rhythm was steady, fearsomely steady. Apart from the legs nothing moved on the dusty hillside. The grass was short. It barely covered the buttercups. The path wound round a granite outcrop. A few bushes grew out from the untidy boulders. The place was wonderfully signposted; there was a different colour for each suggested route and a little red sun with an arrow directing ramblers to the worthwhile view. Further on, he got a better sight of the legs. They ended in tight pink elastic-bounded knickers. Beyond the knickers the body was properly still: arms flat out sideways, no suspicion of wobble about the bust bodice, and the head motionless. The eyes were shut; the cheeks needed all the sun they were getting; the mouth was without expression. The legs pedalled; they could go on all day.

'One of them,' Stella said.

'Can you tell from the legs?'

She pointed at the folded newspaper which lay in the grass. Beside it, stockings, skirt and white blouse were neatly piled on top of a pair of walking shoes. The newspaper was covered with big headlines in black-letter type that Harry could not read.

'What's wrong with her?'

'She smells.'

'How do you know she smells?'

'They all do.'

'Just them—or all Germans?'

'All Germans, I feel very Polish today.'

'Don't they ever take baths?'

'Baths are decadent, like Poles.'

'Do Poles take baths then?'

'No, they are too poor.'

They walked higher. The elderly couples in city clothes whom they had stepped to one side to avoid lower down with many an *'Entschuldigen Sie'* and *'bitte schön'* had mostly faded away as if they were fauna endemic to the region below the timber line. Up here the passers-by wore shorts, except for a few country people in breeches and leggings.

'It's a rabbit warren.'

'We Germans believe in using our countryside. It is like a great outdoors lounge to us.'

'Not lounge.'

'Lounge is *gemein, nicht?*'

'Why do they all have feathers in their hats?'

'It is the custom. You must not laugh.'

'Can I yodel?'

'Only a true German can yodel. Mind out.'

He looked at her with surprise as she gripped his arm. Malice frisked out of her bright, black eye; her pointed nose quivered; she yodelled. It was a hideous enough noise to start with, but distorted and enlarged by her cupped hands it achieved an overpowering eructational vulgarity that at the same time epitomized every yodel in the history of the Central European massif and gave all future practitioners a fresh mark to aim at. It summoned up jumbo-bellied brass bands and dirndl-bursting *Mädels* spilling *Glühwein* over snow-blinded tourists and folkloric professors and elderly *jeunes premiers* with lagery lips calling from rickety rocks in touring productions of Alpine operettas.

Yet the beauty of her voice could not be confined within such easy mockery. She could not keep out an echo, a reverse image of the real thing, the lyric purity buried deep and long beneath its commercial degradations. It was there in the jangled music of her parody like the pure blue of the jay's feather in the brim of the snappy tyrolean hat from Wertheim's. The cruel brio with which this yodel was unleashed made the contrast between the true and the false more poignant still. That painstaking striving after simplicity, that life-consuming aspiration to purity, those laborious attempts to extract from Nature some sap of strength and spirituality were all reduced to nothing by a yodel.

Nature took its long delayed revenge for being so used, patronized, appropriated. Strassburg Cathedral was graspable —that was the work of man—but the spires of rock and fir were not so easily claimed. They refused to be communed with by sparrows masquerading as eagles. As the weekend ramblers walked through the villages strung along the lower slopes, they occasionally came upon a small factory below the road—a cement works blanketed in white dust, a lumber yard or a textile mill with its dyeing shed perched above the forest. These establishments provoked the ramblers. The smoke, the dust, the smell, the *industry* spoiling all the good solitude. Of course it was light industry and it did provide employment but . . . Harry, on the other hand, took to this cottage pollution and the dark aggrieved gnomes who worked in these populous foothills. They were at least engaged in serious contention with Nature, burning, blasting and sawing the old witch out of her hidey-hole with no nonsense about respecting her privacy. They did not pretend to a rusticity that was not theirs. They did not, as a rule, yodel.

As the last elegiac gurgle of her first effusion was expiring, Stella turned to face back down the path where they could see the legs still bicycling at the same steady rate. She let another one go, even more bloodcurdling than the first. The legs stopped. For a moment they stayed frozen in the air. Then they started again.

'I thought you'd got her that time.'

'We Germans are made of sterner stuff.'

'And Poles?'

'Poles are lazy . . . hopeless . . . would still be munching acorns if it was not for us Germans . . . They drink, they beat their wives. Poles are almost as bad as Czechs. Czechs are the worst. Shall I tell you humorous stories about the living habits of the Czechs?'

'No.'

'Very humorous stories. We all have good laugh.'

'No thank you.'

These steep hills, these narrow prospects sealed by mist began to press in upon him. He could understand that wanting to get out, to struggle up into the clear thin air above the trees. But the mist pressed down from above too. They were hemmed in. *'Grüss Gott!' 'Servus'. 'Entschuldigen Sie'. 'Bitte'. 'Bitte sehr'.* This mountain was crawling with people. He had never seen so many people and all so polite and healthy. Gulp in the air, expand the lungs, bicycle with the legs; there is nothing like mountain air for the lungs, good for the circulation and even the kidneys also. Here on the mountains it is good.

The clouds lifted. A yellowish gleam lightened the horizon. Far off he could see the grey-green glimmer of a vast plain.

'What's that flat bit over there?'

'That flat bit is Poland, the homeland of the pig-Slavs. No, wait a moment, we're looking the other way. The flat bit is the valley of the Oder, our own dear Silesian river. It waters the heartland of the German nation. We Silesians . . . ah, we Silesians are the makers of culture. You have seen our Breslau . . . it is very nice, is it not? We Silesians brought culture to these mountains. We drove back the Mongol hordes while the Poles were hiding half-naked in the forests. In fact long before the Poles came, the Vandals roamed here. And who were the Vandals? Germans of course. Very nice, the Vandals. Breslau is the centre of the civilized world, you know. My schoolmaster told me. Just look at the map. Our dear Breslau is halfway between Madrid and Moscow, halfway between Rome and Leningrad, halfway between London and Constantinople. You never heard of anyone going from London to Constantinople by way of Breslau? No matter—in the Middle Ages Breslau was the greatest city in Central Europe. That was all good German work.'

'Do the Poles know about all this?'

'Poor ignorant peasants. What do they understand? They even have the *Frechheit* to claim that they were here first. Our dear Breslau they call Wratislawa or some such nonsense. They say the Polish kings called in the German farmers to do their work for them. A typical Polish legend. Only the Poles would admit to such idleness. That's why I feel so Polish today.'

'But what does it all matter?'

'Matter? Are you mad? Do they teach you nothing in

England? Have you not heard of Ladislav the Short and
Boleslav Crookedmouth? Have you never heard how cruelly
history has treated our great country?'
    'I heard it was partitioned.'
    'Partitioned! Virgin of Cracow defend us! We have been
massacred, murdered, and he can say only . . .'
    'Let's go down. It's too cold up here.'
    'No, we must go to the top.'
    'I want to go down. I want a drink.'
    'No, no, you must see the view.'
    'I've seen the view.'
    'You haven't seen the view from the top.'
    'The view from halfway up is good enough for me.'
    '*Entschuldigen Sie.*'
    '*Bitte.*'
    On and up and down the ramblers went in their good
walking-shoes, politely squeezing past. How lovely the view was,
how helpful the signposts were, there was so much to exclaim
over, with sensible enthusiasm. They were rather strange, these
two persons arguing when the view was so fine. People should
not argue in the open air. It was not good.
    'From the top you can see Breslau.'
    'From the bottom you can get back to Breslau.'
    'Harry, please.'
    '*Gnädiges Fräulein.*'
    '*Bitte schön.*'
    'I am going down.'
    'No.'
    'Yes, I've had enough.'
    'You are easily bored. You think nothing matters.'
    'Of course I don't think that rubbish matters. But if people
bother to make it up, it must matter to them.'
    'It does.'
    'And that is sad.'
    'Worse than sad.'
    'To have no country and want one.'
    'Or to have several and need none.'
    'How can you be so detached?'

'If you can't understand that, my dear Harry, you can't understand much.'

'I'm not your dear Harry. And I'm not as thick as you seem to think. I can see the trouble coming. Anyone could.'

'I know, I know,' said Stella. 'But it's not your trouble, not yet. What do you think you can do about it, anyway?'

'Nothing.'

'The real truth is that you don't care.'

They started down. Her irony had turned to anger. She battered his descending back.

'No, it's not . . .' he bleated over his shoulder.

'You don't care about me, or my family. You don't care about anything. You just have a good time.'

'Who said I was having a good time?'

'You do what suits you, you take holidays . . .'

'I hate this kind of argument.'

'That's bad luck. You can't always have light conversation. Sometimes we must be serious. And I'm not detached.'

'All right, bitter then.'

'Bitter . . . that's what you think.'

The market-place was quiet. Harry savoured the oaten hardness of the stein on his lip, the first cold rush of beer over his tongue, rapture never recaptured as he drained the great mug.

'Show me the sights of wherever this is.'

'I don't feel like it.'

'Don't sulk.'

'There are no sights.'

'What's that over there then?'

'That is the monument to my father's dear friend Dr Ludovic Lazarus Zamenhof.'

'A sight.'

'Of a kind.'

'Who is Dr Ludovic Lazarus Zamenhof?'

'You do not know who was Dr Ludovic Lazarus Zamenhof?'

'You have found my weak spot.'

'Dr Zamenhof was a great and good man. He invented the universal language.'

'Ah.'

They walked over to look at the marble bust. It could not be more than a few years old, but already the mountain damp was settling in the crevices. The bald dome and the lofty brow still gleamed, but the thick moustaches and the imperial beard were tinged with green mould, giving the saga a curiously malevolent and decrepit appearance. He looked like a disappointed academic cheated perhaps of his due chair, his great work insufficiently recognized or the notes for it left behind in a train and never recovered. The inscription was partially obscured by a swastika scribbled across it.

'Can you read . . .'

> *'Sur neutrala lingva fundamento,*
> *Komprenante unu la alian,*
> *la popoloj faros en konsento*
> *Unu grandan rondon familian. . . .'*

'The Esperanto hymn. We were taught it as children. I've forgotten the language now, though it really is not difficult. My father used to read it a lot, but there are not many books. He was a sweet man, Dr Zamenhof. He always brought me chocolates.'

'Was he like your father at all?'

'Yes . . . no, Dr Zamenhof was much harder but also much more hopeful. Esperantists must hope. It's one of the rules.'

'Your father does not hope?'

'Not much.'

'And you?'

'I'm on the side of gloom.'

They went down to wait for the little electric train to take them back down to the city. They had set out early with sandwiches, a crisp morning of early summer. Around them in the compartment other hikers had congratulated themselves on the clemency of the prospect. Boots scraped on the metal steps at each halt; despairing wails of '*Kaffee! Bratwurst!*' from the refreshment carts down the platform and the morning smell as the carts rumbled nearer.

This perfect setting—so agreeable, promising so much pleasure—showed only how difficult things were between them.

Far from drowning in the ointment, the fly buzzed spiritedly. What was wrong, what was it? He had thought nothing at first. The journey had been long, a day to get to Berlin and another six hours on top of that and the country had been so strange—the Hansel-and-Gretel houses with their steep roofs and brightly painted shutters pierced with hearts and diamonds and the tall towers with onion spires seen across flat fields, then the little huddled hills and the steepening valleys and the black woods closing in. He felt he was crawling down the burrow of some unfamiliar animal not knowing whether it bit or nuzzled, was solitary or gregarious, sleepy or full of furry bounce. The compartment was hot. He could not see how to open the window. The ticket-collector pretended not to understand. Harry fell asleep. When he awoke in a stale fug, he was there, or rather as far as he was concerned, he was nowhere. Bleak suburbs, playing fields, workers' dwellings in dingy concrete, factory chimneys, a few red-brick Hansel-and-Gretel villas, dull, airless heat—nowhere. Why had he come?

Then out of the sour-smelling crowd on the platform, there was a thin, dark girl in a large hat looking feverishly in at each doorway discharging its travel-worn quota. He was excited as he could never remember. The possibility of Stella seemed like something he had not thought of, something unimagined, unimaginable. Her smile was as nervous as the flick of a whip. She was pale in the dusty sunlight streaking through the glass roof. Each word of greeting—hullo, how was the journey? I've been longing to see you, my parents are sorry they couldn't come to meet you—was, well, he wasn't ready for any of it. All this life, he said to himself as if the phrase contained some deep significance, all this life. He felt himself stumbling along the platform like a peasant heavy with cider, stupefied, red in the face. She was . . . no, not pretty . . . anyway. Perhaps he was going to faint. A glass of schnapps would set him up. Faced with it in the station buffet, he could not trust himself to keep it down. He looked at her and they began to calm down. She stopped babbling. Her smile stopped trembling. He recovered himself. He had been living like a monk recently; that must be the cause. Stella was just a girl, after all. What a horrible phrase, he didn't mean that at all. But now he could look at her straight. He did not see the passing of this moment as a turning-point. Why should it be? You could not stay greeting each other on Number Three platform in the Hauptbahnhof for ever.

Yet from then on there was something of an uphill struggle about the whole business.

'And how is Evelyn?' Stella's father asked. 'I have not seen him for, oh, twenty years now, before the war.'

'I imagine much the same. He is well preserved.'

'Preserved, I like that expression. Like jam. So he is. A clever man but . . . timid. Other rich men will not or cannot see. He sees but he doesn't want to.'

'He's been very generous to me.'

'To us too. He is a generous man. I remember . . . he was a quiet little boy. Shy, like his mother. His father was a monster. Very strong, big, vulgar. His mother was a mouse.'

'He said he was happiest here.'

'Ah to be happy here, you must . . . is that why he sent you to come and see us? No, you have come to see Stella, not us.'

'He said something about his reasons. I couldn't quite make it all out. It was to do with nostalgia. The lime trees, the landscape, the atmosphere.'

'The atmosphere.' Stella's father sniffed with wry satisfaction. He was a drooping leathery man with Stella's shoulders and her electric flickering mien. He had concentration, also the remnants of energy. His body like hers seemed ill-equipped for carrying him. Nothing he did had, it seemed, quite worked out; at the same time he had not failed. The textile wholesale business he had expanded from his father's shop had risen with the tide and ebbed with it. By a smart exercise in retrenchment he had managed to hold on long enough to sell out to the new cartel for at least a quarter of what the business had been worth at its peak. The same with his marriage, according to Stella. Working too hard, inclining to move in intellectual circles, getting into the habit of stopping off at the Vier Jahreszeiten on his way home for a *Breslauer Korn*, he had slipped away from his wife. It took a sustained effort for him to return to her, not so much in the physical sense (his mistress, a liberal doctor's even more liberal wife, had pushed off without rancour) as to grant her sympathy and attention. Nothing came easy to him. His quickness of mind and eye had a way of leading him into places he soon found uncongenial. Life was a matter of continually doubling back, making fresh casts.

'The atmosphere . . . *echt* ghetto baroque, as you see.' He waved a hand round the small sitting-room crowded with heavy furniture. Every piece—armchairs, tables, desk—was encrusted with scrolls and curlicues, echoing the botanical improbabilities of the floral upholstery. The tables were teeming with photographs in heavy frames of metal or velvet and *bonbonnières* in pierced silver. Most of the objects needed polishing. Dust lay on the parquet. Some of the herringbone strips had cracked or come away leaving shallow heel-traps.

'The atmosphere is not what it was. Before the war now, but everything was better then. You must drink in what we have left. . . . go up in the mountains . . . go to a concert in the Jahrhunderthalle . . . take a ship up the river, see it all while there is still time. Nothing lasts for ever.' He sniffed again and filled Harry's glass, looking round the table with a certain pride in the melancholy in which he had swathed the company. He did not enlarge on his theme. Still less did he snap out of it. He seemed content, more than content, to leave people, particularly his own family, feeling one degree under.

He took it as the privilege of patriarchy to set the temperature, but he was also ready to exercise his skills outside the family circle. Harry had not been in the room for more than five minutes before he found a gentle hopelessness stealing over him. Things were on the slide. There was nothing to be done. Horrors had occurred, would occur again, as inescapable as the east wind. Had Harry ever tasted *Schlesisches Himmelreich*, a baked flan with apples (was flan the right word?). Delicious, with *Schlagsahne* of course. That's right, Silesian Bliss, a charming title for a dessert. There was something peculiarly lowering in the way Stella's father followed each prophecy of cataclysm with a gastronomic titbit, as if in face of the ineluctable disaster the nurture of the stomach was the only rational activity. The vagueness with which he deflected Harry's requests for information was in contrast to the precision with which he tossed him the *bonne bouche*. 'I believe things are very bad in Berlin, very bad indeed. They could hardly be worse. Have you ever had *Berliner Eisbein*, pickled pork knees? Now what should one say, not knees, knuckle, yes, knuckle... In Upper Silesia the situation is naturally different but the future is black, very black. The Poles are no better, some would say worse. You know, they have the most northerly vineyards in the world there. It is said that the wine is so sour that only we Silesians can drink it.'

He pursued this digestive tract as if testing to see how much Harry could take. When he talked about his constipation, it was not as in C.L.'s case a plea for sympathy, a transferred appeal for love and pity, but rather a topic of general interest likely to stimulate conversation. His sluggish metabolism appeared to be a traditional family butt, playing as it were the role of a local bureaucrat from whose pettifogging all present might have suffered: 'My bowels only open once a fortnight, like the Emigration Office.'

Yet Harry did not feel that Stella's father was really imposing himself on his family; somehow he seemed to suit them, or at any rate to suit their present mood. Stella, her mother and her younger brother sat in complaisant silence during this low-key monologue, showing no enthusiasm at any point—enthusiasm would hardly have been apt—but acquiescing in the turn of his talk. There were none of those sidelong glances, ostentatious fidgets with bits of bread, half-controlled sighs by which subjects in a patriarchy usually register non-violent dissent. It was not a question of putting up with a tyrant. If anything, the problem seemed to be for the tyrant to put up with himself. If any strain was visible, it was in the awkward way the father accommodated himself to the world. It was a strange performance to have arrived at, this mixture of weary pessimism and culinary patriotism, but apparently a necessary performance, for it became clear that he departed from it at his peril.

He began to talk about business, how tariffs were ruining trade, how the traditional outlets for finished goods were all blocked up now. He was lucky to have got out. Half the business-men he knew were living on charity. And he didn't know how much longer he himself could keep going. Harry could not have guessed how much this venture into detail would upset all of them. Stella and her mother were anguished, staring down at their plates. From her brother sitting next to him, Harry heard an odd noise like a mast creaking. A quick sidelong glance showed the eighteen-year-old boy rubbing his thumbs across his clenched knuckles with intense ferocity. Stella's father himself trembled; his cheek twitched. The vibrations seemed to come from all round the room as if the father had been speaking not for himself but as the voice of the familial organism and so his distress had sent shock waves through the whole body, disrupted its carefully achieved balance. Harry gazed in desperation at the reproduction of 'September Morn' on the wall facing him. The girl in the picture seemed to be shivering too. Stella managed a smile as she caught his eye.

After saying goodnight Harry lay on his bed, inhaling the dust of his small room. By his bed there was a little table of fake Biedermeier type. On it stood a heavy cut-glass carafe. The water tasted as if it had been there for some time. Under the carafe there was a finely embroidered napkin to protect the wood. The napkin was yellowing at the edges. Its twin was spread on the bow-fronted chest-of-drawers; on top, there was a cut-glass bowl containing a potpourri. By putting his nose into it, he could just screen out the smell of the floor which, unlike the rest of the flat, had been freshly polished, presumably in his honour. The room was quiet and close. He opened the shutters. Outside seemed just as airless. The noise of the city was distant, irregular, minimal. He walked up and down listening to the floor creaking at each step. What were the chances of getting to the other end of the corridor without being caught? It was too early yet. He had better give them an hour at least. Still, he hadn't come all this way just to . . . Three-quarters of an hour. No more. He was a man to be reckoned with.

He looked at the bookshelf: *The Pickwick Papers*, *The Forsyte Saga*, *The History of Mr. Polly*. Either this was where they dumped all the English books or it was another thoughtful touch. The former probably; that kind of thoughtfulness was at a premium in this house, witness the water in the carafe. Perhaps they were just the ones that happened to be available in the cheap edition. He stared at the disintegrating yellow backs and then took out *The History of Mr. Polly*. He began to read about Mr. Polly's indigestion. The whole world seemed to have indigestion—C.L., Stella's father, everyone.

Quite soon he stopped reading and listened again. Down the corridor they were still creaking and mumbling. Outside, the dribble of noise dried away. Breslau went to bed early. Harry closed his eyes. When he next looked at his watch only thirty minutes had passed. The hell with it. The creaking had stopped. Might as well try his luck.

The floor exploded beneath his feet with every step he took. Outside the dining-room the racket was like a firing squad. At first he essayed a delicate tiptoe. Then he switched to a full-footed slow march. This made just as much noise and increased the risk of tripping. He reverted to the mincing step. As he passed the open door of the sitting-room, he saw a figure at the window silhouetted by the light from the street. It was Stella's father. Harry jumped lightly, landing on his points like the ballet prince on first seeing Sleeping Beauty bat an eyelid. Then he saw that the old man was facing the other way, looking out of the window. He was in his dressing-gown. Harry tiptoed on down the passage.

'I was nearly asleep.'

'Were you really?'

'No. Why so long?'

'There were people about. Your father is still on guard.'

'He doesn't sleep much. Spends a lot of time looking out of the window. During the day too.'

'Why?'

'What else is there for him to do? He doesn't go to business. And the situation . . .'

'I like this situation.'

'Glad you came? Don't answer. I'm glad.'

She smothered questions by the fierceness of her love. Her warming frenzy left him satisfied but estranged. Ghetto baroque. You're a cold fish, he said to himself.

Next morning they met a young man on the stairs: young,

good-looking in a flat sort of way, rather slight, manner gawky, embarrassed as if he would rather have been somewhere or someone else. He spoke in short phrases: how long are you here? —You like Germany?—I want to go to England. The obvious explanation was that his English was poor. Yet his accent was good. He drawled like a fop of the nineties, letting the end of each sentence trail into silence as if he was already tired of it.

'That was Geza. He has always lived in these apartments. When he was younger he used to tell me he was of noble birth. I do not think he would say that now. His father is a dentist. They are suffering.'

'Why, have teeth stopped falling out in Breslau?'

'No, but in hard times people stop having them filled.'

'What does Geza do?'

'Not much. I see him in the street sometimes. He has a kind of gang. He used to admire me.'

'Still does, I think.'

They walked through the narrow alleys, stepping on to the cobbles to avoid the groups of men standing on the pavement. There were a considerable number of people about but little bustle or noise except for the clanking of iron-wheeled carts. One or two women were leaning out over the wooden balconies on the upper floors. Occasionally they would call down to someone in the street, without exuberance. Harry and Stella came out into broader thoroughfares under round-arched arcades to enter a commercial city revving up: cars, bicycles, trams, shops, street-sellers. It was cool in the arcades. They sat down at a café in the great market place and watched the sun climb over the gables of the tall houses. He bought the only English newspaper on the stand, a *Continental Daily Mail* of two days earlier.

'What sort of gang?'

'You'll see, I expect.'

An outsider had won the Derby, picking his way round Tattenham Corner like a polo pony: April the Fifth owned and trained by Tom Walls, *the* Tom Walls, the moving spirit of the Aldwych farces. Which was the first one he saw him in? *Rookery Nook*? No, *A Cuckoo in the Nest*. Harry had been to it in the holidays from school. Gorged with chocolates, he had nearly been sick when he had failed, as George Robey would have put it, to temper his hilarity with a modicum of reserve; he had given way to markedly unbridled mirth in the passage where the puritanical landlady berated the young lover who had written a false name in the visitors' book: 'You don't write very clear'— 'No, I've just had some very thick soup.' Tom Walls . . . he could visualize the poker-faced dandy leading in his Derby winner, hectoring the enchanted crowds in his loud bark, his poached-egg eyes swivelling to extract the maximum laugh from each gag.

'There's your friend.'

Harry waved at the flat-faced young man. He was walking fast across the square. He was looking in their direction but he gave no sign of having noticed them. Stella did not wave.

'Geza is very short-sighted.'

'He didn't look short-sighted to me.'

'You can't always tell by looking. Let us start walking. I want to swim.'

'Can't we sit here a few minutes longer? I haven't finished my paper.'

'No, you can read your paper later. Hurry up.'

On the corner of the arcade leading to the river was a little stall selling raspberry cordial and lemonade, an assortment of rusks studded with sugar or caraway seeds and a few bootlaces of licorice. Bestowed out of the sun to avoid the gnats from the river, this frugal cantina had attracted instead a swarm of small boys. Skirting them to catch up with Stella, Harry ran straight into a man coming the other way. He stepped back to apologize and found himself unable to speak; the long gaberdine, the broad-brimmed hat, the black sidelocks—costume familiar in reproduction—struck him in reality with a force that he could neither describe nor master. The dress was in itself no stranger than that of priest or policeman, far less exotic than that of a beefeater or guardsman, yet he had never seen anybody who seemed to stand out more sharply from his surroundings. The face, fine and bony, aquiline rather than Shylock-nosed, the bright black eyes and the general intensity of expression were all rehearsed in embryo in the adolescent boy at his side, the features there less fully developed and the hair on upper lip and chin still wispy. The boy had a chalk-white skin with apple-red cheeks like a doll's.

Unlike those special uniforms whose sole purpose is to mark profession, religion or nationality and which are kept in tiptop condition by wife, batman or sacristan, their garments were shabby, they were among other things simply poor people's working clothes. In the worn hems and the dull shine of the cloth there was that ancient permanence which only poverty keeps alive. The vestments of poverty are still charged with meaning, with life being lived. In this case the poverty was not a calculated reproach to society such as the barefoot friars had offered. It was an historical circumstance, the cause of the challenge not the challenge itself. Because they were poor, they had not changed. And that was the challenge and the reproach. They had remained themselves, an excluded alternative, an image of what might have been if man had chosen to concentrate his energies inwardly upon himself rather than upon the outside world. Better or worse, that was not now the question. They were all too conspicuously different—old and revering ancient authority, poor and scorning material goods, unchanging and despising change—the very qualities that were now unsaleable. There were other disqualifications besides and other resentments to be appeased, scapegoats to be identified. It took no great experience of life to understand how that particular kind of ill-feeling was worked up. But he had not expected to find hanging on in the cracks in the wall an organism so old and fragile and yet so unmistakably alive. He knew that Jews were hated because they were rich; he had not known they could also be hated because they were poor. He very much wanted to explain to her his confused feelings, if only for his own benefit to pin down something important. As he looked at her waiting for him, her shut, tense face told him that he would never manage it.

The man bowed in acknowledgement of Harry's apologetic sidestep. The boy stared stonily straight ahead. They moved on. Stella laughed.

'You thought—her Uncle Mendel and her Cousin Levi.'

'No, I didn't.'

'You did. You thought here are her *jiddische Landsleit*. I am sorry to disappoint you. We are all good Germans in our family. Good Catholics, very modern. We speak only the best *Bühnendeutsch*. You know what our friend Adolf asked himself when he saw his first Jew in a kaftan, in Vienna. He says to himself "is this man a German?" Very nice.'

'That wasn't what I thought.'

'A little bit yet. Come on, Harry. You don't have to be ashamed. It's natural.'

'In fact, what I was thinking was how different they were from all of us, you and me. More a question of "are these people living in the same century?" '

'It comes to the same thing.'

'For God's sake.'

They came to an avenue of limes. The sticky scent already had the dust of summer in it. The spring sheen had gone from the leaves. The grass was criss-crossed with chalky scars—short cuts, children's diggings, dogs' scuffings. It was well-trodden ground. Only at the water's edge was the vegetation thick and green, stippled with the rushes and the underside of the willow leaves silver-grey against the jade-green river. Here and there, narrow shingly sandspits ran out into the water, most of them balancing the bent figure of a fisherman or a few small boys throwing stones. She sang, hummed almost, the words barely audible:

'. . . *wo vor einer Tür mein Mägdlein steht.*
Da seufzt sie still, ja still, und flüstert leise
Mein Schlesierland, mein Heimatland.
Wir seh'n uns wieder am Oderstrand.'

'She stands before a door, quite still and flusters . . .'
'Whispers.'
'My Silesia, my homeland, we'll meet again . . .'
'On the banks of the Oder.'

'Sounds like Loch Lomond.'
'Surely in Loch Lomond they do not meet again.'

Further on, one of the sandspits broadened out into a peninsula large enough for a café and several bathing rafts.

There were steps down from the embankment to the shore. A couple of planks bridged the narrow channel, little more than a trickle, that separated the shore from the café. At the top of the steps were standing about a dozen young men. Some were propped against the parapet; some faced the other way leaning over it, looking down into the river. One or two of them were chewing long stalks of grass. They looked threadbare but not slovenly; their air of nonchalance was less than convincing.

'They're here already. I'm glad you're with me.'

'What am I supposed to do?'

'Look manly.'

'And aryan?'

'That would help.'

'I'll do my best.'

As they strolled nearer with equally unconvincing non-chalance, there was a murmur from the youths. Harry suddenly noticed the flat face in the middle of the group. In the same instant Geza turned his back on the two of them and muttered to the group who huddled round him, all turning their backs as if simultaneously afflicted with the need to relieve themselves, except for a couple of outflankers who seemed not to have cottoned on. One of these, a tall youth in spectacles, shouted something as Harry and Stella hurried past clutching their bundles of towels and bathing-costume like a medical team called to the scene of an accident, all haste and dignity. The other one spat.

'What'd he say?'

'*Knoblauch*. Garlic.'

'I wonder why the others . . . Geza must still be keen on you.'

'Please. The idea makes me ill. No, it is your manly vigour that kept them back.'

'Perhaps he doesn't want trouble at home.'

'Perhaps he thinks my father can give him a job. Very likely.'

'Perhaps it is just too early in the day to start persecuting.'

'Yes, it will be worse in the evening.'

'Or perhaps . . .'

'Perhaps, perhaps. I don't care.'

'Can't we go somewhere else?'

'We are not welcome in the city swimming pools. This is the only place.'

He was not surprised to find her trembling but he had not thought her pale cheeks could flush so red. She stumbled slightly on the plank bridge. He felt himself trembling as he followed her up the path.

He stretched out on the swaying raft, a beached Ulysses, and watched her slip over the side of it until only her head was visible. With her hair scraped under her white bathing cap, her face looked naked. She held on to the raft with one hand and splashed water across her face with the other. The water was bright metal on her mossy skin. The face disappeared. The raft bucked slightly, then settled back to ride the current of the green water from the mountains. The sun cleared the tops of the willows. The trace of breeze fled downstream. Harry watched the first beads of sweat gather on his skin and roll round his ribs. He listened with lazy interest to the buzz of talk around him. He heard names he knew, the names of footballers, film stars, musicians . . . Münzenberg, Jakob the panther, Garbo, Furtwängler . . . *famos, fabelhaft, kolossal.* Too hot to talk. Only the chugging steamers assaulted the languor. After each one had passed, its wash lapped under the raft, slapped gently against the sides.

> *'Palästina vielleicht . . .'*
> *'Jawohl . . . das nächste Jahr sicher . . .'*
> *'Immer das nächste Jahr.'*
> *'Doch ist die Auswanderung etwa sozusagen . . .'*
> *'Mein Onkel sagt, in Amerika . . .'*
> *'Das Kibbutzleben gefällt mir eigentlich nicht.'*
> *'Nu, scheust du dich vor der Arbeit?'*
> *'Palästina . . . Palästina . . .'*

The dark heads nodded under their bathing caps. Now and then a gesturing hand rose from the prone figures on the duckboards, trawling the vast possibilities of America and Palestine across the sky. There was always emigration.

They took a steamer upstream from the little jetty on the far side of the island. The Gothic spires of the city seemed to twitch in the midday haze like needles on a dial. The boat passed under a suspension bridge between high mercantile buildings. The banks began to open out. On one side a park came into view. The guide patrolled up and down the boat whining through a megaphone. Stella translated into Harry's ear, her arm hooked round his neck. Through his shirt he felt her shoulder, still warm and damp from her bathe.

'On the left you will see the animal-rich Zoological Gardens. The elephants fell as a sacrifice to the war, but there is a mark-worthy collection of apes. In the neighbourhood is the Jahrhun-derthalle. It is 41 metres high of iron-concrete. Its cupola spans 65 metres. Inside there is an organ which cost one hundred thousand marks to build. That is much for an organ, ladies and gentleman. It was made to celebrate a hundred years since the Freedom War. It was here in Breslau that the King made his famous speech "To My People" and started the Iron Cross for courage. The Hundred Years Hall is the biggest concrete concert hall in Germany. It is famous for its acoustics. You cannot leave Breslau without hearing our thousand-strong choir.'

At the top of the steamer's run, it tied up to allow the passengers to get out and stretch their legs. They were out in the country now. In some of the fields old men with sickles were already beginning to cut the hay. By the landing stage there was a restaurant sheltered by a belt of poplars. All dopey from the sun, they sat in the shade and had lemonade and cakes in silence. Most of the other passengers had beer. The party began to liven up. There was singing and more beer. Some of the young men in bathing-suits jumped into the river to cool off. One of them clambered back on to the boat over the stern. He sat by the little flag-staff to get his breath back, shaking the water off him like a dog. Then he stood up grinning, stuck out his bottom and wiped it with the black, red and gold flag. The older passengers already sitting in the boat ready to go were uncertain for a second and then burst into laughter, looking at one another.

Harry dreaded the return. He saw Stella flush red again as

they got off the boat, but when they climbed back up the steps, the gang had gone. They walked home through drowsy streets in the late afternoon.

'Perhaps he'll be waiting for you on the stairs with a bunch of flowers.'

'In the language of flowers now, how would you say I'm sorry my friend spat at you?'

'Garlick and roses.'

But there was nobody on the stairs.

> *'As I was going up the stair*
> *I met a man who wasn't there.*
> *He wasn't there again today.*
> *I wish, I wish he'd stay away.'*

'What's that?'

'A rhyme, of sorts.'

Stella's father did not come into dinner that night. He had, it was said, a touch of his old trouble. He would have to take a cure in the mountains soon. It was hard to find out precisely what his old trouble was. It seemed to affect different organs or combinations of organs at different seasons. The general nature of the complaint, in this case the right word, was apparently derived by a process of elimination. As he believed passionately in the specific claims of each resort, his logical refuge was to complain of those ailments which his last port of call had not pretended to remedy. A ferrugineous spring which dealt so effectively with his anaemia was therefore sure to leave him prostrate, a few weeks after his return, with malfunctioning kidneys, neuralgia and even something which he liked to diagnose as gout though the doctors were reluctant to confirm it on the grounds that you could have gout or you could have anaemia but you could not have both.

A session at Bad Elster with its carbonic acid and chalybeate springs might smooth out his heart tremor or alleviate his rheumatism, but he found his digestion ground to a halt under the regime there. Lowland spas brought out his tendencies to asthma, excursions to the 'Saxon Switzerland' grated on his nerves. His nervous condition and what the spa brochures so amiably described as 'complaints of senility' were in any case made worse by the fact that he could no longer afford or thought he could no longer afford—which came to the same thing—to take a full-length cure at a first-class hotel with his family and was reduced to taking a cheap day return ticket from Breslau to one of the somewhat run-down local spas in the mountains. He said that the good work done by the waters was immediately undone by the jolting about in the train and that in any case a proper cure demanded time, regularity, order. It was not so much the liquid itself that did the trick as the routine: the ten-minute walk up the 'heart-way' (thus called because at no point did it diverge from the horizontal by more than four degrees and hence could be recommended to even the most delicate cardiac patients), the light meals served at unvarying times, the steady temperature. A day trip, however regularly repeated, could not match these conditions.

These assertions, all in themselves quite reasonable, were at the same time completely unreasonable in that they were based on the premise that he was fifteen years older than in fact he was but doing the work of a man twenty years younger. This premature assumption of senility was proclaimed by his shuffling step mimicking that of a clockwork toy duck and by his exaggerated pauses for breath in speech as well as in gait. He stuttered as if searching for a word, usually one made quite obvious by the context. To start with, Harry had thought it courteous to supply the missing word. He soon realized there was more to the game when Stella's father greeted each intervention with a sugary '*thank* you, kind sir' or even 'my dear Harry, you are too quick for me.' He clammed up. But Stella's father would not be cheated of his sport. Instead of leaving a blank and waiting for a volunteer to fill it, he would issue a positive request for information: 'I was sitting in the café when I heard they had shot the Archduke at, at, at . . . what was the name of the place, Harry, you're an educated fellow?' Harry, rather too eagerly: 'Sarajevo.' '*Thank* you.'

The fact that Stella's father did not appear for dinner the second night could have had several specific causes: genuine illness and hypochondria in their varying compounds, or pique

6

or boredom or despair. But it was without doubt a serious gesture. The desire not to be left out, not to miss anything, was strong in most people; in someone who relished the opportunities that conversation provided for the exercise of power as much as Stella's father clearly did, it must be overwhelming. To stay away from a meal which involved a trip of only five yards from the bedroom indicated an even stronger counter-motive, if only an intense dislike of Harry in particular or of the human race in general. The signs of distress the night before were not to be laughed off, but he could not judge for sure just how bad things were from one edgy evening. Now he had more to go on.

They were asked to be quiet while going to bed so as not to disturb 'Vati'. Harry made a point of tiptoeing as noisily as he could, punching the balls of his feet at the cracked parquet, this not perversely (or not entirely) to annoy the invalid but rather to make his intended return trip sound by contrast no more than the house settling or the night breeze rattling the shutters. He had a soothing forty minutes in his bedroom with Mr Polly. He was developing a taste for the water in his carafe; it had a slightly mineral taste. He had just reached the passage where Mr Polly tells his landlord that he intends to get married—or as Mr Polly puts it 'have a bit of a nuptial'—when the mumbles and the creaking seemed to be finished for the night. He set out. This time he wore thick socks, to deaden his footfall and as a precaution against splinters, and pursued a zigzag route, avoiding the more heavily mined patches. As he passed the sitting-room, Stella's father put his head out.

'Come in. I am glad to see you. The others have gone to bed, I fear. You are wearing thick socks, I see. So sensible. Most young people do not understand the danger of catching a cold in the feet. Even in June . . . Most of all in June.'

'We . . . missed you at dinner.'

'Missed me at dinner? So? I do not believe you. You had a good time, a better time without me, much better.' He was delighted. He spoke as if his absence had been the signal for riot and orgy, as if they had drunk all his wine, kept him awake with their racket, probably convulsed one another with pitiless imitations of him.

'No, no.'

'*Doch, doch.* I am an old man.'

'No . . .'

'You are a civil fellow. Nu, where have you been today?'

'Up the river. We met Geza's boys on the way.'

'Ah, they are very bad, those boys. Up the river, you say. To the old restaurant. Did you try the, the . . .'

He lapsed into silence. Harry could not tell whether he was playing the forgetting game or whether the thought of Geza's boys had genuinely obliterated the name of the delicacy from his mind.

'We had some wonderful cakes.'

'Cakes, yes.'

There was nothing more to be said on that topic. The cakes had turned to ashes.

'A long time ago, I hoped that . . .'

'Yes?'

'But now . . . now. This Silesian Bliss. You really must try it before you go.'

He stood facing Harry, not quite looking at him, gaze to one side and a little downwards, then turned towards the window. He did not at all resemble the Jew by the lemonade stall although they must have been about the same age.

'Listen.'

Harry could hear nothing. They crouched side by side facing the open window like milers waiting for the starter's gun. Still no noise. Then some way off, perhaps near the crossroads at the top of the street, the sound of footsteps on the cobbles. A dozen people, not many more. The footsteps had almost faded away again when only just within earshot Harry heard the tinkle of glass breaking, and fainter still, running feet. Then silence again, deep, long, airless, constraining silence. Stella's father stretched himself as if he had come to the end of a good day's work and closed the window.

'I think you had better go home,' said Stella, later.

'Don't be silly, Stella. I'm enjoying myself.'

'You can't be.'

'Come with me. Let's go now, as we did at C.L.'s.'

'It's different here. I can't leave them.'
'Come when you can, as soon as you can.'
'Is that worth saying?'
'It can't be as bad as that. There'll be some way.'
'They won't go. I've asked them.'
'Do they expect you to . . .'
'No, no, they told me to leave long since.'
'Well then, later perhaps. They may change their minds.'
'You think so? All right, we'll see. We may be knocking on your door before you know it.'
'Come with me now.'
'I believe you. Don't repeat yourself.'

Intercessional

'The papers say there were riots in Germany last night. Against the poor bloody Jews. Did you see any riots when you were there?'
'No, but that was years ago,' Harry said.
'No riots at all?' Froggie looked at him with some severity.
'I heard some people breaking some glass.'
'That's nothing. Like undergrads smashing windows.'
'Not quite like that.'
'Expect you're right. Thing is, I wouldn't know. Never had none of the advantages of a university education. I was curled up in suburban respectability at the time, dreaming of winning the novice hurdle at Punchestown.'
'Why don't you introduce me to your friend?'
'There you are, you see. No manners. An absence of refinement. This is Louise. She's French.'
'I don't believe it,' Harry said. Louise did not look French. She had bright blue eyes and a scarlet cushion of a mouth. She looked young but battered.
' 'allo, *chéri*.'
'You see,' said Froggie, 'she's French.'
'I am vair' pleased to meet you.'
'*Enchanté*', Harry said with a courtly flourish.

'Come again, *chéri*.'

'Froggie's girls.'

'This one's new,' Mossy said. 'He hasn't brought her in here before. I expect he'll propose to her before the night's out. But of course he's still hopelessly in love with your cousin.'

'Kate? Does nothing ever change? Are we doomed to spend the rest of our lives listening to Froggie's tedious laments?'

'She's still putting him through the wringer.'

'He insisted on being put through.'

'So he says. But it always takes two.'

'Being crossed in what might laughingly be called love doesn't seem to cramp his style in other directions.'

'That's not the same thing at all.'

'Perhaps not. I might drop in on Kate. I'd like to see her.'

'Perhaps you might,' Mossy said, not without a touch of frost.

'And then again . . .'

'You go and see her.'

They looked across the room. Froggie was telling the girl a story: he was riding a race, tugging his clenched fists in towards his chest, got a handful there, rising in his seat to meet the fence, horse makes a mistake, nearly dumps him, clinging on for dear life, cap over one eye, then settling down to ride a finish, heels and elbows driving in the Galway Blazers style, right arm flailing at his flank in the last few strides, flop forward on the horse's neck, had he made it? Won by a short head at three to one, begob, and not a penny on it.

As Froggie leant back to bask in the anecdotal afterglow, the light caught his face. The pouches under his eyes were seaweed pods, the broad mouth drooped like a surrealist pillar box. The bounce had gone out of him. He was not wearing well.

The Pyjama Club itself had not weathered the passing of time much better. Perilous holes had developed on the stair-carpet leading to the attic quarters where Harry continued to reside in chaste proximity to Mossy. The red plush on the bar-stools was coming adrift and the notices on the landing curled outwards to flick the coats of passers-by.

He was tired in the evenings when he got back from the races and needed a couple of quick ones before opening up. The early-evening crowd were not a convivial lot. Later on, he usually drank free and freely. Of all the barman's skills he had developed, the most notable was the ability to pour himself a free drink before he had finished thanking its donor. The club had become a home to him, offering every comfort except love. The girls who replaced Stella were no replacement. There seemed to be something about a barman, unlike a sailor, which kept nice girls at arm's length. At least it would make a change to call on Kate.

Blindfold, Harry could have drawn a picture of where Kate would live—a tall block of grimy brick flats in a buffer zone between the bourgeoisie and the dosshouses. She might herself have planted the ailing but not dead spotted aucuba in the asphalt forecourt, herself blown a couple of toffeepapers but no more across the steps, chipped a little paint off the ironwork in the front door and cracked not broken its reinforced glass; she inhabited with such precise determination this region between the spruce and the decayed, giving nothing away to the sanctimonious vigour of the one or the slaphappy romance of the other. Her notion of being free involved more complex constraint than any dictator ever thought of. 'Being free' was not how she would have put it, far too sentimental an aspiration for her taste. 'Being on my own', 'looking after myself'—Harry thought that if he really tried he would get some such phrase out of her. That at least he did not intend to try.

'There just isn't much to him,' she said.

'Don't be so condescending.'

'He's a nice chap, a decent fellow, is that what you want me to say?'

'Why do you go out with him then?'

'He takes me out.'

'You could stay in,' Harry said.

'I've told him I don't want to go. He says it gives him pleasure.'

'And so you're just being kind to him. St Catherine the Martyr.'

'I'm not kind to him at all. The only alternative is cutting off my telephone. The whole thing's a waste of time, but I suppose I have to eat somewhere.'

'Even martyrs must break a crust from time to time. Where do you graciously consent to be fed? Do they crucify you at the Dorchester or stone you at the Savoy?'

'He tries to take me to . . . those places. But they won't let women in slacks in. We usually seem to end up at some Italian place.'

'Well, at least that prevents the poor boyo from bankrupting himself. Do you know how hard up he is?'

'It's his decision. Anyway, I don't notice him working over-hard.'

'How do you spend your valuable time then?'

'What would you like me to say?'

'Just answer the question.'

'Call it social work if you like.'

'I neither like nor dislike.'

'Well, you wouldn't be interested. It's sort of organizing.'

'Organizing what?'

'People.'

'To do what?'

'To fight together.'

'Against whom?'

'You I expect.' Kate released her deep, gurgling laugh, drained her glass of beer and thumped it down on the plain table. She jumped to her feet and aimed an imaginary gun at him. He put his hands up.

'Do I have to fight back?'

'That is part of the plan.'

'I wouldn't mind driving a train. That must have been great fun. I am sorry I was too young. You know they can go as fast backwards as forwards.'

'Next time, we shall control the railways.'

'It sounds to me more like politics than social work.'

'You cannot separate the two.'

'And Froggie—I suppose his soft white throat will be bleeding in the gutter next to mine?'

She grinned and all the accumulated ease of their childhood meetings came back to him. Not that they had shared any particular confidences but they had been comfortable in each other's company. At tidy teas in her parents' house she would smooth his path. When he came into the cold hall, shivering with fear, she would calm him with her latest lavatory joke whispered into his ear while he was shaking the large, cold hands of strange grown-ups claiming old acquaintance with him. She was always quick to his rescue. If he got jam on his face, she would smear jam on hers. Such acts of solidarity were not without parallel in the unceasing war of children against grown-ups. Duller children whom he hardly knew would make similar gestures of complicity. Yet when Kate smeared jam across her round, jolly face (her first appearance as a thin teenager of severe aspect had startled Harry), there was something miraculous about the way she did it. She was so brave, so debonair, so unrestrainedly friendly. She had mastered all the masculine playground skills. She could belch to order, make a farting noise by rubbing her hands together, she had a wonderful way with blackheads, frowning for the merest second before nipping out the invader and presenting it with a flourish to the admiring patient. These skills, so often used by the male sex as mere instruments of domination, she modestly placed at the service of her friends purely for their entertainment. Later on, her swinging walk, her rough way of talking, had led baffled young men, Froggie not the first or the last, to attribute masculine tendencies to her.

Harry, admitting his ignorance of such matters, could see no evidence of this. On the contrary, to him she had always seemed to represent the female ideal of warmth, receptivity, sympathy. At the same time, he could not help noticing other sides to her. For so intelligent a person, she was slow or perhaps unwilling to look beyond what was most immediately presented to her. She was impatient with explanations, let alone excuses, put forward on behalf of somebody she thought selfish or dishonest. Subtlety and qualification were suspect. She would not tolerate the slightest hint of gush, so that a nervous visitor who, fumbling for a word of thanks, hit upon one which was too much for its occasion, would be condemned irretrievably as a fake. Yet this insistence on absolute standards of plain and sincere speech did not make her forbidding. The opposite. Filtered by this honesty, her good spirits came through as clear as spring water. Her friendliness, her smile which gave the impression of being rarer than it was, shone in their childhood like nobody else's. She was all one. Her integrity had an almost mathematical purity, recalling in earthbound terms the mathematical perfection attributed by Dante to the divine.

It could not last for ever. Honesty, however, being to some extent tolerated if not encouraged in children, it flowed on more or less unmuddied until it was too late. By the time she had gained some idea of how universal and considerable were the concessions most people made to public opinion and private tranquillity she was too far gone to dream of making them. Yet she did not wish to be unkind, to hurt even those people whom she regarded as hypocrites and shams. So she took to silence as lonely women sometimes take to drink, against their will, finding little pleasure in it even at the start. At the same time she could not let her silence give assent to that hypocrisy. She became very slightly sly.

'What do you live on?'

'I work in a shop, part-time.'

'Must be a nice shop to let you work part-time. Most people in shops work very long hours.'

'I'm just starting.'

'Part-time.'

'Yes, what's wrong with that?'

'Nothing, nothing.'

'You think I'm playing at all this, that I'm just a——'

'I didn't say anything.'

'Well, what have you got to say then? I'm busy and there's no more beer.'

'In that case, Cousin, come out to the pub,' Harry said.

'Can't. I've got other fish to fry.'

'Such as? Can I come too?'

'No. Mind your own business.' Again the deep gurgle, the echo of distant conduits trickling under the umbrella leaves of

6*

the gunnera in the water-garden, sapping the dam they had made with sticks and mud. Nobody could rebuff as well as Kate, refuse so bluntly without giving offence; her refusal was more exciting than the compliance of others. Slightly to his surprise, he wanted very much to know where she was going.

'Off to organize somebody, are you?'

'Don't be nosey.'

'There must be no secrets between us.'

'Yes, there must. Now off you go. I have to lock up from the outside.'

'I see the bourgeoisie is still protecting its plunder.'

'Don't be silly. I haven't got anything worth stealing. But there are some papers which—'

'Papers, papers . . . the secret naval treaty with a Foreign Power? The master plan of Aldershot Barracks?'

'I knew you wouldn't take it seriously.'

'It all seems just a fraction irrelevant when we're about to be landed in the biggest war in history.'

'Oh there isn't going to be any war,' said Kate, 'at least not the kind of war you mean. That sort's out of date.'

'Glad to hear it. I'll just let the War Office know. I don't think they've been notified yet.'

'Off you go then. No, not that way and don't pretend you thought it was. Anyway, there's nothing to see.'

There was not. No second toothbrush in the mug. No male pyjamas on the narrow bed. No photographs, ornaments or pictures. No teddy bear. No make-up or medicines. Two hair-brushes and a large bottle of shampoo. She liked to look after her hair. That apart, a nun's cell.

'You see. Nothing. But come again when you're not so nosey.'

'She wouldn't play,' Harry said.

'Who? Oh, Kate. I haven't got time for that now,' said Mossy. 'I have problems of my own to deal with. You see this coat?'

'I see this coat.'

'It belongs to Tom Dunbabin.'

'Who else? It matches his face. The subtle shade of old rust.'

'Do you know what I found inside the pockets?'

'What were you doing looking inside the pockets?'

'Don't interrupt. He asked me to send it to the cleaners . . . Well, I thought it ought to go to the cleaners . . . anyway, this letter.'

'Ah, a letter. Not addressed to you?'

'Hell, of course it's not addressed to me. He's never written me a line in his life. It's to this girl.'

'I suppose it would be.'

'You knew, you knew. Why didn't you tell me? You treacherous——'

'No, no, I hadn't any idea. I just thought if you were so angry, it must be to a girl.'

'Don't try to be so bloody clever. It's that little French tart Froggie brought in yesterday.'

'I don't think she's really French, you know.'

'Of course she's not French. I just called her French to identify her.'

'Her name was Louise, I think.'

'I do not intend to use her bloody name. Anyway, it seems Tom's been having her for ages, practically all along in fact. The whole time. Do you understand what that means?'

'Five years, perhaps six?'

'I don't mean on the calendar. I mean that it's all been bogus between us. Listen to this.'

'I don't think I ought to,' Harry said.

'Well, you're going to. I want a witness. *My own dearest darling, how long it seems since you tiptoed out of my little nest to spread your wings in the great world. When will you come back to your own Tom-Tom? I peeped into my larder this morning and saw that dear little wheat-germ loaf you left behind.* Jesus, she's a health crank too. *Your Tom-Tom only eats those horrid cakes, so he can keep Loafie to remind him of his dearest darling. Perhaps I'll call you Loafie too. Would you like that, my pet?* Loafie, for Christ's sake. *I could certainly eat you all up. When will you come and see me again, my own dearest? You mustn't worry about that other person. She is just an old friend. I know she has a funny way of talking but she is good at heart. You are quite right about me staying up too late and drinking too much at that place. I know how you hate nightclubs and that sort of thing.* That sort of thing. That girl was born flat on her back in a whorehouse. *But honestly I will try and be better in future, I really will. When you see me next, you'll see a new me. But please, darling, don't make me wait too long. Every minute you're away is a stab at my heart—* with the breadknife I suppose—*so hurry back to your very own Tom-Tom. There now.*'

'That's bad. Worse than Froggie.'

'A thousand times worse. With Froggie it's just hullo, howsyerfather and goodbye. With Tom, if you knew what I'd been through . . . Tears, promises to be good, the whole works . . . then Loafie. *Loafie.*'

'Why did he leave the letter in his pocket? Absent-minded, I suppose.'

'Absent-minded nothing. He wanted me to find it. He can't stand the guilt on his own, so he has to unload it on me. Everything has to come out. Everything.'

'Even that stuff about the old friend with a funny way of talking. He meant you to read that?'

'Oh that's all part of it. I get angry. He throws himself on my mercy, tells me how he really loves me best, how ashamed he is, how he has degraded himself with The Other Woman . . . and so on and so on. Life's too short. I'm not staying here to play stooge to him. I'm off. To America.'

'That's the spirit. Who's paying?'

'I've had an offer.'

'That's always nice. What's he like?'

'A professional offer.'

'What profession?'

'You didn't know I was a painter?'

'Never an inkling. What do you paint?'

'Murals. You must have known,' Mossy said.

'I promise. Your modesty . . .'

'I did the Isola Bella Tearooms in the Tottenham Court Road. I can't imagine how you can have—'

'Upstairs or downstairs?'

'Upstairs. There aren't any murals downstairs.'

'That's what I thought. I've never been upstairs.'

'You ought to go. Tom used to be a regular customer. That's where we met.'

'You with the palette, he with the cream buns. Very romantic.'

'He doesn't go there any more. He says he can't stand the décor. It reminds him of me,' Mossy said proudly.

'What will happen to the club while you're away?'

'Oh that. They'll find someone else to run it easy enough.'

'They?'

'Boy and his partners.'

'Boy Kingsmill. Does he own the place?'

'Of course he does. You mean, all these years you thought I . . . well, that is a nice idea. I only wish I did. As it is, my dear, I'm just clinging on by my eyelashes.'

'In that case I can't stay here,' said Harry with dignity.

'Don't be so pompous. Stay put till they throw you out.'

'I shall be sorry to see you go. In fact, to be truthful I really only moved in to begin with because I hoped that perhaps you might some day . . .'

'Not this trip. But you can do something for me if you like.'

'Pleasure.'

'Take this letter and this coat to him and tell him I never want to see him again.'

'A delicate mission.'

'Not a bit. He won't be satisfied with you for an audience. He'll be round here in a flash. But if you could give me half an hour to make my getaway. . . . I'm already packed.'

'I suppose she wants me to go and see her,' said Tom Dunbabin.

'On the contrary, she said she never wanted to see you again.'

'She wants me to go and see her. The trouble is, my dear Harry, that I am rather weak.'

'Weak is a nice way of putting it.'

'No, no, your cruel allusion to my moral state is all too apt, but I'm talking about my physical state. Just now I'm not too good, not too good at all. I'm living under strain.' He looked up at the cracked ceiling as if strain were the name of the ground-floor tenant. He was thinner. The orange rust seemed in recollection healthy compared with his present complexion which was nearer the colour of rotting hay. He was sitting in an armchair with a rug over his knees. The room smelled of damp books.

'You don't think much of this subterranean retreat, Harry. Too tumbledown for your tastes, I expect. But there is honour in dirt. Cleanliness is next to deadliness. That's why I like Mossy so much. Not that she's dirty exactly, but one feels she doesn't worry about baths. That's all over now of course. I have spoiled a beautiful thing. You know, Harry, our relationship worked. We really got on together. And now I have trampled on it with my clumsy hobnailed boots. I am a selfish—'

'Tom—'

'No, Harry. Don't interrupt me. I know what you were going to say. You were going to offer me easy comfort, to say that there must be faults on both sides. I cannot take that easy way out because I know the truth. I know that the fault is all mine. I have wasted my life. I have dribbled away this dreary decade.'

'But your work . . .'

'Second-rate stuff, a raree show of all the cheap philosophers' tricks of the past hundred years—a bagful of metaphysical wind, a dash of know-all scepticism pinched from the Positivists and a theme borrowed from old Hegel's Grand Historical Pageant which has about as much relation to the truth as a village fête's production of Our Island Story. No, I should have been a parson.'

'A parson?'

'I am clergy-boned. I come from a long line of parsons. The age has denied me my vocation. I would like to be remembered as the Very Reverend Thomas Fitzwarren Dunbabin, Dean of Towcester, a grand preacher and a hard man to hounds, the only man in the Church of England who could drink Sydney Smith under the table.'

'Fitzwarren?' Harry ventured idly.

'A genealogical quirk of my father's. He liked to fancy that we were descended from Alderman Fitzwarren, Dick Whittington's father-in-law, though there is in fact an unbridgeable gap in the eighteenth century. If a girl, I would have been christened Alice. Do you like this coat?'

'No.'

'What a pity. I was proposing to give it you as a memento.'

'A memento of what?'

'Of what indeed? These things are too fragile to be put into words. They crumble as we attempt to analyse them. A memento —leave it at that. What can I give you instead?'

'It's not my birthday. I'm not here for presents. If you are so ill, oughtn't you to see a doctor?'

'I fear that the subject of my health does not interest me, that of other people still less. I complain about it, of course, but it does not interest me. Have you noticed that people who are interested in health are seldom really interested in anything else? I do not mean that they are hypochondriacs. Often the reverse. Hypochondria may be the sign of a great capacity for enthusiasm; if one does not care about oneself, what can one care about? But to be obsessed with the general subject of health as such is to be obsessed with mere physical survival. It's rather like being interested in money; in fact, it comes to much the same thing. People who are interested in money, particularly people who've made some, cannot really take any other subject seriously. Gambling, on the other hand, tends to indicate a lack of reverence for lucre. Anybody worth knowing who has ever inherited a bean has got rid of most of it at the tables— Thackeray, Tolstoy, Dostoevsky, all the Russians in fact. You and I differ from these great men in that we have inherited nothing to speak of, in my case barely enough to stand my round in the Senior Common Room, if anyone ever did stand a round in that dessicated symposium, in point of fact an unheard of practice. It might even make a Bateman cartoon—The Man Who Stood a Drink in the Senior Common Room.'

'It wouldn't take a moment to have a general check-up. I have to have one each season. The National Hunt Committee won't let you ride without it.'

'That is their prerogative. But I have no fences to clear, only a few stumbling novices to chivvy round the course set by the examiners. Anyway, check-up is a vile phrase; it sounds as if one were a bill of lading. Perhaps one is. In that case, I am a bill of my own lading and intend to remain so, even if I am labelled "Goods damaged in transit." You're quite right about that coat. It lacks character. I've thought of something much better.'

He jumped out of his chair as if he was demonstrating his fitness before a medical panel and threw himself into the mouldering canyon of books at the far end of the room.

'Here now. The Collected Poems of Charles Cotton, your ancestor. No demur. You are as much descended from Charles Cotton of Beresford Hall—the Younger of course—as I am from Alderman Fitzwarren. The parallel is too good to miss: the fine horseman, the desperate gambler, author of that most excellent treatise The Compleat Gamester, no less sweet-flowing than his contribution to The Compleat Angler, and above all the drunkest of poets and the poet of drinking.

> *'Sobriety, and study breeds*
> *Suspicion of our thoughts, and deeds;*
> *The downright drunkard no man heeds.*

> *'Let me have sack, tobacco store,*
> *A drunken friend, a little whore,*
> Protector, *I will ask no more.*

'Imagine asking anyone, let alone Cromwell, for a drunken friend when most of us spend our time trying to escape from them. Yet what is drinking without friends who are just as drunk, no, preferably a fraction drunker than oneself? By the way, you couldn't by any chance . . . no, better still . . . round the corner there is . . . I don't feel quite up to going out . . . would it be too much to ask?'

'If you're feeling so weak, shouldn't I get something else as well?'

'I've got a first-rate fruit cake. All I need is something to wash it down with.'

Outside the Jug and Bottle, Harry counted the money in his pocket—fifteen bob, enough for a whole bottle and the fare home. Against that, fifteen bob was fifteen bob. On the other hand, Tom was a friend. It was a fine judgment between friendship, health and parsimony. Half a bottle would leave Tom a few lengths short of oblivion, a whole bottle might leave him permanently stuck there. Harry bought a half-bottle of Johnny Walker. When he got back to the basement Tom had the fidgets. It took him a couple of gulps to restore his spirits. Three, and he let Harry go with scholarly ebullience, roaring up the stairs after him:

> *'A night of good drinking*
> *Is worth a year's thinking,*
> *There's nothing that kills us so surely as sorrow;*
> *Then to drown our cares, Boys,*
> *Let's drink up the stars, Boys,*
> *Each face of the gang will a sun be tomorrow.'*

As Harry walked along the passage leading to his attic, the door to Mossy's room was open. She was sitting on her bed. There were two suitcases by the door.

'What happened? I can't wait much longer. I've got to catch the boat train.'

'He said he was too tired to come.'

'For Christ's sake, what a . . . well, anyway, come in for a moment. I've got some drink left.'

The next day, Harry moved out of the Pyjama Club. He went to lodge with his great-aunt in Canonbury. There, behind lace curtains and sustained by Irish stew and scones, he lay low. For days, no word came of him. He was a lost man. Rumours flew from the Pyjama Club to the jockeys' room and back again—he was imprisoned for debt . . . drunk for a month . . . fled to South Africa with an heiress . . . joined the Secret Service. Word of his disappearance even reached his parents. Search parties of a more official sort were sent out, but as Harry's parents were not on speaking terms with this aunt, the bloodhounds were not pointed in her direction and the only effect of their researches was to alert Cod Chamberlayne. Cod was furious. Against his better judgment, as he put it, he had allowed Harry to renew his credit. Harry had lost no time in stretching that credit to its limit. When he disappeared, he was almost back to the point at which Henriques had rescued him five years earlier. Not surprisingly, Cod assumed that the purpose of the disappearance was to escape his vengeance and accordingly sent out his private bailiffs. But this legendary pack did no better than the more conventional agents dispatched by Harry's parents.

Not until Harry telephoned Froggie to confirm a detail about the pedigree of Pretty Polly did the truth emerge. He was writing. To be precise, he was writing an article about brood mares for *Horse and Hound*. Froggie was dazzled by this enterprize and bustled round their mutual haunts to report that 'Harry's turned scribbler and is living like a hermit in the East End.' But in fact Harry had only wanted to get away. His great-aunt had suggested writing as a way of passing the time. He himself was more interested in the rhythm of composition than in the finished article. What he really liked were the slow, sober days sitting in the Canonbury bedroom watching the ducks flight in over the New River; he refused his aunt's offer of a fire, preferring to savour the shiver of sobriety. In the evening he listened to her tales of youth in an Indian hill station.

The article was accepted. On the strength of this success, he came out of hiding. When he got the cheque, he took Pauline out to dinner. The evening went well. He had made a break.

The Last of England

'You were right to get out of the club, you know.'

'I thought it was time for a move.'

'I hear there are funny goings on there now,' said Froggie.

'What sort of goings on?'

'Boy has film shows for his friends.'

'Perfectly harmless. What does he like—Chaplin, Garbo?'

'It's not quite like that, Harry. He takes the films himself, of his friends.'

'Amateur movies. Beach scenes, family croquet. Dull, I agree, but wholesome surely.'

'These are the less wholesome kind of amateur movies.'

'Oh . . . do the performers know they are being . . .'

'Some do, some don't.'

'How did you hear all this?'

'Girl I know told me.'

'And did she herself . . .'

'Good heavens no. Heard the whole thing from a friend . . . she said. God, I feel ropey.'

'Stop the car then,' Harry said.

'No, throwing up doesn't do any good. I've been feeling ropey for weeks. I need a change.'

'Try sea air.'

'No, a whole new life. I feel so bloody old. Even when the race begins, I don't get that kick any more. I'm just thinking about how to get round in one piece.'

'A seasoned campaigner, that's what you are.'

'There's no pleasure in anything now.'

'And the almond tree shall flourish and the grasshopper shall be a burden and desire shall fail.'

'There are times when I feel like calling it a day even in that department. Are our salad days over, do you think, Harry?'

'No, just curling at the edges.'

'God, I feel ropey. If I were a horse, I'd be shot.'

'If I were your horse, I'd put in for a new rider.'

'Is that kind now to a poor Irish jock trying to make his way in a cruel world? Isn't it bad enough luck to be born in that sod-awful island with her terrible geographical position without having me equestrian skills pissed upon by a tight-arsed Englishman?'

Frogmore descanted upon the wrongs done to the Irish in general and himself in particular until they reached the race-course. 'Going: soft' the paper had said, which was an under-statement, the place being a mire although according to the foliage it was still autumn. In the jockeys' room Joe greeted them with malice undiminished by the years.

'Got yer toe-paint, have yer, mister? And Cod Chamberlayne's still after the pair of yer.'

'Just me, Joe. Mr Cotton gave up playing the horses years ago.'

'That's what you think, mister.'

'Harry, you haven't . . .'

'Just the odd coup now and again.'

'Jasus, I don't know whether our friend will bail you out a second time.'

'It won't come to that.'

'Of course it will. It always does.'

'Not always. Look at the Hermits of Salisbury Plain—they got away with half a million. Look at Old Man Wootton and Deaf Wilkinson.'

'You are not Old Man Wootton or Deaf Wilkinson. You are a mug.'

'No more of a mug than you.'

'I am only a small-time mug. You are the Aga Khan of mugs.'

'Don't be so priggish.'

'I don't care for the look of this day now.'

The day did not improve with age. As Froggie weighed out, the clerk of the scales, a mild man with spectacles pushed up his sloping brow, put his pencil down on his clipboard, cleared his throat and said:

'This calls for celebration. I've been doing this job seventeen years and I've never come across anyone putting up that much overweight. Are you sure there aren't two of you on the scales?'

Going out to the paddock, one of the other jockeys said to Harry:

'What are you on in this one?'

'Something called The Last of England.'

'Old Nasty Lasty. Made your will, have you?'

The owner said: 'It is most awfully good of you to step in at such short notice. We've had some trouble finding a rider. He's a good sort of horse but you have to know him. He needs the race, so don't be afraid to have a go. I called him after the picture, d'ye know it? A lovely thing.'

The trainer said: 'Thanks, old man. Look after yourself. He takes a bit of steering.'

The stable lad holding the horse's head said: 'He's a dog that one, he'll have yer goolies for breakfast if yer don't watch him.'

The nature of the problem defined itself immediately. The Last of England was a knobbly, evil-eyed horse, the kind usually described with professional litotes as 'plain'. Strong quarters, his only presentable feature, boded ill. As soon as Harry was in the saddle, he found himself tested with a brisk buck and lunge by way of preliminary. The Last of England's reputation for hypersensitivity was patently deserved; the necessary rapport between horse and rider seemed unlikely to be established. Going down to the start, Harry felt his stomach being tossed like a cockleshell in a hurricane. At each break in the rails, The Last of England spurted for the gap and needed a ferocious tug to be hauled back on course. At the post, Froggie was laughing so much that he fell off and was trampled on by his own horse. He recovered sufficiently in time to observe the start.

The Last of England led by a street before refusing at the first fence. When presented a second time before the obstacle he bounded over it and caught up the field in a trice. From then on he jumped like a stag but at an increasingly acute angle to the fence. With Froggie's former mount, now untenanted, coming from the other side, the remaining horses were caught in a pincer movement from which only the most surefooted escaped. Harry zigzagged round, pursued by a chorus of oaths. One fence from home he was looking forward to coming in a shaken but respectable third when The Last of England put in an unheralded and uncontrollable burst, surging at his preferred diagonal into the last fence between the two leading horses. jamming one against the rails and sending the other cannoning into the fence on the far side. The Last of England himself landed neatly, straightened his line and ran in a comfortable winner to a silent reception from the crowd, except for several lunatics on the popular side who cheered and waved beer bottles presumably out of general sympathy with anarchic behaviour—judging by the odds, nobody could have gone so far as to put money on the animal. The general silence was maintained as he piloted The Last of England into the unsaddling enclosure.

As Harry jumped off, the man riding the second horse said to him:

'If there was any justice, you *and* your fucking donkey would both be put down.'

He did not have to wait long for the summons: 'Mr Cotton, the stewards request the pleasure.'

'Wash yer face and brush yer hair. Always makes a better impression if yer tidy.' Joe buzzed round him as thrilled as a dresser preparing the star for a first night.

The official led him down the passage and opened the door at the end. 'Mr Cotton, sir.' There was a long pause. The official had several goes at shutting the rickety door. The bang-bang-bang sounded like a ragged firing squad. The three stewards sat at their table with bowed heads, quite motionless in the darkening room. They looked like an exhibit in a natural history museum, defects of stuffing being hidden by the dimness of the lighting. The silence was so long that Harry began to fancy that this might be one of those tortures supposedly practised by the Japanese in Manchuria, where the prisoner was kept in silence and darkness until his nerve cracked and he confessed to crimes he had never committed.

Eventually the man in the middle said: 'The stewards have called you before them because they have never witnessed a more disgraceful exhibition.'

Another pause. Then the steward on his right said 'Disgraceful.' The third man did not speak.

Harry thought it time to enter some sort of plea. He extracted a sound from his vocal chords, more of a tuning-up noise than articulate speech: 'Errgh—'

'You have not been asked to address the stewards.'

True enough, nor he had. The room seemed to be very hot.

'You deliberately interfered with both the leading horses, nearly bringing one of them down and risking severe injury to its rider. This deplorable display of rough-riding in front of the stands brings steeplechasing as a whole into disrepute and there can be no excuse for it. Not only have you been riding in public for long enough to know better but you are supposed to be a gentleman. Your conduct leaves us no alternative but to disqualify the horse and report you to the stewards of the National Hunt Committee with a strong recommendation that you be suspended. That is all. You may go.'

'Thing is, I expect it'll be nice to be on foot for a change. Slow down, take things easy, go bust in comfort. Riding races is for younger chaps.'

'I'm not going to go bust, Froggie.'

'You're bust already.'

In the last race of the day Harry fell off. At least that was how it was described in the racing prints the following day. What happened in fact was that the jockey who had ridden the second horse in the first race matched him stride for stride until they reached the far side of the course out of range of the stewards' glasses. Now and then through the noise of hooves and the wind Harry could hear him growling '. . . uckin' donk . . .' As they came to a stiff brush fence, the other jockey took off at an abrupt angle. Harry was forced so far to the side that his horse cannoned into the wing. He gracefully let go of the reins and soared through the air in the embryo position, coming to rest in the brushwood where he lay stretched out like a gipsy's handkerchief drying on a hedge. The horse trotted round the fence and went on down the course.

Harry made no attempt to move. He basked in the concussive's trance, listening to the wind flap the slack of his shirt, until the arrival of hearty voices and the jolting of the ambulance brought him down to a world of pain. Froggie sat in the back of the ambulance with him, dispensing medically inadvisable anaesthesis from a flask.

'See what I mean, you're too old for this kind of thing. Much nicer on foot. Hobble around on sticks boring your grand-children about the day you rode Ampersand.'

'I may not live that long.'

'He never rode Ampersand,' said the ambulance man, taking another nip from the flask.

'Don't say that. You'll give him a seizure.'

'Never. That's Sears's mount, that is. I seen him ride that horse in every one of his Gold Cups.' The ambulance man lit a second cigarette from the butt of his first.

'Would you mind,' said Harry, 'there's a sick man in here.'

'Ampersand—never. That's the concussion talking, that is.'

'Who is this madman who keeps contradicting me?' said Harry.

'Concussion, you see, concussion,' said the ambulance man settling into his evening paper.

'You know nothing about concussion,' Harry said. 'I, on the other hand, am an expert on the subject.'

'Don't see nothing much doing for Lingfield tomorrow,' the ambulance man said to Froggie.

'You don't appear to see much at any time,' Harry said. 'And the first thing to get straight is that I rode that horse. I rode Ampersand.' He raised himself on one elbow like a dying tenor and blared the words at the ambulance man's outspread newspaper, ruffling its pages with his indignant breath.

With a sudden briskness, the ambulance man put aside his paper and pinned Harry back down on to the stretcher, hissing the while: 'Now see here, matey, you want to get some rest.'

'Not at all,' said Harry dreamily. 'It is you who want me to get some rest. And if you ask my opinion, I think a little concussion would do you the world of good.'

Looking out of the window, Froggie reported on the dispersing scene: 'There's Cod now in his ill-gotten limousine, soused as a herring, must have had a good day grinding the faces of the poor . . . and there's Old Man Wootton climbing into his *ill*-gotten limousine . . . and there's C.L. climbing into her limousine . . . all God's chillun got limousines except you and me, brother . . . C.L. does not look the picture of health, agitated, distinctly agitated, there'll be hell to pay when she gets home, hard-boiled eggs thrown all over the place, now she's putting her head out of the window and really letting poor old Evelyn have it. I wouldn't ask him for a favour for a day or two, she looks as if she's going to explode. "Extraordinary tragedy on the turf, spontaneous combustion of well-known owner." I wish you could see this, she's really lashing that car, mud flying in all directions, whoosh here she comes . . . Jasus, look out, you old cow, this is an ambulance bound on an errand of mercy, she nearly had us in the ditch that time. Harry, wake up, . . . well, that's a merciful release, I wouldn't care to be conscious with a couple of broken ribs in this old boneshaker—he wouldn't be dead by any chance, would he?'

But Harry was only placing his bets: five thousand each way

on Pearly Gates, Honest Pete always pays, a pleasure to do business with you, my dear sir, there must be some mistake, surely Cod shouldn't be holding the keys to heaven, the Jockey Club ought to be told—a wonderful sunset, yes, we always have wonderful sunsets up here, the view of the Valley of Sin is famous . . .

'Have you ever seen such a sky?' said Froggie. 'The shepherds must be creasing themselves with delight. Those clouds are as red as the fiery furnace. The woods round Nuts Grove look as if they're on fire. Perhaps C.L. has exploded after all. Look back there.' Reckless of his patient's health, Froggie opened the rear door of the ambulance and propped Harry's head up with his other hand. The cold air of twilight banged at his forehead. His skull felt as soft as rice pudding. The bumpy road unreeled behind them like a fire-hose trained on the woods round C.L.'s house. The tops of the trees were brilliant deep scarlet crests tossing above the black trunks. As they came closer, the whole sky burst into flame, the empyrean shading through carmine into crimson, staining the plum-coloured clouds a more sullen purple. A great black plume spouted up from behind the trees.

'I think perhaps,' Harry murmured to himself, 'something really is on fire.'

'This is a very grave case,' the police officer said. He had a queer humorous mouth and protruding eyes. Harry thought he looked more like a comedian dressed up as a policeman. At any moment he might vanish from sight in the witness box and pop up again wearing a false nose and convulsed with mechanical laughter or in the costume of a ballerina or a deep-sea diver. He read the summary of the police case with exaggerated solemnity: 'I must remind your worships in this connection that the deceased, I beg your pardon, the defendant stands charged with arson, malicious damage, attempted murder and cruelty to animals.'

'Cruelty to animals, Inspector?' The chairman of the bench sat up straight, shocked by this ultimate imputation of wrong-doing.

'Yes, sir, the horses were terrified by the blaze.'

'I let them out first.' Kate's voice was low, almost mumbling, yet clear. Her hair straggled down her thin cheeks. Waiting outside the court, Harry had watched the comings and goings for what felt like an hour. How clearly life had separated the sheep from the goats. The people in trouble were all misshapen, out of proportion, oddities: very tall, very thin or very short and fat; faces green, white, yellow or purple to mauve-brown; their eyes shifting, turning all the time or glaucous and still. They walked with dragging feet, some out of seeming defiance, some from narcotized despair. As they reached the waiting-room benches they mostly split up into groups, individual family likenesses sharpened by the great family likeness of defeat.

In amongst them between the benches, chivvying, calming, consoling, explaining, bustled the other race of men—energetic, busy, their well-being assaulting their clients and charges like a hail of punches. A few must be barristers, professionally called on to display a degree of aggression, but more were solicitors, court officials and detectives in plain clothes, the latter immediately identifiable with their uniformed colleagues by a withdrawn watchfulness, a trained impersonality. They were all alert, they knew how to pay attention. They found difficulty only in restraining their impatience when they could see their client's eyes wandering, his vestigial self-interest swamped by inertia. Across this great divide between the good and the bad and/or between the well and the ill—depending on how you looked at it—there was little traffic. To cross the border was hazardous and usually irrevocable. Once through the barbed wire there was no easy way back. The bent copper no less than the lag going straight had to turn his back for ever on the old country. As soon as Kate stepped into the dock, Harry saw that she had got through to the other side. She was no longer playing, if she ever had been. She looked as ill as the rest of them. He noticed that she had stopped looking after her hair.

'Well, Miss Cotton, you have refused legal representation and you have asked for bail. Now the police oppose bail because they believe that it would be dangerous to the public for you to be released before your trial. So I must ask you if you have anything to say.'

'I let the horses out first. I didn't hurt anybody and I didn't intend to.'

'The police say that you have a grudge against your former employer and that you might do her further injury.'

'That's rubbish. She treated me well by her lights. I bear her no ill-will.'

'In that case, why did you——'

'I thought she had too much.'

'Too much . . . I see. Bail refused. Defendant to be remanded in custody for fourteen days.'

Harry had been watching the magistrates. By the time he turned to look for the white face in the dock, it was gone.

The newspapers spread themselves on the trial. The way C.L. spent her millions was always good for a few paragraphs; Kate's exploits were an additional godsend. The slight air of mystery surrounding her motives gave just the right amount of scope for alarmist speculation. Her target was obviously the existing order, but it was not quite clear exactly from what quarter she was taking aim. Did she receive her orders from Moscow or Barcelona or Berlin? Was she the spearhead of a vast conspiracy or a solitary eccentric? Newspaper articles by 'A Harley Street Nerve Specialist' and 'A Former Intelligence Officer' cast further, though dim, light on the business. It was, however, generally agreed that Kerosene Kate, as she was called in the tabloids whenever lay-out permitted, represented in obscure but threatening guise The Shape of Things to Come. As far as her motives were concerned, Kate herself did not enlarge on what she had said in the committal proceedings. She received no visitors and would not give interviews to journalists. In court she persisted in conducting her own defence and concentrated on establishing that she had taken great care to avoid any hurt to man or beast. The stable lads whom she cross-examined all had to admit that she had given them ample if rough warning through a loudhailer that the whole place was due to go up in flames in two minutes.

She got five years. A solicitor Harry met in a pub said that sounded rather steep for a first offence and that there might be more in the case than had been said in open court. On the other hand, he hadn't practised for some years and was out of touch.

One morning Harry woke up and found he was thirty. Thirty plus five months, to be precise. His birthday had passed with little celebration and less thought. The milestone was not inked in on his mental map until he opened the newspaper and read that Tom Dunbabin was dead. The paper gave Tom, or at any rate the manner of his passing, plenty of space, a page lead with a blurred, scarcely recognizable picture. The story said:

STARVED TO DEATH
IN BLOOMSBURY

A university professor starved to death in a London basement, a coroner's court was told yesterday. The body of Dr Tommy Dunbabin, a 36-year-old lecturer at London University, was discovered in his flat at Mecklenburg Row, W.C., last Thursday, but doctors believe he might have died as long as a fortnight ago.

His landlady, Mrs Elvira Pietroni, said that her suspicions were aroused when she noticed that his dustbin was empty: 'there were usually a lot of bottles etcetera sticking out of it. He was a bit of an absent-minded professor.' She said that he was a very good tenant but she was worried about his health as he never seemed to eat anything but cakes.

Dr Connell McTaggart, giving evidence, said that this was a remarkable case. The deceased was undoubtedly a heavy drinker, but that was not the immediate cause of death although it had probably helped to reduce his appetite. The real culprit was malnutrition. 'In layman's terms, the deceased had starved to death. It seems incredible that an intelligent man in this day and age should have been ignorant of the need for a properly balanced diet.'

Galley Slaves

Many of the symptoms displayed in this case were associated with the disease commonly known as scurvy. The deceased was markedly deficient in all known vitamins and had also been receiving a deplorably inadequate supply of protein. This might have been acceptable among the galley slaves of yore who had no access to fresh vegetables but it was a scandal that it should occur in the twentieth century in the heart of the metropolis.

In returning a verdict of 'death by starvation' the jury called on the authorities to promote greater public knowledge of the importance of a balanced diet.

Friends and college colleagues of Dr Dunbabin said last night that as far as they knew he had no particular worries. They described his future as 'brilliant'. He was a bachelor.

'Makes it sound as if the old boy was a bugger.'

'I remember him at Oxford, though he was a bit older than me. He was tight as a tick the whole time.'

'He said I was the rightful King of England.'

'He must have been tight.'

'No, I promise you, my dear. He asked me if I knew anything about my people and so I had to admit that there was this *story* that Parrott was really just a *corruption* of Perrott and the Perrotts were said to be rather big cheeses in Pembrokeshire. So he looked at me in that awfully mad way and said, "the biggest cheeses of all, my dear Pip, none other than our true sovereigns". Apparently the Perrotts were the real heirs *male*, but the vile Tudors put it about that they were the merest grocers and anyway not absolutely the right side of the *blanket* and Good Queen Bess gave them a castle at the far end of Wales to keep them quiet, a sort of hush-schloss. Well . . . you can imagine how all this was music to my middle-class ears. I always used to stand him a drink after that.'

Harry had not been to the Pyjama Club much since he had resigned his post and moved out of his attic. The zest had departed from it. Mossy was in America. Tom had taken to his bed a few weeks earlier; some said Louise had taken to it with him, but she could not have stayed there long if the cause of death was anything to go by. On the other hand, she was not to be seen in the club either. Nor for that matter was her first protector, Frogmore O'Neill. The racing bums generally had drifted elsewhere; their place had been taken by bums from the BBC. Despite these absentees, Harry called in for a memorial jar and found an angular, not quite young man in a beret holding court to three or four regulars who were got up as theatricals but, if pressed, would admit to employment, for their sins, on the fringes of commerce.

'Another drink, Pip?'

'Sorry, must be running along, my dear. We're on manœuvres this afternoon. Armageddon on Pirbright Common.'

'That where the International Brigade's finished up then?'

'No, my dear, just the Territorials.'

'The good old Terriers.'

'Harry ought to join up. He's got such a soldier's bearing,' said one of the BBC bums.

'Harry already has,' said the man himself. 'I'm the new secret weapon of the Wessex Light Infantry.'

'I think it's so important to be in the *Light* Infantry,' the BBC bum said.

Later that year Harry got married. Pauline wanted him to be married in uniform, but his colonel said that it wasn't on for part-time soldiers.

As a wedding present Evelyn Henriques paid off Harry's gambling debts again. In his letter he said that Stella's parents still refused to leave Germany. They said they were too old to move, and anyway they were Catholics.

CHAPTER FOUR

PEOPLE said my father should have stayed in the army after the war. It was not a view he took himself. People liked to think of him in the grip of military life because they thought it might keep him out of trouble. He rejected the suggestion for the same reason. Regular soldiering with its grumbling rhythm of fatigues and leaves, its alternation of activity and inertia was not up his street, but the war was different. How it was different must be precisely stated; there are few slights more cruel than the careless condescension of posterity. It is too easy to imagine that the war came just in time to give meaning to the lives of a generation of misfits. This was exactly the stereotype from which my father and his generation tried so hard to escape. They hated the prospect of bloodshed; they hated the reality; above all, they hated the glorification of it. Their anti-heroism was not just a modish pose, like that of schoolboys pretending to have done no work for an exam; it went down deep. They were wary to the bottom of their boots; they searched out bombast and cant with the professional mistrust of a customs officer; they touched patriotism only with a bargepole; nor did they expect to find personal redemption in battle. Even now most of them do not speak of their experiences, except glancingly as of something it would be affected to avoid speaking of; they are whippet-quick to forestall the boredom of the young by changing the subject. Ordinary veterans of the last war do not go in for pushing pepper pots around to illustrate the dispositions at Alamein; that is for the generals.

Yet in one way they did like the war. From that angle they are vulnerable to those who like to needle the elderly. They took satisfaction in the dull certainty of their allegiance. They hugged that certainty close to themselves like a girl-friend's photograph. That is why, hard though it is now for us to reconstruct the feeling, people of my father's stamp felt an overwhelming relief when France fell. To be alone was to be completely certain. Certainty was enough; to introduce the idea of a political cause at this late date is only to confuse things. This certainty was graven on the celtic cross in every village. Here there were no displaced persons, no oscillation of place-names between Teuton and Slav, no spring tides of militarism erasing landmarks and leaving islands of stunned cattle to wait for the humane killer. Men here did not lose their papers or their families; they could lose only their lives and those who rode back safe from the war in their demob suits knew that the bus was carrying them home. Untroubled landscape. Never the knock in the night, the official boots on the stairs, the whispered consultation in the back room. The certainty of a good night's sleep.

With the resentment of those for whom sacrifices have been made, we pretend that this certainty weighs upon us, oppresses us. If you are looking for thanks, never save anyone, above all not your children or your children's children. From Odysseus onwards, the homecoming hero has had a dusty welcome. To avoid disappointment, there is a lot to be said for the approach adopted by Alexander, of Tunis not Macedon, who when looking in on his club after the liberation of Italy and asked what he had been up to replied 'just soldiering'. The mystery is the identity of the man who asked the question. In what Happy Valley, what *embusqué* arcadia had he been spending the past four years? Was he perhaps the same clubman as the one who was much distressed by the outbreak of war on the grounds that it might interfere with the St Leger? Such a lack of interest in current affairs would be deplored by right-thinking persons in the present no less than in the preceding generation. Yet the refusal of my contemporaries to contemplate the facts of heroism is just as perverse. The massacres are enough to fill a lifetime's nightmares, the political failures and betrayals a lifetime's remorse. But the heroes are also on the grand scale, too monu-mental to be shaken from their perches by spite or hindsight.

There is a conspiracy of silence between the generations. Those who fought will not tell, and those who come after will not ask. I cannot deny that my father and I were as much part of that conspiracy as any father and son. He was muted by my silence. I lived in the shadow of his certainty. Yet I too had my certainty. I could not, cannot wriggle out of the conviction, however secretly and resentfully held, that what my father and his generation did was right and worth doing and that because it was right there is no dodging the conclusion that life is arduous and cannot be lived without effort and renunciation. We are a dull lot, the children of a people's war.

Barrack-room Ballad

'I can see too many bulging bellies round this table,' the new co said. 'Unfit men never won a war. From now on, this battalion is going to be the fittest in the division—bar none,' he added menacingly. There was no dissent, even from C Company, commonly known as the Cripples' Rest. 'I have requisitioned some bicycles from the local cycling club. I expect all of you to put in a couple of hours a day on them.'

The old co had kept up his soldiering because he liked the comradeship of the annual summer camps. The manner of his successor indicated that there was a war on, representing in himself one of its less agreeable faces.

'Another thing . . . I've been looking at the mess book for the past year. I was appalled.'

'I am a qualified accountant, Colonel,' the adjutant said.

'I do not refer to the quality of your book-keeping, but to the quantity of liquor consumed. We are an engine of war, gentlemen, not a speakeasy.'

He had a presence, no doubt about that, even if one would have preferred his absence. He was short and square where his predecessor had gangled, his nose a pale button where the old co had drooped a mauve snapdragon. He did not look much older than Harry.

'We must be ready for action. In this mess I want to see officers ready to lead their men in battle at all times.' His eyes swivelled, not without desperation, round the room, fixing finally on Harry's old tennis shoes as the epitome of the prevailing state of unpreparedness.

7

'Did you win your game, Mr . . .'

'Cotton. Six-love, four-all. I think he would have beaten me if we had gone on.' Harry was used to this kind of stuff. Languid innocence was the standard counter.

'I am glad to hear it. I only hope Herr Hitler will be so sporting.'

'Oh do you think he will?'

'I am afraid that some of you seem to have fallen for all this talk about the phoney war. I can tell you that some of our chaps out there are having a pretty rough time at the moment.'

'Sir.'

'Very rough indeed.'

'Sir.'

'Now then, next item on the agenda, I've also had a look at the hotel register. As far as I can see, most of you seem to spend more time there than here. I must remind you that your place is with your men. An efficient fighting force cannot afford a gaggle of camp-followers. I can't stop you billeting your women-folk wherever you please, but I can and will declare the upper floor of the hotel out of bounds to officers.'

He pedalled up the hill out of the little town. The Hercules bike made hard work of the incline. On the top of the high down he settled back in the saddle. On either side, the corn was still green. The plough showed through in patches. Buttercups, dandelions and vetches spotted with yellow the roadside grass beneath the canopy of hedge parsley. Harry was hot. His khaki trousers rubbed against the inside of his legs. Already that strange material, its colour and texture redolent of military life, was working up its heavy smell of sweat and sour marmite. He freewheeled off the main road down the track which led to the barn. She was sitting outside in a clearing amid the bramble bushes. The rabbits had cropped the grass close. In her billowy landgirl's dungarees she looked like an enamelled princess on a lawn waiting for the touch of the unicorn. Harry jumped off the bike, letting it fall to the ground, his steed shot from under him. The front wheel spun to a stop. Its whirring broke the silence of their kiss.

'I'm afraid, you'll have to move. You're out of bounds.'

'Here? I don't believe it.'

'No, at the hotel. Wives are forbidden fruit.'

'What a pity. I thought I was respectable at last. Anyway, there's one consolation. That rude woman in the next room will have to move too. I didn't much care for the look of her lover either.'

'Did you get his name?'

'No, he's a small man with a crown and a pip on his shoulder. Snub nose.'

'The colonel and his lady.'

'More like Judy O'Grady. She hasn't got a wedding ring.'

'Aha.'

He unbuttoned her denim blouse as she lay sleepy in the sun. It was the first real day of summer. All that spring they had met in the barn, lying low in the straw. In the distance they could sometimes hear the tanks on manœuvres or the booming of the guns on the artillery range, martial counterpoint to marital idyll. He liked the secrecy of the arrangements. They departed separately as they had arrived. He waited till she had flagged down the bus at the top of the hill before he rode back to the camp, drifting down through the high banks of hedge parsley like a weary insect.

At the guard-post he waved to the sentry who was sitting on an old box with his boots off airing his feet on the Keep Out sign. As Harry wobbled through the gate, he nearly crashed into a staff car coming the other way with the sun gleaming on its bonnet as on a knight's helmet. In his room, there was a message for him to report to the co.

'Where have you been, Mr Cotton?'

'Putting in my bicycle practice, Colonel.'

'You should have informed the duty officer. I want to be able to lay my hands on my officers at every moment of the day and night. The General was most disappointed.'

'The General?'

The co made a parade of looking through the dog-eared papers on his desk, dropping his brusque voice to an absent coo: 'Yehss, yehss, making one of his famous surprise visits, helps to keep chaps like us on our toes. I had to show him round your mortar platoon myself. He was most interested. But he was sorry to miss you. Said he always liked to talk to the man on the spot . . . when he is on the spot, that is. Now what I really wanted to say was that this casual coming and going just will not do. I saw the baker waved through the guard-post this morning without even the pretence of a security check. I'm not saying the baker's a German spy but we shall look pretty silly if the boche just walk in and . . .' He cast around for a homely illustration and finally came up with 'and drink all our gin. When the balloon really goes up, first-class perimeter security will be essential. Now I'm going to appoint you Security Officer, Mr Cotton. At least it will stop you swanning about the country all day. I want a record of every single person who enters or leaves these barracks and of their reasons for so doing. Nobody is to be allowed in or out without good and sufficient cause. I shall be away this evening—summoned to a signalling con-ference at Brigade for my sins—but I want a full report of all movements of personnel, military or civilian, on my desk by 0900 hours tomorrow morning. Is that clear, Harry?' He ejected a first-name smile.

'Clear, Colonel.'

They drank deep in that velvet night. Yeomanry faces shone like harvest moons. Buttons were loosened. Glasses crunched heavily on the table cloth.

One man took his shirt off without removing his coat. Nobody else knew the trick. Everybody had a go. The telephone rang.

'Guard-room here, sir. Corporal Quill. Request a word with the Security Officer.'

'The what?'

'Security Officer, sir.'

'Security Officer, the s'curity awffcer. He wants to speak to the s'cewffity . . .'

'The squiffy officer.'

'We're all squiffy officers here. Let's toss for it.'

'Now it all comes back to me. I'm the Security Officer.'

'Harry, you're raving.'

'It's a fact. Read your Part II orders.'

'Anyway, it's the squiffy officer they want.'

'He'll do.'

'What's up, Corporal?'

'We've arrested a suspicious character, sir. He fell off his bike at the west gate. He appears to be drunk. Claims he's the new CO.'

'How is he dressed?' Harry asked briskly.

'In civvies. Somewhat dishevelled.'

'Keep him under close guard till I get there.'

'I'm afraid he's giving us some trouble, sir.'

There was the sound of a scuffle.

'Will you tell this damned fool to let me go, Cotton?'

'Who's that speaking please?'

'Don't be so bloody silly. It's your Commanding Officer.'

'What has happened to Corporal Quill?'

'Stop blathering about Corporal Quill and get me out of here.'

'If you're the CO, why are you dressed in civvies?'

'I had a . . . a private engagement.'

'Aha.'

'What?'

'I said aha.'

'Well, don't.'

'I said aha because I happen to know that the real CO is at a top-secret signalling conference at Brigade. My God, what have you wormed out of me now, you devil? The real CO warned me about this sort of thing. He'll have my head on a charger.'

'Stop play-acting. I had a private engagement after the conference. I changed at GHQ. My uniform is in my bag which that idiot corporal has impounded.'

'Come with your disguise, have you? Well done, Corporal, if you can hear me, you've bagged one of their top men.'

'Stop fooling about and tell him to let me go.'

'If you are the officer commanding this battalion, which I personally beg leave to doubt, you will know very well that I cannot possibly give the order for your release over the telephone. I have to make a full investigation and report myself to the real CO when he returns from Brigade to the bosom of his brother-officers.'

Harry walked with meandering step through the sweet

summer night. By the time he got to the guard-room, the CO had fallen into a deep sleep. Corporal Quill watched over the comatose figure on the truckle bed like a marble dog on a crusader's tomb.

Sleep was indeed a reconciling, and though the CO did not exactly rise smiling, he had hardly set fair the night before. He was in any case not in a position of sufficient moral strength to take the matter further. War, like peace, was rarely total. Harry managed to steer his bicycle down paths of dalliance beyond the colonel's reach until summoned with his brother-officers for a special briefing.

'GHQ has been asked to circulate this letter which I hold here in my hand.' He pointed to it with his other hand as if he intended to perform a conjuring trick with it, make it disappear perhaps or turn it into a hard-boiled egg. 'The instruction comes from London, from the highest quarters. I cannot say that I myself carry it out with any great enthusiasm. What's more, the DAAG tells me that GHQ takes much the same view. Be that as it may, the letter asks me to collect the names of all those who are prepared to volunteer for special service. Among the qualities demanded are apparently pluck, physical endurance and fitness, marksmanship and self-reliance—those qualities which I think I may say I have in my humble way been trying to instil in this battalion. It seems rather hard that, after all our efforts, our morale should be undercut in this irregular fashion. However, ours is not to reason why. Volunteers will be required to achieve proficiency in all the military uses of scouting—ability to stalk, to move across any type of country by day or night, silently and unseen, and . . . er . . . to live off the country.' He paused, apparently driven to the verge of nausea by the sequence of Boys-Own-Paper phrases. 'The letter continues in the same cloak-and-dagger vein. I shall post it on the notice-board. I observe that prospective candidates will be interviewed naked—but not by me.' He walked out, much moved.

Harry was surprised to find the list blank when he put his name down the next day. Two days later his was still the only name except for '6174343 Corporal A. L. Quill, HQ Company' written in tiny neat handwriting.

'You realize,' said the CO, 'that you and Lieutenant Cotton here are the only men in the entire battalion to have volunteered for this charade. You know what that means, don't you?'

'No, sir.'

'It means that ninety-nine per cent of my officers and men care more about making this battalion into a superb fighting machine than about having a good time. That's what it means.'

'Sir.'

'It's hard slog that wins wars not flashy heroics. You'll come to see that. You a family man, Corporal?'

'Yes, sir.'

'And you, Mr Cotton . . . of course you're newly married. Well, God help your wives. What's your trade, Corporal?'

'Magician, sir.'

'A magician and a jockey. God help the army.'

Corporal Quill was slight and fair. His hair was beginning to recede. To start with, he did not speak unless spoken to. They sat in silence in the hot train rattling slowly through open country. The tops of the hedgerow elms were already full-blown. Dead flies streaked the carriage windows like yellow rain.

'What sort of magic do you do?'

'Mostly small local dos—Christmas parties, British Legion meetings, church socials. There's a fair bit of work to be had when your name gets known. Oh you mean, what sort of tricks?'

'Yes.'

'The usual routine with cards and handkerchiefs. Sausages too but they take up too much room for my liking.'

'Rabbits?'

'I used to but I find doves are no more trouble and they display better. The fluttering wings always set the audience buzzing. But a rabbit—well, if you don't hold it firmly, it gets away and if you do, they think you're being cruel. What do you think it will be like?'

'No idea. Like basic training, only more so, I should guess.'

'Things have a way of turning out much the same, however hard you try to make them different.'

Harry looked at him, surprised not at the reflective nature of the remark but at its implied regret. He had noticed that

Corporal Quill was both quick-witted and thoughtful; he had not noticed a streak of melancholy.

'Always, do you think?'

'Usually, in my case, at any rate. That's why I became a magician.'

'Surely quick fingers, a natural gift for the patter, things like that . . .'

'I might flatter myself I had those even if I don't but they weren't the reason. The reason was to be different, so that when people, like the co, like a girl, like anyone, said, "And what's your work", I could say back smartly, "Magician". But I was disappointed, I'm sorry to say.'

'But isn't it different—when you've sawn the lady in half and the applause thunders up at you, don't you feel then . . .'

'Oh that's nothing much, that's your reward. But the business of it is the same as anything else, making pipes, anything.'

'Making pipes?'

'Anything. It's all arguing about money and doing the same movements over and over again and dressing up the trick to make it look more difficult than it is.'

'By those standards almost any line of country is bound to repeat itself.'

'This won't. This is unrepeatable. That's why I went in for it.'

'I hope you're right. It could be unrepeatable like a bad joke.'

'Even that would be better. Habit's a terrible thing. Habit's a killer.'

He spoke with force, thin face turned away from Harry at a broken-necked angle, pale eyes staring out of the window. They had stopped at a small station. A porter was sitting motionless on a trolley on the empty platform. The name of the station had been picked out in tiles on the brick wall behind him. Several coats of black-out paint had not entirely concealed the shape of the letters: PELSTONE, RADSTONE, REDSTOKE, something like that. The brick terraces of the small Midlands town stretched up from the station in graceless curves. Alder bushes pressed their flowers through the buff palings. Behind the station there was a half-eaten coal tip, its crust weathered to a paler grey. There was an immeasurable listlessness, no, not listlessness, an absence of feeling, a negativity about the scene. Quill turned back to look at him.

'You know, I believe in this war.'

'So do I.'

'There's not many men would answer the question like that, so quickly. Most would say, "What do you mean?" or put you off with a joke. I might myself if I was in the mood.'

'Well . . .'

'What do you think it will be like?'

'I said I didn't really know.'

'Sorry, so you did. I'm a bit keyed up . . . Sir. You don't mind me sharing this compartment with you, do you, sir?'

'I asked you in, didn't I?'

At first Harry thought that Corporal Quill knew what was what. Then he thought he might be a bit cracked; there was something to be said for habit, after all. Then he thought again Corporal Quill did know what was what; there was something to be said for being a bit cracked too. Not much but something.

The training school was much more so than basic training. It was much wetter, much tougher and went on much longer. 'That little fellow of yours will never stand it,' the commandant said, looking at the white face of Corporal Quill. The other volunteers seemed to be extremely fit already. One man in Harry's team fell down a crevasse. 'You're lucky,' the training sergeant said. 'We lost three men in the last lot.' By the end of the course everybody except Corporal Quill looked weatherbeaten, clear-eyed and well. Corporal Quill continued to look white and ill.

After a time, boredom with its ally rain, interminable celtic rain became the chief enemy. The tests of initiative and physical fitness grew more and more elaborate. The men began to get on each other's nerves; fist-fights broke out. When it finally came, the voyage relieved the tension. Even writhing in the hold of a landing infantry assault ship seemed preferable to further imprisonment on this sodden isle peopled only with sheep and muscular calibans.

Mussolini's Tits

The lorry bounced away from the quayside along the dusty road into the desert. The men stared vacantly out of the back of it. The Arabs looked back at them without interest. Inland, the ground was littered with rusty metal—old barbed wire defending forgotten compounds, burnt-out trucks and tanks, corrugated iron roofs, abandoned jalopies, the legacies of war and poverty mingled beyond the grave. As they came nearer to the camp, life began to flicker in the waste. In the patches of thorny scrub there were groups of Arabs cooking and conversing. Here and there a mangy palm tree, a more solid habitation, a well, a fuzz of arbutus. On the edge of a small palm-grove there was a soldier sitting on a jerry-can reading a book.

'One of ours. Ask him if he wants a lift.'

'Do you want a lift?'

There was no reply. The man was small and rather fat. He had very red knees. His green beret was stuffed through his shoulder strap. In its place he wore a panama straw hat.

'Jump down and ask him, Corporal. He may be deaf or something.'

Quill clambered down and went over and repeated the invitation. The man looked up. He had the butt of a cigar between his teeth. He took out the cigar and said in a precise and not unmelodious voice:

'Go away.'

'Rude fellow. Who is he, anyone know?'

'Wigg, Wogg, some name like that, sir. He writes books. I remember him from the training school.'

'Before my time, I think.'

'He was reading Keats's poems,' said Corporal Quill.

'They can't put him in the glasshouse for that. I have a taste for Keats myself.'

There were not many people about at the camp. A tall lugubrious officer in spectacles said:

'Oh you're the reserve, are you? I can't tell you what you're supposed to be doing because they're all asleep at the moment.

I should just settle your men in and wait till they surface. You were meant to be here last week, you know. You've missed the big show. They came back the night before last.'

'How did it go?'

'Badly. They should never have been sent in when they were. That's our trouble. You can divide our missions into two classes —hopeless and useless.'

'And this one was hopeless?'

'Three-quarters of our best men thrown away. They did manage to get quite a few of the others off. But . . .' He withdrew into silence.

The force commander said: 'We'll see if we can lay something on. Trouble is, our little raids are in rather bad odour at the moment. The whole Eighth Army is desperately short of men and they want to use us as general dogsbodies. But I think we might be able to arrange a night out for you, to get your hand in.'

Two days later, he said: 'I've got something for you. Mussolini's Tits. These two little pimply hills here. They're only lightly held by the Italians at present, but they dominate our forward positions and if they bring up heavy artillery, they could command the town too and it would be all over with the siege before we've got the slightest chance of relieving it. We must move quickly, say tonight. The chaps up there will show you around.'

They drove up to the front line, their minds still blurred by the exhaustion they had seen. Harry went round the hospital with Corporal Quill. The words of greeting and encouragement came haltingly from chapped lips and recognition slowly from glazed eyes. He had never seen men so tired. It was this fatigue as much as the bandages and the peeling skin that prevented him also from recognizing immediately men he must have met at the training school. All that confidence that had been injected into them through days spent scrambling up cliffs and swinging across cataracts on ropes had drained away on the bare hillside under the dive-bombers.

'I suppose we'll be like that,' Corporal Quill said.

'If the same sort of thing happens to us, yes.'

'Funny how long it takes to build a man up and how short a time to pull him down.'

'He can always be built up again. I've seen jockeys break every bone in their body and get their nerve back in no time. Anyway, think what this lot have been through.'

'Oh yes, I know that. It just took me aback to see how . . . fragile we are, that's all.'

The captain commanding the raiding party was not inclined to such thoughts. He talked about beagles, harriers and fell hounds and the hills he had hunted them on, about how to pick up the scent again after puss had swum a beck or scuttled over a drystone wall. The words tumbled out of his sunburnt face with nervous gaiety. When he ran out of reminiscence, he sang, mildly, to himself: 'Two little babes in the wood, two little babes oh so good . . .' Harry joined in. The captain stopped singing and looked at the map.

It was dark by the time they reached the rendezvous but only the dark of the desert. The guides and sappers from the forward positions stepped out from behind the boulders. They did not need to flash their torches. Their shapes stood out clean against the sky; every third man had a hump on one shoulder where he carried a groundsheet worn like a bandolier to serve as a stretcher if needed, a platoon of quasimodos. The party split into two, the smaller group to create a diversion in front of the stony paps, the larger to creep round the shoulder of the right-hand one and knock out the post from behind. The Italians were nestling between the two peaks, like a brooch on a land-lady's bosom. The captain took Harry and the rest of the reserve, bar Corporal Quill and a dozen private soldiers who went with the other officer. It was the first time that they had not been together since they arrived at the training school. Quill gave him an awkward wink, ducking his head into his shoulders; Harry half-raised a hand. They walked briskly in their rubber boots. It was like an English summer evening. Occasionally the still not departed glimmer over the horizon caught the barrel of a rifle or the blade of a bayonet. Once or twice Harry stumbled on the broken ground. He thought of the stumbling stroll he had taken from the mess to the guard-room a year before. That seemed more like real life. He shivered. He could just feel the chill creeping into the air or his heart into his boots.

When they came within a hundred yards of the top of the right-hand hill, they halted to wait for the diversionary attack to begin. Their breathing was heavy for fit men. Then the machine-guns and the mortar opened up from below them. They ran at full tilt round the back of the hill, boots clattering on the scree. Thirty yards from the Italian rear, they formed into line, caught their breath and, as the first sleepy challenge came from the Italians, advanced down the gulley, firing rifles and tommy guns. Figures reared momentarily out of the dark, then bolted out of sight again into the dug-outs. They had settled on a password, 'Jock', to prevent them shooting each other in the dark and above the noise of the firing there rose a weird bark of 'Jock, Jock', croaked and shrilled and bellowed, alternately battle cry and enemy plea for mercy. Harry saw the captain rush towards the sound of a machine-gun and saw the butt of his tommy-gun rising and falling against the sky; between the grenades exploding in the dug-outs, he could hear him grunting 'Jock' each time the butt came down.

The answering fire stopped. There was nothing to be heard but groaning and cursing and the rattle and crash of boots sliding on loose stones. The captain shouted, 'Home, Jock, home'. They ran straight down the hillside; they were told they could only reckon on ten or fifteen minutes before the Italian artillery realized what was happening and began to shell the position. As they slithered back down to the place where they had halted, Harry looked at his watch: thirty-five minutes from start to finish, glory won, nothing to it, a dozen eyeties dead and not a broken leg between the lot of them. He felt as fresh as a daisy as he watched the Italian heavy guns pound the graves of their own dead men. The diversionary party were there before them; they had had a much shorter walk.

In the shadow of the rocks, two men were kneeling beside a groundsheet. A torch flashed. The fair hair was sticky with blood; the head lay ducked into the shoulder, broken-necked bird on green winding-sheet. 'Don't quite know how it happened.

There was heavy fire from three o'clock. Then we lost . . .' The other officer was almost talking to himself. Harry shuddered, a long convulsive trembling; he felt it would never stop. He was stained, contaminated; that brief moment of exultation slithering down the scree was something that would not be washed off. He had not seen the enemy's face. Perhaps if he had seen a startled dark eye . . . no, that was not enough, he would have had to see a split skull, brain porridge spilling out over the bare ground. Men like him had to be brought up hard against the ultimate horror before they could understand. They had to poke their stubby fingers into the bleeding stomach. But he had seen nothing, felt nothing until it was shown to him in the dead body of his friend, hardly a friend though, an acquaintance, an original; he did not even know his Christian name, how could he write to his wife, he ought to write to his wife.

Action, as he supposed it must be called, was so unreal, ambiguous, haphazard, so quickly done with, permanent only in its consequences. Harry did not even know if he had killed a man. He had emptied his magazine but only at obscure shapes, rocks perhaps, a desert Quixote tilting at stony windmills, petrified sheep. He had had one man in his sights, but that man had shouted, 'Jock, Jock' and Harry had lowered his gun. Yet it could have been his bullet ricocheting down the gulley like a pinball that had done for Alan Quill, that was his name, Alan. No, the range was too great; besides, such stretched fancies were mere self-indulgence. What had happened had happened, its consequences not exactly foreseen but allowed for. He had been committed to it. He wanted to offer to help carry the ground-sheet but he could not form the words. Anyway two hefty Scots made nothing of the burden. He lasted the walk back to the lorry, but he could hardly lift himself over the tailboard. He sat on the bench with his head beneath his knees, coughing a low dribble of a cough. The man next to him felt his violent shivering and put one of the other groundsheets round him. By the time they got back to the asphalt road, Harry was sure he was running a high fever. He took out his handkerchief to wipe his forehead. It was spotted with blood. He stared at it in the dim light of the swaying lorry amid the silent, dozing men.

The MO said: 'I expect you thought it was nerves—shell shock.'
'That kind of thing.'
'Well it isn't. I'll tell you straight. I'm ninety-nine per cent
certain you've got TB. You're not the first by any means. I don't
know why this place brings it out.'

He lay in the long, white-washed ward, listening to the breeze
shuffle through the bamboo slats of the blinds. The small man
with red knees came to visit him.

'I hear you like Keats. Would you accept this slightly foxed
but serviceable copy?'

'Thank you very much. That is very kind of you.'

'I thought the gift appropriate to your condition, although I
trust that your disease will not run the same unfortunate course
as the poet's. May I sit down?'

Harry floated in an airy languor while the small man reported
the gossip from London. His talk animated a world which Harry
knew mostly at second hand, whose edges he had barely
touched: cocktails, plate-glass, titled transvestites, Roumanian
exiles, Bugattis, suicides and religious conversions. It was hard
and bright and bitter, very modern and very tragic. The vulgar
necessities of war and politics were not to be mentioned in the
same company. Harry listened with delight to the stylish
phrases, their old-fashioned syntax enlivened by twenties slang
dropped into place by inverted commas as neat as pincers. The
small man's voice had the same quality; behind the public man
opening a garden fête, there lurked a small boy pulling at his
coat-tails and relieving himself into the flower-beds.

'I understand that Pip Parrott has been mentioned in
despatches again. Veronica is much distressed. She said it was
too boring and why couldn't they mention someone else for a
change. By the way, I must congratulate you on the success of
your mission.'

'I don't expect it did much good.'

'You met the enemy in battle and slew him. One can ask no
more.'

'I don't feel much like claiming scalps, if indeed I had any
to claim.'

'You will find that attitude unrewarding. It is in the claiming of scalps that the art of the war hero lies. His lines of communication run directly to the popular newspapers. Not surprisingly, this facility for attracting public attention tends to excite jealousy within the bosom of the general staff. One recalls the stinging rebuke administered by Charlemagne to Roland; no doubt it was well deserved. Oliver, on the other hand, was obviously a mere war correspondent, probably for the Beaverbrook press. Hence his insistence that Roland should blow his horn.'

'Did you see much of that in your show?'

'Alas, there were no scalps to be claimed, except our own. Ours was a freak show, a *lusus naturae* of the most extreme variety. Prodigies of cowardice and stupidity were performed, the enterprise was aborted as soon as conceived. The island should never have been attacked, if attacked not held, if held not left without reinforcements or air cover. Nothing, however, will be said. The villains will be propelled upstairs. The boobies will write their memoirs. It is clear to me now, if it had not been clear before, that the people who will do well out of this war will not be hard-faced men but soft-faced trimmers. Advancement will come only to those who possess both the knack of survival and the skill of ingratiating themselves with authority. There is no place here for reckless misanthropes of the old school.'

'You place yourself in that category?'

'I do not find it easy to be nice.'

The MO said: 'We've got a hospital ship sailing tomorrow. I've managed to get you on it. I'm afraid you'll have to go the long way round.'

The SS *Cythera* was an old ferry-boat. The purser said it had been tramping round the eastern Mediterranean since before the First World War. Orange rust stained its white gunwales, railings, davits, bridge. The name-plate in the wheelhouse had not been polished in years, not surprising since it carried the inscription *RMS Arrochar Queen*, John Brown and Company, Glasgow, legacy of an earlier role from which it had been translated to these torrid climes.

Harry tired easily now. He had lost weight and appetite. He

began to run a fever in the middle of the day. Most of the time he lay below. He made a point of not inquiring after the ship's progress. After three days he felt a little better and asked where they were and was told somewhere in the middle of the Red Sea. He was disappointed like a child on a long journey who shuts his eyes hoping that he will be home when he opens them again. In the morning he took to reclining in a chair on the covered deck, sheltered from the sun. The boat moved just fast enough to work up a breeze. In the evenings there was a sweepstake on the length of the day's run. Harry opted for the low field. He won two nights in succession. The boat had been ordered to cut its speed to conserve fuel. They could not be sure of refuelling off East Africa because U-boats had been reported along the coast. They would have to make for the Cape by way of Ceylon.

The other passengers were too ill to talk. The doctors were silent men. The nurses were busy. He was left alone. He paddled in a solipsistic sea. He thought to himself, now I can think about everything—after the war, Pauline, with luck the child, not inconsiderables to live for. But the future did not seem very real. Nothing seemed real except his own thoughts if you could call them thoughts, rippling silent like sargasso weed in a motionless sea. There was nothing to attach himself to, nothing to brace himself against. He was hardly even a geometrical point, no more possessing position than magnitude. His name was writ in water like the poor poet's but in a giftless hand.

He wondered if he was reaching the crisis of his disease. Was his the sort of disease that had a crisis? The doctors had told him, but he could not concentrate at the time. Had he come to the stage at which it was appropriate for the patient to put up a tremendous fight for life? Himself, he felt more like the girl in the story—why struggle? The man in the next bed in Cairo said they had invented a wonderful new drug, in Canada, but you couldn't get hold of it in England. That would be annoying if it came too late to save him. But then illness was annoying . . . annoying and tedious. He could not manufacture any real interest in his condition. The war must be won; and he must see Pauline. These things apart, he might just as well watch the spray spring and fall and pattern its salt traces on the deck. He was in no hurry to live.

The *Cythera* came out into the Indian Ocean. He felt stronger. The doctors had warned him there might be a false dawn shortly after the disease took hold of him. There was a long way to go yet. All the same, he asked if it would be in order to read for an hour or so a day. His mind, left to itself, ran in such slow circles, becoming a little more agitated on each lap. The same practical problems began to repeat themselves in less and less promising form—money and family and occupation and years wasted and years to come; he was caught in a web of neglected obligation. Would there be horses to ride after the war? Would he be there to ride them? Who could say? He had made no sense of these questions when he was well. Now was a worse time to brood. The sensible plan was to sit and watch the flying fishes, if they were flying fishes. It was sometimes hard to tell whether he was looking at a distant shoal curving in the white light or at a curtain of spray falling on to the deck. His eyes were weak. Even so, he could not watch the flying fish all day; he must occupy his mind. The purser came round with an armful of books.

'Doctor's orders. No more than an hour a day. I picked these out myself. I'm quite a reader. Do you like old Galsworthy, probably read him already—or *The History of Mr Polly*, now that's a funny little book. And here's a Zane Grey, this one's a cracker though more for the ors, I suppose. If you want something a bit more up to date, try this, *Brave New World*, awfully interesting, tells us how we're all going to end up.' Harry took *Brave New World* and the Zane Grey which was all about Red Indians who could walk through forests without snapping a twig. He was supposed to have learnt this trick at the training school, but when he tested it out his tracker's tread seemed to make just as much noise as his ordinary walk. He soon wearied of the book; the Indians were so unmitigatedly noble. He dozed a little and then opened *Brave New World*. Almost immediately he dozed off again, this time verging on real sleep, his hand keeping the book open at the title page.

He awoke with a start and looked about, half expecting some

dramatic change in his surroundings. But nothing had altered: the churning chug of the engine, the splashy thud of the wash, the motionless figures under the rugs parked in a row alongside him and the sun frying the open deck outside, from the kitchen behind them an occasional whiff of onions or the clatter and chuckle of the Eurasian cooks. He creased his eyes against the glare of the white page and drowsily began to translate the epigraph from the French:

'Utopias appear much more realizable than we used to think. And we now find ourselves confronted by a question which is agonizing in a quite different sense: how to stop them being realized? . . . Utopia can be realized. Life marches towards utopia. And perhaps a new age will begin, an age in which intellectuals and the cultivated class will dream of how to avoid utopia and of return to a society which is not utopian, less "perfect" and more free.' He read on for some time, then went to sleep. He dreamed he was trapped in a chanceless utopia. Gambling was forbidden, so were chance meetings, coincidences, puns, accidents and pinball machines. He couldn't stand it. He seemed to have joined up with a gang which was plotting to get out. As they discussed tunnels and ropes and ladders and disguises, his fellow-plotters took on the faces of old friends, of Frogmore and Mossy and Tom and Stella. Their schemes and laughter grew louder; their faces began to shine like suns, hotter and brighter and hotter and brighter until suddenly he woke up with a headache and sweat dripping off his face. He asked a passing steward to help him below.

The next day the steward woke him early.

'Look outside.'

Harry knelt on his bunk and squinted out of the porthole. The sun had already laid its net of diamonds on the water and beyond it shimmered a mirage city, its waterfront a splash of whites and oranges and ochres and terracotta, a forest of boats tossing in the harbour and beyond the town the true dark forest curling its glistening sappy embrace round the bay. Everything seemed to be moving and shining and glistening as if the breeze and the sun and the rain were one.

'That's wonderful,' said Harry, 'Will you be going ashore?'

'No, there is nothing here for us.'

'Nothing here? I don't quite understand.'

'We are not wanted.' The steward spoke without feeling.

'I see. That's a pity. I was hoping . . . some souvenirs.'

'You give me money. I go buy from boats.'

Harry watched the boats cluster round the hospital ship, husks bobbing and clashing in the swelling silver water like barley pouring through a girl's fingers. The bodies of the fishermen and the boat-vendors swayed to the rhythm of the water, the colours of their head-dresses and clothes as bright as though they were the effect of light on water, sheer prismatic liquid. His eyes grew tired and he lay back on the bunk.

The steward knocked.

'I buy you these. And here is cable.'

He handed Harry a small ebony elephant with ivory tusks and a larger one with ivory toenails as well as tusks. The cable was from Pauline. She had given birth to a son. He wrote out a reply in shaking capitals: WELL DONE CHRISTEN HIM ALDOUS COLOMBO STOP HURRAH STOP ALL MY LOVE NO STOP

Back of Beyond

'There's not much going just now for someone in your state of health,' said The Man Who Could Fix Things, 'But I could always fix you up as a government agent. Would that interest you at all?'

'An agent,' said Harry eagerly.

'Not exactly E. Phillips Oppenheim stuff, I'm afraid. In fact, the work might sound rather humdrum to you, but it has its tricky side.'

'Ah,' said Harry.

'You see, neutrals are always prickly. And in dealing with the Irish, history is hardly on our side. Do you know Ireland at all?'

'I've ridden there.'

'Then you'll know what I mean. Some of our chaps over

there seem to be a bit adrift. Let me pass you on to the people who are running the show and you can decide for yourself.'

The Assistant Secretary, Recruitment, Eire, at the Ministry of Supply looked neither more nor less helpful than the succession of dry men Harry had faced across a desk since he had come to London to re-enlist in the defence of civilization, X-rays cleared, energies somewhat restored.

'I want you to be a fisher of men.' The Assistant Secretary had evidently used the phrase before. He used it again. 'A fisher of men.'

'Yes,' said Harry.

'The munitions industry, the coal mines, the steel mills, the farms—all are desperately short of manpower. In Eire, on the other hand, there is still widespread unemployment. The inference is obvious—let the men move to the jobs. The logistics are, however, not so simple. There is the question of Irish neutrality. Employment exchanges over there cannot be expected to display vacancies received from a belligerent government. And then there is the turf.'

'Yes,' said Harry, puzzled at the mention of this familiar terrain but ready to display his expertise in such matters.

'They must keep enough men to cut their wretched turf. We have to proceed with tact. Perhaps I had better explain the system.' He shifted into higher gear for what sounded a well-thumbed rubric: 'Minsupp UK suggests importation of Irish labour to British firm . . . firm notifies UK employment exchanges . . . notifications approved by Ministry of Labour which passes them through Minsupp HQ to Minlab HQ which processes them through to UK liaison officer Dublin—very able chap—who allocates a weekly quota to each agent in the field who then recruits his Paddies through local contacts by inviting them to register at relevant UK exchanges . . . Irish Minlab processes applications, passes them to Liaison who refers them back to Minsupp London who sends Paddy his tickets and what-have-you and off he goes.'

'It seems rather complicated.'

'It is,' said the Assistant Secretary with grim satisfaction. 'You must understand there is a reason for each step.'

'Of course.'

'You would be most ill-advised to try to short-cut the system.'

'No, no, I was just thinking aloud.'

'As it happens, we do have a vacancy at this moment. Drop-forgings sub-control agent, Leinster region. How does that appeal to you?'

'Very much,' said Harry. There seemed nothing else to say. He wondered vaguely what a drop-forging was.

'You'll pick up the business as you go along. But I have one very important word of advice to give you before you take up the post.' The Assistant Secretary stood up to emphasize the importance of the advice. 'Certain of our less responsible agents have caused the Department Grave Embarrassment. Naturally an agent, if he is to be effective, must build up his contacts, but in most cases the offer of a half-pint will, I believe, suffice to establish cordial relations. The Department will in future take a serious view of any excessive expenditure.'

'I understand.'

'Good. Well, your instructions are quite straightforward. After you have picked up your flimsies, indents and the rest of the bumph at Liaison, you are to proceed to Devlin's Bar in Knoxtown and make yourself known to a . . . a,' he squinted at the writing on the paper, 'a Mr Birch, one of our most valuable contacts. I'm told you'll find he's quite a character. Devlin's Bar, don't forget.'

Peace or war, the Irish Mail remained the same: the pools of sick, the empty Guinness bottles clinking as they slid across the table, the palsied tenors keening 'Danny Boy', in fine, the image of misery afloat. Only the khaki of soldiers returning home on leave marked the date. Harry lay on his bunk. In the berth above him, a man in braces snored an irregular, impatient snore. On the other side of the bulkhead, he could just hear horses turning in their stalls. Racehorses, the steward had said. Who on earth could have got a movement order for bloodstock in the middle of a world war?

He woke into a calm, grey dawn. The country women sat by their baskets on the cobbled quay. Men in trilby hats sauntered into the refreshment room to get a cup of tea and a ham roll and then sauntered out again to catch a breath of the mild air. The little train backed slowly into the siding as if it had all day. People here looked different, thin in the face certainly but not without serenity, at least by comparison. At Dublin he changed into a bigger train. Knoxtown was only half an hour away, but the smell from the restaurant car was so good that he had the full breakfast.

Devlin's was a large melancholy place, half bar, half general store. When he came in, the bar was so quiet that he could hear the rumble of potatoes being poured on to the scales in the other half. The three or four men at the bar clung on to their glasses as they turned round to look at him. Harry ordered a drink and asked where he could find Mr Birch.

'Mr Birch? There's nobody here of that name.'

'I expect I'm too early to catch him.'

'You may be and you may not. I do not know the man.'

'He's supposed to be a regular customer. Birch.'

'Nobody of that name here.'

The men at the bar clasped their glasses more firmly and turned away from him.

'He could—it's only a theory now—but he could be wanting a Mr *Burke*,' said one of them.

'Tim Burke the horse doctor? What would he be wanting with him?' said the barmen.

'I was thinking more of Joseph Burke the English spy.'

'That's a different thing altogether. But it would be a queer sort of joke to send a stranger in here looking for Joseph Burke.'

They laughed.

'I think,' said Harry, 'that Joseph Burke the English spy might be my man.'

'If that is so, then you must go to Devlin's Bar up the other end of the street.'

'But isn't this Devlin's Bar?'

'Not at all. I grant you the name is still over the door but it is not Devlin's Bar.'

'Devlin's moved up the street, has he?' Harry hazarded.

'Mrs Devlin has moved up the street. Mr Devlin has moved to another place, another place entirely.'

They laughed again. Harry finished his drink quickly and left.

At the top end of the town he found a much smaller establishment, little more than a cottage. On the board nailed to the roughcast wall it said 'Devlin's NEW Bar'. He asked the woman behind the counter for Mr Birch or Mr Burke. A short round man in the corner toppled off his stool and put out his hand.

'Joseph Burke at your service, Captain. I am sorry that you find me rather negleejay. This emergency takes the stuffing out of you.'

'You have an emergency on then?' Harry asked.

'This war, that's what we call it over here, you know, though of course we also have our own local emergencies—Mary, serve the gentleman, will you—we have to be prepared. Come in this corner for a moment and let me show you a thing.' Mr Burke led him into the darkest corner of the room and with his thumb twitched open one pocket of his raglan. Harry peered down into the murky hollow. At first he could not identify the knobbly glint at the bottom.

'Service Luger,', said Mr Burke, 'none better. I expect you found that to be so on the field of battle.'

'We didn't do much shooting where I was.'

'Did you come across Sergeant Mulligan by any chance? Sergeant Mulligan, Military Medal. In the Fusiliers he was. Or Captain Ryan, Distinguished Service Order.'

'No, I don't think . . .'

'I like to keep up with the gallantry awards. The newspapers do them very well here. Captain Ryan was posthumous, of course. Another jar? That is kind of you indeed. Mary, repeat the order please.'

Refreshed, Mr Burke leant forward with bottle-nosed dignity: 'Now then, Captain, the trouble is you're here and you're not here. You must show your face, make friends, entertain a little, otherwise you'll get no customers. But then again, you must not make yourself too conspicuous or there will be complaints lodged. Let me tell you a thing.' He leant further forward until his raglan cloaked the light. 'The wives are bad enough, but the priests are the worst, and I am a Catholic that am telling you this. They put the fear into the wives with their stories of the fancy women and the booze and the betting over in England— as if there were not a loose woman in all Ireland nor a drop of whisky nor a priest having a few bob on the dogs. It's "wadya let your darlin Seamus leave this isle of saints with the turf to be cut and the harvest still not in?"—oh they know how to get round a woman all right. But five pounds a week is a powerful argument and if you can get the support of some of the considerable people in the neighbourhood, well then it will be "I'm sorry father, but I've a family to feed and I'm catching the Liverpool boat in the morning".'

'Can you introduce me to some of the considerable people?'

'It would be a pleasure.'

'Tomorrow?'

'Well now, tomorrow it's the yearling sales. And I hear you're a racing man yourself . . .'

'I want to get on with it,' Harry said.

'That shows admirable spirit, admirable. I was only going to suggest that if you would care to accompany me, we might make some advantageous meetings around the ring. We might also see some good young horses.'

'All right. Are you in the bloodstock business yourself?'

'Not professionally, Captain. But I dabble now and then.'

He made a dabbling motion with his stubby fingers, then stared at his empty glass as if he had seen a scorpion at the bottom of it. Harry ordered two more doubles. He was beginning to appreciate the circumstances that had given rise to the Assistant Secretary's warning, though he had no idea of how to heed it.

'You being anxious to begin operations, Captain, we might perhaps have a bit of a reconnaissance around the town, spy out the land, so to speak.'

Over the next few hours Harry met a great number of persons. They did not visit the other Devlin's Bar, but the gap in the itinerary was hardly missed. The town was not short of bars, nor Mr Burke of friends. On the whole, these friends seemed unlikely to volunteer for employment in the drop-forgings industry, belonging as they did for the most part to the superannuated or derelict class. Mr Burke himself, however, showed remarkable stamina and capacity throughout the reconnaissance; the phrase 'hollow legs' leapt to mind.

On the drizzling morrow he was at Harry's hotel on the dot of nine. He showed total recall of the personages met on the night before, most of whom in Harry's mind had already merged into a collective blur. It appeared that they were all notables in some field or other: 'You remember Brian O'Dowda, that wee feller with the cast in his eye we met in the Sportsman's, a very considerable man in fertilizers, a man to be reckoned with, that . . . the big man standing next to him, that was big Michael Browne, regional manager for Gallagher's, very influential . . .'

The catalogue continued as they walked through the crowd surrounding the sale-ring, Mr Burke softly punching some old friends in the kidneys and removing his glove to shake the hand of other, presumably more reverend acquaintances. As they reached the rails, Harry stood still, entranced. He had not seen a thoroughbred yearling for years. A bay filly was pawing the sanded ground while the stable-lad holding her head stopped to talk to a friend.

'Now here's a very big man in the bloodstock business, Captain. Mr Frogmore O'Neill.'

There was a snap to Froggie's trilby. His voice had taken on a brogueish lilt.

'So you're the recruiting officer, Harry. I don't want you pinching my stable-lads now.'

'Your stable-lads?'

'I've got quite a thing going here. You must come and see my place, or rather C.L.'s place. Don't laugh, but I'm her racing manager.'

'What happened to Henriques then?'

'You didn't hear? Shot himself the day after the fall of France.'

'I never heard.'

He watched the filly begin to trot awkwardly round the ring. Her hooves raised little spurts of sand.

'And Nuts Grove?' Harry asked.

'You *are* out of touch, old boy. After your dear cousin burnt the yard down, Miss L. had to board her horses all over the place. In the end she got fed up with the bother of it. So she moved the whole lot over here. Last two-year-olds arrived on the Mail yesterday.'

'I'm sorry about Evelyn Henriques.'

'He was a lovely man. Left C.L.'s affairs in a hell of a mess, though. We've had quite a time sorting them out, what with the emergency—'

'The war.'

'All right, the war. How've you been getting on then? You look dreadful thin.'

'I've been ill.'

'You always were thin.'

Another yearling came into the ring and ran side by side with the first one.

'Remember that day at the sheep sale?' Froggie said. 'You were a gone man that day.'

'You were fighting drunk yourself. Not a pretty sight.'

'Had to defend my honour. Careful, boy.' One of the horses had knocked against the rickety rail. 'By the way, I don't care for your fat friend.'

'Joseph Burke? He's an enthusiast. I've taken to him.'

'Bit of a troublemaker if you ask me.'

'I didn't.'

'Thing is, his war propaganda has put a lot of people's backs up.'

'Oh, come off it, Froggie.'

'You'll have to learn what it's like over here. It's no picnic being neutral. Look, come back after the sale to C.L.'s place and we'll have a jar.'

'I'll have to bring Mr Burke with me. He's my mentor.'

'If you must, you must.'

C.L. had neither shrunk nor mellowed. If anything, she had swollen to the proportions of the giants of Irish legend.

'Are you recruiting for that tiresome war?' she said by way of greeting.

'Not for the war exactly. For factories in England.'

'I wouldn't go back to England if you paid me. People get so stuffy there whenever you buy a horse. They keep on saying "there's a war on"—as if I wasn't keeping racing going almost single-handed. And I can't say he's much bloody help either.' She pointed at her new racing manager with a finger which did not seem to promise him an unruffled career.

'But you must have seen *some* action,' a woman with pop eyes said to Harry accusingly. He started to tell her about Mussolini's Tits, then, warmed by the liquor, went on to tell her about the death of Corporal Quill.

'Isn't that the tragic thing now,' said the pop-eyed woman, fidgeting with her glass. 'Look, there's Froggie O'Neill. I always think he's the sort of man who ought to wear a bow-tie.'

'I will not wear a bow-tie.'

'Get along with you, a broad man like you, a bow-tie would give you presence.'

'I find them too wearisome to tie.'

'You could wear a made-up one.'

'The woman blasphemes. A made-up bow-tie is not the thing, not the thing at all.'

Mr Burke appeared, towing a considerable citizen behind him.

'Let's get out of here,' Harry said to him.

'Right away, Captain. Mr McWeeney here has a fine motor car. Mr McWeeney, let me tell you, is a hell of a name in the income tax.'

'I hear there's a fine party starting in Clondalkin,' said Mr McWeeney.

'Oh there'll be dancing in Clondalkin,' said Mr Burke. 'It's the back of beyond here. Clondalkin is the place to be.'

The next morning Harry woke in the Sportsman's Arms to hear the first putative recruits to the drop-forgings industry knocking on his door. Luckily they were not talkative. With a head like Harry had, it was as much as he could do to get their names down right. But as the days went by, he found to his surprise that he took to the work. He liked arriving in each fresh grey town towards noon and strolling down the single long main street on a prolonged reconnaissance with Joseph Burke at his side. He liked the red-cheeked young men with big hands and the proud, garrulous mothers who chaperoned them to his hotel room. After they had gone, clutching their leaflets and application forms, he would drop a line to Pauline while Mr Burke slept to restore his energies for the evening's patrol.

When they had completed their week's quota, Mr Burke would borrow a boat and they would row slowly round the nearest lough. Harry trolled negligently for pike while Mr Burke held the oars and talked about the war:

'And how is Mr Neville Chamberlain keeping?'

'I'm afraid he's dead.'

'Is he now? Well to be sure, never a sweeter man rested in Abraham's bosom, and that's a fact.'

Harry found no shortage of recruits. In fact there were more men eager to work across the water than there were jobs going. When his assignment ended a couple of summers later, he wrote to Pauline: 'The invasion you read about in the newspapers is nothing compared to the Irish legions I have unleashed during my time here. The drop-forgings industry will never be the same again.'

CHAPTER FIVE

THE souvenir programme for the victory celebrations was hastily printed, but its crossed union jacks and deckled edges sported a plucky festivity. Luncheon in village hall: cold ham and corned beef, green salad and pickles, apple tart and custard, two sittings, please be punctual, bring your own knife, fork and spoon. I went to the children's afternoon tea: buttered, or rather margarined, buns, jelly, a few, not very many, cakes with the ineradicable taste of powdered egg. At ten o'clock in the morning the bells began to ring. At eleven there was a united service in the church. The other Harry gobbled into his prayer book at twice the normal rate in celebration of the peace, or perhaps he was excited by the throng of Baptists and Methodists in the usually unpeopled pews, divining in their presence a surge of religious feeling out of gratitude for the late deliverance.

The small gang of Italian prisoners-of-war or ex-prisoners-of-war who were mending the roads sat respectfully at the back, mystified by the unfamiliar rites, yet sharing in the elation because of the prospect of going home soon. One of them made me model aeroplanes out of scraps of tinfoil which he melted down with a blow-lamp. He used to hold the delicate sliver of silver between his roughened fingers and ask me to come and look. As I grasped for it, he would pull it just out of my reach, flashing a mouthful of gold-capped teeth before he finally presented it to me with a flourish. The aeroplane had its charms, but I liked its maker more, or not himself but the way he gave it to me, the exotic ritual. When his black-stubbled, olive-skinned head popped out of the trench they were digging outside our house, it was the apparition of a tutelary spirit. 'Can I get down and go and see the prisoners?' 'You mustn't stare at them, Aldous.' 'I don't stare at them, I *talk* to them.' 'Italians love children.' 'Even this child, do you think, Pauline? All right then.'

In the afternoon the sports started: Tots race, potato race Mixed, balloon sticking Ladies, thread the needle Mixed, over sixty Ladies, over sixty Gents, pillow fight Boys—prizes 5/o,

2/0, 6*d*. The sports went on for the rest of the day. Evening was closing in as I went home on my father's shoulders twisting round to see the last pillows being thrown across the playing field like great white moths. Then the bells began again, ringing some donkey-trot peal which may have been too much for the elderly ringers, the younger ones not yet back from the war; the ringing sounded like an old man crying, short of breath.

I was told to rest before the procession. I lay on my bed as stiff as a soldier on sentry duty, showing exaggerated obedience in response to the patriotic colour of the occasion. I would not even turn my head to see if the window was lit up by the glow of the torches. But I was nowhere near sleep. My mind was filled with vast processions streaming in all directions: Italian prisoners stumbling across the desert with a ferret-faced man in a beret with two cap-badges glaring down at them from his jeep, great battleships steaming across the Channel leaving silver trails like the snails on our terrace, Russians plodding through the snow, an endless file of Japanese still winding through the jungle. Then I heard my father running up the stairs humming *'I'm gonna get lit up when the lights go up in London, I'm gonna get so lit up I'll be visible for miles* . . . come on, hurry, they're starting.'

The procession began a little way down the road. The cudgels with their heads wrapped in tar-soaked cloth were like giant matches. They were stacked in dozens in barrels outside the church porch. The Italian prisoner who made me aeroplanes was lighting them from his blow-lamp. As each torch flared, it lit up his gold teeth and his red, laughing mouth and his sparkling eyes. His face was a jewelled reliquary turned up to the clear night sky. As I came to the front of the queue, he began to pull out a torch, then seeing me, thrust it back into the barrel and from another barrel pulled out a much smaller one. He set fire to this child's torch, held it out to me, then for a second took it back again like the aeroplane before putting it gently into my hands, closing them firmly round the rough bark with his own.

We set off swinging down the road, a ragged regiment, lit up within and without. After the so-called village green, marked only by its red telephone box and peeling notice-board, a stream banked with sandbags ran beside the road. As the procession paused to re-group, I looked down and saw flickering streaks of light reflected in its muddy waters, as if the moon had been furrowed by a great rake, bringing to mind the local legend of the rustics who had hidden smuggled brandy in the village pond and when caught by the excise man searching for it with their rakes fobbed him off by asserting with an air of goofy innocence that they were raking the moon.

The legend belonged to that ancient category by which the apparently simple yokel outwits the city slicker, representative of authority, ministering like most legends to the self-esteem of the aggrieved. At the same time, there was an alternative version in which the yokels were genuinely under the impression that the moon they were raking was a large cream cheese. It might be thought that this latter version would be more often told by outsiders but not so. The locals themselves liked to maintain the ambiguity as to whether they were or were not as dumb as they looked, an ambiguity which was in any case close enough to reality. If asked what they were doing with their torches, in their present condition several members of the procession might well have been tempted to answer 'setting fire to the sky'.

As we passed our own house on the way to the victory bonfire on the hill, I moved to the side of the procession so that I could see my mother who had promised to be at the gate. We came round the corner and I could not see her. Perhaps she was hidden by the angle of the hedge. But then we got closer and she was still not there. She could not have forgotten or wearied of waiting; we had only been a few minutes. I felt that lurching, banging feeling which is the prelude to disappointment like the clanging of gates in a high-speed lift before it starts its giddy descent. She wasn't there, she had forgotten. Then, just as we were passing, I saw her. She had been there all the time. The angle of the hedge was sharper than I had thought and had blotted her from my sight. She leant against the gatepost with her arms folded, smiling, slightly ironic but enjoying it. As we strode by, I waved with one hand, nearly dropping the torch out of the other. She waved back, then put her hand to her eyes to shield them from the glare of the torches.

I do not want to say much about my mother. Hers is another story. She married my father and died young. Their marriage startled some of my father's friends. Either they hardly knew her or hardly knew that he knew her. If the wedding had taken place a few months later, it would have been said that the war had hastened their courtship. As it was, even the possibility of war might have had something to do with it. My guess is rather that my father had reached that age when he not only wanted to get married but also could see very clearly who it was that he wished to marry. At such a moment there is no purpose in delay; in fact delay is a kind of coquetry. Nor do I wish to speak of their marriage; the adjustments and renunciations demanded if two people are to live together in concord no less than the rewards earned are not only private but delicate matters, not easily assessed by the satellite egos of their children. If judgment there has to be, it is better attempted from outside. I can bear reliable witness only to the fact that as a child I was sheltered from everything except happiness; the sun shone, the rain drenched the hazel outside my window; I saw my parents kissing by the gooseberry bushes, giving rise to a mental confusion which only puberty finally dispelled; the tensions and anxieties which hindsight imputes did not come near me, and when the disaster happened I was not even there.

The summer holidays after I left school were too long for me to loll about on the sofa listening to the afternoon play on the wireless. At least so I was told; I should be learning something, improving my German, for example. My father believed that arrangements could be effectively made only through friends; official channels were not only useless but dangerous, liable to turn up old convictions. He would write, he said, to a pre-war friend in Germany who would fix something. How could he remember the address? Oddly enough, he remembered the address exactly. Of course, he had heard nothing of her for twenty years. She might have moved, or anything; it was a long shot. But he remembered Breslau as a fine city; anyway, he would like to know what I thought of it; I could always move on somewhere else if I didn't take to the place; besides, he would like to know what had happened to Stella.

8

Within a fortnight he got a reply, phrased in abrupt but friendly terms as if the writer was pressed for time. Stella said my father did not realize how lucky it was that my letter had reached her. It was a chance in a million ('That's what I said,' my father interrupted). She would be delighted to see me if I didn't mind a camp-bed in the passage, but she didn't think Breslau these days was the best place to learn German. 'Why on earth not?' said my father as he read the letter out loud. I pointed to the Polish stamp. 'Poland, Poland, why is she in Poland?' We looked at the map and slowly traced out the dotted line which wandered up the valley of the Oder, then branched off up the Neisse until it reached the Czech frontier. About a hundred miles to the east, there was a solid line running roughly parallel. The strip between the two lines was inscribed 'Under Polish Jurisdiction'; in the middle of it was marked the city of Wrocław, underneath, in brackets, Breslau. 'Well, well,' my father said, 'She is in Poland. I had forgotten. Perhaps I never knew. Ignorance is a wonderful thing. All the more reason for you to go and see what it is like.'

'What about my German, though?'

'Doesn't matter about your German. You can talk German to her, if you want to. And take some coffee with you. She says you still can't get decent coffee in Breslau. Why does she go on calling it Breslau, I wonder? Like talking about St Petersburg. Well, why shouldn't she?' He ended up arguing with himself. I was still looking at the map. 'Whatever happened to her parents and her brother? You must ask and . . . you must go to the old quarter and walk through the arcades and see the . . . what is it called . . . the Jahrhunderthalle . . .'

She had last seen her parents on the platform of the Central Railway Station in the summer of 1939. She had eventually married a doctor who had been studying in Breslau, a Pole. She was going back with him to eastern Poland to meet his family. It was lucky she had been baptized a Catholic, she thought he would not have married her otherwise, and if he had not married her, she would have been waiting with her parents on the same platform three years later, proudly clutching their permits for resettlement in the east; like them, like everybody on that platform, the same platform from which her father used to take day trips to the spas in the mountains, she would have been re-settled for ever in the sandy soil a few weeks later. It was luckier still that she and her husband had been caught on the Russian side of the line which divided the occupation zones in Eastern Europe. Her husband became a doctor in the 'Polish Army in the East' and when the tide of battle swung full circle, if tides could be said to swing—her English was rusty (not at all, I said with limp sincerity)—they found themselves back in Breslau looking after the victims of the terrible days of Easter 1945; it was again lucky that he was not a military man or the Russians would have shot him years earlier. And the greatest luck of all was that when she arrived in the city, empty, ruined (she or the the city? Both, she said), her old house was still standing and she had the key to the front door in her pocket. It was an extra-ordinary thing, the furniture was still there and some of the glass was intact, protected from the blasts by the heavy shutters of Silesian oak. She was very, very lucky. In fact she was almost the only person in the entire city of 400,000 souls who was living in the same house as she had done before the war. Her husband had died two years ago. Exactly why she did not know, nor did the other doctors; people did not live long under such conditions, the times wore them out, but at any rate she had space to offer me and that was scarce enough. Did I know that nearly three-quarters of the city had been destroyed in the spring of 1945? I knew only what I had read in guidebooks; was it like Hamburg and Dresden? It was longer, she said, but it was just as hot. It was so hot that the bells melted in the belfries. Had my father ever spoken of a young man called Geza, who used to live in the flat below?

'Geza, yes, I think so. Didn't he spit at you?'

'His friends did. But Geza himself had a friend, a man only a few years older than himself, a man called Karl Hanke. You have heard of Karl Hanke?'

I had not.

'It is so strange. We live among monsters and we do not even know their names. Karl Hanke was the Gauleiter in this region. He was a fanatic. When the Russians came the mayor wanted

to surrender to save lives. He had the mayor hanged. Geza did
the job and between them they organized a defence to the death.
They made the city into a fortress and sent the civilians away.
They called it the Barthold Project after some legendary general
who was supposed to have defended Silesia against the Mongols
in the Middle Ages. Geza loved stories like that. When he had
no job, he used to go to the city library and read stories. He
would stop me on the stairs when I came home from the music
school and tell me what he had read that day. Barthold was one
of his favourite heroes. The name must have been his idea. I was
told later that Barthold never existed; he was just a character in
a romance. A whole city murdered in honour of a person in a
novel! But they did very well. It took the Russians three months
to move a mile. When they got here they found only ruins and a
few thousand corpses, not many. The rest of the people had been
moved to the west. Geza and Karl had created *Lebensraum* all
right but for the other side. They had done the Poles' work for
them. All the same, the Führer was very pleased. In his last will
and testament he made Karl Hanke Supreme Head of the SS to
succeed Himmler. Oh Geza would have been a famous man if
only . . .'

'What happened to them in the end?'

'In the middle of the city by the Kaiserbrücke, they built an
aerodrome. They destroyed streets and churches and houses to
make it. And all the time the Russians were bombing night and
day. You can imagine the cost and the suffering. But Barthold,
this person in a novel, said that there must be an airfield. And
there was. And the day before the city surrendered, the first and
last aeroplane took off from this airfield. Only Geza, Karl and
the pilot—it was a little aeroplane. A whole airfield just for
Geza and his friend. When the Russians got here, the birds had
wandered.'

'Flown.'

'Flown. My English is rusty. I work in a translation agency
but I do not speak to any English people. So they vanished into
thin air. They were never seen again. We heard the usual
stories. Someone said he had seen them in a Russian concentration camp. Someone said they had been shot by the Poles. Some

aeroplane wreckage was found in the mountains; but there were so many aeroplanes wrecked. Nobody really knew. At any rate, I seem to be a survivor. I bear a charmed life. Here I am, a Pole in an all-Polish city. I have come into my own. And I do not know a single soul.'

I thought of the bells melting in the belfries, great drops of molten metal spiralling down the bell towers, crashing through the wooden floors, hitting the pavement as cannon-balls. I thought of the bells at home, on the same night near enough, jangling out their breathless donkey-trot and the victory torches reflected in the muddy stream. These themes of fire and blood and iron and water had a terrible simplicity; they were far outside my range. Themes of that sort were for scholars to pluck laboriously out of ancient texts or resurrected to divert well-dressed people in theatres. They were not meant to come alive in our own time. Yet peoples and cities had been consumed by fire, the evil dwarfs had vanished in the flaming ruins of Valhalla and the iron curtain had clanged down.

And Stella herself had been saved by a few drops of water splashed across her face when she was a few days old, and by a magic ring placed on her finger, ancient symbols charred with perverted meaning by the holocaust. It was very terrible to have to take Wagner seriously; my father was an undeviating Mozart man. Stella too was all irony, melancholy, elegiac elegance. She was very bent now, a little old woman. At her jaw and forehead and round her mouth there were sharp lines running across the natural drift of the wrinkles, the impress perhaps of intense and prolonged suffering upon the normal silt-lines of age.

The flat had been divided into two. She showed me to the space in the passage up against the hardboard partition where I was to erect the camp-bed. She herself slept in the sitting-room.

'Even so I have more space than most. When I think of . . . your father used to say this floor was like a minefield, it creaked so badly, at night.' She raised her eyebrows in mock horror. 'Is your father happy?'

'Yes, on the whole, I think so, considering.'

'At your age, how can you know? It was a stupid question. After he had gone, I thought that I was in love with him. At the time he irritated me. But it was probably a good thing that he did go. We were too different, although I suppose that was why he liked me. Me.'

Her self-deprecation had a glint of pride in it, not in her appearance but in her past or in her survival. I liked her company.

'At that time I would not leave my parents. So I said, but if he had pressed me . . . he did press me . . . even if he had gone on asking me, no, I would not have gone. I did not want to leave. That is funny. I knew what was going to happen and I did not want to leave.'

'Did you want to share in . . . whatever was going to happen?'

'No, I was not that morbid or that brave. I was just interested. It was . . . interesting. Vairy inneresting.' She imitated a Gestapo heavy. 'We see British war films here now. I do the subtitles sometimes. The old concert hall—the Jahrhunderthalle, your father would remember it—is now a cinema.'

'And when you married, did you mind going—'

'We didn't know we would be caught. We thought we could get back. I was in an odd state. I did not care greatly about living, but I did not want to die either. I just wanted to see everything. That was why I got married, I think. But I liked my husband. He was a nice man.'

'In England I suppose you would not have seen much.'

'No, I suppose not. Thank you very much for the coffee. It's just the ticket. I'm sorry, my slang must be out of date. I will keep it under my bed to be safe. There are bandits about. You must be careful in this city.' We were standing side by side in front of the camp-bed. The struts running along the stained canvas stretcher stuck out like broken bones. Only a couple of them were fitted into their sockets. 'I fear I must ask you to put the camp-bed up. I am not strong enough. The metal parts are rusted. We used to take it when we went camping in the Riesengebirge before the war, my brother and I.'

I looked at her. I could not get the question out. She spread her hands out slowly, then compressed her shoulders in a shrug so quick it was almost jaunty. Later she pointed out the re-production of 'September Morn' which hung in the sitting-room now (the old dining-room was part of the other flat). They had had a joke about it in the old days, she said. The frame had warped and the colours faded. It did not now seem like a picture to joke about.

Through the hot August days, I wandered in the ruins south of the Gartenstrasse, beyond the railway station. Ten years had blurred the edges of the desolation. The upper storeys must have been levelled to avoid danger to passers-by. Only the occasional fireplace or patch of flowered wallpaper on the first floor was left to remind me how recently people had lived there. For the rest, these might have been the ruins of imperial Rome. The broken arches, the jagged courses of brick were already sealed and smoothed by grass. Ragwort carpeted the floors, transformed the piles of rubble into yellow dunes. The streets were silent. Hardly a cat moved. The creaking of a bicycle on the cobbles could be heard for half a mile. In parts the desert stretched to the river. Poplars railed the horizon. Stella said that at the height of the bombing people ran to and fro across the bridges like cornered rats until the bridges became so jammed that some of them jumped in and, unlike rats, broke their necks in the fall. I tried to find out where I was from the pre-war city map, but every German street-sign had been removed. The blank spaces on crumbling plaster street-corners were plainly visible. Throughout the city no single mark of the Germans survived; they had built this place, stayed in it for a thousand years; now they had been rubbed out.

When I got back to Stella's flat, she handed me a telegram from my father announcing my mother's death. I had not known she was so ill. At the time I resented the kindness of not telling me; now I think I would probably have done the same. Stella offered consolation with odd dignity, like a public widow. I was numbed and stiff. She put her arm around me. We sat down to supper, discussed what I should do—letters, telephone calls, travel tickets. I stared into my alphabet soup, watching the glutinous white letters swirl round in the thin broth, looking for an omen. After supper, another telegram from my father arrived. It said that my mother was seriously ill. The unspeakable hope rose for an instant only to be stamped on with the finality of the date stamp; the second telegram had been sent off a day earlier than the first one, an error had crept into the address at some stage and caused it to be delivered later. I explained this to Stella, holding the two telegrams side by side in my hands. She said, 'It's just like the war,' got up and walked quickly to the sofa. She sat down and burst into a long, convulsive sobbing. Her grief unlocked my own. Soon afterwards I went to bed. As I lay staring at the wall, I could hear her crying in the next room, mourning a woman she had never met, others too I imagine.

I met my father at Victoria Station. We had a cup of tea in the cafeteria. At once it was clear that I had not begun to understand. I had thought of what had happened as a loss, a taking away which was catastrophic and irreparable but which could at least be isolated and defined. I had thought we were bereft, precisely that. I had not imagined that everything had changed, utterly and for ever. A certain moment had arrived, an irreversible process had taken place. Although I was more or less grown up, until that moment I had continued to think of myself as a sickly child and my father as a vigorous guardian, never mind his oddities; I had lolled in the tyranny of the weak. All at once my father was somebody to be protected, a person for whom I was responsible. This moment is all the more alarming because it is in the same instant that we realize that we are alone. Solitude and responsibility are the two sides of the same coin, a hard currency. My father put his hand in his pocket to pay for the tea. He had come out without any money or had spent it all over the road. I had just enough left. The journey had almost cleared me out.

For something to say, I told him that the picture of 'September Morn' was still there. Stella had said he would remember. He did not remember. I gave him a brief report on my trip. From time to time, he muttered something or other. By the end, he was staring at the table, hardly listening. Then with an unexpected burst of coherence, he said, 'And Mr Polly? Did you read Mr Polly at all?'

After my return, I used to meet my father rambling about the house at all hours of the night. We exchanged mumbles: 'the sound of the waterpipes' . . . 'left a book down here' . . . 'ah, not a burglar then'. Often he was wearing his tattered sheepskin over his pyjamas, his bare feet wet with the dew. When there was a moon, I could see him walking very slowly across the lawn. I went down to the garden and called him to come to bed. 'No, no,' he cried hoarsely as if I had handed down a terrible verdict on him. Once I ran into him in the dark hall. I recoiled from the wan ghost. I could not look him in the face. Neither of us spoke.

The house began to fall apart. Neither of us felt like dealing with leaks in the roof or patches of fallen plaster. Light bulbs went phut and were not replaced. I was shaving one day, looking out of the bathroom window with one foot on the lavatory, an attitude I found helpful to cerebration, and the lavatory bowl crumbled beneath my foot, dissolving into grainy dust like the slow-motion replay of an explosion. I stood startled with one leg still in the air, recalling incongruously my father gripping the lectern and drenching Ecclesiastes in autumnal melancholy: 'Or ever the golden bowl be broken, or the pitcher be broken at the fountain, or the wheel broken at the cistern, then shall the dust return to the earth as it was.' The garden went back too. The gooseberries ran wild. You could not get close enough to pick them for the thorns. Occasionally I mowed the lawn, but there was no weeding done. The jungle advanced.

My father did not spend much time in the house. When the pubs were shut, he went on expeditions. I watched him pass the window, head thrust forward, lips pressed together, eyes blinking in the rain which seemed to fall incessantly that year. I lay on the sofa like a Victorian consumptive, glad to be back with the afternoon play: 'Can you hear the waves, Winifred?'— 'No, George, since he went away, I have not heard the waves.' I was not receiving the waves very well either above the crackle. The wireless needed an overhaul too. It is difficult to realize how much effort is required to keep a house going until that effort is abandoned.

One by one, activities were closed down. Hens and cats were given away. One or two rooms were locked up. The wireless finally surrendered to neglect. I ate alone off corned beef and
8*

tinned peaches and Russian novels, waiting for the end of the holidays. Among other projects permanently shelved at about this time was my father's Life of Charles Cotton, poet, angler, rakehell and putative ancestor. This was a long-running project. Materials for it had accumulated all over the house. My father rarely went into a bookshop without emerging with a fresh edition of *The Compleat Angler*, of which Cotton wrote the second, less famous, part. Editions of the poems, manuscript notes on them, and the scant previous memoirs were also scattered around the house. We had even, not many years earlier, gone on a trip to Cotton's native haunts, so vividly evoked in his verse. Izaak Walton, his closest friend, as well as his collaborator, used to stay with him and said of the place: 'the pleasantness of the river, mountains and meadows about it cannot be described; unless Sir Philip Sidney, or Mr Cotton's father were alive again to do it.' The day started fresh and cloudy. As we drove over the hills, my father pointed out distant valleys where he had once hunted. We passed the white rails of racecourses curving in shallow ellipse on the edge of market towns and he told stories of famous upsets and broken collar-bones. He wore the landscape with the familiarity of his tattered sheepskin.

It was Cotton's fishing-lodge we were after; the house itself had been pulled down. But above the fireplace in 'my poor fishing-house, my seat's best grace', we would be able to see carved the initials of Cotton and Walton and above the door 'Piscatoribus Sacrum 1674'. It was a pilgrimage worth making. We strolled along the scarcely untrodden ways beside the Derbyshire Dove. From time to time, we met walking parties with bulging rucksacks. My father said they reminded him of hikers in Germany before the war and look what became of them. He was restless and dry after the long drive. Even if there had been a pub nestling in the mossy verdure, it would not have been open. Water gurgled down the ferny clefts in the lime-stone and trickled across the path in zigzags down to the noisy river. As we ducked under overhanging alders, we dislodged miniature showers from the leaves. The air was already damp; it soon thickened into a drizzle and then into a curtain of water.

Our macs were treacherously permeable. We tried sheltering under a rocky overhang, but the water dripped off the underside with the persistence of an embryo stalactite. Our gullets were the only dry places for miles around.

The situation was grim, going on desperate. Any moment now, I would find myself saying 'Water, water everywhere and not a drop to drink' and my father would be correcting me 'nor any drop to drink'. This was almost his favourite mis-quotation, second only to 'human kind cannot bear too much reality' which provoked him to say '*very* much reality—it's obvious that nobody could bear too much,' though if in the mood I might argue that you could have too much of something without being unable to tolerate it, drink, for example. The point remained debatable. Meanwhile, we were dry and getting soaked.

Round the next bend the path reached a place where a by-road crossed the river. At the side of the road, there was a cottage surrounded by dripping trees. On the patch of lawn leading down to the river were some chairs upended for protection from the rain and two or three green tin tables with folded sunshades stuck through a hole in the middle. A badly painted sign said TEAS. Underneath, a rusty black-and-yellow disc nailed to the wall proclaimed the endorsement of the Cyclists Touring Club. A family in plastic macs were clustered around the window of the lean-to at the back. The window was open only a few inches at the bottom so that the leader of the party had to bend down and twist his head to make himself heard in what looked like the kitchen.

'. . . toilets.'

'This is not a public convenience.' The voice of the unseen proprietor was slurred but resonant.

'Be reasonable, squire.'

'This is a teahouse.'

'My little girl has—'

'She should have throught of it earlier. Look, tell you what I'll do. I'll charge you five bob a go.'

'You can't charge more than a penny. I know the law.'

'There's no law which says your little girl can piss in my house.'

'There's no need to talk dirty.'

'Why can't she go in the trees?'

'My little girl's been properly brought up.'

'In that case, my lavatory is no place for her. Thing is, you're creating a bloody awful draught.'

The window was slammed shut. The party in plastic macs huddled together for a minute, exhaling their outrage on the sodden air before withdrawing to consider their next move. My father went up to the window and rapped on it hard. There was a great groan from inside. The window was thrown up as high as it could go and a vast red face was thrust out, filling the entire frame.

'Who the hell do you—'

'You were damn rude to those—'

'Harry.'

'Frogmore. I thought that voice was familiar.'

My father clasped the enormous jowls with both hands. The face broke into a smile the size of a pillar-box.

'Wait a minute.' The head withdrew again. In due course a short man waddled towards us out of the back door. His belly reared up from his knees. He wore an open-necked shirt, considerably singed across the chest. His face glistened with sweat.

'Sorry to be so unmannerly. Thing is, I've had a mountain of washing-up to do, and Louise hasn't been feeling too good.'

'I find washing-up broadens the mind,' my father said. 'Sink's the only place where you have time to think.'

'Not when you've got a hundred bloody cups and saucers to finish before the next lot. Stiffens your finger-joints, that's all it does. Louise!' He bellowed back at the house.

A crumpled face appeared at an upper window.

'Don't shout. I've got another migraine.'

'Come down, these are friends, not customers. This is Harry Cotton and his boy. That's my wife Louise. She's French.'

'I remember.'

'You remember?' He looked surprised, then nettled. 'I didn't know you knew her. I knew Tom Dunbabin knew her. But I didn't know you knew her.'

'You introduced us once.'

'Good, good.' He seemed relieved.

'Extraordinary luck coming across you like this.'

'Yes, tremendous. Come in out of the rain and have a drink before the mob get here, though on a day like this . . .'

'I knew we'd get a drink somewhere,' my father said.

We went into the kitchen. There were plates, cups and saucers stacked everywhere. It was hard to tell which had been washed. On the draining-board stood a half-empty bottle of whisky. Frogmore took three cups and poured a generous helping into each.

'Rather short of glasses, I'm afraid. This is the nerve-centre of the operation. If the sun's out and it's a weekend, we serve a hundred teas in a day.'

'A hundred teas.'

'A hundred bloody teas. A hundred fucking teas. Think of that now.' He banged his fist down on the draining-board, making the crockery jump.

My father and I sat at the table in the middle of the room, emptying our cups, rapidly. Froggie came and leant over us, the corner of the table swamped by his paunch.

'Thing is, I hate them. Louise hates them too. But I hate them more.'

'What's that, *chéri*? Where's the booze?'

Louise looked much less crumpled at ground level. She had tidied herself up. She jangled slightly as she walked—bracelets or earrings presumably but I couldn't see because her shirt was frilly at neck and cuffs. Froggie introduced her again and then quickly turned away to pour her a drink. He had the air of someone who had lit the blue touch paper and was now retiring.

'You must be the same age as my son. Do you know my son?'

'I didn't know you had a son, Froggie,' my father said.

'Very nice boy,' said Froggie.

'He's not your son, *chéri*.'

'Louise.'

'Only by law. He bears your name. But he is not your son.' She talked to him as to a schoolboy who has forgotten his lesson.

'For Christ's sake, what does it matter? I took him on when I married you, didn't I?'

'We must be honest. If everyone was honest with each other, there would be no more wars, don't you agree?'

'I hadn't thought about it.'

'Don't be so timid. You must not be timid. Englishmen are always timid. Timid and hypocritical.'

'Not always,' I said, trying to prove her wrong.

'Always. Now I'm different, *chéri*. I speak my mind. My trouble is that I just cannot help telling the truth. And the truth is that my son is not Froggie's son. He is the son of a very dear friend of mine, the only man I ever really loved.'

'You don't mean—'

'You would not even know his name. He was a great philosopher. He died just before my son was born.'

'Not Tom Dunbabin?'

'You knew him?' She did not appear pleased.

'He was a great friend. In fact, he's indirectly the reason why we're here. Aldous and I are looking for Charles Cotton's fishing-house and it was Tom who first put me on to Cotton because he thought we might be descended from him.'

'Ancestors. That is all you English think about.'

'In fact he was a poet.'

'A poet? Ah, that is different. I'm crazy about poetry. Tell me some of his poetry, *chéri*.'

'Well, there was one verse that I remember Tom was very fond of:

*'A night of good drinking
Is worth a year's thinking,
   There's nothing that kills us so surely as sorrow;
Then to drown our cares, Boys,
Let's drink up the stars, Boys,
   Each face of the gang will a sun be tomorrow.'*

There was a pause.

'I don't call that poetry,' Louise said.

'More of a drinking song really,' Froggie said nervously.

'It is very fine verse,' said my father.

'I liked parts of it,' Froggie said. 'A night of good drinking is worth a year's thinking. That's good stuff.'

'What do you know about poetry? You are just an old soak.'

'Thing is, Harry likes it.'

'What does he know about poetry either?'

'He says Tom liked it too.'

'He did not know Tommy like I knew him.'

'That would be difficult.'

'Tommy had soul and spirit.'

'And spirits.'

'God, if you knew how bored I am of your stupid jokes.'

'I would prefer it if you did not insult me in front of my friends.'

'Your friends. You have no friends.'

'Harry is a very old friend.'

'So old that you haven't seen him once since we were married.'

'I met Froggie in Ireland once.' My father said. 'During the war. He was C.L.'s racing manager then. By the way, whatever became of that?'

Froggie turned from refilling the cups to launch a ferocious kick at the ceiling. 'What do you think, old boy? The B-O-O-T, of course.'

'You see, he cannot keep a job,' said Louise. 'It was a good job too, that one. But do you know how long ago that was? Fifteen years ago. You call that friendship?'

'Absence makes the heart grow fonder,' Froggie said. 'We used to ride races together, Harry and I. Once we nearly rode Ampersand, or rather one of us nearly did. It was a question of who was the lighter.'

'You have no friends now,' said Louise. 'He is not a friend now. He is here by chance.'

'I did ride Ampersand,' my father said.

'No, no, you never rode him,' said Froggie with a vehemence I had not expected. 'Thing is, you were going to ride him. But you never did, because C.L. changed her bloody mind at the last moment, as usual.'

'I didn't ride him in the race. But I schooled him the morning before. That's when I rode him.'

'No, no, you *nearly* did. That's the whole point.'

'You have no friends at all,' said Louise. 'You have not seen him since the war.'

'I rode that horse.'

'I know the feeling, Harry. You dream something so often you begin to think it actually happened. Like the Prince Regent telling everyone he fought at Waterloo—do I mean the Prince Regent?'

'For God's sake, I'm telling you, I did ride the horse.'

'What the hell are you two arguing about?' Louise got up to pour herself another drink. The bangles chinked against the cup.

'We're not arguing,' said Froggie. 'We're just having a friendly talk about old times.'

'If you're such old friends, why are you shouting at each other?'

'The privilege of friendship. It shows what old friends we are.'

'I rode Ampersand,' my father said.

'Christ, don't go on about it. Don't flog a dead horse.'

'I didn't flog him. It was like sitting in an armchair.'

'Shall we drop the whole argument?'

'You can't argue about questions of fact,' my father said.

'All right, if that's what you want to think, you go on thinking it.'

'If this is your oldest friend, I dread to think what your enemies must be like,' said Louise.

'The rain's stopped,' I said. But the water was still dripping on to Froggie's cracked lino from the hem of my mac. It was the old navy-blue gaberdine with the despicable buckle, the one that had long since ceased to be fully waterproof. Friendship was no more reliably proof against oblivion. Time—ubiquitous, corrosive, unrelenting—permeated its fabric, crept in at the seams, rusted the metal buckle. Nothing was to be depended upon.

Perhaps my father never had ridden the horse. Perhaps all his stories which so lightened my days were not quite fantasies but incidents that had just failed to happen, not invented but improved. Perhaps Ampersand had never existed. No, there were records, but that was all. I had read of some ancient civilization whose only surviving documentary traces were stone tablets giving the chariot-racing results. The Assyrians was it? Probably not.

We got up to go. My father invited Froggie and Louise to walk on with us towards Cotton's fishing-lodge. They said they were too busy, but we must drop in again whenever we were passing by. We said we would, and they must do the same whenever they were down in our part of the world.

No meeting in fact took place until my father read in the paper that Frogmore O'Neill, former amateur jockey and now proprietor of the Wishing Well Café, Dovedale, was in hospital with stab-wounds. He went to visit him. The patient was comatose, presumed moribund, surfacing only briefly to mutter, 'Never get stabbed in the stomach, old boy,' and a few minutes later, 'don't blame Louise too much. Thing is, she's French.'

The shelving of the Cotton biography represented a terminal stage in the process of closing down the house. Soon after my father had collected his notes and put them away in a drawer, the inevitable over-delayed migration to London got under way, inevitable not because anyone, least of all my father, would claim that city life was a cure for unhappiness but rather because cities attract the unhappy, offering possibilities of submersion and concealment which smaller settlements deny. He lived in Oakley Street for a few months. He said that everyone lived in Oakley Street at some point in their lives, he saw no reason why he should be an exception. Some time later, he moved in with Mossy and later out again and then in once more. A couple of years after that, my own hospital visiting began.

Cheerfulness sang down the corridors of the place. There were flowers on every window ledge and through the windows there were more flowers to be seen in the well-stocked borders beyond the lawns. The walls were painted in contrasting pastel shades. The corridors were hardly corridors at all in the institutional sense, more like tunnels of good-humour. Feet going down them made a jaunty thwat-thwat sound on the colourful rubberized flooring—no cold ring of hobnail on stone here.

And jauntiest of all was Dr Mukhija with his hopping gait and his birdlike twittering and gleam. 'It was a piece of good fortune you bumped into me. I'll take you there myself, no trouble, not the slightest, I was going there, anyway, we can talk on the way, I would like to talk to you about your father and

234 THE MAN WHO RODE AMPERSAND

I can show you how we handle this shooting-match mmm.' At the end of each burst of affability he emitted a pleasant tenor hum, perhaps to maintain the level of cheerfulness while he considered what to say next: 'And now we are going through Nicholson House, some of our more difficult patients reside here, difficult but not downhearted, that's right, isn't it, Walter?'

We overtook an ill-shaven ancient in a dressing-gown who was walking very slowly along the corridor keeping close to the wall and looking at the ground. Dr Mukhija patted him on the back. The old man stopped but did not look up. Round the next corner, we picked up a trail of blood. At first there were only a few spots, but the trail soon thickened into a solid red line. The blood stayed with us for a full hundred yards, then branched off at right angles and disappeared under a door. From the far side of the door came a banging noise. 'Oh dear,' said Dr Mukhija, clicking his tongue. 'Difficult you see, but responding well to treatment, very well. Your father of course is a hopeless case, quite hopeless. No purpose in him being here at all. Very nice fellow, we all like him. And we hope, we hope very much that he likes us. Sometimes I feel, but I may be wrong, I may well be wrong, but I do receive the impression that I am not quite getting through to him. However, it is always a pleasure to have conversation with him. Mmm.' We passed into a lower building which seemed to be a lavishly converted nissen hut with a big television and tables for cards and ping-pong. 'I thought we'd find them in the wrecker. Mmm.'

Seated at a card table by the fire at the far end of the recreation room were my father and a huge old man in a wheelchair who looked as if he had once been even larger. My father got up and extended his arm to me in a gesture halfway between a handshake and an embrace. He looked very well. His eyes were clear. It was ten days since he had come out of the straitjacket. He stood there smiling, pleased to see me but as unable as I was to think how to begin. Dr Mukhija came to a halt by the card table, still bouncing lightly on his toes. 'I expect you two will have a lot to talk about. Have you thought over what I said to you yesterday?'

'No.'

'Now you must be a good man. Mr Cod here, he always listens to what I tell him. He is a good patient.'

'Ay, you run along then, Mucky. We've 'ad enough of your jabber-jabber for one day.'

'I do not want to miss the O.T.'s match. The hospital fellows badly need support. We may meet there later perhaps. Mmm.'

'That's as may be, Mucky. You 'op it.'

'Such a good patient. Mmm.' Dr Mukhija skipped out of the room.

'I can't stand that man,' my father said.

'You don't want to take him so 'ard, my dear sir,' said Cod Chamberlayne, shuffling the cards.

'All that nonsense about my childhood. What could he understand about my childhood? My major hand.'

'Mumbo-jumbo, don't let it get you dahn.' Cod's great flippers dealt the cards like a sea-lion shaking itself. His cheeks had caved in, folds of flesh buried his little eyes and hung about his jaw as if waiting in vain for a chin. His mouth drooped open, now sumptuously flabby. His gadoid appearance had reached its high point in extreme old age.

'Point of five.'

'Good. Trouble with Mucky is that he will 'ave it we're all off our chumps and come in 'ere to be put straight. But we ain't, you know. We're just refugees from an 'ard unfeeling world. Orphans of the storm. I tell him that's what an asylum's for, ain't it—shelter.'

'Quart major—and a tierce. Fourteen jacks.'

'Good enough. Nought to poor old Cod. One. Two, and now let's see if you've got the little lady. If I 'ave a regret, young Aldous, it is for the days when I used to work the race trains before I became a monarch of the turf, before your dear dad's day even, I dare say.'

'You worked the three-card trick, did you, Cod?'

'Find the Lady, my dear sir, Find the Lady. The three-card trick is what the beaks calls it, not the professional man. But those was lovely times, Harry. You was your own master. None of the burdens of the businessman, no office to run, no paperwork—it was the paperwork that was my undoing, I could have managed all right if it wasn't for the paperwork. I'd be out there on the rails now giving as good as I got. My wife, my 'ealth, my 'ahse—all gone, just because of the paperwork. Three. Four.'

'Twenty-seven. Twenty-eight. Twenty-nine. I made a quid spotting the lady once. He let me win the first time and I said that's enough, thank you.'

'Five. Six. He must 'ave been a novice that one, letting the punter win the first time. The proper way to draw your man on is to make him lose the first, win the second, lose the third, then you've got him 'ooked, and even if you 'aven't you're still ahead of the game.'

'They're very nice here, the people,' my father said to me. 'One of the night staff is rather a bully but otherwise they're all right. And the food's good. Sometimes we go down to The Hero of Inkerman for a drink.'

'A drink?' I said.

'Just a lager. We aren't really supposed to, but . . . the theory is, we try and help each other.'

'Ay, enough of that, play up now. Seven. Eight. Nine.'

'Thirty, thirty-one, thirty-two. And one for the last trick. Thirty-three. Your cards—nineteen, which leaves you just three short of the rubicon.'

'Poor old Cod, left 'igh and dry again. Like when Miss L. left you in the middle of nowhere wivaht yer 'orse.'

'As it happens, I got a lift home on the trainer's hack. But you remember that, do you, Cod? However did you find out?'

'There wasn't much I didn't find aht in them days. I 'ad my informants. And anyway you may recall we was engaged in negotiations at the time, very difficult negotiations?'

'We were.'

'And then later on, there was even more difficult negotiations.'

'There were indeed.'

'So your prospects was a matter of concern to me.'

'I quite see. So you remember the time when I rode Ampersand.'

'Course I do, Harry, you don't forget a thing like that. Rode him nicely too, my informant said. Gave him plenty of room. Sears 'ad a nasty way of pushing him at his fences.'

My father tried to appear nonchalant in deference to my presence, but delight slipped its leash and coursed all over him.

'You remember that, do you now?' he asked, like a lawyer anxiously coaching an unreliable witness.

'Course I do. Great 'orse Ampersand. And you rode 'im nicely.'

'You've got a wonderful memory, Cod.' My father stared at the old man as if he had travelled through many strange lands in search of this mnemonic paragon and here at last was journey's end. Here was permanence.

'Ay, thank you, thank you. I may get a bit muddled up other ways, but me memory's still 'ot as mustard. Take wine. I can remember the vintages like me own muvver's face—that 1920 'ock and there was a good Krug that year too though the burgundies wouldn't wet a baby's arse.'

'You know who else is here, Aldous—the other Harry. I saw him yesterday. Dr Mukhija tells me they closed down the little home he was sent to, and they've had to dump him here, in a terrible place . . . wooden bunks one on top of each other like boxes of apples.'

'The docs don't have to worry about the MSNs you see,' Cod said. 'Poor sods can't write to their MPs. And their nearest and dearest don't come near 'em more than they can 'elp. Chappie 'anged himself the other day because he thought they was going to transfer him to the subnormal wing. In fact he was cured and they was going to let him aht, or so they said afterwards.'

'If we go down to the playing fields we might see him. He sometimes holds an open air service in the fields.'

'It's the Bin against the O.T.'s. Mucky reckons the Bin ain't got a prayer, the O.T.'s is so fit.'

'So they should be,' said my father. 'Those ghastly exercises.'

'Who plays for the hospital?'

'Doctors and nurses mostly. A few patients. There's one man who used to play wing-three-quarter for the Harlequins. He's still got a wonderful turn of speed. The only trouble is he sometimes stops and bursts into tears. But he's much better playing football than not. He's far worse watching the gogglebox. We had a party political broadcast on in here last night—both channels, of course, no escape—it was Boy Kingsmill talking about pensions—and he blubbed throughout.'

'D'ye mind pushing me,' said Cod, 'this chair's a fair weight.' It was. The wheels bit deep into the gravel. Beyond the flower borders stretched broad playing fields. The game had already started. The trim-waisted team all in white must be the occupational therapists. The other team came in various shapes, sizes and colours. My father pointed out the man who used to play for the Harlequins. He had crinkly hair and oaken thighs. He was wearing a faded multi-coloured shirt and shorts held up by an old pyjama cord. He ran very fast. He did not speak to anyone. The other players talked a great deal. Half a dozen spectators well wrapped up occasionally gave out mournful cries of 'Come on the O.T.'s' or 'Brackenfield'. My father shouted 'Up the Bin,' twice, hoping to annoy Dr Mukhija who was hopping up and down the touchline keeping level with the play. But Dr Mukhija was completely absorbed in the game. He shouted, 'Heel, boys, heel' or 'Keep it in', striking gloved fist into gloved palm to express his frustration when some manœuvre failed to succeed, dancing along the touchline with arms raised when the Brackenfield backs started a movement.

Despite this encouragement, the hospital seemed to be losing. Then a smart sequence of passes across the field sent the ex-Harlequin rocketing away down the far side, his heels winking at the leaden sky. He evaded the last despairing challenge. There was nobody between him and the line. All at once, he stopped in his tracks as quickly and neatly as he had been running. He let the ball slip from his listless grasp and covered his face with his hands. Dr Mukhija immediately ran across the field at a brisk pace, his well-polished black walking-shoes slipping on the muddy ground. As he ran he tugged out of his coat pocket a small satchel not much bigger than a wallet. When he reached the ex-Harlequin, he put one arm round his shoulder and fumbled in the satchel for something which he popped in the weeping player's mouth. The other players were arguing.

'I think we should have a line-out.'

'But the ball's still in play. Whenever play stops for an injury, you have a scrum.'

'This isn't really an injury.'

'Severe schizophrenic depression is no joke.'

'I didn't say it was a joke, I said it wasn't an injury.'

'Well, if you think a pathological condition resulting from a chemical imbalance isn't an injury——'

'Come off it, Neil, the whole thing's basically sociogenic.'

'Balls.'

'Anyway, we had a line-out the last time it happened.'

'But that was because the ball rolled into touch after he dropped it.'

The ex-Harlequin rejoined his team and Dr Mukhija jogged back towards us. My father pulled my sleeve: 'Come this way for a moment. I think that's him.' We walked towards a plantation of fir trees at the end of the playing fields. The November air was already thickening into mist. The young fir trees were glistening in the rough grass. A few yards in front of the fence stood a small man in a long overcoat. He had his back to us. We went round the side of him and I could see that it was the other Harry. His hair was silver now. He had a bald patch on his crown, giving him a ragged tonsure. He was gobbling into a battered old prayer book, occasionally snorting as he caught his breath in mid-gobble. He did not move his head, but his eyes flickered sideways towards us and then back again to the book. There was no sign of recognition. We withdrew a few yards.

'The fir trees are . . .'

'. . . his congregation. More majestic than the empty beer bottles. Time we were getting back to the recreation room. If we start now, we can have a cup of tea in peace.'

On the return walk, my father said: 'I feel a great deal better already.'

'You look a great deal better.'

'I don't think there's any point in staying here much longer.'

'No, that's more or less what Dr Mukhija was saying.'

'I bet he didn't put it like that.'

'No.'

'Well, I'm going to come out quite soon. I can't stand much more of this place. They never tell you the same thing from one moment to the next. Sometimes they say you're ill and then ten seconds later they say you've no one but yourself to blame. When I pointed out the contradiction, Dr Mukhija said that the truth was relative. I said that was just what Pontius Pilate thought, to which he rather feebly replied, did I really want to get better or not? Anyway, I do feel much better. I've had a good rest and I like talking to old Cod. I'm glad he remembered about Ampersand.'

Just as we reached the hospital buildings, we were overtaken by a couple of mud-spattered therapists carrying a stretcher. On it lay the ex-Harlequin. A few yards behind bobbed Dr Mukhija, looking anxiously inside his satchel as he ran. He shouted breathlessly at the stretcher-bearers. I caught only the words 'perhaps the dosage . . .'

For all that their lasting effect upon my father's well-being was small, it was to these spacious grounds and athletic thera- pists that my mind returned with something approaching nostalgia as I sat outside in the passage of Lazarus Ward, the Churchill Grimshawe Centenary Hospital, waiting for the surgeon to finish his examination. I found the bin, for all its cant and disorienting horror, less depressing than the present institution so honourably dedicated to the saving of life. Was it the contrast between the spreading cedars and leisurely routine of the former and the implacable assembly line of damaged bodies presented to the latter? There was that, but that was not all. Brackenfield was at least dedicated to the proposition that such entities as minds existed, had their value, their privileges, even on occasion their dignity to be honoured, but the Churchill Grimshawe traded only in neurons, measured only minute quantities of electrical energy in the skull. The shrinks seemed to treat their patients as old sparring partners, acquaintances admittedly of the most tiresome sort but who had gained a certain right to affection if only by virtue of familiarity. The surgeons by contrast showed as little feeling towards their patients as garage mechanics towards the old bangers backed up into their yard, rather less in fact. A topcoat of sympathy had to be sprayed on to keep the customer quiet, but since they were always busy, they did not make a very good job of it. Their usual manner took the form of a grave rudeness like that of undertakers pressing for payment.

'Here he comes. You go and talk to him, Aldous.'

I got to my feet. I did not feel like talking to him. He did not like being nagged for hourly bulletins. Anyway, I had already got the message. 'You must understand that your father's skull is like a battlefield. It's scarred by old bomb craters. He's probably had several falls already . . . yes. Complained of feeling a wee bit groggy, gone to bed . . . yes, yes. In ordinary language, we would say that this is his first actual stroke but that he's really been brewing up for it for oh six months. This recent haemorrhage was only the last straw, just enough to trigger off the paralysis and so on. In layman's terms . . .' He spoke as if ordinary language was not much better than the mumbling of the brain-damaged and the layman a euphemism for the hemiplegiac. 'He could conceivably make a partial recovery, but the prognosis is not good. At the moment that's all I can tell you. You can go in and see him if you like.'

I returned to the small group sitting on the wooden bench. Mossy asked me to ring home. Pip would be waiting for news. When I gave him the news, Pip said: 'I do wish I could be with you. But there's not a cab to be had. It's too tiresome about all these bombs. There are still sirens going all over the place. One begins to wonder if it isn't the beginning of the end. I almost feel I can hear the distant rattle of the tumbrils, my dear; nearly time to get out one's knitting. And how is your poor dear father? I expect it's just one of his falls, he'll be all right in a day or two. If only he didn't drink quite so much.' For a second I believed him. Then I recognized the familiar false comfort of the second telegram and, in recognizing it, knew that there could be but one end. 'Tell me,' said Pip in a confidential tone, evidently putting his mouth closer to the receiver, 'do you think by any chance, or putting it another way, is it likely that by this evening . . . Mossy was taking me to the theatre and you know how she loves it.'

'I don't think she'll be able to go this evening.'

'You don't? Well, in that case, I wonder if I oughtn't to do something about the tickets.'

'I'll ask.'

Mossy looked bewildered for a moment 'The tickets?' Then caught between a hope that my father might be all right, an ingrained reluctance to cancel any entertainment and a feeling that this was not the time to discuss such things, she eventually said:

'They're on the table in the passage. I'll be late.'

When I told Pip, he said: 'That's not the point. I know where they are. I must know *definitely* if she's coming or not. I can't hang about all evening. If she isn't, you see, I could always give the other ticket to my lodger. I can't very well go by myself, can I?'

As I was coming back to report, a gaunt, elderly woman in a nurse's uniform stopped me in the corridor.

'You must be Aldous. I'm your cousin Kate.'

I stared at her stupidly.

'I work here. I saw your father's name on the admissions list. Is he bad?'

'Yes. Very bad.'

'Was he hurt by the bombs?'

'No, nothing like that. He's just had a stroke.'

'We've had several casualties from the bombs. Some of them are very poorly.'

'That's awful. I didn't know you were a nurse.'

'I never did my exams. That's why I'm still only an auxiliary. I started too late.'

'Oh yes, I remember.'

'Of course you would know. I am so used to covering up. When I came out, the war had already started and I went straight into nursing. I never stopped to take the exams. Do you know why I got such a long sentence?'

'No. My father always wondered.'

'I'll tell you because it doesn't matter now. I had a friend who helped me. They hadn't got any evidence against him except what I could provide.'

'And you didn't provide it?'

'No, he had an IRA record and I knew he would get a very long sentence. They said I would get off lightly if I helped them.

But I didn't. His name wasn't mentioned at the trial because they still hoped to get him and I wasn't going to say anything. But the judge knew. I know the judge knew.'

'Anyway, they didn't get him.'

'No, not until today. He was arrested at the airport with some other people. I just heard on the radio. That's why it doesn't matter telling.'

'Today? He must be quite an old man now.'

She grinned at the implication. 'Yes, only a little younger than me.'

'No, I meant too old to be playing with dynamite.'

'Is there a right age for that? He was always a fool.'

'Why did he think setting fire to a racing stable would help Ireland? I thought the Irish liked racing.'

'I told you, he's a fool. I persuaded him it was a blow against what they now call the Establishment.'

'And why did you . . .'

'You never met C.L.'

'Did you hate her that much?'

'Until the moment when I saw the flames break out over the barn. Then I realized that I had not quite got that kind of madness in me and I looked at Michael rushing around with his blazing torch and I realized that he had.'

'Were you ashamed?'

'No, I don't think so. Am I now? Not really. I took up nursing because I wanted to. It wasn't a penance.'

There was something cocky about her. I didn't much take to her. I gathered from her strange, sly look—strange because it came so puckishly from that gaunt face—that she did not take to me either. Though we were not closely related, I felt we shared a certain family likeness, some quality quite absent from my father's make-up. What was it, not primness exactly, more a sort of distaste for people's imperfections, her version shaped by pride, mine by timidity? The more I thought about it, the less I liked both of us.

'Could I come with you to see your father? I'd like to see him —even like this.'

I nodded, rather put out. I felt she expected gratitude for her concern; I had none to give. We walked in silence back down the corridor to Mossy and Dan. I introduced them. They did not want to go in. The ward was quiet. Those patients who were not in a coma were asleep. I hardly recognized my father. His hair had been shaved off. He looked much smaller. His breathing was heavy, irregular like the bump and flutter of a bird that had strayed indoors and could not find its way out again. Kate bent forward to make the position of the saline drip more comfortable. As she adjusted the clip on his nose (had she the right, I wondered), her attitude of extreme concentration—head on one side, forehead wrinkled, lips pressed tight together—suggested how she must have looked as a child attending to her friends' complexions. From that fancy flowed the memory of my father taking the sleep out of my eyes with the same pursed concentration. Finding the attention tedious, I would try to wriggle out of his grip, but he held me too tight. As my eye began to mist over, he would hold up his catch and say 'there now, off you go,' flicking the pale specks of wax into the air.

We stood either side of the bed listening to the breathing and the noise of the drip. The small body in the bed seemed to be controlled by the drip, like one of those clockwork cars which can be directed by pressing a rubber bulb linked to its exhaust pipe by a plastic lead. I began to feel that my father existed solely in order to amuse the drip, that it was this arrangement of glass and metal and plastic that was the living organism. Kate took his hand and held it. I bent down and kissed his forehead. I could not deny a feeling of rivalry.

Everything is what it is. It is the peculiar disease of our age to confuse things that are essentially consecutive and distinct; we do not much care for distinctions and consequences. We cannot tolerate the proposition that virtues carry their defects with them and defects their virtues. People find it more congenial to pretend that the virtues are not virtues at all, nor the defects, defects. My father was free from this disease. He had a quick eye for the corruptions and absurdities of success but he did not sentimentalize disappointment, least of all his own. He did not try to present failure as a kind of disguised success or to deny that events, as often as not, had their logic. His life was the way he led it. He liked people and places for what they were, which is not the same as saying that he liked them as they were. In his fashion he was a realist.

When we came back down the passage, Dan was crying. I was fed up with the whole lot of them. Who was Dan to indulge his hysteria when there was so much to do? Dan was just a little ballet boy who kept my father out of trouble so long as Mossy let him stay in her attic for nothing. He had no rights in the matter. To cool my rage, I went out for a breath of fresh air. In the mirror at the end of the corridor I saw the reflection of an angry civil servant, tight-lipped, verging on middle age, dry-eyed. My father said he had no time for a man who could not weep. Perhaps only realists can weep.

Not long afterwards I was re-posted from UPARS to the private office of the new minister responsible. Boy Kingsmill greeted me with molten affability.

'I'm glad we shall be working together. I used to know your father well. Pity he . . .'

He jerked an imaginary glass to his lips. I bowed my head.

Kingsmill turned out to be a good man to work for—energetic, balanced, considerate and durable. He had staying power.

The story of the grasshopper and the ant is grim enough as it is. Think how much grimmer it would be if the grasshopper had given birth to the ant. The ant's revenge would be a terrible thing.